THE WHOLE WORLD FOR EACH

KATE MACLEOD

1

AN ELUSIVE VOCATION

It wasn't hard to believe two children had died here. April Nguyen stopped short at the bottom of the steep stairway, pulling her foot back before it touched the narrow catwalk. Through the grating was an inky blackness, with distorted patches reflecting the glow from the emergency lights. Water. She couldn't see the edges of it in the dim light; it lay under the entire network of catwalks and platforms, each with token handrails at waist height but nothing to save anyone who took a tumble. Or anyone shorter than the rail, like a child. No, it wasn't hard to believe they had died here; what was hard to believe was that anyone could actually live here. And yet they did. Entire families, the borders of their homes, the edges of the blankets or carpets they had spread on the platforms, blanket after blanket, with only the narrowest of open floor serving as corridors between private spaces.

April's mother was halfway across the catwalk when she realized April wasn't following. She looked back, waving for April to follow. April gripped the end of the stairway rail and looked past the toes of her faded, too-small slippers at the dark water below. She had exercised as much as she could, but months in free fall had taken their toll. Her legs trembled, and stumbling and falling was a real possibility.

Her mother came back to her, her hands gripping the catwalk railing tightly, and April knew that as weak as she was feeling, her mother had to feel weaker still. *Her* months of free fall had been spent barely stirring from her hammock.

"We'll keep it to the short ceremony," her mother said, low so her words didn't carry to the people waiting for them on the far side of the catwalk.

"It's so dark down here," April said.

"That's good. The red from the emergency lights—it really creates an atmosphere. That's good for you," her mother said.

"I'm going to unveil," April said. "I can't see through all this. It's dark enough, right?"

Her mother frowned as she pondered, then gave a short nod. "Just remember you're not just any teenaged girl; you're the conduit."

"I remember," April said, lifting the front layers of her veils and smoothing them back over the top of her head. Then she set her foot on the catwalk, the bells at her ankle chiming softly. Then the other foot with its bells, and then she was crossing the catwalk, carefully not looking down, hands clasped one inside the other at chest height, forcing her posture to stay tall despite the aching in her back. So much aching, and they'd been under gravity-simulating spin for only an hour.

She could get through this. She had to; the money had run out days ago. If she failed to put on a worthy show, they would have no choice but to sell her reader for food. Her stomach growled loudly even as her heart sank at the idea. That reader, the books it contained—those were her life. She could not fail.

Ted Vasquez, the man they had met in the shuttle bay, led them over four crowded platforms and catwalks to a final platform tucked away in a nest of thick pipes. There was a wall here that reached down into the water, but April suspected anyone brave enough to attempt the swim could get under it, even circumnavigate the station, if they wanted to. The water, in addition to serving the usual functions of water for the people and their plants and animals living on the station, also shielded them all from radiation. It was open water here, where it was filtered and dispensed throughout the station, and where used water was cleaned before being returned to the immense tank. There might be another similar station at a different point along the perimeter, perhaps several others; April didn't know for sure, but the *Triomphe* was certainly large enough for it. But even if there were, it would be a long, dark swim to find it.

"Did they fall into the water?" April asked, not able to pull her gaze away from the rippling surface below them. It looked bottomless, and so dark and cold.

"No," Ted said. "Like I said before, what killed them is a mystery. We just found them dead and gone, arms around each other like they were napping, but they were so cold." He took a deep, shaking breath, then pointed with his chin. "There is my wife, Carmen." He threaded his way along the narrow open space between blankets to the frayed ends of what must once have been a navy-blue wool bedcover. A sleeping bag was curled up in the far corner, not even a head visible, only the lumpy outline of a person inside. The man knelt beside the sleeping bag, his hand finding and squeezing a shoulder as he spoke softly. The figure stirred, and a voice murmured an answer.

April felt eyes on her and looked down at a little girl of perhaps six, staring up at her with big brown eyes from the edge of a blanket covered in vines and roses. April resisted the urge to smile back; she was supposed to be ethereal, otherworldly, not friendly. She lifted her head higher, the bells in her braid tinkling with the movement, and the girl's mouth formed a wide *O* to match her eyes.

"Come," April's mother said, briefly touching April's elbow before leading the way to the far blanket. April gave the girl one last look, hoping her eyes were giving the smile her lips weren't allowed to, then followed her mother.

"Mrs. Vasquez," her mother said as she, too, knelt beside the sleeping bag. "My name is Melena Nguyen. This is my daughter, April. We're here to help."

A hand reached out of the sleeping bag to clutch at the man. He helped his wife sit up, and her head emerged. She was younger than April was expecting, but grief was already etching deep lines on her thin face. She ran a hand over the braids wrapped around her head, loose hair everywhere refusing to be smoothed down.

"How can you help? Nothing can bring my girls back. Nothing else matters." Her voice sounded dead, devoid of emotion. April could sense the scars left behind when all the young mother's feelings had been ripped away, and her own heart ached.

"Tell me about them," Melena said, taking the woman's hand between her own. Her mouth worked, but the words wouldn't come and she slumped against her husband.

"They were perfect babies," he said, his voice muffled as he pressed his face into his wife's hair. "We thought it would be hard, having two at once, but they were angels."

April was standing on the very edge of their blue blanket, hands still clasped as she listened. She felt a tug at her kameez and looked down to see the girl standing beside her, her feet still in the uncovered common area but her toes brushing the edges of the blanket. She didn't speak, just pointed up into the tangle of pipes above them.

"There is a space up there," April said, looking up. "Like a little platform."

Carmen, not noticing the little girl tucked out of sight behind April's legs, looked up with a start. "That was their special place. They would play up there. That's where they were when it..." Then her tears did come. Her husband hugged her close, tears in his own eyes, and Melena murmured whatever kind words she thought would help. April looked down at the girl.

"You've seen them up there?" The girl nodded. "Since they died?" She nodded again.

"We all see them," a soft voice said, and April saw that every family on the platform was looking at her.

"We hear them laugh," another added.

Suddenly, the pipes snaking all around them began to rumble and the water below churned. April's knees nearly crumpled as a sudden wave of dizziness and nausea hit her and she clutched at the nearest thing to support herself, closing her eyes as she waited for it to pass. Was she getting motion sickness from the spinning station? That didn't seem likely; the station was immense, not one of those tiny things where you could feel your feet moving faster than your head. More likely, it was the lack of food for the last few days catching up with her.

She had thought she was gripping the railing, but as the nausea passed and her brain cleared, she realized—being in the middle of the platform—that wasn't possible. She gave herself a little shake and forced her eyes to open, looking down at the sturdy little girl holding her up as she gripped her bony shoulder.

"Are you all right, my darling?" her mother called up.

"Yes," she said, straightening and releasing her tight grip on the girl. "Does this happen a lot?" she asked, pointing at the water moving beneath them.

"Every eight hours," Ted said. "For ten minutes at a time."

"Filtration cycle," someone else added.

"When you see the ghosts, is it during these times?"

Some of the people looked at each other, but the majority were nodding.

"But it wasn't running when they died," the mother said. "Their death... it had nothing to do with the water."

April's mother was giving her a very pointed look and April quickly clasped her hands together, resuming her rigid stance. "This is the time to act, when they will appear," April said. "Quickly, form a circle. Hold hands."

Ted helped his wife out of the sleeping bag, and the others left their blankets to gather in a tight circle inside the space of the royal blue blanket. Melena took Carmen's other hand, but April was on the other side of the circle from the three of them, where she had a view of the platform above. The quiet little girl was clinging to her hand, her face carefully serious.

"Do you play up there sometimes?" April asked in a whisper.

The girl considered, then gave a tiny nod.

"Don't. It's a bad place. Not because of the ghosts, but something else. Something that hurt your friends. Don't go up there, OK?"

The girl nodded gravely, and April gave her hand a tight squeeze.

"I see them!" someone called out and others in the circle gasped. April felt something like a chill running up her spine, but the others were lifting clasped hands, trying to point without breaking contact with each other. Then the pointing coordinated until they were all focusing on the sole catwalk that connected their platform with the others.

April kept her head down, murmuring meaningless words the others couldn't hear. She didn't turn to look. She was afraid she'd see the same thing she always saw, the thing that haunted her, that had driven her to quit doing this work entirely years before. The thing she feared she would still see every time she summoned the spirits of the dead.

Nothing.

"Do you see them?" Melena was asking the Vasquezes.

"Yes," Ted said breathlessly, but his wife was weeping silent tears, unable to speak.

"Call to them," Melena said. "It's time to say goodbye."

The mother let loose one wracking sob, nearly crumpling to the ground. Then, straightening and looking directly at the catwalk, she let loose a tidal wave of rapid Spanish, out of which April could just discern the names Serena and Mariposa. Then she fell silent again, slumping against her husband's shoulder with another sob, like a festering wound that is finally induced to bleed again so it can heal.

April ceased her chanting, putting the little girl's hand into the hand of the man on her right, closing the circle once more as she stepped out of it. She usually did this veiled; she felt exposed standing barefoot on the catwalk in only her shalwar-kameez. She closed her eyes for a moment, picturing what the two twin girls must look like. The feeling of something pressing down on her chest was stronger with her eyes closed, like someone was bear-hugging her from behind, fists locked on her sternum, long bear-beard tickling her spine. She could believe that something otherworldly was standing behind her. It didn't even require belief; she could *feel* it.

Opening her eyes, she turned to face the catwalk. The *empty* catwalk. Her chest constricted tighter than ever, the overwhelming sadness pressing down on her, but still she saw nothing. Yet she knew from the murmurs behind her that the others did, just like every other time she had done this. She raised her hands and threw her head back, her tired back protesting at the formal posturing.

"Serena, Mariposa," she said to the nothingness before her. "It's time to go on. Your mother is going to be all right now. You can go. She's going to be OK."

She stayed in that pose for what felt like far too long, and she worried yet again that her "skill" had failed her. But then the filtration system cut out, and the pipes grew quiet, the water below them returning to dark stillness.

"They went on," Carmen said, her voice thick with tears. "Did you see them? They waved goodbye."

"I saw," Ted said, kissing the top of her head.

"It was beautiful," one of the neighbors said, her face filled with bright happiness despite the tears running from her eyes. "I've never seen anything so beautiful."

April returned to the edge of the blanket, gathering up her mountain of veils and slipping her feet back into her battered slippers. The others started to close in around her, wanting to thank her or tell her about what they had seen or simply touch her. She quickly replaced her layer of veils, her only protection against what always felt to her like an attack. Her mother knew this and left the Vasquezes' side to stand between the clamoring crowd and her daughter.

"Please, my daughter is quite drained by these encounters," she said. "It is tiring, communing with the world of shadows. And we have not yet found a place to stay."

"You're welcome to stay among us," one of the neighbors offered, but his wife elbowed him sharply.

"Look at how they're dressed. They will already have a place up above," she hissed at him.

April's cheeks reddened at her words. When her mother had forced her back into this wardrobe before leaving the shuttle, she had protested every article of it, from the too-small shoes to the faded colors and unraveling stitchery of her shalwar-kameez. And yet, to these people, she still looked rich and fine.

Ted stepped up to Melena, his hands twisting together. "I don't know how to thank you. My wife..." His voice dropped off, but Melena and April both knew what he was trying to say. Carmen, who likely had not left that cocoon of a sleeping bag since her daughters died, was hugging and crying with the friends she had neglected and talking of her daughters finally in the past tense, with warmth in her words and not cold, bitter loss.

"It's what April does," Melena said.

"I have nothing to pay you with," he said. "I was on the docks looking for work, but it's scarce..."

"Please," Melena said, laying a hand on his arm. "We don't do this for the money. Although we do accept humble gifts."

April was glad she was hidden once more behind the veils. No one could see the look on her face as her mother accepted anything the people who lived on blankets in the bowels of a space station saw fit to give her. Even their meager offerings were far more than she deserved.

April Nguyen had done nothing. She was a fraud. Worse, she had betrayed her own self. She had accepted when she was twelve that she was never going to see the ghosts everyone praised her for communing with, and she had sworn that never again would she pretend she could see them, could send them on their way, could end the hauntings that tormented people like the Vasquezes who had more than enough torments in life.

All it had taken for her to go back on her own word was a little poverty.

2

SOMETHING AT FIRST SIGHT

April wanted to gawk—oh, how she wanted to gawk. But you can't be awe-inspiring when you're within the raptures of awe yourself, especially if what's so striking to you is just mundane to everyone around you.

She and her mother had met Ted Vasquez before even leaving the shuttle docking bay and had followed him down maintenance hallways and service elevators and narrow, utilitarian stairs so steep they were nearly ladders until they reached the water treatment area where he lived. Now that the job was done, she was getting her first look at the station itself, and what a sight it was.

April had never been on a station like the *Triomphe*. Not even close. Much of it was familiar: it was just as crowded with people as any place she'd ever been, and the marketplace was filled with the same sorts of smells: mouth-watering food aromas mingling uneasily with the foul odors of inadequate sanitation, both overwhelmed by the personal scents of thousands of people brushing past each other as they bustled through the marketplace. Just another space station designed for industrial or manufacturing work with living areas for all its employees, now made over for the use of far too many refugees from disease-plagued Earth: inner walls torn down to make larger spaces, larger spaces broken up by makeshift walls to make smaller spaces, and shipping containers stacked to make homes for family on top of family.

No, what was different on the *Triomphe* was that everything she was used to just kept going and going. The rotating wheel that simulated gravity would take hours to walk around; the rows of structures off the main walkway extended farther than she could see in each direction, obscuring her view of the station hull until it curved overhead—so far overhead it was dizzying—and the makeshift buildings reached all the way up to it.

She wanted to tip her head back and get a good long look at all the people above her, the lines of laundry crisscrossing the open spaces, people sitting on rickety porches and balconies to watch the crowds as they did small chores. She was afraid it would give her vertigo, looking straight up through layers of people. Mostly, she was afraid her mother would catch her at it; under all the veils, no one could see where she was looking unless it was up, when her jutting chin gave her away.

She wondered if the buildings ever came tumbling down. There were no earthquakes in space, of course, but it didn't look like it would take much of a jolt to knock down one of the spindly supports. And so many of the buildings were buttressed against their neighboring structures that if it happened, it wouldn't take much more to bring entire blocks down.

"Stay light, April. Potential clients are all around us," her mother whispered, her bright smile never dimming despite the annoyance in her words. April swallowed hard and pushed the images out of her mind, concentrating on her walk as she followed her mother through the marketplace. She was supposed to be taking small, gliding steps to make it look like she was floating under all the veils, but her legs, unused to carrying her own body weight, didn't want to do it.

The big-eyed girl gave her hand an encouraging squeeze and April took strength from it, enough to keep walking. The people living on the platform had little in the way of money but apparently were rich in favors. The girl's parents had a relative who ran a bedsit and had sent their twelve-year-old son to lead them there and see them settled for the night. April wasn't sure anyone else had noticed the girl slip away with them. Her brother was walking beside April's mother, telling a jumble of tales about other hauntings on the *Triomphe*. Melena would never do anything so overt as to take notes, but April was certain she would remember them all and look into each on her own later. If half of what the boy was relating turned out to be true, they would be busy here for weeks.

April felt her heart sink and gritted her teeth in annoyance. She had never seen a ghost in her life—did she really think it would be different this time? That somehow not trying to see a ghost for four years would have changed everything and suddenly they'd be there when she looked? Everyone else had seen them, just not her. Same as always. She hadn't realized how much she had been hoping that things had changed until the moment she had turned and seen nothing. Now she felt more of a fraud than ever, and yet she had already agreed that this was what they had to do, at least until they had enough set away to find other work. She had promised her mother that she could do this, that she wouldn't throw the tantrums of her younger self.

She had promised. She might not be someone who could see ghosts, but she was someone who kept a promise. April tried to pull herself up straighter, to walk a little more glidingly, to look like someone who commanded ghosts and who ghosts obeyed. The growling of her stomach helped; it was a nice reminder of why she was doing all this.

"Let's stop here for a moment," Melena said, pointing to a fountain: a series of progressively smaller bowls topped by an elaborate lotus, all dry. There was a bench situated for optimal viewing of what would probably be a lovely sight if the water was running and Melena settled onto it, April perching beside her, careful to still look otherworldly even while she rested her all-too-worldly body.

She must have been doing something right, she considered, as they had attracted a sizable retinue of children as they walked through the marketplace. They hovered a short distance away, and the two children from the platform puffed up importantly at all the attention.

"Hello, little ones," her mother said, always on the job. "Do you know who this is?"

Most of the children just stared back at her, but the bravest, a girl with fine blonde hair gathered into two thin braids, lifted her chin as she answered, "No."

"This is April Nguyen, Mistress of Spirits, Quieter of Hauntings, Cleanser of Sorrowful Places."

"That's a long name," the girl said.

"Have you ever heard of her?" her mother went on.

"No," the girl said, giving a sideways glance at April. "I can't even see her. Is she pretty?"

"She's more than pretty," her mother said. "She can command ghosts."

"To do what?"

"Anything. But the most important thing she does is help them move on. Have you ever seen a ghost?"

The girl shook her head, and a second later her companions did likewise.

"Ghosts are very sad. But most of us can't figure out why. April can, and once she knows why the ghosts are sad, she can help them leave. Ghosts don't want to be here, you know. They just get stuck and need a little bit of help."

"Ghosts are scary," one of the boys said, his voice no more than a whisper.

"Some are," April's mother agreed. "But they don't mean to be. They're lost, and being lost makes them sad and sometimes angry."

"How can she talk to ghosts?" the girl asked.

"It's a gift she was born with. She's always been special."

The girl turned to scrutinize April more directly, unconvinced. "Why is she hiding, then?"

"Like ghosts, she prefers quiet places: not so bright, not so loud. Without her veils, this place would overwhelm her."

The girl's mouth twisted and April knew, without her saying a word, just what she thought of someone so delicate. April kept her eyes up, doing her best to ignore the girl, resisting the temptation to explain that, of course, it was all part of the act. April wasn't nearly so helpless as all that.

"So tell me, children," her mother went on. "There must be ghosts here. Every station has its ghosts. Tell me the stories."

The children looked at each other.

"The bridge," one kid said. "My da said the bridge is haunted. The captain in charge of the station and the whole bridge crew died there and they haunt it because—"

"That's just a story," the girl interrupted with a wave of her hand. "They don't want kids up there, so they made up a story."

"And you're clever enough to figure that out?" April's mother said.

"I think they're all stories," the girl said. "To keep us out of places or to scare us into behaving. I don't think any of it is true."

"I've seen ghosts," the girl from the platform said softly. "They were my friends, but then they were ghosts."

"April made them go away," her brother added. "Now they won't make their ma so sad anymore."

"That's right," Melena said, and April tried not to sigh aloud. If only she felt so sure. Why was she still doing this?

She felt it before she properly saw it: a boy about her age staring daggers at her that struck her like his gaze really could stab into her flesh. He stood at the edge of the fountain square outside one of the shops, but what should have been plenty of distance seemed like nothing as he towered over the people bustling between them; no one else was tall enough to get between his eyes and her. And while the girl before her was staring at her suspiciously, he was doing it with deepest hate. April felt certain if she ripped off her veils, she would be able to see the flames burning in those dark eyes. As it was, she felt their heat and gasped softly, her posture finally starting to crumple. Her mother caught her elbow, and the children rushed forward but then stopped, as if wanting to help but still not willing to touch her.

"I'm all right," April said and willed herself to sit up straight again.

"Maybe we should go on now, get settled in our room," her mother said. "Then rest."

"Yes, let's," April said, getting to her feet. Her knees were shaking, but she took a deep breath and focused until they stopped.

Then, although she really didn't want to, she couldn't help seeking out the boy again. Perhaps she had imagined him. Or perhaps he hadn't been looking at her at all. Such blatant hate... he had to have been looking at someone he already knew, not someone he had never met before in his life. And she knew she'd remember him if they had met. Tall, lanky, untidy Afro, dark brown skin and nearly black eyes; he would have been memorable even in passing.

He was still there, still glaring at her. Definitely at her. Her breath caught again. It was like the veils weren't even there, like he really could see her. He saw every bit of her, body and soul, and his hatred was all the deeper for it.

The girl took her hand once more and April let herself be led away from the fountain and that glaring boy. Normally, April loved market-places; even veiled, she could smell tempting foods, catch glimpses of all the goods for sale. It had been years since she had visited one, and never one close to this size. And yet today it just felt too overwhelming. She needed calm and quiet. She needed to lie down and sleep for a thousand days.

From the central mall, it looked like everything inside the station was jury-rigged from shipping containers and scraps of whatever had been available, but April watched as the boy ducked down a side street that dead-ended at the bottom of a stairway that was clearly original construction. There were two flights of stairs moving first away and then towards each other in an endless zigzag.

"How far up?" Melena asked as the boy started up the steps.

"Seven floors," he said.

April's knees quaked just at the idea.

"Is there an elevator?" her mother asked.

"Yeah, but the gangs control those. They charge, and with how you two are dressed, they'll charge you more."

Her mother took April's elbow and spoke close to her ear. "Can you do it?"

"I'm more worried about you," April said.

"Tomorrow will be easier," her mother said, giving her elbow a squeeze.

April wished they could at least eat something first, but she supposed it would be rude to eat in front of the children without sharing, and what little the Vasquezes' neighbors had given them was scarcely enough for two.

She draped the edges of her veils over one hand, gripping the staircase rail with the other, and focused on putting one aching foot in front of the other. Her mother set a slow pace, so slow the boy was several flights above them before he realized he was alone.

"What's taking you?" he called back down.

"Apologies, young one," her mother called back breathlessly. "We've been in free fall for some time."

The boy ran back down to stand at the top of the flight of stairs they were currently ascending. "Free fall?" he repeated. "I've never been in free fall. Is it fun?"

"Free fall is fun," Melena said as she reached his side. "Coming out of free fall, not so much. Your muscles get weak."

April just kept her attention focused on moving one foot in front of the other and not tripping over her veils. The girl beside her kept a hand on her arm as if ready to catch her if she stumbled.

The boy ran ahead again to get their room arranged. By the time they reached the last flight before the seventh floor, Melena's pace had slowed so that she was walking beside April, the girl between holding an arm of each of them. When at last the stairs ended, April bent with hands on her knees and fought back waves of dizziness. The lack of food was catching up with her, too.

She lifted her head, forcing her eyes to open and look around. They were on a landing that, like the staircase, was part of the original station. On one side, she had an impressive view of the makeshift marketplace and city with its tottering buildings, on the other a series of glass-fronted shops. So even in the original structure, this part of the station had been a shopping area.

Melena touched her arm, and she straightened, settling her veils with a twitch of her hand. They walked through the open glass doors into a sitting room with chairs and little tables and carefully angled lights, perfect for curling up and reading and occasionally looking out the windows at the crowds passing by. On the far end of the room was a hallway, but between them and the hallway was a long, tall desk, and behind the desk was a woman who looked none too pleased to see them.

"Here they are," the boy said, and the woman scowled. But as they drew limpingly nearer, her frown softened into a look of grudging concern.

"We just need to rest," Melena said. "We are most grateful for your hospitality. And I know it was promised as a favor, but in a few days we will have something we can pay you with. You have my word."

"I can spare a room," the woman said. "It's not much."

"We don't need much," Melena said. "Just a place to lie down."

The woman nodded and poked around behind her desk before emerging with an old, battered tablet. "This way."

"We should be getting back home," the boy said as Melena and April moved to follow the proprietor.

"Of course. Thank you for showing us the way. And thank your family and your neighbors for their gifts. We shall be putting them to good use."

April looked down at the girl who was once more clasping her hand. She dropped down to one protesting knee, unthreaded one of the bells from her long braid, and looped it through the tie in one of the girl's pigtails. The girl broke out into a wide smile, the first April had seen from her, made all the more special for the gaps where she was waiting for adult teeth to come in. Then she took her brother's hand and went out the door, walking with a skip to make the little bell tinkle.

"This way," the woman said again, and they followed her down the long hallway to where it ended in a T and down the right-hand corridor to the very end.

"I'm particular about my guests; there are only good people here," she said as her fingers flew over the tablet. "Even so, the doors are programmed to remain locked. The passcode changes between guests. Yours is 3829," she said, tapping the code into the number pad as she read it out to them. The light went from orange to green and the door popped open with a click. "You'll need the same code to get out again, so don't forget it."

"3829," Melena said. "Thank you."

The woman nodded, then turned and marched back to her desk.

April stepped into the room as the overhead light flickered to life. The room was longer than it was wide, with two narrow beds taking up so much of the space there wasn't room to walk between them. April clambered over the overly elaborate footboard and spilled onto the lumpy mattress with a contented sigh. She nearly gave in to the desire to drift off to sleep, but fought it back and sat up, stripping off the layers of veils and kicking off her shoes. Melena stepped more gracefully over her own footboard, settling cross-legged on her bed facing April. She held the mesh bag with the gifts.

"Is there anything left like a tablecloth?" she asked, switching to French now that the two of them were alone. April sat up again, digging into the carpetbag. There wasn't much in there besides her reader and her mother's treasured doll, just a change of clothes for each of them.

"No," she said.

"Mind the crumbs, then," her mother said and started removing items from the mesh bag. A box of slightly mushy crackers (living inside the water treatment system must wreak havoc on food storage), a tube of fish paste, and another of some sort of nut butter. A packet of something that wasn't truly dried fruit but was a remarkable teeth-sticking simulation. There wasn't much, not really even enough for two, but after days of nothing, it was like a feast.

"It won't take long to get back on our feet," Melena said as she gathered up the empty packets. "Your reputation is already spreading, and even though it's been a few years, people will remember you from before."

"They'll be expecting a precocious little child," April said. "Remember, things were already changing before I quit. After my growth spurt, I wasn't what they were expecting anymore."

"That's how this little break helps us," Melena insisted. "You're reinventing yourself."

April sighed.

"April, we really only have two choices. You do this, or I find another man and hope he doesn't dump us out of his ship at the far end of everything, like the last one. There is nothing else."

April nodded mutely. The last man had seemed nice enough, and he certainly had been rich enough. It had been good at first, when Melena had still been in her up phase. But then her personal darkness had cloaked itself around her once more and she refused to get out of bed, not even to eat. Wearing the same clothes for days on end, her long hair grew matted with neglect and her unwashed body took on a sour smell. Then the quiet crying over nothing apparent would become sobs and finally she would just talk with herself in words barely coherent. Even the nicest of men bailed at that point. This last fellow had been captain of a long-haul freighter. He couldn't just leave them, so instead he dropped them off on a tiny asteroid mining colony, a thirteen-year-old girl and her nonfunctioning mother alone among miners who had no time for them.

"April?"

"Did you see them?" April asked, fidgeting with the fraying hem of her kameez.

"See who?"

"You know. The girls. Did you really see them? Or were you pretending because the others said they saw them?"

"Honestly, April. This conversation again?"

"It just seems like I should see them too, doesn't it? I don't understand what's wrong with me."

"You doubt yourself too much," Melena said, brushing stray hairs back from April's forehead. "You need to let go of those doubts, to trust in yourself and your beautiful gift. I think when you stop letting this bother you, when you let go of your doubts and fears, then you will see what we all see."

"But what if I don't? What if I never do? I feel like a fraud, like I'm tricking people."

Melena's cheeks reddened and her voice hardened, as they did every time April mentioned the word. "You are not a fraud. What difference does it make if you can't see these ghosts? Lots of people can see ghosts, it's nothing special. But *you* are the one who can send them on, who can give their families peace and a sense of closure. You may be blind to the other world, but you can touch it all the same. You saw the mother, how changed she was by what you did."

"Yes, I did," April said.

"Then that's all you need to see." She looked around and found the control for the light, then gave April a questioning look. April nodded, and she clicked off the lights.

"But it doesn't make sense that I can't see the ghosts too," April said to herself as she peeled back the covers and climbed into the bed. "I believe just as much as anybody. I want to see, with all my heart. Why can't I?" She curled up under the covers, hands tucked under her pillow.

The memory of those eyes glaring at her in hatred kept sleep at bay for far too long.

3

LOST IN A CROWD

April bit her lip as she watched her mother move about the room, dressing to go out. She moved slowly, each motion deliberate, but April saw the pain in the tight line of her mouth.

"Maybe I should go out instead," April said. She was feeling pretty wrecked herself, but nowhere near as bad as her mother looked.

"No. You are gifted, but sales is not your gift," Melena said, brushing out the long waves of her hair.

"I did OK the last few weeks," April said. She hadn't particularly enjoyed it—talking with strangers always stressed her out, and trying to haggle with them to get the most out of every one of their possessions had really taxed her—but now that she was looking at the prospect of being cloistered again like she had been as a child, she missed the freedom, scary as it had sometimes been.

"You took care of the two of us beautifully," her mother agreed, "but it's better if someone else brags you up."

"Like my mother."

"I'm subtle, you know that," Melena said. "I'll be back with a client, hopefully someone who can give us a gift of coin. I'd like to pay for our own room, and of course there's food,"—April's stomach gave a half-hearted growl in reply to that—"and you're going to need a wardrobe upgrade."

"That's going to take lots of jobs," April said glumly.

"One job at a time," her mother said. "Just focus on that. I think I'll start with that boy's story about the bridge."

April nodded, then reached into her carpetbag to dig out her battered old reader.

"With everything else you sold, you held on to the thing with the least use to us but the most value in coin," Melena said with a frown.

"I also kept your doll," April said. She looked into the bag but then saw the doll resting comfortably on her mother's pillow. She was meant to be some sort of superhero from a story April had never heard and doubted her mother had either. But her purple cape was very eye-catching, only the very edges starting to fray despite its age.

"The doll wouldn't fetch much," Melena said, but the cross look had faded from her face. "The reader is worth a week's worth of meals, at least. Besides, it never answers your questions, it just gives you more questions. Doubts. Sometimes I regret ever giving you that thing. I don't even know why I kept it when I left home."

"I can't live without it," April said, clutching the book tightly to her chest.

"April, always so dramatic."

"No, it's completely true," April said softly.

They never talked about it; after her mother came out of one of her black periods, it was always as if the last few weeks or months had just never been. As if everything April had been dealing with—caring for her mother through lethargic depressions or furious storms of rage—hadn't happened. But when she was living through those days, the stories in her reader were her only escape. They kept her sane.

But of course she couldn't say that. Because that would be talking about what they never talked about.

Her mother was frowning over her, as if trying to puzzle out what April had meant. "I suppose just now it's very handy indeed, if it keeps you in this room safely out of sight while we build the mystery of your persona. I don't know how long I'll be. Hopefully not too long; I know you're hungry."

"I'll be fine," April said, pulling the covers back over her legs and settling her reader on her knees.

April opened the reader's menu and scrolled through the contents, but nothing grabbed her attention. It had originally been Melena's school reader, filled with learning programs and textbooks, as well as every book she had downloaded from the corporate station's archives. April supposed that technically it was stolen and not something Melena should have taken with her when she left her corporate home. Her mother showed so little interest in it that April would bet she had taken it by mistake; she had always gotten the impression that her mother's decision to run away had been very spur-of-the-moment. Melena never spoke of the past, but as April's life had been a succession of moves with little warning, just time to stuff all of their things into bags and catch a ride on the next shuttle, April doubted her mother had been any different as a teenager.

April had long since searched every book the reader contained for information on ghosts. Most of the contents were fiction, but there was an encyclopedia, the part of the reader she spent the most time with, and she followed link after link to article after article. It did often feel like she found more questions than answers. She knew every ghost story from history, the folklore from cultures all over Earth.

She had also read about famous debunkers of ghost stories, people like Harry Houdini, who proved mediums had no real powers, just a variety of tricks. April wasn't sure what to make of those stories. She never did anything to make anyone believe there was a ghost there when there wasn't. She wasn't ripping anyone off, not deliberately, not like those spiritualists had. She didn't research who the ghosts were supposed to be and pretend to talk with them like she knew all about them or anything like that. She did feel like maybe she shouldn't take money for something she wasn't sure she even did, but everyone else was always so sure, and so grateful.

After an hour or so, her stomach stopped grumbling and settled into a tight, empty knot like a stone under her ribcage. At last, April threw back the covers and pulled her other outfit out of her bag. She couldn't sit here alone in this room all day, no matter what her mother wanted. She had never been on a station like the *Triomphe* before, and she couldn't bear not getting another look around, this time out of costume, so she could gawk all she liked. She just needed to stretch her legs a little.

Once she had had bags and bags of clothes, but now she was down to two outfits. The costume she was still wearing was designed to get attention, but today she just wanted to blend in, to be the same as everyone else. She also had a single pair of jeans—cut off and rolled up at the knee and so faded they were nearly worn through, but they still fit—and a plain white kameez that had a sheen to it but would perhaps not draw too much attention. It had the advantage of being long enough to hide where her reader was clipped to her belt, in case the marketplace on the *Triomphe* was a draw for pickpockets. She never went anywhere without the reader close at hand.

She climbed over the footboard and slipped out the door. The landlady was at her desk, gazing dreamily out into the street. She glanced up and April froze. Had her mother left instructions to keep her confined? But the landlady went back to watching people pass in front of her bedsit and April quickly plunged in among them.

A man right outside the bedsit was selling kebabs from a cart, and April's stomach rumbled back to life at the smell of roasting meat. She lingered for a moment, watching him carefully brush a sweet sauce over each piece of meat on the skewers before turning them over on his grill. He noticed her standing there and smiled, but April quickly walked away before he could start talking to her.

She had intended to stay near the bedsit, to walk along the edge of the balcony and watch the activity below, but when she approached the next set of zigzagging stairs, she changed her mind. Her body had been achy when she had started, but the walk was actually making her feel better, and everything she wanted to see was down below.

The size of the place was still boggling her mind. She remembered all the shuttles docking when she and her mother had arrived; they had waited for hours to get an open airlock and the captain had unloaded his ship with great haste because the harbor fee was charged by the minute. Looking around, April started to form an idea why. The *Triomphe* had become a center for trade, not just within its own walls but between all the space stations.

She paused at the bottom of the stairs outside one of the shops that was part of the original architecture. Inside, a man and a woman were consulting a tablet as they packed a crate with a variety of foodstuffs and medical supplies. Then the woman told the man to bring it up to the docks. April looked at the sign over their door: SONG'S IMPORT/EXPORT. That crate was destined to leave on a shuttle.

April walked on, feeling a bit dazed by all the sights around her. Somewhere on the *Triomphe,* there were greenhouses. There had to be, there were so many kinds of fruits and vegetables for sale, as well as bakeries filled with bread of every shape and color. Then something even more amazing caught her eye: a bookstore. She had never seen so many books in one place, boxes upon boxes filled with yellowing paperbacks, battered hardcovers, slightly sticky books for children. She wondered who had sent so many up into space when electronic readers had been prevalent before the first corporate station had even been built, but satisfying her curiosity would involve talking with the shopkeeper. She strolled along the tables he had put out in front of his shop but said nothing and did not venture deeper in to the shadowy depths of his treasure trove. She did look around and note the land-marks. If she and her mother were truly going to be staying on the *Triomphe* for a while, she wanted to be sure to come back. She would never be able to afford a proper book, but he might also have a digital library with things on it that she didn't have on her own reader.

She followed the line of shops around a corner to a narrower section of the ship. The space between the shops here was free of carts and stands; instead people had spread blankets or carpets out on the floor and arranged their goods on the ground. They were handcrafts mostly, jewelry of beads and silver wire, hand-knit sweaters, and uncut woven cloth. A woman sat on a square of rough canvas, piles of machinery parts and broken appliances around her, a tablet computer open on her lap as she tinkered with its insides. A small tray of tools sat beside her, and her tongue was just visible at the corner of her mouth as she adjusted something improbably small.

April wished she could learn how to fix things. It must be so rewarding to finish and turn on something that had been nothing but dead weight before you touched it.

"Hey, girl."

April froze, telling herself no one was really talking to her, but reluctant to turn around and be sure.

"Girl with the black hair, come here for a minute," the man said again. He spoke English, but with a strong accent she couldn't identify.

Still April tried to ignore him, moving away from the repair-woman's canvas and heading back toward the busier shops, but a hand caught her arm and detained her. April stiffened, her hands curling into fists she had no idea what to do with.

"Hey, take it easy," the man said, letting her go and holding up his hands in proclaimed innocence. "I don't think you heard me. I wanted to talk to you for a second."

"I don't know you," April said, not relaxing.

"I wanted to make you an offer," the man said.

"An offer for what?" April asked. Was this a job? Did he know who she was?

"That hair of yours," he said, reaching towards her but letting his hand drop when she flinched away. He smiled at her in a way she was sure was meant to be disarming.

"What about my hair?"

"Sister, do you know how much hair like yours would sell for? That length, that color, that shine. It is real, isn't it?"

"Of course it's real," April said, pulling her hair forward over her shoulder and twisting it between her hands.

"You must eat well, to have hair like that."

"Sometimes," she said, not adding, *Not lately.* "I'm not selling it."

"I'd be willing to go quite high," he said. "I have a few clients in mind already. And what would you be out, really? It'll grow back."

"No, thank you," April said and turned her back to him.

"Come on, we can at least negotiate a little. You can't just say no and not talk it over."

April didn't answer, just kept her hair pulled tight in her hands as her walk became a jog. She didn't want to look back, but she felt like he was getting closer. Was he planning to tackle her, to steal her hair?

"Stop following me!" April said, then broke into a run, pushing back into the thickest part of the crowds. She collided with person after person, upsetting more than a few and leaving quite a ruckus in her wake. Then the crowd thinned out and she could run again. She ran until a stitch in her side made her stop, hands on knees as she tried to catch her breath. Her hair swung forward over her face and she brushed it back in irritation. Then she straightened, turning and turning as she looked at everyone around her, trying to figure who else might be wanting her hair. She quickly combed through it with her fingers, then braided it, wrapping the braid around her head and tucking the end back through itself. Without pins, it was sure to fall sooner rather than later, but hopefully it would catch less attention this way. She should just go back to their room and wait for her mother to return. She had had enough adventure for one day.

Her stomach gave a sickening lurch as she realized she had absolutely no idea where she was. She tried to walk back the way she had come, but the path she'd taken as she ran through the crowds had been nothing like a straight line. She had been on the seventh level, that she remembered, but looking up she could see that most of the balconies above her didn't connect. They stopped and started at regular intervals; she would need to find the exact staircase she had come down in the first place.

She tried to remember what had been at the bottom of the staircase. The import/export business for sure, but what else? A bakery? The bookstore had been farther down, but she had paid more attention to those surroundings. She could probably find the bookstore again and, once there, figure out the way back to the room. That would be better than trying to find the room itself.

April kept walking, resisting the urge to cover her hair with her hands. Suddenly everyone seemed to be looking at her too closely, too long. She told herself it was just her imagination, but she didn't like it. She longed to have the layers of veils once more between her and the world. She wanted to be back in her room, alone.

April twisted her hands together. She was going to have to ask for help. She looked around. When she'd first stepped into the market-place, the tableau of cranky shopkeepers chastising the street kids with harsh words or even quick cuffs to the head had been entertaining, at least in its shock value. Now the prospect of trying to talk to one of them was positively frightening. She didn't want to get yelled at, or worse, cuffed. But she wasn't sure asking one of the street kids was a better option; the first words out of her mouth and they'd surely know she wasn't one of them. She could understand their patois well enough —each station had its own variety, though they were more similar than not—but she didn't think she could speak it more than haltingly.

As if in answer to her thoughts, a phrase carried through the hubbub, a trick of the market acoustics, a snatch of unadulterated English. She turned to find the source but at first saw only what she'd been seeing all afternoon: a mass of people wearing all manners of clothing and hairstyles, speaking every sort of language and somehow making themselves understood to each other.

April felt a thickness in her throat as tears threatened to spill, and she closed her eyes tight, willing the feeling to pass. She could deal with this. The only reason she didn't know what to do was that she'd never been on her own in a strange place before. It wasn't because she was helpless.

Her quiet moment of centering herself was shattered by the feeling of someone else's hand exploring the pockets of her pants. Her rather *tight* pants, she couldn't tell in the moment if the person was trying to rob her or molest her. She let out a cry, flailing her arms and backing hurriedly away. She didn't see the culprit, but that feeling of everyone staring at her was now a certainty. She ducked her head to hide her flaming cheeks, patting a hand over her stomach. The reader was still there. She wasn't sure if that was comforting or not; it was nice to still have it, but she didn't like the way that answered the robber-versus-molester question.

She couldn't stay cowering against the wall of the spice shop forever. April lifted her head and looked at each person around her carefully, listening and watching, hoping to find someone who spoke English or, failing that, French. But even if that didn't work out, surely she could speak and gesture and be understood the same as anyone else.

Then she found him, the voice she had heard speaking English, and her brief flame of hope blew out. It was the boy from the day before, the one who had glared at her with such hate in his eyes.

4

____

A QUICK STUDY

HE WAS SITTING ON A TATTERED BIT OF CARPET, CROSS-LEGGED, IN A FADED pair of canvas pants that barely reached past his knees and a dashiki of red and orange that looked new, if a bit too large for him. There were six game boards sitting on the carpet in front of him, each with a different opponent frowning over the pieces. April crept closer, watching as he shifted his attention from one to the next, addressing one man in the patois of the space station, another in what she thought was Arabic, and a third in English. His face was younger than his voice; he couldn't be more than a year or two older than she, maybe eighteen at the most. She could still ask him for help. Without her veils, he wouldn't know her.

April crept into the alley, making sure no one was near or watching her, and took out her reader. She held it up, taking a picture of one of the game boards. The encyclopedia shuffled, then matched the image. They were playing a game called Othello or Reversi. She read over the basics of the game as she watched the boy play six simultaneous games. The board was divided into sixty-four squares and the pieces were white on one side, black on the other. Each player set a piece down on the board with his color up, and any of his opponents' colors between that piece and some other piece of his would be flipped over, now part of the player's color. It seemed simple enough.

April watched as three players lost, one after the other. The patois-speaker grinned and handed over a large, nicked coin. The Arabic-speaker stared at the board as if trying to figure out where he had gone wrong but, at the boy's prompting, handed over a few shiny, flat bars stamped with some sort of image. That was money April had never seen before; it looked new. The English-speaker paid up but demanded a rematch.

"I'll have you this time," the man said, taking out another coin from the pocket of his emerald-green waistcoat and setting it on the carpet as the boy removed all the pieces from the board except four in the middle, two white and two black. Then he added another black piece, turning over the white one between, and the game was on.

"I've got him this time," said the woman at the end, spreading her hands over the full board. "Thirty-three to thirty-one. Count it."

"No, you're right," the boy said, digging the recently acquired coin out of his pocket and handing it to her. "Again?"

"That makes me one for ten, but maybe it's the start of a roll," she said with a grin, and they reset the board.

They were all so engrossed in their games that April was able to draw nearer without fear of calling attention to herself. She tried to figure out the strategies the players were using. The last few moves of each game always involved huge numbers of pieces changing color in rapid succession. Everything could change right at the end. So how did one decide where to play in the beginning?

April leaned in closer to watch a woman with a fierce tangle of dirty blonde hair and a very ripe smell make her move. This was the closest of the matches, and April spotted what seemed to her to be the obvious move, but the woman didn't take it. The boy glanced up at April and she realized she had made a little noise of disapproval. There was no way for his opponent to come out with a win now, but the woman didn't concede and the boy scarcely waited for her to turn pieces over before making his own moves to win the game.

The woman was infuriated. She spoke a patois so coarse April could barely understand it, but the man next to her did.

"No cheating here, amiga. He beat you fair and square. You pay up," the man said, his face smiling but his voice holding just the slightest nuance of threat.

The woman said something else, and April gathered that she still thought she'd been cheated, and that perhaps there was some question as to the boy's parentage. The boy was unruffled, moving from board to board and removing the pieces to set up for the next games. The woman didn't like being ignored, though, and she jumped to her feet and kicked over the game board. She towered over the boy, arms waving as the words came fast and loud, but when he refused to even look up at her, she screeched and stormed off.

"Hey, amigo, she didn't pay," the patois-speaker said.

"It's not a thing," the boy said. "Rematch?"

"Yeah, but hold on a sec," he said and hopped up, jogging out of sight down the lane that led to the market. The Arabic- and English-speakers were already making their opening moves.

"How about you?" April jumped, realizing he was talking to her. She had been so sure she was invisible.

"Oh, no. I haven't any money."

"Don't worry about it. I have an open board, and I don't mind the practice."

"I've never played," she admitted.

"You've figured it out, though, right?" He looked right into her eyes. It was a completely different experience than the day before. Yesterday had been nothing but harsh disdain; today his eyes were appraising but not judgy, and when she nodded, he narrowed one eye in half a wink as if saying he knew she had.

"I understand how the game is played, but I'm not sure I get how to win it."

"You'll pick it up." He extended a hand to the place opposite him on the carpet and April sat down, adjusting her reader under her kameez discretely. She picked up a black piece and set it down, turned over the white in between, then looked up at him. He put down a piece of his own, turned hers over, then shifted his attention to one of the other boards. April tried to puzzle out what play would be best, but they all seemed equally valid to her. At last she picked one at random, turned over the piece between, then waited as he worked across the other boards.

The patois-speaker came jogging back, handing the boy a thin bracelet of tarnished silver. He took it without comment and the two settled over the opening moves of their game.

"I'll give up my place if you get another paying customer," she said when he came back to her.

"Don't worry about it," he said, making his move.

April once more studied the board. Nothing jumped out at her as being the obvious choice, so again, she picked one at random.

The game ended with her only having three pieces left showing black.

"I muffed that," she said, brushing a stray hair out of her eyes and sending the loose braid tumbling down her back. She didn't bother wrapping it back up.

"But you learned something," he guessed.

"The corners are important," she said. "You got all four corners, and you crushed me."

"Try again. You're white this time. That means you play second." April nodded and watched him make his own first play.

April tried to take the corners this time, but they never seemed to be available to her. She lost again, but this time she had ten pieces showing white.

"The sides. Almost as good as a corner. It's not impossible for you to turn my piece, but it's harder."

"Good," he said, waiting for her to make her first play before making his.

April was vaguely aware of the other games going on to her left. The boy lost a few but won most. One by one, his opponents called it quits and left. Shopkeepers at the end of the alley were beginning to pack up their wares. April's stomach gave a sudden growl, as if reminding her that she had missed breakfast and lunch and was, at that very moment, missing dinner. She ignored it, focusing on the game. Soon there were only two active boards, hers and the one belonging to the man in the green waistcoat.

"This is going to be my last game," the man said as they set up the board. "It's getting late."

"Sure," the boy said, making a play on each of the two boards.

"You did good today?" the man asked, pointing at the boy's pocket with his chin.

"I did OK," he allowed.

"Slow road to riches," the man said, and the boy shrugged.

April frowned over her own board, trying to pick between two options. Either would let her turn over three pieces. Then she realized if she picked the first option, she'd leave herself open to losing six, whereas with the second, he could only take one. She put her piece down with a grin.

"You're getting the hang of it," he said as he made his move.

"I'm getting more of a sense of where I want to put my pieces," she said.

"The real leap is when you realize you should spend more of your time thinking about where you want me to put my pieces."

"Yeah, I just figured that out." She made another play, and he took the last open space. April counted up her pieces and realized she had just won.

She looked up at him. He was smiling at her.

"Why did you let me win?" she asked.

"I didn't let you," he said, the grin fading. "I'm offended you would even think such a thing. I would never disrespect the game like that."

"I really won?" April counted up her pieces again. She had.

"Quick study," the waistcoat man said, watching her reset her board. "You could have her work with you, twice as many boards. Double your money."

"Yeah, but then we'd be splitting it," the boy said, making his play on the man's board. Then he looked up at April with a smile that seemed to say "No offense" in case she thought he was accusing her of elbowing into his turf.

She tried to smile back but wasn't sure what answer her smile was making. She was suddenly acutely aware of how little time she had spent in the company of people her own age. She was mostly with her mother, her mother's friends, her mother's boyfriends, and clients.

Occasionally, children were there when she did her work, but when veiled, she wasn't supposed to interact with them.

And she was beginning to suspect that the little behavioral cues she was used to interpreting when dealing with adults weren't quite the same in teenagers, or at least not in this teenager. She thought he liked her, but the memory of that first look of burning hate made her unsure.

The man in the waistcoat just shrugged as he made his play. "You might be in the wrong line of work. Have you heard about the quieter of spirits?"

"The who?" the boy asked. April shrunk down, fidgeting with the remains of her braid until her hair fell over her face.

"This woman arrived yesterday, all decked out in layers of veils and bells for jewelry. She was silent as a ghost but for that tinkling. She was like a wisp of something ethereal, just gliding over the ground." His eyes were bright as his hands tried to demonstrate the smooth glide.

"I saw her," the boy said, his lips twisting as if the memory left a bad taste in his mouth. "And I heard the woman with her, talking her up to a pack of kids. Playing up her 'magic powers' with 'ghosts.' That's a loathsome way to make some coin, taking advantage of people grieving."

"I've heard the story of what happened," the man said. "There were two dozen witnesses who all saw the same thing. They all saw the ghosts of the girls right there in the hidey-hole where they used to play together."

April shrank down further. The story that was spreading wasn't even correct; everyone had seen them on the catwalk. Everyone but her.

"You heard a story," the boy reiterated.

"People saw something," the man insisted. "How is it possible to fool so many people in the same way at the same time? They agreed to every detail, what the girls were wearing and everything."

"It's ridiculously easy to fool people," the boy said, placing a piece on the game board and turning over his captured pieces. "Especially people who want to believe."

"You're saying they are all making it up?"

"No, I'm sure they all really think they saw something. But they are reinforcing each other's perceptions without knowing it. The mind is easily fooled. You can remember things that never happened, see things that aren't there. Your brain rewrites your own memories; it feels like you're remembering what actually happened but the data has been corrupted. Scientists used to study such things, back when we still had scientists."

The man shrugged and made his play. "Well, she's supposed to be here for a while. Maybe you should go watch her next performance."

"'Performance' is exactly the right word for it," the boy scoffed.

"You've never seen a ghost?" April dared to ask.

"Well, of course not. There is no such thing as ghosts. Just lonely people who miss their loved ones, who are maybe more than a little afraid of the way we live now, up in space in aging stations and ships we are quickly forgetting how to repair. I get being scared, and I get missing your loved ones. I miss my parents every day. But I would never sully their memory with a game of pretend."

April felt her cheeks flushing and quickly ducked her head. She had never heard anyone say such things before, and with such conviction. She had read Houdini—always searching for the supernatural, always disappointed when he uncovered yet another charlatan. But this boy was different.

And, like her, he had never seen a ghost. She wished he would be there the next time she worked. She wanted him there at the moment when everyone was gasping and wowing. It was possible he had never seen a ghost because he had never been in the presence of one. Would that change if she summoned one for him? Or would he still not see but finally realize he was missing out on what everyone around him was experiencing?

She realized he was still talking, his eyes on the game piece between his fingers. "I could never take comfort in some bit of nonsense that is so far removed from an actual solution to the problem. Take those two girls whose 'ghosts' everyone saw. How did they die?"

"The hidey-hole they used to play in had a valve in the back between two pipes," the man in the waistcoat said, to April's surprise. How had he come by that information? Was it any more reliable than his version of her ceremony with its wrongly placed ghosts? "They must have bumped it somehow while they were playing, enough to fill the space with some sort of odorless, poisonous gas. They died pretty quickly, I understand. Nothing could be done."

"And I bet there are still kids living down there," the boy said. April remembered the little girl she had given one of her bells to. She had never asked her name. "And I'm sure those kids know all about the dangers of ghosts and nothing about the dangers of their actual environment."

"There are hundreds of people living in groups wherever there is enough space to spread a carpet and call it home," the man in the waistcoat said, his voice turning hard. "There is nowhere else for them to go. So what's your 'actual' solution to that problem?"

"Obviously, there is no easy fix. That's what makes focusing on the emotionally gratifying ghost business so appealing. Every station in the solar system is overcrowded. It's only going to get worse, and the Earth is lost to us. We need to build more stations."

The man laughed. "We can barely maintain what we have, and you want to build more?"

"There are still people out there who have the skills. But every year there are fewer. If we don't act now, we will be lost, all of us."

"You're a cheerful one," the man said, finally turning his attention back to their game. He played a piece, taking his only available move. "Well, I'm definitely going to try to watch," he said as the boy quickly dominated the board between them and took both of the coins. "I really am skeptical, whatever you might think. I don't know if I believe she can do what they say she does, but I want to see for myself."

"I don't think she likes to be watched," April found herself saying. Her cheeks reddened again; she could feel their heat and grew more embarrassed with the realization that the two looking at her knew she was embarrassed. "I mean, with all the veils. I think she doesn't like to be looked at."

"It's part of the show," the boy said. "The real world is too much for her. She's so delicate. I bet when she 'works' she takes all those layers off, opens herself up to the world beyond this one." April bit her lip. He was downright eerie with his guessing. "These are very old cons." April remembered the things she had read about Houdini uncovering all sorts of con artists, but the unfairness of it hit her hard. She had never tried to deceive anybody. Being veiled might be an old con, but it was just a coincidence that she wore them, too.

But the veils had been her mother's idea. She had done a lot of research putting together April's look and the aspects of her ritual, combining elements from folklore from every corner of Earth. Her mother had always said that April's skills were real, but that selling her image was important to get her skills out there. You couldn't tell by looking at April what she could do; the costumes and trappings were just a part of bringing people to the truth of what she could do. And people were comforted by things that reminded them of the life on Earth none of them had ever had but had heard tales of from their elders. It felt a bit dishonest to April because she had never seen proof of her own skills, but not to her mother, who had seen the ghosts. If her mother believed, then she wasn't conning anyone either.

That was all true, but it didn't make April feel any better.

"Maybe she's just ugly. Or blind. Or both," the man said, getting to his feet. "See you tomorrow evening, then."

The boy returned his wave. April turned her attention back to the board, but it was as if it had all suddenly grown foreign to her. She made a play, the wrong one.

"You saw that woman yesterday too," he said. He was trying to catch her eye, but she kept her gaze on the board.

"Yeah, kinda," April said. Her throat was dry and her head was starting to swim. She had gone longer than this without food many times; it shouldn't be hitting her so hard. She made another bad play, and he made his last move. There was no need to count up the pieces; it was not even close.

"What did you think?" he asked. He wasn't looking directly at her, just glancing at her now and again as he packed up all six boards inside a large bag.

"Um," April said, twisting her braid. She had no possible answer to that question. "Listen, I'm actually incredibly lost I saw a bookstore this morning. Do you know how I can find it again?"

He put the last of the games inside the sack and cinched it closed. He froze there a moment, hands still on the closure, and just looked at her for a long moment. Then he straightened and rubbed at the back of his head. "Bookstore?"

"It's near where my mother and I are staying. I can find my way back from there, but I got a little turned around after passing the bookstore this morning."

"I know which one you're talking about. Come on, I'll show you. It's on my way."

"Thanks," April said, grateful both for the guidance and for the change of conversation.

"My name is Hakim, by the way," he said, putting out a hand. She took it and gave it a quick shake. It was warm, and the way his long fingers wrapped around her hand and squeezed felt right. Almost familiar. She felt herself blushing again.

"April," she said, not quite flinching. He said he had seen her mother; it was possible that he had heard her saying April's name. But it wasn't particularly unique. Perhaps he wouldn't connect the two.

"Pleased to meet you, April," he said and slung the clattering bag of games over one shoulder, then stooped to roll up the carpet. He wrangled the carpet up onto his opposite shoulder and indicated with a nod of his head that they should start walking.

"Can I help you carry something?" April offered.

"I've got it," Hakim said. "It's more bulky than heavy. And you look like you're still getting your gravity legs."

"That obvious, huh?"

"You've been in free fall for a while?"

"Nearly a year off and on. But we're going to be staying here from now on."

"A year, that's not good for you."

"Yes, I know. There was no way around it."

Hakim looked at her carefully, and April resisted the urge to cover her still-pink cheeks with her hands. "Did you just arrive today?" he asked.

"No, yesterday," she said, then wished she hadn't.

"The same as the woman in the veils," Hakim said, and April didn't meet his eyes. Then her stomach growled loud enough for even him to hear it. "Hungry?"

"Yeah," she admitted. "But my mother will have something for me when I get home."

"You don't sound sure," he said, still trying to catch her eye.

"She probably will? She's very resourceful."

"Hold this," Hakim said, dumping the carpet onto her shoulder and putting the strap for the bag around her neck. She struggled under the sudden load; despite what he had said, she found them both heavy and bulky. She had just gotten them situated when Hakim was back, taking the carpet from her shoulder. "I bought some fritters."

"I really can't..." she started to say, but he just sighed and then put one of the fried bits in her mouth. The golden batter was pressed against her tongue, hot and oily, and she lost the will to resist. She bit in, catching the remaining half with one hand while Hakim took the bag from her other shoulder. The inside was soft and hot, something she couldn't identify. "What is it?" she asked around her full mouth.

He shrugged, reached into the paper cone, and popped one in his mouth. "Zucchini," he said after chewing.

"It's amazing," April said, putting the other half in her mouth. The batter tasted like corn, and the oil had a pleasantly fresh taste. "Thank you."

"Have another," Hakim said, shaking the cone at her.

She was about to refuse when a sudden loud cry of her name made her freeze in place.

"April!" her mother called again, finally appearing out of the evening market crowd to march towards her. April caught a glimpse of the bookstore over her mother's shoulder; she had nearly made it home.

"I got lost," April said.

"Lost? You weren't even supposed to go *out*!" Melena said.

April cringed, not from the shouting but from the look of deep hurt in her mother's eyes. "I'm sorry I worried you. Really, really sorry."

"I don't know what to think. This just isn't like you, running around with boys!"

April glanced at Hakim, hoping he wasn't offended by the notion that she had been "running around" with him. His eyes were narrowed, his gaze just as dagger-like as the first time he'd clapped eyes on her.

"I *thought* you waffled that answer," he said. "Should have trusted my instincts. Of course you're her."

"I'm... sorry?" she said.

"Say goodbye now, we have a client to meet." Melena, arms crossed, hovered over her daughter as she waited.

April turned from her mother's impatience to Hakim's disdain. "Bye," she said, barely above a whisper. He scoffed. Melena shot him a look and April was prepared to sink into the ground if she started to upbraid his manners. But her mother just took her arm and pulled her away, chattering on about the man she was taking April to meet and how important he was and how much money they were about to make with the job he had for them.

April looked back over her shoulder. The crowd had already closed between them, but Hakim's Afro was still in sight, disappearing down one of the cross streets.

He hadn't even looked her way.

5

———————————————————

WARM CLOTHES AND HOT FOOD

April hadn't expected to be leaving the *Triomphe* again so soon, but they never even went back to the bedsit.

"Your things are already on the shuttle," her mother said as she set a brisk pace back to the docks. "Our client is waiting for us. Luckily, he's an important man. He can make others wait for him.'

"Where are we going?" April asked, nearly out of breath by the time they reached the elevators. Her stomach gave another loud growl.

"Earth," her mother said, taking April by the shoulders and turning her around so she could finger-comb her hair and rebraid it. "Well, low orbit over it. It will take a few days to get there There is a small station, completely abandoned, because it's cursed. You're going to get rid of the ghost so our client can salvage it."

"Who's the client?" April asked. She didn't normally care, but her mother was showing definite signs of being smitten again.

"He's actually a very old, dear friend of mine."

"Have I met him?" Her mother's boyfriends had never made repeat appearances before.

"No, I knew him when I was your age, still living on the corporate station with my parents. I haven't seen him since, but he recognized me straightaway. His name is Ivan EchoHawk." April guessed Russian and Native American from the name, but given what she knew about that particular corporate station, there might be a few other ethnicities mixed in as well. Her mother's parents were Vietnamese and Bengali. April didn't know what she was on her father's side, or if he had even been from the station or was someone her mother had met after running away.

"Why did he leave?" April asked.

"Limited opportunities," her mother said. "Their loss; he's made quite a success of himself out here. He got his start converting unused space on stations into agricultural habitats to decrease everyone's dependence on Earth produce. He also salvages ships and converts them into living space and has some projects underway to build expansions onto existing stations. There is a very high demand for more living space."

"That's so amazing," April said. It was just the sort of thing Hakim had been talking about as an alternative to her own work. She supposed it was just a coincidence, but a part of her wanted to see it as a sign, a possible new future opening up for her. *If* she did her other job well enough to impress him first. Her mother was giving her a puzzled look, and she quickly added, "We need more living space. It's overcrowded everywhere."

"We're going to be spending more time with him than we do with most of your clients," her mother said.

"I don't have to keep up the act the entire time, do I?"

The elevator doors opened, and they floated out into the dock hallway. Her mother consulted the map on the wall, then led the way to the right.

"I shouldn't think so," her mother said. "He's what you would call a skeptic; he's only hiring you to set his workers' minds at ease."

"He doesn't believe there are really ghosts?" April asked, and her mother gave a dismissive shrug. "I've never met a person who didn't, and now today I met two."

"Anything you can think of in this world, you'll find people who believe in it and people who don't," her mother said. "I've tried to keep you apart from such arguments—they can get ugly. Now, Ivan is a disbeliever, but not an unkind one. He respects his workers and their beliefs. One of them actually gave him your name; his cousin was there yesterday and told him all about you. I told you your reputation would build fast. This worker with the cousin found me while I was still trying to find out about the bridge haunting and brought me to speak to his boss. Imagine his surprise when he saw it was me; he had no idea you were my daughter."

April nodded along, but she had stopped listening at the word "skeptic." That was a relief. She wasn't sure how she was going to go through the motions with Hakim's words still echoing in her head, the burning accusation in his eyes. She wished they could have talked more. She wondered if he had ever been in a place where everyone saw something he didn't. Would he still trust what his own eyes told him, despite everyone else's opposite experiences? But it was more than seeing. April had felt things that weren't of the norm: the pressure in her chest, the chill up her spine, the overwhelming sadness that fell over her like a blanket. If he had been there, would he deny those things as well? Or would he feel them but have some other explanation for them?

What explanation could there be? Those things made no sense. But then neither did not seeing the ghosts everyone else saw. April rubbed her head as if that could calm her thoughts running in anxious circles.

"Ah, there he is," Melena said, pulling April along behind her as she pushed off from the wall, sailing across the hallway to the airlock opposite. The man waiting for them looked like a character from a film, perfectly coiffed, stunningly handsome, smiling at them with friendly warmth. Under his tailored suit was hard muscle, perhaps from work, but more likely from access to a gym. April wondered if this was what wealth had brought him—or if looking like a Greek god come to life brought wealth to him.

"Ivan, this is my daughter April," her mother said, clinging to Ivan quite a bit longer than was necessary.

"Pleased to meet you," April said, holding onto a rung near the airlock so she could shake his hand.

"Likewise," he said. "We should get going. My pilots are standing by."

"Sorry to have kept you waiting," April said as they climbed into the airlock.

"Not a problem," he said as he shut the door behind them and spun the lock. "The *Triomphe* is full of distractions. I get sidetracked often myself."

He opened the other side of the airlock and helped them through the narrower space into his shuttle. April glanced to the left, where she could see the two pilots watching them board from the open cockpit door. She smiled, and they raised their hands in hello. Directly in front of her was a little kitchenette full of gleaming appliances. She followed her mother and Ivan to the right, past an open space with a table set into the floor and screens built into the walls. Beyond that was a narrow hallway with small hatches on either side, two high and three deep on each side.

"The sleeping quarters are cozy but private," Ivan said, spinning the hatch on two of the doors. "I put your things inside. There is a toilet and a shower at the end of the hall, but not much more space there. Mostly, I find it more comfortable in the common room when I'm awake."

"It's awesome," April said, crawling into her sleep space. It was like being inside a box of her own; a sleeping bag was tethered to the far wall, a screen set into the wall above it. Her bag had been secured in a cargo net that ran down one side of the space. The opposite side was filled with square cabinet doors which, when she opened a few, she found to be filled with pants, T-shirts, hoodies, and soft slippers.

"I had my assistant pick up a few things in your size," he said. "It's pretty generic stuff, but it's just for this journey. When we get back, you and your mother are going to have more than enough time and money to do all your own shopping. Well, I'll leave you to get settled in. Once we're underway and the pilots can take a break, we'll all eat."

April nodded, stunned by the sudden wealth of clothing options, then remembered to thank him. He nodded with a smile and shut her hatch, his words to her mother abruptly cut off as the door clanged shut. April pulled out every article of clothing, mixing and matching until finally making her choice. The cotton was soft and fresh; these clothes were all new. No one else had worn these before, not even once.

But the decadence of the clothing was nothing next to that of the food: hot buttery noodles with chicken, mushrooms, and nori. April wolfed hers down so quickly that Ivan made her another.

"You look like you've been having some lean days," he said as she dug in to the second bowl.

"Yes, a few," April said, glancing anxiously at her mother, who was eating her food much more daintily.

"Well, those days are over now," he said. "This station is not the only salvage of mine with a tainted reputation. You're going to be a big help to me for a long time to come, I think."

April chewed while she considered how to respond to that. How best to lay the groundwork for eventually doing other work in his company? "I like to be helpful," she said, trying not to wince at how stupid that sounded out loud.

"We have a few days before we get there, but would you like to see where you're going?" he asked.

"Yes," April said. "I know it's orbiting over Earth, but that's it."

"It's called the *Moreau*, and it's one of the oldest stations orbiting the Earth," Ivan said, floating across the room to touch one screen to life. His fingers flew through the options until he brought up a schematic of a ring-shaped space station. "It was one man's personal residence, a very exotic getaway in the early days of people living in space that weren't part of any nation's space program. The man was wealthy beyond imagining, and the station has long been rumored to be full of treasures. But then there is the killer ghost."

"Killer ghost?" April repeated. That was a new one for her.

"The stories say those who go too deeply into the station never come back out. The man was a hermit; he didn't like guests, apparently."

"April has dealt with angry ghosts before," Melena said. Ivan nodded, but April could tell he was humoring her. She remembered what Hakim had been saying about other solutions.

"Could there be something dangerous in there that's killing people, I mean, besides a ghost? Like a gas leak or something?"

Ivan looked surprised at her question, but glanced at his notes before answering. "The station is no longer spinning, and I'm not sure if any of the power or life-support systems are still online. You'll be going in there suited up, so you don't need to worry about gas."

"But there might be something else going on," April persisted.

"You just need to focus on what you do best," her mother said. "The rest will take care of itself."

April bit her lip, not wanting to contradict her mother, but in no way reassured by her words. Ivan looked at April thoughtfully, but said nothing.

After dinner, April went back to her berth and took out her reader. She searched the encyclopedia for the name "Moreau," but the results were all images of paintings of religious and mythological themes by a man name Gustave Moreau, plus one mention of a character from a book. Which might give her a hint into the mind of the station's creator, but not a very direct one. Not a helpful one.

She slept comfortably in her sleeping bag cocoon but woke up early, stomach growling loudly once more. She dressed and gently opened her hatch, poking her head out. It was dark in the hallway, but she could see the light from a screen in the common room. She floated down the hallway and hovered in the doorway, watching Ivan moving through a three-dimensional schematic of the *Moreau*.

"You're up early," he said. "Hungry?"

"Very."

"I left some oatmeal packets out in the kitchenette. Just add water from the spigot and wait a minute."

"OK," April said, pulling herself into the kitchenette. There were several bowl packets on the counter held in place by a strip of cargo net. They listed different flavors, and she read over each before deciding on the one with pecans and cranberries. She peeled back the cover, pushed the bowl up around the spigot, and turned on the water. Then she sealed the cover again, found a spoon, and floated back into the common room.

"I've been thinking about what you said about other dangers," he said, rotating the model on the screen. "This guy was an eccentric. The schematics don't show it, but it's certainly possible he set up booby traps of some sort in there. I think I should come with you."

"I'll take it slow and be careful," she said. "But I want to go in alone. There's no one here who's going to get any catharsis out of this ghost leaving, so I'd really rather do my ritual thing without a bunch of people watching me."

"I don't think—"

"But we're going to go over those schematics first," she interrupted. "Find every possible danger so I know what to watch out for. I will be thoroughly prepared for anything. You can help with that."

Ivan just looked at her for a long time. April put a spoonful of oatmeal in her mouth, warm and sweet perfection.

"You're not what I was expecting," he said at last. April smiled and took another bite of oatmeal. Then Ivan turned back to the virtual model, rotating the image to center on the airlock and zooming in. "The entire space station is one continuous flow of rooms, no hallways or side spaces. So let's start at the beginning."

April looked at the dizzying array of colored lines that represented all the systems of the station. It was a jumble of overlapping images to her now, but soon she would be able to read all of this as easily as she read novels.

Her future outside the world of ghost dispelling started now.

6

―――――――――――――――

BELIEVING IS SEEING

April looked out the window at her destination. She could barely make out its shape from the glare of the sun reflecting back at her.

"Why is it so shiny?" she asked.

"It's completely covered in brass," Ivan told her. "And the airlock has no way for another ship to dock with it. Eccentric hermit. You've gone EVA before?"

"I lived in a shuttle colony once, where we traveled from airlock to airlock in inflated bubbles," April said.

"But never in a spacesuit?" he asked.

"No, those are way too rare."

"Well, you're getting part of your payment in advance," Ivan said, opening a cabinet between the kitchenette and the cockpit. He pulled out a sleek white jumpsuit and floated it to her.

"This is brand new," she said, catching the fabric and pulling it to her. It was so light. She could feel circuitry running between two layers of fabric. The cooling system? "This goes under the suit?"

"Honey, that *is* the suit."

"Just this? That's not possible," April said.

"It's not pressurized by gas," Ivan said. "You'll have a lot more mobility. The gloves are an absolute dream."

"Where did you get this?" she asked.

"I know a guy. This was the latest design just starting to hit the market when the plague happened. There might be warehouses full of them down on Earth, but up here they are a real rarity. My guy has been trying to work out a way to replicate the design, but materials are hard to come by. In the meantime, this is too small for any of my workers, but it will be perfect for you. Go suit up."

April took the suit with her back to her berth and stripped out of her jeans and T-shirt. It was a tight fit—the fabric with its built-in circuitry had no give and pinched over her curvier parts—but she managed to seal it all the way up and snap the neck ring closed. The suit reacted to that click by coming to life, like hands running all over her and squeezing in a slightly uncomfortable hug. She braided her hair, pinned it around her head in a tightening spiral, then floated out of her berth.

Her mother was chatting with Ivan when she glided into the common room.

"This is amazing," April said, spinning in the middle of the room.

"Let's get the helmet on so you can start pressurizing," Ivan said, tossing her the cap. She pulled it on, her mother floating over to help her tuck all her hair inside before snapping it closed under her chin.

"Were you serious when you said this was part of my payment?" April asked.

"Part of the payment?" her mother repeated. "This is the first I'm hearing of this."

"I'll admit it's a bit self-serving on my part," Ivan said. "I need someone willing to do some work for me in that suit, and it's too small for any of my current employees."

"What kind of work?" her mother asked. "Are there more ghosts in free fall?"

"Is it salvage?" April asked, barely daring to hope.

"We'll talk about it when you're back," Ivan said, passing her the helmet. He helped her seal the helmet to the neck ring of her suit. Her air tanks were on a backpack that buckled around her chest, the hoses connecting directly to the helmet. He double-checked everything, then patted her twice on the helmet, and she gave him a thumbs-up. She climbed into the airlock and Ivan shut the hatch behind her.

Nothing to do now but wait as the airlock around her was slowly depressurized.

"How's it feel?"

She jumped at Ivan's voice inside her helmet. "I have radio?"

"You'll be in contact with me the entire time. You can access the suit parameters and instructions from the control pad on your left wrist."

"This is amazing," April said, scrolling through the text and pictures on the features of the new suit. "And you were right about these gloves."

"You can see why I invest so much in my friend's work. Imagine if everyone had a suit like that."

April whiled away the hours reading the owner's manual on usage and maintenance of her suit until she was finally ready to head out into the black.

"Make sure to stay tethered at all times," Ivan said over the comm in her helmet. "You have enough tether to take you out to the station. Don't worry about that. And if your jump off the shuttle takes you wide, just redirect with your air canister. But you've grown up in free fall. This is the same as anyplace else you've been."

"Just a lot bigger," April said as the outer hatch opened beyond her floating feet. "And with no walls."

April carefully drifted to the edge of the hatch and secured the end of her spooling tether to the anchor by the door. Then she tipped her head back and the space station filled her view. It gleamed in the sunlight, too bright to look directly at, even brighter than the glowing Earth behind it. April pushed off from the shuttle, one hand near the spinning spool of her tether in case she needed to deal with a snag, the other holding her pressure canister. Her initial jump had been good; she didn't need to redirect her trajectory at all, only turn herself about to catch the hull of the station ring with one outstretched hand. Ivan was right, some things were just instinctual.

She hit the hull feetfirst, then caught on to a rung. The entire surface was indeed covered with brass. Just to be pretty? Up in space back when nearly everyone was still down on Earth, who was it being pretty for? Did they realize that whenever the sun touched it, it was impossible to look at?

April crawled along the rungs, looking up at the Earth and not at the blinding surface below her, until she reached the station's only airlock. She had never seen a station so small that still bothered with the ring shape designed to simulate gravity. And yet the station wasn't turning; that was odd. Someone would have had to deliberately stop the spin. Why? Perhaps some occupant preferred floating to the unsettling sensation of one's feet moving faster than one's head. The ring was small enough for that to be a real possibility.

At last she reached the airlock hatch and examined the controls. The screen was dead and didn't respond to her touch—not surprising, as someone had left the crank for manual entry in the door. April attached her shorter tether to an anchor ring under the dead panel and braced herself with both of her feet and a hand before turning the bar. It was a strange mechanism; she had to rotate the crank while something like a clockwork moved inside the door. She felt vibrations through the crank as each of the heavy bolts was separately engaged and pulled back, one by one, until after the fourth, the door swung open.

"I'm in," April said, hooking the end of her long tether to the anchor point and detaching her short tether after pulling herself into the tiny airlock. "Definitely a hermit; there's only room for one in the airlock."

"Is the power up?" Ivan asked.

"Hold on," April said, struggling to pull the hatch shut behind her. Without the glow of the Earth bathing everything around her in golden light, it was completely dark. She turned on her helmet light and looked around. "No, the control panels are all dead. I'm manually opening the inner door now."

The inner door swung into the airlock, which left barely enough room for her to squeeze past and get inside. She pulled the door shut behind her and latched it. If the life-support systems were still functioning, she'd fire them up. She'd rather poke around without her helmet on if she could. More peripheral vision, better hearing.

"I'm in," she said. Then she turned to get her first look at the interior. "Wow."

"What is it?" Ivan asked.

"It's gorgeous." She was still holding on to the rung near the door, turning her head slowly to let her helmet light play over everything around her. "I think this must be wood, but it's so shiny."

"It's been polished. It's all in the specs," Ivan said.

There was a huge difference between reading "interior constructed of polished wood paneling, brass fittings, and etched glass" and standing in a room with walls that glowed a warm honey color all around her. She felt like she was in the heart of a living tree, the walls living wood flowing with sap. This space was just for storage, being closest to the airlock, but the storage lockers were concealed within long benches of polished wood with pillows of some soft green material tied to brass fixtures at the back of the benches to keep them from floating away. To her right, the entire wall above the bench was a sheet of thick glass, too murky to see through with her helmet light mostly reflecting back at her. To her left, two separate glass panels divided that room from the next, glass etched with white flower trellises and two elegant, long-necked birds mirroring each other, the clear glass around them giving her a glimpse of the even grander room beyond.

April opened one of the lockers, but the space within was completely empty. She could see places where pillows were gone as well.

"Someone who came here left alive," she said. "Things are missing."

"The stories are pretty specific that the ghost is in the farthest rooms, the bedroom and beyond."

"Territorial ghost," April said, pushing her way past the glass doors to the next room.

"Aren't they all?"

April didn't answer, lost as she was in the next vision of wonder. The wood still surrounded her—walls and ceilings all aglow, the floor carpeted a deep, rich blue—but here, instead of paneling, the walls were shelves holding a wealth of treasures. "Books," she said, still floating in the doorway, overwhelmed. "Real books. And they're still here."

"You can, of course, help yourself to anything you find interesting," Ivan said. "But save the browsing until the return trip."

"Thanks," April said, pushing away from the door to catch the edge of the first shelf. The books were all in the two rows of shelves nearest the floor. Then there was an open space where even the wood paneling stopped, a long strip of glass that ran down both sides of the room barely two hand spans high. Above that were more shelves behind glass doors, but these were mostly empty. April examined the few remaining items, elaborate, needlessly beautiful instruments of various kinds. She recognized a very old microscope, a spyglass like a sailor would use, other things with delicate arms and moving parts she guessed were various types of navigating equipment from back in the days before computers. She saw a little plaque on one shelf that read "differential machine", but the space was empty.

In the center of the room, a book lay open under a glass case. She leaned in to take a closer look. The left-hand page was text in a fancy font she didn't recognize; the right-hand page was an illustration of a collection of creatures, half man, half animal, but the animal halves were from all sorts of different animals. She leaned in closer to examine the expressions on their gruesome faces until the glass of her helmet visor met the cabinet. They were tormented, howling in pain and rage. She glanced at the top of the text page. THE ISLAND OF DOCTOR MOREAU/H. G. WELLS. That explained the name of the space station; it was the literary reference, not the arty one. She had heard of Wells but never read him. Looking at that picture, she wasn't sure she wanted to. The eyes of one man-dog in particular caught hers and wouldn't let her go. She could feel his torment, his anger.

Then something moved, not in the book but between the two sets of shelves, a flicker of motion like something hiding from her. She gripped the glass case, holding herself still as she looked around, her light flashing rapidly from place to place, but she didn't find the source of the movement. She added her handheld light to the light on her helmet and forced herself to calm down and look more carefully. She hadn't disturbed anything; all the objects in the glass cabinets were floating in space, just as they had been when she'd entered the room. And yet something had moved. She pushed off the display case and floated back to the shelves. Then she leaned in, taking a closer look at the glass band that ran around the room. She couldn't see anything inside, just a greenish murk.

"Still in the library?" Ivan asked.

"Yes, I thought I... never mind," she said. She looked around the room one more time, but everything was as it should be. She was letting a picture in a book give her the willies, that was all. She pushed away from the shelves and towards the door to the next room. "I would love to live in a place like this."

"It's a lot of space for one person," Ivan said.

"He must have been lonely, whoever built it. But I can see a family living here," April said, her hands pressing against another pair of glass doors. These were in a metal frame that made the shape of inter-locking arches, the clear and frosted glass alternating in a complex pattern.

"I can see ten families living there," Ivan said. "After I finish remod-eling the interior."

"I suppose they'd be moving through each other's homes to get in and out unless you built a hallway."

"Exactly."

"But to build a hallway, you're going to have to pull everything out of here. It's not laid out to have a corridor unless it's down the middle, which would make the rooms too small," April said

She pushed past the doors; the next room was a dining room. She looked at a tangled mass of crystal that sparkled in the light from her helmet. She couldn't make sense of the shape until she realized that if the station were spinning, the artificial gravity would be pulling it down to hang over the table: a chandelier with crystal droplets in successive layers.

"Some of it will stay," Ivan said. "Most of it, I'll bring back to the *Triomphe*."

"To sell?"

"Or use in my own home, if I like it," he said.

"You'd be crazy not to like this," April said, running a gloved hand over the long oval of the wood table. She imagined it felt smooth and warm. If only she could get out of her suit and explore properly.

Beyond the dining room was the kitchen. It had been thoroughly ransacked: cabinets hanging open, the interiors empty. She wondered what the plates had looked like. Fine china? Solid gold? What sort of food had he prepared in his little kitchen?

Something flashed past the corner of her eye again. April quickly turned and pushed back the way she'd come, back into the dining room, but nothing was out of sorts. The walls were still wood panels split down the middle by the band of glass. She looked again but could see nothing beyond but murk. It wasn't an exterior view, so why the glass? What was she meant to be looking at? Nothing should be moving on its own; nothing could possibly still be alive after all this time, and without so much as the smallest puff of air, nothing nonliving should be stirring either.

"I want to find the lights," April said. "My flashlights aren't penetrating the nooks and crannies very well."

"If they are still functioning, the main control panels are just beyond the kitchen," Ivan said.

"I'm heading there now."

April pulled her way through the kitchen, past another pair of even more elaborate glass doors, the geometric pattern on these even more complex. The room beyond was a narrow hallway between storage lockers. She pushed open one of the ajar doors, but the space within was empty. "I'm in the storeroom," she said. "A lot of things have been taken from here. If the ghost is meant to be protecting his stuff, he's not been doing a very thorough job of it."

"The real wealth was always rumored to be in the deepest room," Ivan said. "What the wealth actually was is vague and changes from story to story, but its location in the farthest room either with or just beyond the ghost—that's always the same."

"Everything in here is treasure to me," April said, pushing another locker door shut so she could pass. The narrow space between lockers met a cross hallway halfway down the room, the controls for all the station systems tucked out of sight. April caught the edge to pull herself into the right-hand branching hallway, her helmet light focused on her hand as she found her hold.

When she looked up, the world flashed bright around her, a glimmering white vision filling the hallway before her. Her breath caught, and she gripped the corner of the wall tightly, stopping her momentum before she plunged into the shapeless white form before her. It was billowing, filling, rippling. She couldn't make sense of what she was seeing, but whatever it was, it was moving towards her. Then it reached for her, flowing an appendage forward, glowing ever brighter in the light from her helmet as it approached her visor.

April pushed back hard despite the awkwardness of her grip on the corner, desperate for that thing not to touch her. She collided with the bank of lockers, the corner of a bottom-row door digging into her lower back just before the back of her helmet cracked hard against the top-row door. She scrambled for a hold, panicking as she drifted back across the hallway towards a locker with its door opened wide, as if waiting to swallow her whole. She put a foot out to stop herself, then clung to the door, breathing hard as she watched the place where the hallways met, waiting for the white form to come for her.

7

SEEING IS BELIEVING

"APRIL? YOU OK? WHAT WAS THAT BANG? YOUR BREATHING SOUNDS stressed. April?"

Had she just seen what she thought she'd seen? What everyone else had been seeing all the time? She thought it would feel different, more real, or surreal, or something. The way it had moved had been beautiful and terrifying at once, but now that it was out of sight, she wasn't sure.

She would have to look again.

April took a deep breath, then let it out slowly. Her heartbeat was not so easy to control, pounding loudly in her ears as she forced herself to get moving, to grasp the edge of the last locker and pull herself around to look into the hallway.

The bright flash of white startled her yet again, the groping appendage still flowing before the main body of the form. The shape reminded her of pictures of jellyfish she had seen on her encyclopedia. She watched it float and tried to remember how big they were. She thought that most had been much smaller, but some kinds had been big. She could feel her reader against her belly, but being that it was inside her suit, it was useless.

"*April?*"

She reached out a hand, touching the end of the appendage. Even through the thickness of her glove she realized the feel of it was all wrong. Then suddenly her perceptions reordered themselves, like making the picture of a duck turn into a picture of a bunny. She grasped the whiteness and pulled hard.

And the sheet rippled after, flowing after her hand in a long twist that looked nothing like a jellyfish, or that other thing she had feared first but wouldn't name, not even in her own mind.

"I'm OK," she said, wadding up the sheet and stuffing it in one of the lockers. Even completely alone, her cheeks reddened, embarrassed at how stupid she had just been. The station was weird, creepy, and she was keyed up. She needed to calm down and be rational. "Just checking out the life-support systems now. There is definitely some air in here. I can see things moving in the currents."

"That's a good sign," Ivan said. "One less thing I'll have to fix."

With the sheet out of the way, April could see the large vent at the end of the hallway. She couldn't feel anything through her suit, but she was certain there must be a draft, just enough to float a sheet about. Over the vent was a wall panel that lit up at her touch. She turned up the air flow as well as the heat. The status indicators declared the air mix breathable, but the temperature was -25°C. April decided that wasn't too bad and unsealed her helmet, gasping at the sudden cold.

"April?"

"I'm taking my helmet off so I can hear and sense things. I can't really do my thing sealed off in my suit. I'll radio if I need you."

"If you really need me, you won't be able to get your helmet on in time to radio. I should have given you a handheld; I didn't think about you needing to... sense things. Is that really necessary?"

"I'll give you an update in ten minutes or so, OK?"

"Happy hunting."

"Thanks."

She removed her helmet, the cold biting at her cheeks and ears. She expected she would get used to it as it slowly grew warmer.

The space station didn't smell like anything. That was strange, and a bit of a shock. Everyplace April had ever been had suffered from too many people crammed into too small a space. She was used to smelling a plethora of body odors, a smorgasbord of cooking styles that individually might be mouth-watering but all together were anything but. Some stations were cleaner than others; some had some truly vile smells that lurked just underneath the other scents, like footnotes in a book. But this place smelled like nothing. She had brought her own funk inside, and there was an undercurrent of oranges from the space shuttle.

It was unsettling, that lack of smell.

She looked over the panel again, then found where to touch to turn on the power. Light suddenly filled the station around her, and distantly she heard music come to life, a woman singing an old blues torch song. She recognized it as one her mother liked to sing: "Ne me quitte pas." The singer was sad but resolute. Heartbroken, but soldiering on. April buckled her helmet to the back of her suit belt and continued through the next set of glass doors, these a geometric pattern of colored glass that obscured the room beyond.

This room was a sort of sitting area, with sofas wrapping around the perimeter and overstuffed chairs dotting the center of the room. She pushed herself from the doorway to one of the sofas to take a better look at the glass ribbon that still ran down the length of both outer walls. Light from an unseen source filled the space beyond the glass, and although it was still murky, she was certain it was an aquarium. Specks floating in water didn't look any different from specks floating in free fall, but she was sure that's what it was. Something bigger must still be floating in there. That would be the movement that kept catching the corner of her eye.

But the specks in front of her now weren't moving, just floating. If there was a current moving things about enough to make them catch her eye and then disappear, it should be affecting these specks too. Unless it was some sort of intermittent thing, something necessary for aquarium maintenance, necessary enough to be part of the emergency systems that were still running when the rest of the power was off. April didn't know enough about aquariums to know for sure.

The next set of doors matched the colors of the last pair. The room beyond was an exercise room; some things like the treadmill and the free weights were useless in free fall, but others like the bike with straps to hold yourself on it and the resistance strength training equipment were still useful. It seemed like a lot of equipment for just one man.

The next set of doors matched the pair between the kitchen and storage room; she was beginning to see the pattern. She was in a bedroom now, and the music was loudest here. She saw the player set in the wall over the head of the largest bed she had ever seen—big enough for a dozen people to cuddle up in—but decided to leave the music playing. It was comforting in its aching sadness. She touched the edge of the bed. The bed frame had a lip that held the mattress in place, the sheets and blankets tucked in tight. It was almost as if it had been designed to stay neat in free fall, which was insane, since it served no purpose in free fall. It was puzzling.

This time she definitely saw something moving behind the glass, something which pressed up against it momentarily, then darted away. She pushed herself closer. There were lights inside, but they were recessed somewhere up above. She pressed her cheek to the cold glass and tried to look up and then down. The strip of glass was only a hand width long, but the actual space beyond the wall was much bigger. She couldn't see the top or bottom. Then something floated up to look at her, eye to eye.

She yelped and pulled back, sending herself out into the middle of the room. Her first thought had been *alien*, what with the protruding bits all over, but even before she caught the edge of the bed to stop her motion, she knew she was being silly again. Fish. It was an aquarium. A strange aquarium, built only to be barely looked at. It was almost as if it was designed for the convenience of the fish, who only occasionally wanted to watch the humans.

The glass strips ran along both walls, and from what she could see, the aquarium filled the entire space between the wall and the hull of the space station. Had it been built for insulation against radiation? She didn't think it was thick enough for that, but then she already knew from the wheel being too small that the designer hadn't been good with those sorts of details. Why fill it with fish, though? And what was keeping them alive? The glass was cold to the touch; how did they stand it? The life support was still on in the human part of the ship, and there must be some sort of filter keeping the water breathable for the fish, but what were they eating in there?

She remembered the H. G. Wells book in the library. Did some rich eccentric first come up into space because he couldn't find an island remote enough to conduct his crazy fish experiments unmolested?

She would think she had found her ghost, but she couldn't see how fish in an aquarium could kill twelve people. Unless they had mind powers. April chuckled to herself nervously, but the sound of it set her even more on edge. She moved on through the next set of doors, the geometric arch pattern this time.

The cold air that puffed out to caress her face carried a foulness with it. April recoiled at once, pushing away with her feet as hard and fast as she could, but the smell stayed with her. She put on the helmet and sealed it, but still the smell lingered in her suit, in her hair. She had been near many a butcher shop selling questionable meat, not just from nonstandard animals but old and turning green. This was worse, so much worse. Sealing her helmet didn't help, and she clung to a bedpost, eyes closed tight, breaking out in a sweat all over as she struggled to just breathe, breathe and not vomit in her helmet.

The smell didn't fade, but she slowly mastered her gag reflex. She knew beyond this last door were the twelve missing treasure hunters. And they were so very dead. Whatever had killed them was there as well.

She had expected some sort of heart of darkness, but what she found was a very elaborate bathroom. It was as if all the elements in the rest of the station met here and exploded in a cascade of brass fixtures, sunburst patterns, etched glass and mirrors, and warm honey-colored wood. Six people could fit in the bathtub.

And as April moved around the glass panel, she realized they had. Six bodies, all clumped together, floating. April pulled back, looking around for signs of what had killed them. Had they died here or been pulled here? They were all huddled together, so she was guessing someone had pulled them here. But what had killed them?

Not seeing any other clues in the rest of the opulent bathroom, she went back to the tub. The six were all men, two with helmets still on but four bareheaded, their hair floating around like kelp in the ocean. She had jostled them before; they were moving because she had touched them. She had to repeat that to herself a few times to slow her heart down. The rational part of her brain knew it was true, but the other bits had their own ideas, and those bits were the ones making her adrenaline go into overtime.

April reached out for the nearest body and grasped its shoulder. They were all floating with their faces turned away from her, and it was beginning to freak her out. It felt like they were hiding something from her. Taking a breath, she turned the one she was touching over.

His face was frozen in a paroxysm of pain. His skin was sallow in the flashlight and a bit sunken, but he didn't look decomposed at all. It was as if he had just died. Died in a moment of great pain and fear. Had the cold preserved him? But then there was the smell. April was vaguely aware that she was muttering something under her breath, but she couldn't stop her hand until she'd turned them all over. All of them, even the two in helmets, had died with the same look of horror on their faces.

One of the fish in the walls was floating steadily at the level of the glass strip, staring at her.

Then she noticed the line tying all the bodies together. Had someone intended a burial in space out the airlock? But they would have wanted to finish this journey first, to get to the treasure, and they'd never come back. There was nothing to be done but go on to the very last room, past the doors once more etched in a pattern of a pair of elegant birds.

If the bathroom had been the crescendo of the art déco design, the last room was like the last notes of the score fading away into the silence before the applause. It was soothing, and it would probably be a nice place to just sit and relax if it weren't for the other six corpses cluttering up the place.

April looked from face to face, each expression caught in a moment of torment. She lingered in the doorway, reluctant to touch them. This was the last room. This must be where the killer lay in wait. But where was it?

She craned her head, trying to see anything besides the corpses. The far wall was glass, but on this side it was broken glass. That made no sense; if anything had broken the glass she'd seen when she'd first come through the airlock, she would have heard it. That had been the whole reason she'd taken off her helmet in the first place. But she had heard nothing but her own breath and rantings.

She looked again. Were there two sheets of glass in that wall, the far one intact and only the near one broken? Something else was in the air besides the dead people: little bits of rock that sparkled in the beam from her light. Decorative bits of rock, small like gravel.

Another aquarium, then, but not connected to the one that enveloped everything. Where would the water have gone? If it had been broken more than a decade ago, but the air filters had still been running all that time, could they have pulled it all from the air? Or, if she touched the people here, would they feel wet?

She reached out to test her theory when something else caught her eye, a small brownish blob. No, not a blob; it had a back, a long row of spines. Then she saw other things: something puffed up with spines all over, a look on its face like it too had died in an agony of fear; a delicate brown and white fish with long tendrils floating off of it in neat manes.

Then she realized with a start that the space was filled with tiny for-real jellyfish, scores of them just floating among the human and fish corpses. They were barely moving about on the tiniest of drafts, but she backed out of the room and shut the door, suddenly deeply freaked out that something was going to bump into her no matter how careful she was.

April had a suspicion that she had found her ghost, but she needed her reader to prove it—the reader tucked into the front of her pants, pressing against her belly.

April took a deep breath, then pulled off her helmet, opening the front of her suit and sliding it down far enough to pull the reader out. It caught on her waistband for a moment before coming free, and she couldn't hold her breath any longer. The smell was so intense it made her dizzy and she took the smallest possible breaths, struggling to seal her suit back up as quickly as she could. The smell lingered, and she was nearly in tears. She couldn't wait for the nausea to pass this time; she was certain it wouldn't now that her whole suit was filled with the stench.

She pushed the door back open but stayed in the doorway—she was close enough. She thumbed on her reader and moved closer to one of the ghosts, training her flashlight on it with one hand while she snapped a picture of it with the other. The encyclopedia mulled it over, then pulled up an entry. STONEFISH, it said. Venomous spines. Very dangerous. She took a picture of the other spiny one, appropriately called a PUFFERFISH. That one was deadly if eaten wrong. The delicate fish was a LIONFISH, another venomous, spiny fellow. The jellyfish brought up a specific jellyfish entry, IRUKANDJI BOX JELLYFISH. They could fire stingers full of venom.

No one up here in space would have held onto anything as obscure as fish antitoxin. Those that might have weren't on stations that were close by. Had this eccentric really been experimenting on fish? Why else collect deadly specimens and use them as wall decoration? So many dead people here—had these fish been bred to be super-venomous?

April looked closer at the bodies. Now that she was looking, she could see where spines had pierced their hands. Had they died trying to grab the fish? Some had spines in other places and must have died bumping into the fish. Or the jellyfish had fired their stingers. She suspected these four had come in after the first six had already smashed the aquarium and died. Some of these creatures remained venomous long after death. These four had pulled the bodies out, come in to find the treasure, and been killed by the already-dead fish. It was a theory. She would have to warn Ivan; there were still fish living in the walls aside from these deadly corpses.

So why smash the aquarium? If the treasure stories were true, someone must have found what they were looking for and gone off with it; April could see no sign of anything valuable now. Had they made it before or after these twelve?

Then she had a darker thought. There had never been a treasure at all. They had smashed the aquarium looking for nonexistent treasure and released these biological mines to float about the room. It wasn't a killer ghost; it was a school of killer corpses.

What Hakim had said was starting to make some sense. While they were looking for ghosts, people missed all the real dangers.

8

CARBONARA DREAMING

Ivan came over personally with one of the pilots to do the delicate work of removing all the fish from the *Moreau*. April lingered in the library, examining each of the books and trying not to look up as fish disposal gave way to human body disposal. There had been no way to figure out who these people were or how long ago they had died, although a few names could be guessed from the many stories about the murderous ghost and its victims. April stared unseeingly at the book in front of her, unable to stop the vision of those bodies tumbling down to burn up in the atmosphere of the Earth below or spinning away forever into deeper space.

"Have you picked your reward?" Ivan asked, startling her out of her reverie.

"Oh, I..." April looked about. She hadn't been thinking about that at all. She trailed off helplessly. The book in her hands was some sort of biology textbook. She set it back on the shelf, but that left her hands with nothing to do. The bodies were still tumbling in her mind's eye, tumbling forever in a school of dead but deadly fish.

"Most of this will be picked up later by the salvage crews, so if you want to go through it again, you'll be able to," he said, casting a quick glance around the room. "Do you know what I think?" He moved easily from the bookshelf to the glass cabinet in the center of the room and felt around for the catch. The glass hinged open like an egg hatching, and he reached in and closed the book inside before grabbing it and floating back to hand it to her. "I think this would be particularly appropriate, don't you?"

April looked at the cover. She was pretty sure it was real leather, and the letters were stamped in gold.

"It's too much," April said. "This with the suit—"

"You're an investment," he said. "Was there anything else that caught your eye, or are you ready to head back?"

"Head back," April said, tucking the book inside her suit just above her reader, then zipping up and sealing her helmet.

When they returned, they found that her mother had a celebratory dinner already waiting for them. Ivan brought up the model of the station again, this time to show them his plans for renovating the space. He had a long waiting list of families ready to move in as soon as he was done.

"It wouldn't be possible without you," Ivan said, toasting her with his container of carbonara.

"I told you she could handle it," Melena said, beaming at her daughter. "Even the angriest of spirits hears her call."

April felt her cheeks reddening and dipped her head, suddenly focused on her own barely touched container of pasta. She could feel Ivan's eyes on her, observing her, weighing her response.

"April?" her mother said, touching her elbow until April looked up. "Was it too draining for you, this ghost?"

April shook her head, unable to say the words out loud that she was more certain than ever that there were no ghosts, not really. But her mother's worried frown needed some sort of response. "A lot of people died in there," she said. "I keep thinking about them. Their last moments of life were truly horrible."

Ivan made a sound in his throat, wordlessly agreeing. He had seen the faces, too.

"No more are going to die now," her mother said, smoothing April's hair back from her face. It floated right back, but there was still some comfort in the gesture. "You did good. Do you want to rest now?"

"Yes," April said, looking down at her half-eaten container. "Save it for me. I'm just not that hungry right now."

Ivan gathered up the rest of their little feast to carry it back to the kitchenette while Melena helped April open the hatch for her sleep berth.

"Are you all right?" Melena asked in a voice no more than a whisper. "You seem different this time. Did you see something?"

"Yes," April said, blinking hard to dispel the vision of the bodies stacked in the bathtub. "But not a ghost."

"Next time you don't go alone," Melena said, and April nodded mutely. Nothing would have been different if others had gone with her, except for the real possibility that someone would have blundered into that cloud of fish and met a venomous end before she had figured out what was going on.

April climbed into her sleeping bag and spent a long time staring at the wall before a fitful sleep took her, but that last thought haunted her dreams and she jerked awake from a nightmare of Ivan and the two pilots writhing in agony as fish came to life to swarm all over their bodies and she floated hopelessly by, frozen in fear, unable even to scream.

She took deep breaths until her heart slowed to its more usual rhythm, then felt a sudden stab of hunger and remembered the half-finished carbonara waiting for her in the kitchenette. She zipped out of the sleeping bag, snatched her floating hoodie out of the air and slipped it on, and then opened her hatch as quietly as she could.

The shuttle lights were dimmed to nighttime levels, but a smaller light still shone brightly in the common room. April pulled herself along the hallway to see Ivan in front of his work screen, frowning as he moved through images and typed in a smaller box off to one side. He glanced up as she floated noiselessly into the room.

"Hungry?" he asked, and she nodded. He turned his attention back to his work, and she pushed hard enough to sail across the room to the kitchenette and find her half-eaten carbonara. Even reheated, it was still the perfect combination of carbs and fat. She finished it off far too quickly, then went back to the refrigerator to find the dessert she had never even touched. Chocolate pudding with whipped cream swirled throughout. She was sure it was all simulation, as dairy was so hard to get in space, but never having had real dairy products, she found the simulation good enough for her tastes.

When she was done, she cleaned up and emerged from the kitchenette to find Ivan looking her way. She hesitated, not sure what that look meant. He rubbed his chin, then said at last, "You don't like what you do."

She felt herself blushing again but forced her spine to straighten, to meet his gaze. "No, I don't," she admitted.

"You do it for your mother," he said.

"Yes. Well, we need the money." She chanced a look up at him. "I'd rather do something else, something like what you do. You make useless things useful again—that's cool."

He tipped his head, acknowledging the compliment, but his face was still serious. "Your mother has a strong personality," he said.

"That's putting it mildly. You knew her well, when you were kids?"

"I was completely in love with her," he said with no sign of embarrassment. "She scarcely knew I existed, of course. That's how those things always go when you're young."

"Did you know my father?" April asked as casually as she could.

"I don't think so. What's your birthday?"

"April 1, 2179. She named me for my birthday."

"Your middle name is First?"

"Yeah," April admitted.

"That's more than a year after the last time I saw your mother. I'm guessing she's never told you his name?"

"No. I'm pretty sure she was alone before I was even born. She doesn't talk about it. Like, at all."

"I might have known him; she left with one guy and shortly after two more of her... paramours left the station as well. I don't know how close she was with any of them. It might have been one of them, or it might not have."

"It could be anyone at all," April sighed.

"Does it bother you, not knowing?"

"Not really. I mean, not profoundly," April said. "I just wonder. I'm different from my mother in some significant ways. I assume I must be like him then. Sometimes it would be nice to talk to someone else like me in those ways."

"You don't see ghosts," Ivan said. April felt her eyes go wide. "That was a stab in the dark, but I see I'm right. That might be something you share with your father, true enough, but it's also something you have in common with a great many people."

"Really?" April asked. "It always seems like everyone sees something but me."

"I think you've been kept among a very exclusive group of people," Ivan said. "It's understandable, given the work you do. It would attract a certain sort, wouldn't it? And you don't get out much outside of your work. I know your mother believes strongly in the need for you to maintain the mystery, to be a remote figure, apart from others, closer to the spirits. You don't really see this need; I bet that's been lonely. But I think you're starting to outgrow the cocoon your mother has been keeping you in."

"It's not quite like that," April said. "You make her sound so controlling."

"No, you're right. That's not what I meant. I just know your mother. She has an effect on people, like the way light bends around a gravity well. It's not something she does, it's who she is."

April didn't know what to say. No one had ever talked to her about her mother before. She had never gotten an outsider's perspective.

"I guess you probably have sensed that I feel the same as ever about your mother. She's... when she's around, everyone else is in black and white and she's in full color. But this time, she knows I exist."

"Yeah, she does," April agreed. "But I've seen her like this before. Lots of times. Things change. She changes."

"I remember what she was like," Ivan said. April shook her head and opened her mouth to speak, but he kept going. "Everyone has their ups and downs, of course, but your mother has them tenfold. I know, I remember. But she doesn't have to be like that."

"What do you mean?" April asked.

"I have a friend who's a doctor. He works on the *Triomphe* and he has access to a lot of supplies, pharmaceuticals and everything, from Earth or one of the corporate stations, I don't know. But the point is, I think your mother has a condition that makes her how she is, and there are medicines that can help her. They can smooth out her mood swings."

"Medicine can do that?"

"Yes, medicine can do that. If you find the right one, which my doctor friend can do."

"What if," she said, "when you fix her, you change the thing that you love about her? What if the medicine makes her black and white?"

"I don't think it will," he said. "But you know the love that is that spark of emotion, that's just the beginning. After that, love is the decision you make every day to be with someone, to care for them and be cared for, in turn, to build a life together. The medicine won't change that."

"It sounds like a fairy tale," April said.

"Says the girl who fights ghosts," Ivan said.

"Too good to be true," she clarified. "Sorry, but it's been like a couple of days. A couple of days when she's in a good place and a memory from your youth."

"Fair enough," he allowed. "But all I'm saying is, it looks like your mother and I are going to be together for a while, anyway. And while we're together, there is no reason for you to do any jobs you don't want to do and every reason for you to pursue other things that interest you. The *Triomphe* is filled with opportunities for those with a little motivation."

"You said you need me for more ghost jobs," April said.

"Correct. I have other spaces like the *Moreau* that are disrupting my work crews. I could use you, if you're willing. But I've seen how your mind works, and I noticed how hard you worked to follow what I was saying about those station blueprints. I never had to explain anything to you twice. Frankly, with a little time invested in training, you could learn to do anything."

"I'd like that," April said. "Learning a real skill. Any skill."

"Why stop with one?" Ivan asked, and April grinned.

She was going to learn *all* the skills.

9

———————

REMATCH

Once upon a time, April and her mother had been, while not exactly rich, well enough off to afford a day of shopping and lunch every now and then. April had always loved those days, free of the trappings of her mystical persona, out in the world with people who didn't know what she did. Inevitably, some of the purchases would be items for her job, another veil or tiny bells or perhaps a candle or incense. But mostly it was just a day to be herself with her mother, hunting for the perfect clothes, sampling all her favorite foods.

The nicest of those days years gone by had been nothing like this day.

April had woken up to find the shuttle already docked, just holding a berth while she and her mother finished sleeping. The extravagance of that was mind-boggling enough. But then Ivan walked with them down to the marketplace and showed them some of the nicer shops clustered around the dry fountain, then given her mother a bulging sack of coins.

"I'd love to spend the day with you, but I've been too long away and need to catch up on some projects," he said. "Have fun without me. I'll see you when you get home. You remember how to find it?"

"Of course," Melena said with a bright smile. He smiled back, but

April saw it waver just a little as he hesitated, as if he feared if he let Melena out of his sight, he might lose her again.

"I can't wait to see your home," April said, hugging her mother's arm. "If the things I saw in the *Moreau* would fit in there, it must be gorgeous."

"It's a work in progress," Ivan said. "But that's a shopping trip for another day." Then he kissed Melena on the cheek and was gone.

He could have given them the money and sent them down from the docks on their own, but the way the shop proprietors rushed to wave them into their shops and show off their best wares, April suspected he had wanted to put on just a bit of a display. He was well known on the *Triomphe,* not just for being wealthy but for the work he had done to earn that wealth and the free hand he had with spending it.

April couldn't wait to start learning his trade. This was so different from her previous life: only going out in secret, getting sidelong looks from shop owners who weren't convinced she could pay for anything she was looking at or touching. Ironic that going "in secret" meant just being herself, not wearing the costumes of her job. If she had shopped in her ghost-dispelling finery, not only would they have known she could afford whatever she chose to buy, they would likely try to get her to take it as a gift. April, the dispeller of ghosts, was always getting gifts. But if she worked hard one day, she could be like Ivan, with just one persona instead of two, and people could know who she was and what she did with no secrets.

The morning flew by as they went from store to store. Soon April's carpetbag was bulging with purchases, and her mother had to buy her another larger bag, as well as two for herself. Finally, they stopped for lunch at a tea shop on the second floor over the shoe store. They sat on the balcony overlooking the dry fountain and drank tea and ate little sandwiches.

"I told you it wouldn't take long," Melena said. "Although even I hadn't thought we'd do so well, so fast."

"It's more your doing than mine," April said. "I told you there wasn't even a ghost there."

Melena waved away the objection before taking a bite of cucumber sandwich. "Ivan tells me he has more work in store for you."

"Yes," April said, watching the light reflecting off the surface of her tea.

"There is a renovation underway that involves squeezing into tiny spaces to get at what needs fixing, and you in that fancy suit of his would be perfect, he says."

April looked up at her mother. "Really?"

"There are some things you need to learn first, but yes. Surprised?"

"Totally," April said. "I mean, he and I had talked about it a little, doing something like that. I thought you might feel differently about it." She watched her mother's face carefully. The soft smile never changed as she poured herself a second cup of tea and swirled in the tiniest amount of sweetener, then stirred it over and over again. She tapped the spoon on the rim of the cup and set it carefully on the saucer.

"You know I believe in your gift," Melena said. "That hasn't changed. But I think maybe you have a path in front of you that isn't clear to me. You don't believe in your own gift. I think you're at the age where such crossroads usually appear, and whether you go one way or the other isn't up to me. I do hope, I really do hope, that with some experience out in the world, you will start to see the value of what you do, not superficially but deeply, in your soul. I've told you again and again to look into the faces of those you've helped and see just how much you've done for them, and I know you do look and you try to see. I know you do. But you don't feel it, not like I and the others feel it. And I don't see how you can go on without finding that feeling."

"You think I can find that feeling working salvage?"

"I think you're about to try all sorts of different things, and some will suit you and some won't. But I think in the end you'll know what your calling is. You'll be sure. That's my fondest wish for you."

April looked down at her tea, then picked up the cup and took a long sip. "And if in the end my path isn't working with ghosts?"

Melena smiled. "Well, we'll see. I call it your vocation, you know what that means. It's going to keep calling to you. That's what I believe. But we'll see."

"I guess we will," April said.

Then their server returned with a three-level tray of cookies and sweets and their conversation took a more culinary turn.

They lingered at the table until lunchtime was long past, but when at last they emerged back out onto the street, April felt all shopped out.

"You don't even want to find that bookstore you were so fascinated with?" Melena asked.

April blushed a little; she had mentioned her longing to visit it more than once on the trip out to the *Moreau*. But her body was aching, being back in spin after yet another spell in free fall, and she shook her head. Melena shouldered her bags and led the way through the crowds, April trailing behind.

Then she saw him out of the corner of her eye, down the end of one of the many alleys off the main street, once more on his carpet, playing six opponents at once. It might even be the same alley as before, April couldn't recall. She stopped so suddenly the person behind her collided with her, then moved grumblingly around her. Melena came back.

"Not feeling well?"

"I'm OK," April said.

Her mother followed her gaze. "That's the boy from the other day," she said, and April nodded. Melena frowned at her for a moment, then gestured for April to give her both her bags.

"What?" April asked, but her mother just gestured again until she handed them over.

"Go ahead and talk with him," Melena said, grunting a little under the weight of all their shopping. "In another few blocks, this main street crosses another large one; there's no fountain in the square but it's still a large open space. Follow the cross street to the left and it ends in doors that are part of the original structure of the station. That's where Ivan lives. Just knock and the doorman will let you in."

"Doorman?" April repeated.

"If you get lost, ask anyone the way. Everyone knows his name."

"Yes. Thanks, Mom," April said.

"Just don't be long. Be back before dinner. Which would be sooner than you could pry yourself away last time," Melena said.

"I was lost last time," April said. "I won't be late, I promise."

Melena kissed her cheek, then readjusted the bags on her shoulders and disappeared into the crowd.

April twisted her braid between her hands. She doubted he even wanted to talk to her again, now that he knew who she was. And while she was still wearing the clothes Ivan had provided for her on the shuttle—nothing like her work finery—the unstained whiteness of her canvas shoes and the unfaded colors of her jeans and T-shirt still made her stand out from the crowd. She could imagine what he would say about ill-gotten gains. Her mind came up with all sorts of awful things he could say to her, but even imagining the worst of them, she still had to talk to him. Taking a breath, she stepped into the alley.

This time she had coins in her pocket, change from a few of the stores that her mother had asked her to collect while she was sorting things into their bags. April lingered across the alley until one of the opponents abandoned his board and she slipped into his place, dropping to sit cross-legged on the faded carpet and placing one of the coins next to the game board.

Hakim looked her over and some of the things she had imagined he would say came back to mind, but in the end he said nothing, just placed his own coin opposite hers and waited for her to make the first move. She placed a disk on the board, turned one of his over, and looked up at him. He played his own piece and moved on to the next board without meeting her eye.

April lost eight games, then won two, before he finally said a word to her.

"The ghost business must be doing gangbusters," he said, and she realized he was annoyed about losing to her twice.

"No ghost," she said, trying not to look too smug as she took his coin and set up the board for another match. "Fish."

"Fish," he repeated.

"Venomous fish," she clarified. "One was poisonous, but I don't think anyone tried to eat it."

He gave her a puzzled look, but moved on to his other games. When he got back to her, he pretended to consider his move. "Explain," he said.

"There was a space station that was orbiting Earth, completely useless to everybody. My employer sent me in to clear the space, which is what I did. A month or so and there will be ten families living there."

He made his play. "You went to dispel a ghost," he said pointedly.

"I went in to find out what was killing people, and it was fish."

He looked at her like he didn't quite believe her, then moved through another round of the other games.

"I don't do the ghost thing anymore," she said while he considered her play. "Before the other day, I hadn't done it in years. And before I did it that time, I had sold off everything I owned until there was nothing left and then I went without food for days. Have you gone days without eating, ever?"

"Yes," he said.

"Then you know what that's like."

He grunted noncommittally, then made his play.

"I won't be doing ghost work anymore," she said when he came back around. "I'm learning another trade."

"I don't know why you feel like I need to know this," he said.

"Don't you?"

His eyes swept over her face, but she kept her shoulders back and forced herself not to crumple under his assessment. "No," he said at last.

"I saw you glaring at me when I was at the fountain with my mother. Like I was the most loathsome thing in the universe. Like I murdered babies and got away with it. But you don't know me. You've not walked in my shoes."

"Those shoes?" He gestured at the gleaming brightness of the white canvas tucked under her knees.

"No, the ones I was wearing the last time we played," she said. "The ones that were far too small, that had been repaired so many times, little remained but my mother's stitches."

"Ah," he said. "The ones like everyone else's. Those shoes."

"You seem like you're doing OK yourself," she said, gesturing to his leather sandals. "Not new, certainly, but it must be a chore and a half finding that size. Your feet are huge."

"Are we playing or what?" one of the other opponents griped, and Hakim quickly made the next plays on all the boards.

"I took space going to waste and made the first step toward converting it into a home for ten families. That's how I earned my shoes. And thank you, they are quite nice, aren't they?" April said when he came back to her.

"You're awfully touchy," he said. "You should focus on your game. I'm going to have you in two moves."

April refocused on the board and saw he was right. She conceded, leaving her coin next to his and adding a new one before resetting the board.

Winning another match seemed to turn his mood around. "So now you're in the renovation field," he said as he made his first move.

"Just starting out," she said. "Lots to learn."

He played through the other boards and returned. "I was just looking at getting into that area myself."

"Really?" she said.

"My sister and I have been stuck here for months trying to earn enough to repair her ship, but now she's nearly ready to go. We're headed out to a science station orbiting the moon, the *Chandrasekhar*. There was a major disaster there after the exodus from Earth that took out the entire station population, but the bones of the structure are still strong and a crew is working to convert it all back to livable space. You should check it out if you're into that now; they're looking for anyone with those sorts of skills."

"That sounds cool," April said.

"You sound down about it."

"No, it's cool," she said, forcing herself to brighten up. "It's just, I don't actually have any of those skills yet. I do have a spacesuit, and it's pretty sweet, but I'm not much good in it until I learn how to fix things."

"Your own spacesuit," he repeated. "Nice like your shoes?"

"Better than the shoes," she said and couldn't help the grin that spread across her face. "And I'm going to learn to do things in it that only I can do because I'm small."

The noise from the street at the end of the alley was growing louder. April made her plays and tried to figure out what she could say to convince him to meet her again when he wasn't working his game boards, when the two of them could talk alone. She had never tried anything remotely like that conversation before and didn't know how to string the words together without sounding like a virtual shut-in who didn't know how to talk to people. Then she noticed the other players were all finishing up their games and leaving.

"Oh, no—is it late?" she asked, lifting the hem of her shirt to take a quick peek at her reader screen. Not even dinnertime yet.

"It's a festival day," Hakim said. "They celebrate refugee arrival day. Or days, really; the shuttles arrived continuously for a week. It sounds pretty cool, actually. Each day they celebrate whichever part of Earth the arriving shuttle was from with food and music from that culture. Tonight is the first night, which is—"

"Russia," one of the last remaining players said.

"And Ukraine," the other player added, finishing off his game, then waiting for his friend to finish his before they headed off together. April and Hakim were now alone, a row of abandoned boards between them. April found herself helping Hakim to pack everything back up in his sack.

"Did you want to check it out?" he asked, not quite looking at her.

"I'd love to, but I'm supposed to be back home before dinner."

"Where's home?"

"We're guests of Ivan EchoHawk..."

"Ah," Hakim said, nodding. "That explains the shoes."

"He's going to be teaching me his trade."

"That's cool." He cinched up his sack and slung it over his shoulder, then rolled up his carpet and hoisted it over the other shoulder. "Shall we?"

"Shall we what?"

"I'll walk you home."

"Really?" April found her braid in her hands again and forced herself to let it go. "I thought you hated me."

"How could I hate you? I've never seen anyone grasp the intricacies of Reversi so quickly. It was amazing, watching your eyes as you discovered strategy after strategy. Then you *beat* me."

"Just the one time," April said. Knowing that she was blushing like mad only made her blush more.

"You recognized me, that first day. And still you sat down and played. Then again, today." He looked over at her, waiting for her to answer his unasked question.

"Yes," she said slowly. What was she supposed to do, say out loud how much she felt driven to understand him? How desperately she wanted to see the world through his eyes, just a glimpse? That she wondered how she would be different if she had grown up knowing him rather than cloistered among only true believers?

She couldn't say any of that. "Before you saw me play, though, you did hate me," she said instead.

Hakim tipped his head, looking her over in slow assessment while he chose his words. "That first time I saw you, of course, I didn't know you. I was just reacting to what you represented."

"What I represented?"

"You get all costumed up like that, you can't be surprised that you're a symbol."

April bit her lip, then nodded. "That's fair. I hadn t thought about it before. I was doing that sort of work since I was five, a lot of it—I've never thought about the why of it all. But symbol, yeah. At any rate, it was definitely a costume." Her mother must have known exactly what she was doing, choosing all those clothes. "But still, you were beyond angry. You don't think you were a little extreme?"

Hakim set the carpet and sack back on the ground. The street was a mass of partying people in brightly colored clothing, laughing and dancing as the music echoed down from the plaza. The alley they were standing in was like a bubble of softly lit quiet.

"Look," Hakim said, then turned to sit on the roll of carpet. April hesitated a moment, then sat beside him, waiting for him to speak. "I don't usually tell people this, but I died myself once."

"You died?" she repeated, not sure she had heard him correctly.

"I was helping my sister try to repair a faulty door mechanism. We both got hit with a massive jolt of electricity. Both our hearts stopped."

April gasped, but he just shrugged it off. "But you recovered? How?"

"We were trying to get through the door to rescue some people. There were others there with us, and someone had brought a defibrillator along with the first-aid supplies to treat the people on the other side of the door. But they ended up using it on us. It took a minute or so, but they got both our hearts going again."

"I suppose that was lucky, then," April said, "that there was a defibrillator already there."

"No," he said, his voice thick. "The people we failed to rescue were my parents. My sister nearly didn't make it back at all. 'Luck' is not the word I would use."

"You're right. I'm sorry."

"My point is, I saw the tunnel and the light at the end of it. That's a function of your brain shutting down when it doesn't get enough oxygen. I know, I looked it up. But then I came back out of the tunnel and I was awake. Nothing else happened."

"You didn't see anything?" April found herself asking wonderingly. "Nothing at all?" He shook his head, not looking at her. "So that's why you don't believe in ghosts."

"Ghosts don't exist," he said. "It's not a matter of believing or not believing. Empirically, they don't exist." They were quiet for a long moment before he spoke again. "You're not going to argue with me?"

"Everyone sees ghosts," April said, but she couldn't make herself sound sure. "Everyone I've ever met has seen ghosts. And not just telling me stories; I've seen them seeing ghosts. I can't believe so many people are lying, or deluded, or whatever. Not that many."

"You said it's been a few years since you did this gig. You were younger then. You might not have noticed as much. Especially if your mother was always there to hush up and chase away any skeptics."

"I would have noticed," April said, but he just shrugged.

"There are a lot of natural phenomena that trick our senses. They can be hard to suss out. I'm sure the idea of chalking it all up to ghosts is easier. Especially these days; we don't have the right sort of equipment to pin down the other causes." He looked over at her. "You're awfully careful with your wording, focusing on everyone around you like their perceptions are more trustworthy than yours. You've been doing this business since..."

"Since I was five, but..." Her voice dropped to barely more than a whisper. "I've never seen a ghost. I've been there when others have, though. Lots of people all reacting to the same thing. Only me, outside of that experience. I stopped doing it a few years ago because I was afraid I was crazy."

"Not crazy, just not taking to the indoctrination," he said.

"It's not like that," April said. "My mother has never told me what to believe. I'm not brainwashed."

"These things have degrees," he said, and she could tell he was carefully choosing his own words to soften her anger. Only then did she realize she was angry, her hands in fists and her face hot. She took a deep breath to calm herself.

"I don't see anything. Well, sometimes little blurs out of the corners of my eye, but they go away when I try to focus on them. But I do feel things. Like the other day, down in the water treatment area, I felt weird. Something was pressing down on me, this immense weight, and it made me so sad and... uneasy, I guess. I had no reason to feel those things. It was like I was lost in a fog of someone else's emotions. I didn't see anything, but that feeling was very unsettling."

Hakim nodded.

"I feel like I want to do one more job, just so you can be there and tell me what you see happening."

"You don't have to do that," he said. "I think we both know I won't see any more than you did. Come on, I should get you home."

April nodded, and they stood back up. The noise of the crowd had been growing as they sat together, and it was impossible to talk during the walk to Ivan's house. The rowdy crowd churning around them made April more nervous than she wanted to show. She caught the dangling strap of Hakim's sack and held it tight, determined not to lose him.

He glanced back at her and put an arm back, keeping her tucked close behind him as he skirted behind the food sellers' tables, avoiding the center of the plaza. The party was just as thick in the wide cross street, but it had thinned out by the time they reached the large double doors built into the original structure of the station. April let go of the strap and fought the urge to twist her braid. Hakim didn't seem to know what to do next, either. The obvious thing was to knock on the door, but neither of them stretched out a hand to do it.

"Listen," Hakim said at last. "My sister and I are going to be leaving soon, but I would like to see you again tomorrow if that's cool. I see you have a reader; I could copy some of my book files onto your device. Things you should read."

"You have a reader too?"

"On my sister's ship in the repair dock," he said. "I don't carry it with me. It's not as easy to hide as yours."

April brushed a hand over her belly where her reader snuggled under her waistband. She liked that she could always have it with her, like a protective talisman.

"Does tomorrow morning work for you? The books I have to give you, you're going to want to start reading them right away."

"OK," April said. "But I'm pretty much like that with all books."

The corner of his mouth twitched like he was almost going to smile. "Till tomorrow, then."

April watched him go. He was nearly across the plaza before she lost sight of him, tall as he was. Only then did she turn and knock on the door.

10

CROSSROADS

April jerked awake, unnerved by the sense of open space around her. Being back in spin was odd enough after so long in free fall, but the bed couldn't be softer, both the mattress underneath her and the mountain of blankets and comforters over her. No, it was when her eye opened ever so slightly and she saw no wall close to her nose that the sudden disorientation scrambled her brain. She sat up, looking around until she saw each of the walls around her, the ceiling above and the thickly carpeted floor below. It was all so far away from her on the bed that was bigger than most of the rooms she had slept in. All of this space, all for her. It felt beyond strange.

Her stomach gave a soft grumble, and she climbed out of the enormous bed, digging through the piles of clothes she had pulled from the bags the night before but had not yet sorted and put away. She found lime-green leggings with a slightly darker green tunic but left her feet bare, enjoying the feel of the carpet, and she didn't bother combing out and rebraiding her hair. That could wait until after breakfast.

April opened her door as quietly as she could and crept down the dimly lit hallway to what Ivan called the great room. A collection of sofas and stuffed chairs made two separate conversation nooks on her left. The right side of the room was half formal dining area and half kitchen, stocked with appliances for cooking she had never seen before, let alone knew how to use.

She thought she was alone, but she drew up short at the bar that divided kitchen from dining area. Ivan was there, hands clasped behind his back and head bowed. He looked up at her, looking infinitely weary, but still managed a welcoming smile.

"You don't sleep much, do you?" April asked.

"Indeed, I do not. Hungry? Want some eggs?"

"I can heat up some oatmeal..."

"Nonsense. That's adequate for free fall, but here at home we eat proper food. And to be honest, cooking relaxes me."

"All right then," April said, sliding into one of the stools and pouring herself a cup of coffee from the machine at the end of the bar. Ivan turned a knob on the front of the stove and an actual flame sprang to life before settling down to a soft glow. He unhooked a heavy pan from the rack over the cooktop and gave it a little spin before setting it over the flame. Then he went to the refrigerator and took out a container of eggs and started cracking them open, one after the other, emptying the contents into a shiny stainless steel bowl and then whisking them all together with a little shot of what looked like cream but was probably a soy-based substitute. He poked his head back into the refrigerator, examining the contents.

"I'm thinking smoked salmon," he said at last.

"That's fish, right?" April said.

"You've never had it? You're in for a treat." He uncovered a small bowl and scraped the pink contents into the eggs. Then he added a little olive oil to the pan on the stove and swirled it around. The moment the eggs hit the pan, their aroma filled the kitchen.

"I could get used to living like this," April said, taking another sip of rich coffee.

"Yes," Ivan said absently, and April glanced up to see the weariness once more contouring his face.

"Has something happened?"

"I have had some very bad news, in fact," Ivan said, poking at the eggs as they curdled in the pan. "One of the businesses I operate in the Belt. The man I left in charge..." He blew out a harsh sigh and shook his head. "I wish I could say I had some inkling he was not to be trusted, but I didn't, not even for a moment."

"Did he rob you?" April asked.

"Yes, but that's not the bad part. I don't have all the details, and what I've been told is a garbled mess, but the gist of it is that the man is a tyrant, treating workers like slaves or worse. I have to go out there at once and sort all this out."

April stared mutely at her coffee. The Belt. She had struggled for a long, long time to get her mother and herself out of the Belt. Her heartbeat in her ears grew too loud, like a rhythmic rushing of wind. She was back in a world where she didn't know what was going to happen next. Or she had never really quite left it.

"This is the worst possible timing," Ivan said, turning the eggs over in the pan. "I'll be away for months, at the very least.'

"Bad for business?" April asked.

"Business? No, I was thinking about your mother," Ivan said. He divided the eggs between two plates and pulled up a stool across from April. "And you, of course. This is awkward for all of us, not the time in a relationship for this sort of decision. Certainly not on an empty stomach; eat up."

April forked up some eggs. They were nearly too hot to eat, but the salmon and fake cream were so rich she immediately put another forkful in her mouth. Ivan watched her enjoy her breakfast with a sad little smile and April forced herself to pause long enough to say, "If you ask her to go, she'll say yes."

"You think so?"

"I know so," April said, and she put more eggs in her mouth before she started talking about how her mother always said yes to everything this early in a relationship.

"I know the two of you just came back from the Belt, and it wasn't an easy journey back. She hasn't told me the whole story, but I gather you were abandoned there by her last man."

April nodded.

"I can promise you it won't be like that this time."

April nodded again, poking at the remains of her eggs.

"Of course, it's possible you don't want to go at all, not even under the best of circumstances," Ivan guessed.

"I like it here," she admitted.

"We wouldn't be taking my shuttle for a journey that far," Ivan said. "My long-range freighter has living quarters under spin, all the luxuries you enjoy right here." April put the last of her eggs into her mouth rather than giving an answer, and Ivan switched their plates so she could finish his own half-eaten eggs. "I sense there is something more you're not telling me."

"I do have a friend here," she said. "But that doesn't really matter; he's leaving himself today, anyway."

Ivan rested his chin on his hand and watched her eat. "Friends are important. Communication between stations can be unreliable, but it's worth trying not to lose contact."

April nodded, fairly certain he was thinking of all the years where he had no idea where her mother was or what she was doing.

"You are certainly welcome to stay here. My staff would be at your disposal. You could take some time to explore the *Triomphe*, meet people all over the station, figure out for yourself what you most want to do."

"I don't need time; I already know what I want to do," April said. "I want to learn how to do everything that you do, every aspect of your work."

"You wouldn't necessarily need me to start on that," Ivan said. "I have a team of managers I would trust to oversee your apprenticeship as deftly as they run my businesses when I'm away. You would be in good hands."

April gave another little nod, and a smile quirked the corner of Ivan's mouth.

"What?" April asked.

"That nod of yours—it's not necessarily a gesture of agreement with you, is it? You do it when you're thinking something you don't want to say."

April flushed. Was that true? "It's not deliberate," she said.

"Maybe not. But tell me what you're thinking, anyway."

April set her fork down and clasped her hands together in her lap.

"I appreciate everything you're offering me. It's fantastically generous, I know it. It's like being in a fairy tale and suddenly I have a fairy godfather raining wishes down on me."

"But," Ivan prompted.

April searched for words that eluded her. In the end, she only managed, "My mother."

Ivan sat back on his stool, folding his arms as he gave a little nod of his own. "Your mother."

April caught herself about to nod again and reached for her coffee instead. She finished it off, then set it back down next to her plate and folded her hands on her lap again.

"I don't want to come across as the outsider who thinks he has it all figured out," he said at last. "I know it's been years since I knew your mother well, and I can see that she's changed, and you I only know as much as I've worked out in the days we've spent together. And I've never been a parent or even close with anyone who was a parent, not when they were actively parenting, anyway."

"That's a lot of caveats," April said. "You're about to say something you think will upset me."

"Yes," Ivan said. "You're free to disagree."

"What are you trying to tell me?"

"It's not just this ghost business, which, again as an outsider, is damned odd," Ivan said. "It's clear you don't believe.'

"I never said that," April interrupted.

"You don't see, then," Ivan said. "I guess you feel like you want to believe?"

"I don't want to talk about ghosts," April said. "What are you saying about my mother?"

Ivan sighed, getting up from his stool and taking the pan from the stove over to the sink. April was aware that she was glaring at him every step of the way, that the hands in her lap had unclasped and she was now crossing her arms like she was bracing for a blow. She suspected he was stalling until she was calmer, but she didn't want to be calm.

"Don't just leave it there," April said. "Tell me."

Ivan watched the water from the sink fill the pan, then closed the spigot and came back to the bar for their plates and forks.

"Tell me," April said again. Hot tears were pricking at the corners of her eyes. What was so bad he couldn't just say it?

"Perhaps I am your fairy godfather," he said, dumping the dishes into the sink and wiping his hands on a soft white towel before coming back to stand at the end of the bar. His hand twitched as if he was about to reach out and touch her, but opted not to. "You know what I'm offering you are opportunities. You know."

"Opportunities to learn skills," April agreed, her voice hard.

"An opportunity for time away from your mother," Ivan said. "If you want it. And not forever, just a time. April, it would be good for you."

It was the way he said "good," like he was pleading with her, that nearly made her lose the tight control she was exerting over that hot feeling in her eyes, nearly had her crying. She bit down hard on her lip.

"Mr. EchoHawk?"

The gentle voice caught him once more about to touch her shoulder, and his hand dropped again. "What is it?"

"Someone at the door, to see the young lady. A Hakim Little."

"Your new friend?" Ivan guessed. April nodded stiffly, still working hard at not erupting into a flailing emotional mess. It was tiring, like making a fist with her entire body and holding it without release. "Let him in," Ivan said.

April stared fixedly at the counter in front of her and he stepped away from the counter, giving her a moment to pull herself together as he greeted Hakim in the center of the great room.

"Hakim Little, is it?" he said, catching the youth's hand in an exuberant handshake that seemed to catch Hakim off guard. "I'm Ivan EchoHawk."

"Yes, I know," Hakim said, then quickly added, "Pleased to meet you."

"What is it you do, young man?" Ivan asked. "Or are you looking for work?"

"No," Hakim said, momentarily puzzled at the question. April could see why; it sounded like Ivan thought he was there to beg for a job. "My sister and I have a job opportunity on the *Chandrasekhar*. We're leaving today, actually. I apologize for stopping by at such an early hour, but we are leaving as soon as my sister finishes one last repair, and I promised April some books."

"Books," Ivan said with a broad grin. "I see you know her well already."

"Er," was all Hakim managed in response to that.

"You're a big reader too, then?" Ivan asked.

"Somewhat," Hakim said. "My real interest is mathematics."

"Like engineering? I always need more competent engineers."

"Like number theory," Hakim said. "Pure mathematics, not practical applications. Like G. H. Hardy, I glory in the uselessness of my work." April made a mental note to look up who that was on her reader later.

"Interesting," Ivan said. "Do they have much need for that on the *Chandrasekhar*?"

"They have a great need for my sister," Hakim said.

"She's a little more practically minded?"

"She can fix anything, but the smart employer lets her just build from scratch to her own design."

"As it happens, I've heard of what they're doing on the *Chandrasekhar*. They've poached quite a few of my best workers, but I can't fault their decision to go. To have an entire station to refurbish, to live out your days with no worries of overcrowding, with a chance to be part of building an entire society from the ground up. If I didn't have so much invested in my own businesses already, I would pounce on that in a heartbeat."

"Yes, sir," Hakim said.

"You should take April with you," Ivan said, and April jumped. He had said it so casually, was he joking?

"Sir?" Hakim asked, clearly not sure himself.

"April is at a crossroads at the moment," Ivan said. "She has to pick a path now, and I'm very anxious to be sure she picks the right one. You can help me convince her, right?"

Hakim sent a questioning glance at April. She didn't remember standing up and crossing the room, but somehow she was there at Ivan's elbow.

"It's not really up to me," Hakim said at last.

"I've heard they've put a cap on applicants," Ivan said. "But I can send a glowing recommendation. I'm sure they'll have her."

"It's not just that," Hakim said. "It's my sister's ship. It's really up to her if April can come with us or not."

"Then I suggest the two of you go ask her. Not a moment to lose."

"But I haven't met his sister..."

"Salima," Hakim filled in.

"I haven't met Salima."

"I know this is happening fast," Ivan said. "You have a lot of options in front of you and no time to think about which one to choose. I'm sorry about that. But in my experience, the thing my intuition is telling me is the right choice is almost always what I settle on, even when I have weeks to come to a decision. So close your eyes and think: what do you most want to do?"

April started to answer, but he put a hand over her forehead, brushing her eyes shut. She stayed like that for a minute, not sure what was supposed to be happening. Was she missing out on some other mystical experience, like the ghosts she never saw? Was there supposed to be a flash of insight, a feeling washing over her that just felt *right*? Because it wasn't happening.

April opened her eyes. Ivan was leaning against the back of the sofa, that indulgent smile still on his lips. Hakim was watching her with, if anything, more anxiety than she was feeling herself in that moment.

"I think," she said, drawing the words out, still hoping for that magic moment to hit her. But it didn't. "I think I want to try the *Chandrasekhar*."

Hakim just nodded, no words spoken or even a smile, but she got the sense that he was just now breathing again.

"Excellent choice," Ivan said.

"But my mother," April started.

"I'll talk to her. I'll go wake her up now. The two of you go talk to Salima, then come straight back here. Time is short."

Then he was gone and April was alone in the oversized great room with Hakim.

"What do you think?" April asked, her voice sounding so tiny in all that space.

Hakim pondered. "I don't think he's trying to get rid of you."

April made a noise somewhere between a scoff and a laugh. "This is not how I thought this day would go."

"Come on," Hakim said, brushing her elbow without quite grasping it. "Let's go see my sister."

"So," April said as they crossed the atrium to the second set of doors and the station proper. "You like math?"

"Math is life," Hakim said.

11

———————

SALIMA

April had been in and out of airlocks all her life. She had on occasion done this in a spacesuit, the hull of the ship or station under her gloved hands, but more often she had moved from ship to ship or ship to station from two joined airlocks, the exterior shape of the vessel just an abstraction extrapolated by her mind. She had never really thought about how seldom she had seen the outside of a ship until Hakim brought her to the *Triomphe*'s dry dock and she saw shuttles and vessels of all sorts cluttering up a space as large as the marketplace below. She had never imagined such a variety of craft were traveling about in the solar system.

Hakim glanced at the screen of his oversized reader, then led the way along a serpentine craft between the shuttles in various stages of repair or disassembly. April hesitated, watching a man sitting on a dirty tarp putting something together, his hands finding the next piece by touch and snapping or screwing it together, like a kid with a puzzle toy he's solved a thousand times. April wondered what that would be like, to know how things worked so well that it became intuitive.

"April," Hakim called back to her, and she rushed to catch up, bounding more than she intended to in the half-gravity so much closer to the center of the spin. She checked herself on the edge of a shuttle wing, then settled beside him with a nervous flush on her cheeks. "That's Salima over there," he said, and she followed his vague gesture to see a woman nearly a decade older than the two of them but too similar to tall, lanky Hakim for her identity as his sister to be in any doubt. Her hair was cut close to her head, and she wore a utilitarian olive-green jumpsuit with arms and legs both rolled up. She did not look up as they approached, focusing on something deep inside the shuttle engine, leaning in as far as she could reach and fiddling with something she couldn't even see, her face intense in concentration.

"It's a nice ship," April said when the long moment of silence became too much for her.

"Is it?" Hakim said absently. "Listen, rule one of living with my sister: learn when you can interrupt."

"She gets grumpy?"

"Not even; she just won't hear you. My sister in problem-solving mode is uninterruptible. Seriously, she can tune out anything when she's thinking something through. I wish I could do that. I mean, sometimes I can when I'm in a flow, but I can't sustain it for as long as she can. Little things like hunger and other bodily needs distract me."

"She's a bit older than you," April pointed out.

"Twelve years," Hakim admitted. "I didn't know her that well as a kid; she moved out on her own when I was still quite young. Our parents were both engineers on a former corporate station, always reading and discussing all manner of things. I think all the talk is why she left when she was barely fifteen. It's been just the two of us for half my life now. To tell the truth, I miss all the talking from my younger days."

"I promise to talk to you about anything you like," April said. "The books you're going to lend me, to start. You could even teach me some math. I've never gone much past multiplying and dividing."

"You're kidding," Hakim said.

"Most people don't even know that much," April said, but he nearly cut her off.

"That's no excuse."

Then whatever Salima was doing deep inside the engine sorted itself out and she pulled her arms back out, wiping her hands on an already filthy cloth as she approached a heavy-duty computer plugged into the panel exposed on the shuttle's outer hull.

"Salima," Hakim said at last, when it became clear her focus had moved from engine to computer screen without so much as passing over them. She looked up, and it seemed to take a minute for her to recognize her own brother. "This is the April I was telling you about."

"The ghost girl," Salima said, her face unreadable.

"Yes, but remember I was talking to you just last night about how she wanted to change all that?"

Salima gave a vague shrug, her eyes on April. April was acutely aware of just how hurriedly she had thrown on clothes that morning. She had not dressed to impress, not remotely, just acted on a desire to wear bright colors. And when she forced herself to stop twisting the braid in her hands, she remembered deciding not to comb it out and rebraid it neatly until after breakfast. And then after breakfast, not thinking about her hair at all.

"She wants to come with us to the *Chandrasekhar*,' he said.

Salima looked down at the cloth in her hands and then started wiping her hands on it once more. "Not my call," she said at last.

"April works with Ivan EchoHawk, and he's going to put a word in for her. She just needs a ride."

Salima tucked the rag into the pocket of her jumpsuit, glancing from April to Hakim and back again. Then she stepped back to her computer and tapped at the keys as if the two of them had once again fallen out of her notice. April looked to Hakim, wondering if she was supposed to say something, or if he would.

"I'll be done here in half an hour," Salima said, still tapping at her computer. "I can only afford four minutes of dock time. Be there and be ready. I'll send you the details when I have them."

"Of course," Hakim said.

"Half an hour?" April said. "To pack and talk to my mother and everything?"

"We better hustle," Hakim said, bounding back across the dry dock to the elevators. April sailed after him, her untidy braid twirling behind her.

April clutched the elevator rail as they descended once more to full spin.

"You OK?" Hakim asked.

"Too much change lately," April said. "I don't mean... I'm just talking about gravity. Free fall, then here, then back in free fall, then back here, then half-spin for a little bit, back in full..."

"Free fall for a week on Salima's ship," Hakim finished for her. "But then full spin on the *Chandrasekhar*, and once there you'll be in full spin for as long as you like."

"That's true," April said. "I just have to get there."

It was now late enough in the morning for Ivan's assistants to be manning the desks in the atrium that separated his apartments from the main station, a curving stair starting from the left side of the desk and arching over the double doors to his apartments and up to more offices and the apartments where his employees stationed here lived. For a workplace, it had a very homey feel, April thought as she returned the smiles of greeting from the two people behind the desk and nodded her thanks to the man who set aside what he was doing to hold the door open for the two of them.

"I'm making the right choice," April said under her breath. "I'm making the right choice." But was she? She had no idea what to make of Salima, except to feel a little sorry for Hakim, who clearly longed for someone to have an actual conversation with. But then it seemed the two of them had already had discussions about her. What did Salima mean by calling her "ghost girl"? What had Hakim been telling her? If Salima only remembered what he had said after their first meeting and had not been listening to what he said after the second, it couldn't possibly be good.

Ivan and April's mother were both in the dining room, her mother sitting quietly in front of an empty plate and a half-empty cup of cold coffee. Ivan's fingers were flying over his tablet, and from the way her mother was sitting with her arms folded, she got the sense that whatever conversation they had been having, they had paused for Ivan to respond to something urgent. She could almost see the remains of the last spoken words hovering in the air between them, the next words ready to spring the moment he pushed the tablet away.

"Mother," April said.

Her mother turned in her chair, frowning a bit when she saw the state of April's hair. Then her eyes moved on to Hakim and her face fixed into a carefully expressionless state.

"Hakim, this is my mother, Melena. Mom, this is Hakim. I know you met once before. I just wanted to make it formal." Her words trailed off, and she looked down at the toes of her white sneakers. She could only imagine what her mother would say if she had gone out to the dry docks barefoot, as she nearly had before Ivan had sent her to her room to fetch some shoes before leaving.

"Hakim," her mother said, raising from the chair and approaching with hand extended. "Ivan has been telling me about you."

"Oh," Hakim said. "Well, he just met me a few minutes ago, as well."

"And my daughter has met you just three times in total," Melena said. "I would say you must make a terrific first impression, but in fact, I was there the first time you set eyes on my daughter and I saw you, so we both know that's not true."

"I wouldn't call that a proper meeting," Hakim said. "I was seeing the badges of an office and not the girl performing them. But of course you'd know that. Keeping the two separate is important to you."

"Yes," Melena agreed, but her stern posture did not relax in the slightest.

"April, Hakim," Ivan said, joining them in the middle of the great room. "How did it go with your sister?"

"We're leaving in less than half an hour," Hakim said. "You should get packing."

April nodded, but Ivan caught her arm before she could brush past her mother.

"Hakim and I will get your things together. You and your mom take what time you can."

April bit her lip. The idea of the two of them packing for her was not a comfortable one. It wasn't so much that they'd be touching her stuff—it was all still too new to feel like hers yet—she was just afraid something would get left behind. But she had so little time to say goodbye to her mother that she just nodded, and Hakim followed Ivan out of the room.

"I don't think I like that boy," Melena said.

"You're right, he makes a terrible first impression. I wish you had more time to talk with him. He's a mathematician."

"I wish *you* had more time to talk with him. Are you sure about all this?"

"We're riding together out to the *Chandrasekhar*. After that, we'll be in a whole community of people, some of whom Ivan knows. If I'm wrong about him, I only have to spend a week alone with him and his sister and then I'm sure there will be all manners of ways of avoiding them if I feel I have to."

Melena nodded, finally starting to loosen her tight posture. She unfolded her arms and the two of them slumped into the nearest chairs in one of the conversation nooks.

"You can always find a ride back here if you need to," Melena said.

"I will if I have to, totally," April promised. "Everyone here is so kind, and Ivan promised someone would take over my apprenticeship until the two of you returned. I hope I don't have to, but it's a very tempting backup plan."

Melena nodded again, and April remembered what Ivan had said about her own nodding. Did she get that quirk from her mother?

"What about you?" April asked. "Are you sure you want to do this?"

"Oh, you know me," Melena said with a wave of her hand. "I never care where I am day to day. So long as I have food, water, air, and a little good company, I'm content."

"Ivan seems like a good guy," April said.

"You know, I barely remember him from the corporate station. We weren't really in the same social circles there. Weird how life works out sometimes."

"I like him. I think he'd be a good teacher too. I was really thinking about going with you."

"Oh, you don't want to go back out to the Belt," Melena said.

"Don't you want me to go?"

"April," Melena said, leaning forward to squeeze April's knee. "If I thought that going with us back out to the Belt was the best thing for you, I'd absolutely insist that you come along."

"You think the *Chandrasekhar* is better?"

"Well," Melena said, "Ivan certainly thinks so. But like we agreed, coming back here is always an option for you. Either way, you're staying in the Earth–Moon area. Civilization. We fought too hard to get back from the Belt last time."

"I know," April said. "That's why I worry... wonder. Are you sure you want to go?"

"I'll be fine," Melena said. "Don't worry about me. I know you do. And I know why. But you don't have to. I'll be OK. Just like I know you'll be OK. Honestly, I have no worries about you always making do. We have not had an easy life, you and me, and don't think for a minute I don't know how much you've done to take care of me when you had to."

"Mom," April protested.

"No, we both know it. So how could I worry about you? Taking care of yourself can't possibly be any harder than taking care of both of us, and you've always managed to do that. You're going to be just fine."

"But..." April dropped her eyes to the hands in her lap. "Well, like you said. The last time we went out to the Belt. And this time you'll be on your own..."

"Ivan is with me," Melena said. April nodded, this time too aware that she was doing it in lieu of saying everything running through her mind. It was too much at once and her mother knew it all anyhow. "April," her mother said, leaning closer. "There is something else, another reason why I think that you staying here or going on the *Chandrasekhar* would be a good idea, just for a little while."

"What?" April asked, glancing up briefly.

"Ivan has a doctor friend."

"Oh," April said. "Yes, he explained some of this to me."

"I'm not sure if he knew, although I suspect he did, but the drugs he was talking about—I've been on them before."

"You have?" April said, sitting up straighter. "When?" But then there was only one logical answer. "On the corporate station."

"Yes."

"Did you leave because of the drugs?" April asked, her heart sinking.

"No," Melena said. "Not at all. No, quite the opposite. It didn't occur to me when I left that I wouldn't have access to them anymore. Growing up on the corporate station, they were always just there. I heard stories about the wild life on the free stations, but none of the stories had ever mentioned the rarity of pharmaceuticals. Not that knowing that would have changed my mind; never having been off my drugs, I wouldn't understand what being off them would mean until I lived through it."

"So Ivan having a doctor friend is a good thing," April said.

"Yes and no," Melena said. "Yes, in the long term, definitely yes. Once they figure out which drug at what dosage, yes. But the process of figuring those things out, it can be messy."

"Oh," April said, her gaze once more on the hands twisting together in her lap.

"I know it's probably a fantasy of mine," Melena said. "But I'd really like to see you again when I'm well, as well as I can be. I'd like to spare you the erratic mood swings of the next few weeks. I know you'd handle them just as ably as you've handled all my other swings; this isn't about doubting you, April. It's just, I guess, a gift I'd like to give you. The weeks and months to come might get rough, and I'd rather you were learning these skills you're so envious of, and making new friends, lots of new friends. And when I see you again, we'll both be different, but in good ways."

"That sounds nice," April said. "But what if...?"

"Don't worry," Melena said. "Please, don't. Or I tell you what—when Ivan comes back out here, you look him deeply in the eyes and tell me if you think he's remotely like that last fellow. This relationship is new and might not work out, but I don't foresee any future that ends with Ivan EchoHawk leaving me behind on a miner's station with no cash and no way home. Do you?"

"It's a lot to ask, that kind of trust," April said. "I don't think I can get enough out of his eyes to feel OK with it."

"I'm always going to know where you are," Melena said. "And

you're always going to know where I am. We'll get too far apart to talk on a comm line, but we can message each other every day. We're not going to lose touch."

April nodded, her stomach knotting just imagining how she would go about rescuing her mother if things went south again. Finding her and bringing her back to civilization would be twice as hard as bringing the two of them back had been. She could only hope that if it did come up, she'd have friends to help.

"I do have one thing I want you to promise me," Melena said.

"Anything," April said.

"You have a vocation," Melena said, raising a hand at April's sigh. "You are going to explore other things, I know. I just want you to keep an open mind. And an open heart. If there are people around you who need you, don't turn your back on them because of some intellectual argument you're having with yourself. Please. Those people have no one else to turn to."

April hugged herself, not wanting to meet her mother's pleading eyes. Melena waited, never looking away.

Then Hakim and Ivan came back into the room with all of April's things packed into two rucksacks of durable canvas, more practical than her carpetbag had been. Ivan smiled at her and bent to kiss Melena's forehead, but Hakim was looking from April to her mother and back again as if he could feel the unsworn promise hanging in the air between them.

"Time to go," Ivan said. "My personal elevator will get you up to the docks faster, but the dock number Salima texted Hakim is quite a jog from here. I have a man standing by with a transport at the docks, but you don't have a minute to lose."

April nodded and got to her feet, taking the rucksack from Ivan, not meeting his eyes. She didn't want to give anyone any last-minute tests. What was she going to do if he failed—abandon everything? He gave her a tight hug, and she murmured a goodbye. Then he turned to shake hands with Hakim and she was once more standing in front of her mother.

"April," she prompted.

"Yes," April said. "I promise."

She wished promising to help people didn't make her feel so bad.

Her mother smiled her most radiant smile, the tears at the corner of her eyes only making her expression shimmer more brightly. Then she hugged and kissed April, whispering one last farewell in French.

April felt like her vision was tunneling, only allowing her to focus on what was directly in front of her. Then the double doors parted, and they were jogging up the curving stair to the office level, Ivan still beside them, leading the way down the long central hallway to a set of elevator doors that a worker was holding open for them. Ivan bustled the two of them inside and waved one last farewell as the doors hissed shut.

April rousted herself out of her funk just in time to see her mother standing beside Ivan, also waving a tearful farewell. April raised a hand just as the doors clicked together and the elevator floor pushed up hard against her feet, hard enough to make her stumble. Hakim caught her elbow and helped her brace against the acceleration.

"Ivan put us on the fast track," Hakim said, but April just nodded mutely. This time, she had no thoughts to hide behind. She felt numb.

The doors opened, and hands were taking her sack from her before she even emerged from the elevator. Someone was chattering away to Hakim, but her ears refused to make the sounds into words. She put her hands on the bar behind the luggage bin and Hakim did the same beside her. The luggage sled fired a burst of air and they lurched forward, flying down the dock past airlock after airlock.

"It's going to be close," Hakim said to her. "We have to hustle on board the minute this sled stops. You ready?"

April nodded, her tongue too thick to speak.

The sled braked with another burst of air and Hakim unlatched the lid of the luggage bin, pressing one of the sacks into April's arms, then taking the other and disappearing down the airlock. April pushed off the sled to follow.

Her vision picked that moment to widen, her natural curiosity conquering the numbness of this too-rushed departure. She wished it hadn't.

The ship she had seen Salima repairing? Was not her ship.

Her ship was not a shuttle at all. If any part of her ship had once been a shuttle, April couldn't pick it out. No, Salima's ship was a collection of random pieces April couldn't wrap her head around. It looked like something an insane child had cobbled together.

April put a foot out, catching herself on the lip of the airlock. Was she seriously going to do this? Had Ivan known what this was going to be like? Because if her mother had seen this "ship" there was no way she would ever have agreed to let April board it.

"April!" Hakim yelled down the airlock. "We have to go!"

April ducked so that she could see him, her sack hugged tight to her chest. One little push and she'd be gone. He'd have half her stuff, but she'd be here on the *Triomphe*. Safe.

He held out a hand to her. She could feel the seconds ticking by, every one measurable in dock fees.

"April," Hakim said. "I know it doesn't look like much, but my sister is an engineering genius. An artist, not so much."

April smiled, more at gratitude for the attempt at a joke than from any real feeling of humor. Then she put her hand in his and he pulled her on board, holding her tight against him as he closed the hatch door and spun the lock.

Never had that clang sounded so final in April's ears.

12

TRAVELING WITH INCOMPLETE STRANGERS

April hugged her bag close to her chest, reluctant to move away from the airlock even as she felt them drifting away.

"Firing," Salima's voice echoed back from the front half of the ship.

"What?" April asked. Hakim caught hold of her shoulder and tucked her close to his side just before a loud bang shook the tiny ship around them and a series of jerking pushes thrust them back against the wall.

"It's OK," Hakim said when the noise stopped and they were once more freely floating.

"What?" April said again, her ears still ringing from the noise.

"You were screaming. It was just the directional rockets getting us away from the *Triomphe*. Let's stow your stuff before Salima fires the big rocket."

"The big..." April's voice trailed off. Hakim opened a tiny cabinet and April was about to warn him that her stuff would never fit in there when she was seized with a fit of giggles. He looked over at her quizzically as he took out a pair of bungees and shut the cabinet. April forced herself to take a deep breath, but the giggles kept wanting to come back like hiccups. It was the only way she could let off some of the pressure from the panic squeezing her like a giant's fist. This ship was so small, so delicate, the black of space outside so immense. She forced herself to take a breath. Hakim tied her rucksacks together by their straps, then bungeed them against the wall. April took another breath and finally got herself under control.

"Let me give you the tour," Hakim said. "There are two pods. The fore pod is the cockpit, engineering, and kitchen; basically all the electronics run through there. The aft pod we're in now is where we sleep, and behind that plastic curtain is the lavatory. Sorry, it doesn't quite close properly."

"There are no bunks," April said.

"We have sleeping bags stowed in that cabinet there."

Salima's head appeared in the hatch between the two pods. "We're going to be accelerating at half a G for about an hour."

"Sounds good," Hakim said, and she disappeared once more.

"Where do we strap in?" April asked, afraid she already knew the answer.

"We'll just get comfortable on the floor there. Get your reader, let's compare books."

April took her reader out of the waistband of her pants and Hakim helped her settle near the "floor" in an orientation that would feel upright in a minute when the engines started firing. He kept an arm braced behind her, almost around her. He caught her eye and made a jerk of his chin that somehow filled her with reassurance. This was his home, his and his sister's, and had been for years. He felt safe here; there was no reason she shouldn't feel safe too. And yet he wasn't judging her for being nervous. That helped too. She took out her reader, then looked over at his.

Hakim's reader was square and longer across than even his two hands with tapered fingers spread wide. Strips of Velcro on the back held it on his lap once he set it there. When he tapped it to life with his spare hand, the screen was filled with what she recognized as mathematics without having a clue what any of it meant. Like Egyptian hieroglyphics, only she'd probably figure out the meaning of some, eventually. Hakim swiped the math aside and pulled down the main menu.

"I've never seen a reader like yours," April said.

"It's not really designed for reading," he said. "Although I do use it for that. It's more for drawing or working with plans and schematics and things. It used to have a 3-D projector, but that's broken. It's been in my family for three generations. My great-grandfather gave it to my grandfather when he passed his certification exams as a mechanical engineer back in Algeria."

"Wow," April said, running a fingertip along the edge of the reader as if she could feel Earth still clinging to it. A low whine that had been lurking just out of a range she would notice was building to a level she couldn't ignore and she looked to Hakim to see if this was normal.

"The engine," he said. "We'll start feeling it in a minute here. Let me see yours."

She handed over her tablet.

"The screen is cracked," he said.

"Oh no, that's just a screen saver I use to discourage thieves," April said, reaching over to swipe it away. The main menu lit up the smudged but otherwise flawless screen.

"Clever," Hakim said, scrolling through the icons. "This was a corporate school reader."

"My mother's," April said. "When I was a kid I used to work through the programs, pretend I had a teacher. It even gives exams and grades them. It's just not much help when you get stuck and don't know why you're getting things wrong."

"I bet that was tougher with math than other subjects," Hakim guessed.

"Math, and also science when it got complicated enough to need math."

"There are a lot of things on here in French," he said. The whine of the engine had built up to a level where it was just possible to talk over it and April realized the floor that the backs of her thighs had been brushing against was now something she was actually sitting on.

"My mother and I usually speak French with each other," April said. "It was the language her parents spoke with each other. The corporate station she grew up on was very eclectic."

"Hold on," Hakim said, handing her reader back to her and returning his attention to his own. His fingers flew through folders until he found what he was looking for. He opened one and then traded readers with her again. "You can read that?"

April glanced at the title. "Certainly. This is a math book?"

"A very old one, but I've been dying to read it forever," Hakim said. "I can parse some of it by looking at the math, but the text... we should read this together. You can teach me some French and I can teach you some math."

"Cool," April said. The knot in her belly that was telling her she had made a very bad mistake finally loosened ever so slightly when he shared a smile with her.

There was no room for privacy on Salima's ship. The two pods technically had a sealable hatch between, but that was closed in emergencies only. And Hakim hadn't been exaggerating about the plastic accordion curtain that separated the lavatory facilities from the rest of the hexagonal aft pod and didn't quite close. April was used to living in tight quarters with little to no privacy, but always with her mother or with complete strangers she would never see again. Somehow, it felt different this time.

Salima and Hakim seemed perfectly comfortable with it, and their nonchalant attitude eventually wore away her embarrassment. By the time they drew near the science station she was nearly as matter-of-fact as they, waking up in a tangled tumble of arms, legs, and sleeping bags, taking turns behind the curtain, Salima and April dressing while Hakim was behind the curtain, then floating to the fore pod so he could change. Salima heated three coffee bulbs in her little microwave and April took the last of the fruit and nut bars out of the cabinet. She smiled a greeting to Salima, who gave the barest hint of a nod in return. April was still getting used to that being the closest she was going to get to a conversation most days.

Hakim had warned her about his sister's introverted ways, but he had neglected to mention his own. He did indeed like to talk, but not when he was working. She doubted he even realized how many hours passed while he was engrossed in whatever mathematical problem he was caught up in, filling his reader's screen in scrawling numbers and symbols using whatever came to hand as a stylus, occasionally wiping the screen blank with an irritated groan.

Salima took her coffee bulb with her and went back to the nose of the fore pod to her usual post: floating amid an array of screens, usually with something to tinker with in her hands. At first, April had been a bit panicked with the thought that the ship around them was constantly in need of repairs, until Hakim had explained that most of what Salima was doing was more optimizing than fixing. If he ever felt how close death was around them the way April did, he never showed it. He had complete confidence in his sister's ship of her own constantly evolving design. April tried to follow his example but was anxious to get to the *Chandrasekhar* and enjoy the comfort of a proper hull around her.

Hakim emerged from the aft pod just as April was finishing her breakfast. She waited to find out if this was a rare talking day or if he was already hard at work at something in his head and only taking a refueling break before heading back to his reader and stylus. "Ready for some more reading?" he asked, and April smiled.

"I'm not sure I'm much help to you at all," April said. "It's hard to translate concepts I don't understand myself."

"Working through it is good for both of us," Hakim said. "You're never going to forget something you worked that hard to learn, right?"

April didn't know how to admit how much of it still didn't make sense, even after his explanations. "It would probably be easier to just teach you French."

"I'm picking up a lot of vocabulary as it is, but if your reader has a grammar in it, I could formalize my learning a bit," he said to her surprise. "On the other hand, you could use a bit more formal work with numbers."

"I know," she said.

"It's useful for lots of skills," he said. "The more math you have, the better you're going to be at grasping tech."

"I suppose that's true."

"I know the stuff I'm into is kind of esoteric. Don't let that scare you off. You should dip a toe back in your program on your reader."

"I'm so far behind, though. The program has me labeled as a third grader."

"What's a third grader?" Hakim asked.

"On a corporate station, it's the third year of full-day schooling. So an eight- or nine-year-old."

"Ouch."

"Yeah. I've always preferred reading stories, and no one was making me do any of it, so it was easy to stop trying."

Hakim put his entire fruit and nut bar in his mouth and gestured for April to hand him her reader. She unhooked it from her belt and passed it over to him. He chewed as he looked through the settings on her math program.

"I wouldn't really think of it as being eight years behind," he said, giving another one of those assessing look-overs that always made her blush madly. She never knew how she was scoring on these little assessments.

"But I am eight years behind."

"You would be if you were moving in lockstep with a bunch of other students, but there's no reason to leave your app settings on teacher-driven pacing. Look, I'm going to change some of these admin settings. There are going to be things that you already get or will get the hang of very quickly by virtue of not being an eight-year-old. I'm setting it so you go through that stuff very quickly and not endlessly drill what you already have no trouble with. The program is going to focus on things you're having trouble grasping. I bet you find it only takes a year or so to be where your program wants you." He tapped the screen a few more times, then passed the reader back to her with a little spin. "Which, by the way, is a completely arbitrary designation. Learn as much as you like, as fast as you like. It's more meaningful that way."

"I will," April promised. "This is how your parents taught you?"

"Very hands off," Hakim agreed. "My mother said it was the best way to go, especially with highly motivated learners. She had had a miserable education herself, always having to wait for the rest of the class to catch up before moving on to the cool things she really wanted to learn."

"My mother was very hands off too," April said.

"Some guidance is good," Hakim said. "But really, you don't need much. You're more than bright enough to grasp this with just a little help, and you're certainly highly motivated."

April didn't know what to say to that. No one had ever called her bright before. Gifted, her mother had, many times, but never bright. Or motivated, for that matter. She liked the idea of being a bright, motivated person. But then she sighed. "I wish I had done this months ago. I'd be further on my way to getting a place on this station."

"You don't need to worry about it, honestly. You have the recommendation from Ivan EchoHawk, but even that you don't really need. Salima is our ticket in, me and you both."

"But you were invited. I invited myself," April said. She hadn't realized just how exclusive this science station reclamation project was until Hakim had started talking about it a few days ago. The people running the station kept the number of workers carefully balanced to existing life-support systems, and for every person there, they had ten more hoping for a place. April had pushed herself to the front of a long line without even realizing it. What was going to happen when they discovered how little use she was?

"Salima, would you reassure our guest that she has nothing to worry about?" Hakim said.

Salima, bent around a piece of equipment she had removed the back panel of, didn't respond.

"Salima? O sister of mine? Sal!"

"She's lost in a problem. Leave her be," April said, whispering quite unnecessarily.

"She's always lost in some problem or other," he grumbled, then pushed off from the kitchenette to catch his sister in a tackling hug.

"Hakim!" she protested as her multi-tool went spinning across the pod. She patted his shoulder awkwardly, but he just squeezed her tighter. April smiled as they tumbled past her, putting a hand out to stop them from colliding with the top of the open hatch. Finally, Hakim let his sister go.

"Honestly," Salima said, fetching her multi-tool. "Find something to do."

Hakim rolled his eyes, then caught April's hand and pulled her back into the aft pod. "Let's leave her be. She has many important things to get done today."

"Thank you, Hakim," Salima said. Her voice was as deadpan as ever, but April was certain there was just a hint of sarcasm there.

The radio squawked to life. "Salima Little?" Hakim and April exchanged a glance, then floated back to the hatch to listen.

Salima flipped open the mic. "Here."

"Hello, this is Lars Gundelach. We've not spoken, but we've exchanged messages?"

"I know who you are."

"Good. Yes. I'm in charge of recruitment for the station *Chandrasekhar*. First off, the engineering team is very anxious for your arrival."

"They've been pinging me since we've been in range," she said.

"Yes, they are very anxious to get you in a room with them." There was a pause. "There is a problem, however."

April looked to Hakim, who was intent on his sister's face.

"I'm betting more than one," Salima said.

"Ah, yes," Lars said with a little forced laugh. "It's just... as you know, we maintain a very delicate balance on our station. We know to a person how many people we can support, and we are at full capacity."

April clutched the lip of the hatch, as if anchoring her body would stop the feeling that she was tumbling away. The worst-case scenario that had been running through her mind for the last week was about to play out in real life.

"I see," Salima said, not looking up from her work on the component. "No room for me, then?"

"No, we can definitely make room for you," he said. "It's just your plus one. That might not work out."

April's heart started to beat too fast, loud in her ears.

"It's not a plus one now, it's a plus two," Salima said, calm as ever.

"Plus two?"

"Yes, now it's a plus two. You should have received a personal recommendation from Ivan EchoHawk." Salima finished whatever she was tweaking and snapped the back panel back in place, leaving the multi-tool spinning in the middle of the pod.

"Ivan EchoHawk? I don't... I can check my messages. I might have missed that. But still, two, that's just too many."

April felt tears prick at her eyes. She had expected this, but expecting it hadn't taken any of the sting off the moment. Hakim caught her hand and gave it a reassuring squeeze.

"I see. Please give my regrets to your engineering team," Salima said, turning the component over in her hands and pressing a button. The machine beeped and lit up.

"You don't understand. We definitely need you. And arrangements can be made for the others at a future date when space opens up—"

"It's now or never. You're in charge, Lars. You make it happen or you don't."

There was an agonizingly long pause, and April became certain that he had gotten angry and switched off, but at last they heard a sigh. "Come on board. I'll see what I can do. No promises."

"No promises," Salima confirmed, then switched off the mic.

"They think once you get caught up in problem-solving with their team, you'll take their offer," Hakim said. April bit her lip. Having seen how Salima got caught up in problems, that felt like a very real possibility.

"I'm sure that's what they're hoping," Salima said. "But considering the messages they've been sending me with increasing frequency, they really need me. They'll deal." She pulled the cables and wires straight, then folded them up neatly, tucking them behind the unit as she put it back in its space in the wall, catching her still-spinning multi-tool to lock it into place. "Of course, it would help if you could sell yourself a bit. He's going to want to talk with both of you about what you can bring to the station. Try not to seem like dead weight."

"But I am dead weight," April whispered to Hakim.

"Nonsense," Hakim said.

"With everything you know, you could be just as useful as your sister, if you put your mind to it. My only skill is not really a skill."

"You have a great deal of general knowledge from all your time reading that encyclopedia," Hakim pointed out. "And you speak how many languages?"

"I can read five, but I only really speak the two," April admitted.

"Still, that might be useful. Look, go through your reader and think about all the things you know and know how to do. Don't self-edit what you think might be useful. We don't really know what they need besides Salima. Make a list of every possible thing and when we get there, you can hit them with it."

April tried to take his advice, but she was still certain hers was a pathetically short list. Hakim didn't seem to be working on anything similar himself; she could see the French math text open on one side of the screen and he was working through some sort of proof on the other side. It looked like arcane, magical language to her.

She looked over her list one more time, then closed the page with a sigh. She hoped someone could at least give her a ride back to the *Triomphe*.

13

THE DERELICT STATION

April spent a sleepless night planning every possible route back to the *Triomphe*, and for once she was grateful when Hakim woke up in a math fog and she didn't have to make small talk. After breakfast of just coffee now that the fruit and nut bars had run out, she floated in the aft pod, the reader in her hands in sleep mode as she watched Hakim curled around his own reader, one of her hair sticks playing the role of stylus today. How had that gotten out of her bag?

"We'll be docking in about fifteen minutes," Salima called back to them. She had put on her headset and buckled herself before the piloting controls. Hakim grunted, lost in his problem. April put her reader away, but the hair stick in his hand gave her an idea.

"Do you mind if I change?" she asked. "Sometimes that helps me feel more confident."

Hakim looked up from his reader at last. "Not your full bell-and-veil regalia."

"No, not that," April said. "I just want to make a good first impression."

"As you like," Hakim said, floating into the aft pod to hover behind his sister. April opened up her bag, pulling out garment after garment until she was at the center of a cloud of shimmering fabrics.

What did she have that projected serious competence? Dark colors seemed appropriate. She plucked the pastels out of the cloud and shoved them back into the bag. She had nothing in black; her mother was very superstitious about April wearing black. She had some dark blues, but what caught her eye instead was a shalwar-kameez of a deep, dark green, like the heart of an emerald with a simple trim of equally dark gold, nothing bright or shiny. Perfect.

April cleaned up with a scented wipe, not as good as a shower, but infinitely better than nothing. She dressed and then combed out her long hair, very tricky in free fall, but something she had done on too many occasions to count. She braided it, but considering the station would be at full spin, she let the braid trail freely behind her. She put the rest of her clothes away, then took out her little jewelry bag. Nothing too flashy—definitely no tinkling bells, although she quite adored them outside of their ethereal medium context. She chose a pair of gold hoops, thin and only a few fingers in diameter, discreet, she hoped.

She had no way of knowing how they dressed on this station, but she was fairly certain that she looked professional, and in no way like she dealt with people's ghosts for a living.

Salima started firing the directional rockets, and April quickly stuffed her bag back into the cargo netting before floating into the fore pod.

"You might want to hold on to something," Hakim said when another burst of directional rocket sent her colliding into him. April caught a rung and held on with both hands.

"Aren't we docking at the hub?" April asked.

"No room," Hakim said. "Don't worry, Salima has done this before."

"Done what before?" April asked, then Salima pressed a button and braced herself.

Before April could react, she was pressed back, half in and half out of the hatch between pods. It was as if something had caught them by the nose and started dragging them hard. Then everything fell to the floor of the ship.

"Harpooned onto a spinning station," Hakim said, pulling her out of the way as Salima rushed past them to the back of the aft pod.

"We're on the outside of the station?"

"Yes, but no worries. They have a flexible airlock they're bringing our way. We don't have to go EVA."

Something jostled the ship amid muffled clangs. Then there was a brisk knocking on their rear hatch. Salima knocked back, then spun the wheel to open the door.

"Hi! Salima?"

"Yes," Salima said, disappearing out the hatch. April stepped over the lip of the hatch between pods, then across the aft pod to the rear hatch. It was awkward, and she kept her eyes on her feet to keep from stepping on any of the controls, cabinets, or rungs on what was normally a wall and not a floor. She stepped up onto the airlock hatch and through to the other side.

Stepping onto the floor on this side was like walking on an air mattress, and she was suddenly very aware that nothing separated her foot from the vacuum of space but a thin layer of plastic. She could even feel the cold leaching through the plastic and past her slipper.

"Hello, I'm Lars Gundelach."

April looked up, brushing stray hairs from her face with her left hand as she extended her right to meet his handshake. She had expected someone older, far older given the rank he seemed to have on the station, but he was somewhere around hers and Hakim's age.

"April Nguyen," she said with a smile she had no trouble mustering. He was tall and broad, bigger even than Ivan EchoHawk, with even white teeth. Definitely corporate-born. His hair was short on the sides but long enough to curl on top, a bright gold darkening to a honey brown at the roots. More startling were his eyes, a shade of blue she hadn't seen since she had floated over the Earth's oceans outside of the *Moreau*. Her cheeks started to flush as she realized she had been holding his hand entirely too long without speaking, then flushed a hotter red when she realized he had been doing the same.

"And you're Salima's brother," Lars said, apparently remembering himself, although his eyes flicked back to April one more time before reaching past her to extend a hand to Hakim. He was still holding April's hair stick, and she took it from him, twisting her braid around once and anchoring it with the stick as they briefly shook hands. She adjusted the little bun, draping the remaining braid forward over her shoulder, then flushed again when she realized both boys were watching her.

"Sorry," she said, not sure what she was apologizing for. "It's nice to be out of free fall."

"I bet. Shall we?" Lars asked, touching April on the shoulder and showing the way with one sweeping arm.

April climbed up the ladder to where Salima was already in deep conversation with two other people in faded blue jumpsuits. April brushed down her kameez, hoping she wasn't too wrinkled. Hakim came up beside her, then lastly Lars. He dropped a hatch shut over the flexible airlock and spun it closed. He was also wearing a jumpsuit, but his was a crisp khaki that fit better. He glanced at a tablet in his hands, then looked up at April again with a frazzled smile.

"Busy day?" April guessed.

"They all are," he said. "I had a tour planned..."

The engineers stopped talking to Salima to turn on him at once.

"Straight to engineering," one said.

"But..." He consulted his tablet again. April could see message windows popping open almost constantly. She had worried that Ivan EchoHawk had forgotten to send her recommendation, but now could see how easily it could have been missed.

"They can show me the way," Salima said. She already had a station tablet in her hands, one with LITTLE stenciled across the back of it. "I'm sure your facilities are far better than I'm used to. I don't really need to see it all. But please take my brother and his friend around."

She was looking at the tablet the entire time and her tone never wavered, but April felt the phrasing "his friend" had been nowhere near as offhand as it sounded. Was Salima distancing herself from her? She wasn't going to be able to stay, was she? Not as a friend of a relative of someone they needed.

"Of course," Lars said, and the two engineers took Salima with them, steering her around a corner as she scarcely looked up from her tablet.

"She's going to solve all your problems in a week and then where will we be?" Hakim said and Lars gave a nervous laugh.

"Sadly, we have lots of problems, and they breed like rats."

"Sounds like a challenge," April said. He nodded, eyes on his tablet again, but April could see Hakim scowling at her. "We like a challenge," she said, glaring back at Hakim. This was his job-winning behavior?

"Well," Lars said, tucking the tablet behind him and turning his attention back on her. April felt like she was cooking under a very bright, very hot spotlight. "I'll take you on the orientation tour, shall I?"

"Yes, please," April said and fell into step beside him, going the opposite direction Salima had gone. Hakim trailed along behind them, hands in his pockets as he scowled at everything around them. April became desperate to keep Lars's attention on her and not Hakim's unfriendly behavior. "I'm very interested in the work you're doing here. How large is the station?"

"It was built to hold five thousand, the scientists working the scopes as well as support staff. Currently, we've only reclaimed about twenty percent of the space, and our life-support systems can only handle four hundred and twelve."

"Four hundred and twelve—that's a very specific number," April said, her heart sinking.

"It's calculated daily," Lars said, catching her elbow briefly to indicate they should stop at the elevator. "We have a team that acts as a buffer. They help with salvage on the station, but when the number dips, they do supply runs on the shuttles."

"Salima will bring that number up," April said, trying to sound as confident in Salima's abilities as Hakim always did.

"That's what we're hoping," Lars said. "I'll be pushing that point hard when I meet with the founders in an hour to ask for you two to be allowed to stay."

"Are you optimistic?" April asked as the elevator door opened and they stepped inside. She caught Lars's arm and pulled him closer to her so Hakim could pass behind. He slumped against the back of the elevator, arms crossed as he glowered at both of them. What was his problem?

"Ivan EchoHawk wrote a very glowing recommendation for you, and I can be quite persuasive myself," Lars said. "I'll show you around a bit, then we can talk about what you bring to the *Chandrasekhar* before I meet with them. It's rare that they don't take my advice on these matters."

"How long have you been here?" April asked.

"Nearly a year now," Lars said. He hadn't stepped back after Hakim had passed, and April had to tip her head back to look up at him. She would bet he was tall even by corporate station standards. "I was in the second wave of arrivals after the founders. That's the four people who first found this station and started the salvage work. The station was spinning, but had no life support. They lived out of their suits for weeks before getting the first room habitable."

"They didn't have a ship?" April asked.

"They were dropped off by a passing shuttle. They had a crate of tools and supplies, enough to swap out the tanks on their suits and make repairs here. But if they hadn't succeeded in bringing the life-support system back online here, they would have died here. They had no ride back."

"They risked a lot," April said.

"They had nothing to lose. They were from one of the lunar stations built on the surface."

April knew what that meant. No radiation shielding. They probably each already had the cancer that would kill them growing somewhere inside them. Like so many others, maybe even like her. She had spent months in that shuttle village, completely unprotected. The elevator stopped and Lars stepped out, then turned back to wait for her. She gave herself a little shake and put a smile back on her face before he could ask about her sudden change of mood.

"But I guess it was worth it—they are the owners of this place now?"

"We don't really think of it that way," Lars said. "Everyone here has a vested interest in the enterprise that increases the longer you stay, but the four of them make all the major decisions."

"Like who goes and who stays," Hakim said from behind them. "Yeah, they're owners."

April risked shooting him a look. How could he think the surly attitude was helping? But he was looking at one of the doors they were walking past, a sealed hatch with a red light over it.

"Red light means no atmosphere beyond that door yet," Lars said. "Those are not yet reclaimed areas. This part of the station was administrative originally, lots of offices and computers. Those are low priority for us at the moment. Here is the cafeteria."

The far wall was a long glass-covered counter, empty now. Four long tables with built-in stools running down the sides dominated the space. Three people huddled together in one corner of the room, all poring over the same tablet the size of Hakim's, empty plates and bowls at their elbows. One lone woman in a white jumpsuit wiped down one of the other tables and the tops of the stools.

"We can fit about a hundred people in here at a time, so we eat in shifts depending on work crew. Shift four's lunch just ended, but shift one will be having dinner in an hour. The kitchen staff are always busy," Lars said. He led the way between the two middle tables to the counter.

"Do you grow your own food?" April asked.

"That's the goal, but we're not there yet. Reliable food supplies for so many people are hard to come by."

April peeked past the glass, but the food bins were all empty, waiting for dinner. She could see more people in white jumpsuits through the doorway past the counter, bustling about with armfuls of dishes or food containers. They looked hot and tired, cheeks flushed from the ovens and steam, but when two nearly collided they each gave a little laugh before moving on. Maybe it wouldn't be so bad if she ended up there.

"The commons is this way," Lars said, pushing through a pair of swinging doors at the end of the counter to the next large room. There were sectional sofas in two of the corners making conversation nooks, table and chairs in the middle of the room with games scattered about, and, at the far side of the room, an enormous media screen with chairs in rows in front of it. "We organize some entertainment, movie nights and game competitions. We have some exercise equipment in that room there"—he pointed to a door on the far side of the room—"and that terminal there is our sharing library."

"Fantastic!" April said, fighting the urge to run over and start scrolling through its contents. "I love books."

Lars's face lit up. "Me too. Favorite author?"

"Lewis Carroll," April said at once. "I've read *Alice's Adventures in Wonderland* and *Through the Looking-Glass* like a million times. In English and in French, it's poetry in both languages."

"He was a mathematician, you know," Hakim said as if he couldn't help himself.

"Oh, yes?" April said, encouraged that he seemed to be coming out of his funk.

"My favorite is Karen Blixen," Lars said, then added with a teasing glint to his eye, "in English and in Danish."

"*Out of Africa*, right? I've never read her," April said.

"You should. I've put all her works in both languages in the library. She worked such beauty with her words."

"Robert Kanigel," Hakim said suddenly.

"I don't know him," Lars said. April also shook her head.

"He didn't write fiction. He wrote a biography about Srinivasa Ramanujan, a mathematician from a poor family in India that did amazing, sublime work all on his own before he was discovered by academia."

"He's your favorite writer from just one book?" April said, not sure if that should count.

"That book made me who I am," Hakim said, his mood starting to darken again.

"You should add it to our library. It sounds like the sort of thing a few people I know would be very interested in," Lars said, but Hakim just shrugged, as if the topic no longer interested him.

April longed to give his hand a squeeze, but he was too far away for her to do it without being obvious about it. Still, she sensed he was feeling out of place on this station in a way he hadn't expected. She knew that feeling, but she was sure if he just tried, he would be accepted.

"Let's go back through the cafeteria," Lars said, putting a hand on April's elbow to guide her back through the double doors. The people at the table had gone and the woman who had been wiping the tables was now sitting cross-legged on top of one of them, watching a small fleet of mopping robots zip over the floor. She noticed Lars this time and raised a hand in greeting, giving Hakim and April a puzzled smile.

"New recruits?" she said. "Do we have the space? Because Michael is still out on shuttle duty."

"I'll be giving everyone an update tonight after dinner," Lars promised.

"A lot of people are going to be annoyed if we stay, aren't they?" April said. Whoever Michael was, he and some other shuttle worker were losing their places on the station if she and Hakim stayed—places they had undoubtedly worked hard to earn.

"We need Salima. They'll understand," Lars said. "If Salima helps the engineering team get the second life-support station online, we'll be able to have Michael and all the other float workers come back full time. And you being here will be a part of what makes that happen."

"I hope so," April said. "I want to help."

He smiled down at her again, then turned off the main hall into a shorter hallway that took a hairpin turn before opening out into a locker room with showers in one corner and a row of sinks and mirrors. The lockers were oversized, but April saw a pressure suit hanging inside one locker with a half-open door.

"Locker room, of course," Lars said. "Mostly the salvage team uses these, although when the showers in the barracks get crowded, some of us sneak down here to use them."

He led the way back out, then further down the hall.

"All the barracks are the same," he said, pushing past one of a series of swinging doors. "Twenty to a room."

"Everyone sleeps in here?" April asked. There were ten bunks in rows of five, with a central aisle that ended at a pair of sinks under a long mirror, showers to the left, and a pair of toilet stalls to the right. Lockers lined the other walls. "Cozy."

"When we get the time to open up some of the sealed-off areas you saw outside the elevator, we hope to convert those to private rooms, especially for the married couples."

"Are there children here?" April asked.

"Not yet. That's a term in the contract. We can't have kids here until we're much more certain it's safe. There are a lot of risks living here just now."

"That's a shame," April said. "I like kids."

"Someday we'll have tons," Lars said. April felt her cheeks pinken, and he rushed to amend, "the *Chandrasekhar*, I mean. Not us. Of course."

Hakim scoffed, softly, but April was certain Lars had heard it, too.

"Come," Lars said, striding purposefully further down the hall. "We have to go back up to the engineering level. That's where my office is."

No one spoke as the elevator moved soundlessly between floors. April fidgeted with the end of her braid, smoothing out the already smooth tail. She could feel Lars looking at her; she imagined trying to gauge her response to what he had misspoke, and Hakim was still glowering at them both.

The ding before the doors slid open was an immense relief.

"Admin," Lars said, sliding comfortably back into tour guide mode. "It's just the four founders and me up here, so you likely will never be back up here again." They passed a room lit only by rows of screens streaming with data and flashing images. A man with long, dark hair sat alone in the darkness, so intent on the screens before him he didn't even notice them walk by.

"My office," Lars said, opening a door and stepping aside to let April and Hakim precede him. "It's a bit tight."

"You should see the inside of Salima's ship; it makes this look positively roomy," April said, squeezing past the chair nearest the door to the one against the far wall. There was barely room for her knees between the chair and the desk. Hakim folded himself into the chair next to her, suddenly all knees and elbows.

Lars sat down across from them, and the surface of his desk instantly came to life. Sighing, he swiped a number of message boxes off to the left and tapped out a series of notifications, then put his finger on an icon at the bottom, flicked it to the center of the desk, and double-tapped it until it expanded to fill all but the edges of his desk where his messages lurked.

"Salima gave me the impression neither of you had engineering skills," Lars said. "Otherwise, you would have been dragged off with her when you arrived."

"No, nothing like that," April said quietly.

"I assist her with some mechanical work, but really just following her directions," Hakim said.

"That would give you some familiarity," Lars said, fingers scrolling through his screen. "Alas, most of our float staff are also mechanical. We're quite full in that area."

"Hakim is very mathematical," April said. If he wasn't going to speak up for himself, she would.

"Math," Lars said, propping his head on one hand while the fingers of the other moved through lists. "Can you code?"

"I've never tried," Hakim said.

"I'm sure he could pick it up fast," April said. "He's very smart."

Lars looked at her, then at Hakim. Hakim was looking at his own cuticles. "What about you?" Lars asked, his eyes coming back to her.

"I've never really done anything useful," she admitted. She did not want to give him her real work history. "I've done odd jobs in marketplaces, helping to move things or clean, things like that."

"Hmm." He scrolled through more lists. "You're both young and healthy, that's a plus. We need people who will be looking to start families in about a decade."

"Is that how you got this job? Being the right age?" Hakim asked.

"Well," Lars said, "yeah, that and my decade of experience doing this sort of organizing work with my parents. They have helped get a lot of communities like this running all over the Earth–Moon stations." Then he frowned at something on his tablet.

April's hands were twisting together in her lap. She folded them tightly together.

Hakim gave an exaggerated sigh and said, "She has a suit."

"A suit?" Lars repeated.

"Oh, yes. I'd forgotten," April said. "Ivan EchoHawk gave it to me. I can do EVA work. I mean, I still don't really know how to do anything, but I have the suit."

"That helps," Lars said, looking relieved. "We have a shortage of suits and a lot of work that needs to be done in compartments still without air. Excellent."

Hakim looked at April and gave a little shake of his head, clearly disappointed in her abilities to sell herself. How could she have forgotten the suit was in her plus column? She had been too focused on everything in her minus column.

Lars sat up straighter in his chair, engrossed in something on his tablet. April watched his eyes move as he read whatever it was twice, then tapped away at the screen, the beginnings of a smile tweaking the corners of his mouth.

"Good news?" April didn't dare feel actual hope.

"I found the message from Ivan EchoHawk."

"Oh?" She couldn't imagine anything he could say could help. Even the most glowing of recommendations would be about potentials and not actualities.

"Yes, we'll definitely make space for both of you," Lars said as his tablet chirped discreetly. "The founders agree."

"They know Ivan?" April asked.

"By reputation," Lars said with a vague gesture of his hand before returning to tapping away at the screen. "He must think very highly of you, indeed. He's offering us a cargo container full of very hard-to-acquire things, things we need nearly as much as we need Salima."

"Oh," April said again. She wasn't entirely sure she liked the idea of someone buying her a space here.

Lars was still engrossed in his tablet as Hakim leaned close to her ear to whisper, "He bought you an opportunity. The rest is up to you."

April turned to look at him. He had slouched back into his chair, hand to chin and still determined not to look impressed by anything, but he did meet her eyes long enough for her to be sure he had known exactly what she had been thinking and had said exactly the right thing. And was ever so slightly smug because he knew he had.

"I don't see any way around putting you on low-level crews," Lars said at last. "Although even those people all have skills of some sort. That's where we hold people until positions open on other crews. I'm going to be introducing you to everyone after dinner when I give the sitrep, but even with that you can expect some people are going to be resentful. That's to be expected; lots of people are waiting for spaces to open up here to send for spouses or family members. They know we need these supplies, but two people on the station are about to be transferred to shuttle duty. There's no way around that, and people will be upset. You're just going to have to roll with it. Try to make friends, and pick up whatever skills you can. Be useful in every way you can find. We work ten-hours shifts here seven days a week, there's not a lot of leftover time for learning. You're going to have to be very dedicated."

"I will," April said. She felt tingly all over. She was going to be able to stay.

"And you?" Lars said, looking at Hakim. Hakim nodded.

"I'll make sure he does," April promised.

"Actually," Lars said, pushing two of the lists across the desk and spinning them around. "I have to put you on separate teams. You'll be working on a salvage crew, suiting up and clearing debris from unmanned parts of the station. Hakim, you'll be in sanitation."

"Different teams," April repeated.

"Sorry. But you're both shift three—you'll be able to eat together if you wish."

"Thank you," April said. "Thank you for letting us stay."

"I'm sure we'll soon be grateful for more than just Salima," Lars said. "You're going to earn your place here. I have no doubts on that score. Welcome to the team."

14

THE PAST HAUNTS

April sat with the rest of her crew, watching as the electrician and his apprentice checked each other's hazard suits, then passed through the portable airlock into the next room.

"It's too late in the shift for this, boss," said Kyle, always the first to complain.

"Orders are orders," their boss, Sunita, said. "Someone wants this area cleared in a hurry."

"So we can go swimming?" Kyle asked with a grin. "I'd love to try that."

"You'd drown," Sunita said. "This is one of the largest rooms within reach of the reclaimed area. If I had to guess, I'd say they're looking to turn it into another hydroponics farm. Reducing our dependence on foreign foodstuffs is a huge step towards being self-supporting."

"Doesn't change my original point," Kyle said. "By the time we get in there, it will be time to pack up for shift change."

"We'll get as much done as we can before then, yes?"

"Well, yeah. That goes without saying," Kyle said and lapsed into silence.

April had never worked with others before. She hadn't realized that too was a skill until she had been forced into a situation where it was absolutely necessary. The other members of her crew weren't unkind, but they weren't exactly friendly either. The stress of being on one of the lowest-skill teams showed on all of them. The station's balance was constantly monitored, oxygen and CO2, food and water, constantly measured against the number of people currently on board. If the system were too taxed, someone would have to go to restore the balance, and it would be one of them. And the shuttle crews were currently all full. They'd have to go somewhere else and be back on the wait list.

April wasn't the only one desperate to get a better placement, to apprentice with anyone learning any skill if it meant a more secure position. She and eight others had put in for the electrician apprenticeship, losing out to Martha for no reason April could see. To be fair, Martha was learning her trade quickly, and her mentor Willem seemed pleased with her progress. But she hadn't been any more qualified than the rest of them when she had got the position. They must have just picked a name at random.

April knew she was prejudiced. Martha had been at one of April's ghost dispellings at an impressionable age and had recognized her the moment they met. She wouldn't stop telling the others tales of all the things April had done. She pestered April constantly for more stories, more details on things she half remembered or only half heard, but especially on all the stories she had never heard at all. It was embarrassing, all the attention, especially when Martha got others caught up in her enthusiasm and they started asking April to tell them stories, too. While she would have preferred to have gotten the apprenticeship herself, at least with Martha doing that job, they were no longer working side by side on the same crew every day. April could go back to being mostly ignored by the others.

The light over the airlock went from green to red: the electricians were coming back through. Some of April's crew got to their feet, ready to cycle through into the next room now that the danger of exposed wires was eliminated.

Then the light went back to green, and the door opened. Martha was hyperventilating, her face red and blotchy under the tears. She slumped over, hands on her knees as she struggled for breath. Willem was trying to calm her down, putting an arm around her and whispering comfortingly to her. He was calmer than Martha but still looked shaken, his face gray, his eyes too wide.

"What happened?" Sunita asked, her hand on the communicator on her belt. "Do I need to sound an emergency?"

"Yes!" Martha sobbed.

"No, no," Willem said. "We're just a little spooked, is all. Give her a minute."

April felt a trickle of cold run down her spine at the word "spook." She also felt eyes on her, but she kept her head down, letting her loose hair cover her face.

"Is there an electrical problem in there?" Sunita asked.

"It was her! I saw her!" Martha said, then covered her face with her hands.

"This is going to make sense soon?" Sunita asked. People were still sending random glances April's way, as if waiting for her to speak up. She bit down hard on her lip and tried to fade to the back of the crowd.

"She's talking about the first officer, what's her name," Kyle said.

"First officer?" Sunita repeated, clearly still at a loss.

"You know the story. She was swimming laps here when the crash and hull breach happened. Apparently she used to swim laps to clear her mind, and she spent so much time there that when she died there, she haunts it still. Apparently," Kyle said with a shrug.

"I see," Sunita said. "I'm curious how anyone knew this room was haunted when no one has been in there from the moment this station became unviable two decades ago, until just now."

April smiled to herself. Maybe this wasn't about to go bad. Sunita was a good boss; people listened to her. If she was being skeptical, the others would follow her lead.

"I saw her," Martha said. She rubbed at her face, then dropped her hands and straightened up. She was calmer now. The emotion making her cheeks flush was no longer panic. "We went to check the boxes like ordered. It's a mess in there—there were apparently a lot of loose chairs and rows of bleachers that got knocked about in the crash, like the whole room was inside some kid's toy and he shook it really, really hard. And there's water everywhere. We had to be extra careful on account of that. The panels nearest the door weren't live, so we were crossing the room to get to the far side, when I started seeing lights. Not from my flashlight, all around me. I've seen it in movies before, the pattern of light off of water. That's what it was."

"Reflecting off the water on the floor?" Sunita asked with a frown.

"No, not like that. Deep water, water deep enough to move about, like waves. It was dancing all around me, that light."

"Did you see it?" Sunita asked.

Willem folded his arms and considered the floor in front of his feet. "I saw something. I don't know what it was. I've not watched many movies. If Martha says she knows what it was, I guess that's what it was."

"Was there water in the pool then?" Sunita asked.

"No more than anywhere else," Willem said.

"But that's not all," Martha said. "I could hear sounds like water splashing. I would turn my head to find it, but it would stop, then start again when I took a step. Splashing like swimming, you know?"

"Willem?" Sunita asked.

"I think I heard something. It's hard to get a sight line more than a meter or two in any direction before debris blocks your view. It's unsettling, not being able to take a proper look about."

"The far panels have been dealt with?" Sunita asked.

"We didn't get that far," Willem admitted.

"That needs to be done," Sunita said. "We can't send work crews in there until we know there's no risk of shock or spark from exposed wires. We can't cut the power to this room without taking out every light in this sector. That includes main control just above us. We don't have access to the right panels yet."

"I know," Willem said, but Martha quickly drowned him out.

"I'm not going back in there until she does," Martha said, pointing at April.

Everyone turned to look her way, and April felt the sudden weight of their attention crush her.

"She's not trained for this," Sunita said. Because chitchat always died away when the boss approached, April supposed she was the only one there who didn't know who April used to be.

"She knows what I mean," Martha said. "Please, you have to."

"I can't," April said. She meant "won't" but couldn't quite get that word out.

"Someone please fill me in," Sunita said.

"Our little April used to be something of a sensation in the haunting-elimination world," Kyle said. To April's confusion, he sounded smugly proud, like somehow that reflected positively on him. "She can communicate with spirits, does a little ritual and convinces them to move on. Bye-bye haunting, the living get on with their business without the dead being such a nuisance."

"I don't see ghosts," April said. "I don't. I never have. I am—was—a fraud. It was just something I had to do to eat." She dropped her gaze back down to the floor. It sounded so lame to say it out loud. There were other ways to get money for food.

"No, April, you were fantastic!" Martha said. "I saw her work once, at the last station I was living on. Twelve workers had been pulled into the vacuum during a massive hull breach in one of the engineering pods. They had repaired the damage, but no one could work there because those twelve workers were haunting the place. People who tried to work there felt cold all the time, and sad for no reason, and they heard knocking through the hull like someone wanting to come in. Accidents kept happening, little things but getting more severe. People were getting hurt by equipment not responding the way it should, things like that. Then April came. My father was the head of engineering, so I got to be there when she worked her magic. It was beautiful. We all saw them, twelve happy balls of light that came in from the cold of space and gathered together inside her magic circle. She convinced them to move on to the next world and they glowed so brightly." Martha was crying again, this time radiant tears of joy. "We never had a problem again after that, all thanks to her."

"It was a lie," April said, her cheeks burning hotter than ever. "I don't actually do anything. It's just pretend. Was just pretend. I don't do it anymore."

"I don't know why you believe that about yourself," Martha said. "You have a real gift."

April just shook her head.

"I won't go in there again until that spirit is gone," Martha said. "And she can take care of it. She needs to do it."

Sunita gave a nod, not so much of agreement as of acknowledgment that she heard what Martha was saying. She looked around the room at the rest of the crew, some of whom had been nodding along when Martha had said she wouldn't go in there.

"We're ten minutes from shift change, but clearly nothing more is getting done today. Crew dismissed. We'll take this up in the morning. April, a word?"

April watched the others go, wishing desperately that she could be leaving too, just another anonymous member of the crew.

"I know this conversation is making you uncomfortable," Sunita said, gesturing for April to sit beside her on some of the crates waiting to be filled with broken bits of chair and bleacher.

"I came here to leave all that behind me, to do something real and worthwhile."

"I respect that," Sunita said. "But I have a problem. I need my crew in there, working as quickly as they can to get that room cleared for the construction crews to start setting up the hydroponics bay." She paused, seemed to come to a decision, and leaned closer, her voice pitched lower. "I'm casting it in the best light when I say we want to be more independent of outside sources. That's been true since we started, but lately it's less about want and more about need. The supply lines are drying up. Stations that grow food no longer have as much of a surplus, not with every one of them being totally overpopulated. And shipments from Earth are used up before they get anywhere near us. We have to start growing our own food. We needed it yesterday. The agriculture department needs a large space separate from the rest of the station so they can control the environment. The station's existing hydroponic farms are too far away, we have to use this pool.

"So, as I said, I have a problem. And you have my solution."

April clenched her hands together, fighting the urge to squirm. "I don't really do anything. Those twelve lights Martha talks about—I never saw any of that. I don't know why she thinks she did. I really, really wish I did understand."

"I know you just want to be helpful," Sunita said. "I need my crew in there, happy and working. You can give that to me. It doesn't really matter if it's real or pretend or whatever. If they believe it, if it makes them happy and willing to go in that room and work, that's what matters."

April felt a stabbing pain in her chest. She had promised her mother she would be open to just this situation, but now that it was before her, she just couldn't. It didn't feel like the right thing to do. Anguish and helplessness choked her until she realized why she was feeling so reluctant, and then she could take a full breath and properly speak.

"The last ghost I was supposed to deal with wasn't a ghost at all," April said. "It was a collection of fish, deadly fish from Earth. People were dying because whatever steps they took to protect themselves from an angry ghost were useless against fish venom. They weren't prepared for the danger and they died."

"I don't believe in ghosts either, April," Sunita said.

"But don't you see? I could do what you ask and everyone could be content and willing to work, but what if there's really something in there? Something that is dangerous, that we're ignoring because we're too caught up with the ghost idea?"

"Like what?" Sunita asked.

"I don't know. I wouldn't even know where to start finding out. I think you should talk to Willem more about what he saw. Talk to him when Martha isn't there."

"OK," Sunita said. "I can do that. I see your point; I can investigate other potential causes of, I don't know, shared hallucinations or whatever. But I can't stop the work while I investigate. We *have* to be in there, clearing out the space. Can you help me out?"

This time April did squirm, Sunita's dark brown eyes were so unwaveringly intense as she waited for her answer.

"Can I take some time to think about it? I want to talk to some of my friends and think things through."

Sunita sighed, clearly not pleased. "Fine," she said at last. "Until morning. I expect by morning you'll be ready to step up and do your thing. It's probably better if the crew sees you go in there and come back out again, anyway. It doesn't take long, your ritual, does it?"

April felt the threat under those words. She expected, after thinking it over, that she would comply... or what? "It doesn't have to take any time at all since it's all completely pretend," April said, more sharply than she had intended.

"Good," Sunita said briskly. "You better get going or there'll be nothing left for you to eat. I'll see you in the morning."

April went to the locker room to stow her hazard suit. The others had already gone and the silence of the empty space did not help her mood. She had been sending messages to her mother a few times a week, telling her all about her job and her coworkers, but today she was feeling just how much of that was fiction. She was not fitting in the way she had hoped she would. And what would she tell her mother when she messaged her next? Her mother hadn't brought up that promise even once in her own messages, but April doubted that meant she had forgotten about it. Of course, she could just not tell her mother about all this, but she was certain her mother would know there was something she wasn't saying. She always seemed to. April shut her locker door with a sigh.

The cafeteria was full of people eating in groups of three or four. She got a tray and moved down the line, taking her allotment of yellow lentils, canned veg, and canned fruit. No bread today, sadly. She looked around and saw Salima sitting alone, food before her mostly ignored as her fingers danced over a tablet. April made her way over, then sat down across from her. Salima glanced up long enough to give her a quick smile, then turned her attention back to the tablet, a frown furrowing her brow as she puzzled over something. No point in trying to talk to her, then. April sighed and plunged her spoon into the lentils.

A tray slammed down next to her and she jumped, then smiled as she realized it was Hakim. Her smile withered away when she saw he was in one of his moods again.

"Bad day?" she asked.

"No, entirely ordinary day," he said, dumping his vegetables into his lentils and stirring violently with his spoon. "They're never going to give me any computer time."

"I suppose they need all the processing power for station functions," April said.

"Every bit of it, every hour of the day?" Hakim demanded, and April fell silent. Clearly, it wasn't really a conversation he was looking for.

"I want to go into some of the unreclaimed parts of the station, see if I can find more computer equipment in working order."

"Will they let you?" April asked. There were so many rules on the station it was hard to keep track of what was and wasn't allowed.

"I was debating whether I should even bother to ask," he said.

"The worst they could do is say no," April said. "You'd be no worse off than now."

"Perhaps I should say I was debating whether I should bother to ask *first*," he clarified.

"Don't make trouble, Hakim," April said. "We're already at the bottom of the list, the first to go for any reason at all. Don't give them one."

"I'm beginning to wonder what the point of staying is," Hakim said. "I'm not accomplishing anything here. The shifts on the sanitation crew are so long I have little time left over for my own pursuits." April knew he was cramming mathematics into every spare moment in his day and probably further into the night than was healthy. She knew because whenever she did have spare time and sought him out, he was always too absorbed in his tablet to notice her standing there. And this was a rare Salima sighting; April was convinced she slept in engineering, probably catnaps in front of a computer screen waiting for a diagnostic to run.

"We have food and shelter," April said, pulling the little bowl of peaches in front of her. "That's not always easy to come by."

"I've always managed to hustle enough for that before," Hakim said.

"I like it here," April said. Aside from the unabated loneliness, she enjoyed the feeling of being useful, filling her days with work and going to bed tired and achy.

"That explains the gray cloud hanging over your head today," he said.

"I *do* like it here," April insisted. "It's just that something happened today. You remember I told you about Martha? She's the one who saw me once in my other life."

"Martha, your number-one fan," Hakim said, nodding.

"Yeah, that's her." April stabbed at one of her peaches, but it slipped out from under her fork. "She thinks there's a ghost in the pool, and she's freaking out a lot of people on my crew. Sunita wants me to go in there tomorrow morning and dispel it so the others can get to work."

"The pool?" Salima repeated, looking up from her tablet. "The pool is critical. We need that space."

"Yes, I'm well aware." April sighed.

"You said no," Hakim said, as if there could be no doubt.

"I tried to say no."

Hakim scoffed, pushing his tray back and crossing his arms to glower at her. "Tried."

"The pool is critical," April said. "Sunita really needs me to do this. I will go in alone and take care of it. No one will see what I'm doing." Then she leaned forward, pitching her voice lower than the various conversations around them. "Which frankly won't be anything. What's the point? Then I come back out and everyone gets to work as if something magical just happened."

"And you agreed to this?"

"I said I'd think about it," April said, turning her attention back to the last peach floating in the peach juice at the bottom of her bowl. "I don't want to, but I don't see how I can refuse."

"You have to refuse," Hakim said. "Stick to your principles."

"Thanks, that's helpful," April said.

"You know what will happen if you don't," he said. "The number of ghost sightings around here will spike. Your old skill will become your new skill, the one that lets you stay here."

"I have thought of that, actually," April said, irritated. "But the pool is critical. Without it, the food is going to run out."

"That's a nice self-justification," Hakim said, not looking at her but at his half-finished lentils. "Maybe you just miss the life of being a celebrity, grateful dupes bringing you gifts so you can dress and eat better than everyone else."

April stood up without a word, picked up her tray, and left. As she put her dishes into the wash bucket, she caught a glimpse out of the corner of her eye: Salima glaring at her brother, who was eating the rest of his dinner as if nothing was wrong. April stacked her tray on top of the others and headed for the door to the barracks hallway.

The truth was, she did hate wearing the same jumpsuit every day, all of her nicer things packed away in Salima's ship. But that wasn't why she was thinking about doing this, was it? It was about the needs of the station. When it was done, she'd still be dressing like all the others, eating the same food. Hakim was wrong.

She didn't realize how studiously she was looking at her own feet as she walked until she turned a corner and collided with another body.

"I'm so sorry," she said as she and her victim clung to each other and regained their balance. Then she saw who she had run into. "Lars."

"April," he said, and his face lit up. "Actually, I was just coming to look for you."

"You were?" She had barely seen him after that first day. His job kept him almost exclusively in the administrative hallways, and as he had predicted, she never had a reason to be in that part of the station.

"Yes, Sunita asked me to talk to you."

"Oh," April said.

He must have seen her heart sink, because his face grew pensive. "Listen, I haven't eaten yet. I'm just going to grab something and we can go to my office and talk."

"OK," April said. "Do you mind if I wait here?"

"Sure. I'll just be a minute."

April felt conspicuous, waiting at the side of the hallway, although the lone pair of people who came out of the cafeteria and walked past her didn't even seem to notice her there. Then Lars reappeared with his tray and smiled as he approached her. She fell into step beside him through the administrative hallways to his cramped office. He sat down at his desk, setting the tray on the grayed-out screen, and arranged the bowls carefully before picking up the lentils and sitting back in his chair. "Now, start at the beginning," he said, putting a spoonful of lentils in his mouth.

"The beginning today or the beginning of the whole story?" April asked.

"Whole story," he said around his mouthful of food. Then he swallowed. "Some of it I've been hearing around the station, but I'd like to hear it from the source, not in fragments."

April nodded, tapping her fingertips together as she tried to pick her starting point.

"I was five," she said at last, "the first time I did it."

"Dispelled ghosts," Lars offered before putting more lentils in his mouth.

"Yes. No. Let me start again." April sighed, and he nodded his encouragement. "My mother was born on a corporate station, one of the closed-off ones that no one outside ever gets into. But she ran away from all that before I was born. She's not... stable? Someone once told me there were medications that could help her, but outside of the corporate world, they are pretty much nonexistent.

"I don't know who my father was. From my earliest memories, it was just me and my mother and we were always on the move. My mother would just use up a place and we'd have to leave, find a new place with new people. Sometimes we'd be living somewhere nice enough; she was very good at attracting men in a position to offer her things. Other times she was hard for anyone to be around, and those times we would have nothing. I was young. I didn't know why we were sometimes in one place, sometimes in the other. I just knew how hard it was for my mother in those times we had nothing. She would get nightmares, bad ones. The kind where you're kind of half awake."

"Night terrors," Lars said.

"Exactly," April said. "I was five. We lived alone on a shuttle, and she was convinced it was haunted. She talked about it a lot when we were awake, and at night she would wake up and scream and scream and scream." She looked down at her fingers interlocking in her lap. Lars waited for her to continue. "I would try to comfort her, try to wake her, but nothing ever did any good. Finally, one night, I screamed too, screamed at her ghosts to just leave her alone.

"And she stopped screaming, blinked, and looked at me. She was awake, and clearer than I had seen her in a long time. She hugged me and cried, but it was a good kind of crying. She was better for a long time after that.

"She told our neighbors about it. Her story didn't really match what I remembered, but I was five—how was I going to correct her? Then one of our neighbors started feeling like her shuttle was haunted, too. She could hear knocking in the walls and was certain something was trying to get in or out. My mother brought me over and we sat with her for a few hours until we both heard it too, a knocking sound in the hull like someone tapping with just their fingernails or maybe a gloved hand, soft but definitely there. And my mother told me to tell it to go, and I did. And I guess it stopped, whatever it was. I suppose there are lots of things that can make noises like that on an old shuttle."

"Certainly," Lars allowed, setting his empty lentil bowl aside and picking up his mixed vegetables. "But it stopped when you told it to."

"That's what our neighbor said. She never heard it again, she said. I don't know for how long because after that we moved to a bigger station where my mother had some friends. And she now had two stories to tell everyone, and soon more people with ghosts asked me to visit. It just... what's the word?"

"Snowballed?" Lars offered.

"Yeah, snowballed. Weird word. But the truth is, I never really saw anything. I have never seen a ghost. I did this work for years and years. I must have been credited with sending hundreds of souls on to wherever souls go. But I never saw a single one of them, even when everyone else did."

"And now?"

"Well, the last job I did for my mother was on this weird station, some private hideaway for a wealthy eccentric from back before the plague. It was supposedly haunted by a killer ghost. That killer ghost turned out to be some very deadly fish. People went in expecting a ghost and were getting killed by the fish they weren't expecting. And I realized what I was doing was just wrong. I never saw a ghost, not even once. I'm not sure they even exist. I do know I don't want to do what I do anymore without some sort of proof that it's actually doing something. I worry that pretending to get rid of imaginary ghosts is a problem, or that it's masking a real problem."

"Like the fish," Lars said.

"Obviously it's not going to be fish every time," April said. "Did you talk to Sunita? Did she talk to Willem?"

"Yes."

"Because I worry that there really is something going on. Not a ghost, but something actually dangerous. I think Martha's imagination ran wild with whatever was going on in there, but I think there *was* something that needs to be looked into. Why were they both hallucinating? Or if they weren't hallucinating, what were they really seeing? I think that's where our attention needs to be."

"Yes, Sunita said you felt that way," Lars said. "I can certainly see with everything you've told me why you feel the way you do. I'm sure it's very confusing, when what you perceive is in such conflict with those around you. Do you believe your own two eyes, or the twenty eyes around you?"

"Yes, exactly," April said with a grateful sigh. "I want to trust myself, but can I?"

"I think if you were your friend Hakim, this would be much simpler." He was eating his peaches but watching her too attentively to match his casual tone.

"That's true. He would trust his own eyes and never have a moment's doubt."

"But you're conflicted."

"Yes."

"I would even add, if it's not too presumptuous, that you are unhappy. I don't think you enjoy saying no to Sunita and the rest of your crew. It's a small thing they're asking, and the potential benefit is huge."

April blinked. He was good at figuring these things out. She supposed he learned it from his parents. She was briefly envious, imagining such a childhood.

"That's all true," April admitted, "all the way down to how it makes me feel. But there's another problem. I know from the past, this never ends. I might make everyone feel safe going into the pool, but then other parts of the station are going to start feeling strange, too cold or making weird noises or whatever. A lot of people died here."

"136,890," Lars said. "I never forget that number.'

"I can't do this 136,890 times."

"Can't you? Can't you think of it as providing comfort to your fellows?"

She had promised her mother. April sighed, pushing that thought away.

"If I do a ghost-dispelling ceremony, especially at the behest of the administrators, it would be like saying there were ghosts, like that was an official position. People who've been telling themselves they're being silly, getting freaked out by tricks in the lights or faulty wiring, will suddenly have reason to think they're not just being silly."

"You think it will snowball," Lars said, and April nodded. "I'm not convinced. I don't think people's beliefs in these sorts of things are as easily swayed as all that."

"OK, I have very strong moral convictions that nothing I do should be interpreted as endorsing a belief in the supernatural," April said firmly. "I was made to do that as a child, but I am no longer a child."

"But you did spend years acquiring this reputation. You can't expect people to just follow you when you reverse everything."

"I don't want anyone to follow me. I just don't want to be pushed back in that direction. I came here for a chance at a new kind of life."

"I respect that, truly," Lars said. "But see it from the community's point of view. We're not in the personal renewal business, we're in the get-this-place-up-and-running business. It's a hard business. It's going to take all we have not to fail."

"Do you believe in ghosts?" April asked.

"I guess I don't believe or disbelieve," Lars said. "I've never seen one. But then I've never seen a horse, and I'm sure those still exist somewhere down on Earth."

"It's not the same thing," April said. "The records of one are much more rational than the records of the other."

"Lots of people believe in ghosts," Lars said. "All through human history. Could they all be wrong?"

"Yes," April said, but she knew she didn't sound sure.

"But not about horses?"

April dropped her head into her hands, her fingers threading through her hair, then tightening into fists. She wished Hakim were here. He'd know what to do, what to say.

Lars reached across the desk, touching the hand fisted in her hair. "April..."

She looked up at him. He was a lot closer than she had realized. His eyes were really two shades of blue mottled together. For a moment she thought he was going to move closer still, but instead he let go of her hand and sat back, clearing his throat nervously.

"Look, we can go around this all evening..." he started to say, but was interrupted by a deep thoom. The entire space station rocked, throwing April's stomach down towards her feet. The lights flickered, then went out. This was a black unbroken by Earth, moon, or stars. It was total darkness, pressing in on her on all sides. Another rumble followed, a low roar that grew louder as it rushed toward them.

April closed her eyes and waited for the flames to engulf her.

15

CATASTROPHIC FAILURE

THE RUMBLE ROLLED AWAY AGAIN, AND APRIL OPENED HER EYES. SHE FELT giddy, almost drunk, to find herself still alive. Of course, the black around her remained total, and she only knew Lars was still there because of the sound of his breathing.

"What was that?" April asked, barely above a whisper. Then her heart clenched as a sudden thought struck her. "The pool—there really was gas."

"No, the atmospheric unit blew," Lars said with certainty. The lights flickered again but couldn't quite bring themselves back on. April heard the sound of Lars moving, bumping the edge of his desk but reaching the hatch to swing it open with a clang. He was silhouetted against the dull glow of the red emergency lights, and the shrill whine of the alarm system echoed down the corridor to them.

"Blew?" April repeated numbly. Then, not knowing what else to do, she followed him down the corridor. He took a left and ducked through another hatchway into the room with all the screens. The room must have a separate power supply; although there were no overhead lights, every screen was filled with images, data, scrolling graphics. There were already people in that room. She recognized them from her very brief introduction to them her first day: the founders.

They were all moving quickly but surely, tapping the screens on the walls and tabletop, zooming in and out of images and windows of data.

"They said it would hold," Lars said. He stepped into the whirling dance of the four of them moving from screen to screen, falling into the pattern with practiced ease. April stayed in the corridor, peeking in, occasionally glancing back down the hall to make sure she moved if anyone else needed to be in the room.

"They said they *thought* it would hold," the woman said. Marie-Therese was her name, April remembered. "They thought wrong."

"The emergency protocols all fell into place without a hitch," silver-haired Vlad said, his mouth a grim line. "The hatches shut when the alarms sounded; the affected area is sealed off."

"Did any of the personnel make it out to report?" Marie-Therese asked.

"Not yet," Lars said, tapping a screen, then spinning to consult another. "It was second shift, that's half the size of first shift. Thirty people would have been at duty stations down there."

"Maybe more; it wouldn't be the first time our policy against letting off-duty workers hang around the workstations was ignored," Marie-Therese said.

"It's likely there were extra hands down there," Lars said, and April had the sense the two of them were revisiting an ongoing argument. "Everyone with any skill at all has been working this problem for weeks. That would involve a lot of actually looking at the source of the problem."

April's stomach clenched. Salima had still been in the cafeteria when she left, but hard at work at some problem. If she'd thought she had a solution, or needed to look at something... There were a million reasons she might have gone down to the part of the station currently flashing red on the largest screen.

And Hakim might have been bored enough to go with her.

April wondered if the elevators were still working. There must be stairs somewhere, but she didn't know where.

"Well, the problem didn't get solved," Marie-Therese said, "and who knows how many hands we've lost."

"Do we have anything like a damage report yet?" one of the others, Julio, asked.

"All the equipment in that area went offline instantaneously," Vlad said, pointing to a screen. "If I had to make a guess, either the unit blew with enough force to breach the hull or there was another flash fire."

April put a hand to her mouth to hold back a gasp. Either scenario was bad, very bad.

"Either way, the problem was contained to just atmospheric unit number three. The hatches shut, and everything is reading normal on this side of those doors," Marie-Therese said.

"How do we get in to look? With no sensors working on the other side, we can't just blindly open the hatches," Julio said.

"I've already sent what shuttles we have to investigate," said the founder named Ted, the one who had been working in this room the day April arrived on the station. He had up to that point been murmuring constantly to himself, but now that he was looking up, April saw the comm unit nestled in his ear.

"That will give us a picture from the outside, anyway," Vlad said. Ted's hands flew over the tabletop, closing all the screens to open ten new ones, each a camera mounted on a different ship that was berthed at the station's hub.

"Look at that," Marie-Therese breathed, pointing at one screen. The ship in question was just coming around the curve of the station. The black of space over the station horizon was glistening as if the sky were full of diamonds. Then some of the glistens grew larger, resolving themselves into tumbling bits of debris.

"We've lost a lot of water," Julio noted, turning to consult one of the wall screens. "The shutoff valves engaged, but we're still down nearly five percent."

"I don't think that's going to matter," Lars said, and the others nodded solemnly. April bit her lip. She didn't know why it wouldn't matter, but surely that must mean they had bigger troubles.

There was a sudden hiss of everyone around the table sucking in their breath at once, and April risked creeping a bit further into the room to see. Several of the ships were close enough to get a picture now, and it wasn't pretty. The smooth skin of their snug little home had been ripped asunder, torn and jagged remnants reaching out into the black as if hoping to pull away and escape. One of the ships had a view that included two of the other ships, both transport shuttles. It provided a sense of scale that turned April's stomach. It was such a large hole, a gaping wound.

The glistening diamonds were water droplets flying away, and the tumbling debris among them were pieces of the station, furniture and equipment, bits too small to identify. Mostly. Some of the tumbling, escaping objects had once been parts of humans.

"Gods," Marie-Therese said. "Did we lose them all?"

"There might be survivors," Lars said, enlarging a window on the wall screen behind him. "All of this is the area that fell inside the emergency protocols, the locked-down area. But see, there are rooms in here that are far enough from the actual unit; perhaps if someone had been working in there, they would have had enough time between the first hint of trouble and the loss of atmo to shut their hatches."

"Sounds like a long shot," Julio said. "They'd have had to move so fast—"

"But they knew this might happen. They knew it better than we did, I think, on a more visceral level," Lars said.

"We haven't had any calls," Marie-Therese said.

"Not all the rooms have call boxes. Heck, some of the spaces I'm looking at are actually within the ductwork," Lars pointed.

"That hole might be big enough to fly a ship into," Ted said, "but I don't think you'll find a pilot willing to risk it while we're spinning—"

"We're not stopping the spin," Vlad interjected.

"—and even if you could, they couldn't navigate into the sorts of spaces we're talking about."

Everyone hunched over the table, deep in morose thought.

"Salima could do it."

April only realized when all eyes turned on her that that small voice had been hers.

"Salima?" Marie-Therese repeated.

"Salima Little, the engineer," Lars clarified. "She has a small ship of her own design parked on the hull."

"It's much smaller than any of our shuttles," April said. "And I have an EVA suit. I'll go with her. I can search the ducts."

"Wait—you have an EVA suit?" Ted asked.

"Yes," April said. "Don't you?"

"We had exactly two," Ted said. "Guess where they were being used."

April looked at the screens with their images of tumbling debris.

"Call Salima," Ted said to Lars, then grabbed April by the arm and marched her down the corridor. "Time is of the essence. Does your suit have a working HUD?"

"Yes. It's fully functional," April said. He stopped to pull open a hatch. The stairs beyond were so steep they were nearly a ladder. Ted grasped the rails and slid down to the floor below. April turned around before following him so she could also use her feet.

Ted was already out in the corridor, tapping at a keypad on the inside of his wrist. "I'll send you all the schematics to that part of the station so you can find your way around. Do you have a functioning camera in the helmet?"

"Yes, it all works," April said, turning down the corridor that led to her barracks. Ted, never looking up from his wrist, followed her without missing a step.

"Lars is organizing crews on the inside. They'll be working their way along all the walls between the safe and unsafe parts of the station, listening for tapping or the like. If we hear anything, or if we do get a call from a call box, we'll let you know at once. Does your comm work, or just the data on the HUD?"

"The comm works," April said. She tried not to get frustrated at repeating herself; she knew Ted was just being thorough and a lifetime of experience in space had taught him that most "fully functional" equipment had one or two things that didn't work quite up to spec.

"You'll need an hour to pressurize before you can go out. That's going to hurt us. Nothing to be done about that. The crew in the ships are going to observe all they can. I think a few have remote arms; that might help. Keep your comm lines open and I'll fill you in on anything we learn."

"Yes, sir." April had reached her barracks. Ted stayed in the doorway, murmuring with his hand over his ear. April opened her locker and pulled out the carrying case, flopping it onto her bunk and snapping it open. She unlaced her work boots as quickly as she could and peeled out of her jumpsuit. The air in the barracks was cold now that she was just in her underwear, but when she reached for the suit, it was gone. Ted was holding it wonderingly, letting the material flow through his hands. He saw her shivering there and handed it to her quickly, reaching for the more conventional helmet. April closed up the suit, then wrapped her braid around her head, using pins from her locker to secure it before pulling the skullcap over it. Ted handed her the helmet and led the way back down the corridor to the airlock.

"I hope you're not too late," Ted said as she stepped inside and settled herself on one of the long benches.

"Me too," April said. The door shut, abruptly cutting off the blaring of alarms. The sudden silence was startling.

April closed her eyes but was too keyed up to catnap. It was late, and she'd worked hard all day, hauling load after load of debris from the work area to the salvage center. By this time of the night, she was usually collapsed in her bunk and sleeping hard, but she didn't feel the least bit tired. Her muscles were twitchy, anxious to move, and her mind was fully alert, but with nothing yet to focus on. It was torture.

There was a tapping at the viewport, and April looked up to see Lars waving at her. Then he pointed to his ear, and she nodded. She put on her helmet and turned on her comm.

"Nearly time," she said.

"I know. Salima is already out there, but so far even she hasn't found any survivors. We need to get into the tighter spaces—" He broke off with an angry huff of air, then leaned closer to the window. "April, this is going to be dangerous. Are you sure?"

"I can handle it," she said. "I've done a lot of jobs in derelict ships. Not in vacuum, but in free fall."

"But this isn't some ghost hulk that's been drifting in the black since the plague. There is a lot of debris out there, and you're not wearing a hard-shell suit."

"I'll be fine," she said. "The suit isn't pressurized with air, so a tear for me isn't nearly as dangerous. Not that I want to be tearing my suit, mind you." She knew she was babbling, trying too hard to sound upbeat and confident. She didn't need him telling her how dangerous this was; that warm liquid feeling in her gut was already doing that quite nicely.

"Are you hearing me? There are things out there that can pierce your suit and you won't be able to see them."

April tipped her head to look at him more directly through helmet visor and viewport both. He looked genuinely concerned. She had a brief flash of memory, of his outstretched hand trying to catch hold of her as Ted propelled her out of the room. She knew he considered the well-being of every person on that space station his personal responsibility, but there was something in the way he was looking at her that made her think perhaps her well-being was of more particular interest. She wasn't sure, but just the idea took the faux-bubbly attitude right out of her.

"Hakim," she said suddenly. "You said Salima took her ship out, so she's OK, but where is he?"

"I'll find out," he said. The scowl she could imagine on Hakim's face if she asked him to do something Lars-related was completely absent from Lars's. Still, he was here when he was supposed to be organizing work crews. "I'll radio you when I know. I'm sure he's fine. He had no reason to be in that part of the station."

He had no official reason, but April couldn't say that out loud. "I know. I just want to know for sure."

"Try not to let it distract you," he said. "You need to be focused out there."

"I'll be careful," April promised. She put a hand against the viewport and he reluctantly put his hand against the other side of the glass.

"See that you are."

He gave her one last look, as if he might have something more to say, but then he turned and disappeared from her tiny area of view and she was once more alone.

At last she reached a safe pressure and let herself out into the black. It was a long crawl up the hull, rung by rung. Someone had painted level numbers as she climbed higher, so she was able to keep herself oriented. It certainly helped that her weight was gradually lessening as she got closer and closer to the center of the wheel.

She had thought she'd gotten the full sense of scale from the video images, but as she climbed over the final curve and hovered with one hand on the last rung, she felt dwarfed by the size. She had scampered through lunar craters that weren't as immense as this jagged hole.

"April, Salima may have found something," Ted's voice came over her helmet comm. "Do you see her?"

April snapped the end of her tether to the last rung and let herself float away from the station. Her eyes scanned the edges of the damage. The shuttles were mostly further out, towing back larger pieces of debris, but Salima's smaller ship was inside the crater in the station hull, prying at twisted bits of blasted wall with mechanical arms.

"I see her. I'm on my way," April said, pulling herself back down to where she was tethered to the rung, then pushing herself off with a hard kick, sailing through the crater itself.

"I'm isolating channel twelve for communications between the two of you," Ted said. "Ping me if you need me; I'll be checking the transcripts on my end periodically. Good luck."

"Roger," April said. There were small bits of debris in the void around her, but none of it was moving fast enough to prove a danger. She hoped. She looked down at the keypad on her wrist and switched her comm channel. "Salima," she said.

"Can you see what I'm looking at?" Salima asked.

"Not yet, but I'm nearly there." She was also nearly to the end of her tether. She fired a short burst from her air gun and maneuvered herself around to land on an exposed girder. She attached her shorter secondary tether first, then detached the end of her longer tether and snapped it onto the girder to follow back up later. She spider-crawled along the edge of the damage, clinging to the twisted ends of walls and girders until she was next to one of Salima's robotic arms.

"OK, what have you got?" she asked over the comm.

"Straight ahead. The light is flashing."

April saw it right away: the door panel beside a sealed door was indeed flashing, flashing in a pattern as if someone on the other side was trying to communicate.

"Someone is in there," she said.

"I think the pattern is Morse code. I'm copying it over and Ted is looking into it. In the meantime, go get a closer look."

"Got it," April said, pulling herself through the hole Salima had so meticulously peeled back. The fire damage was bad here, the walls blackened and metal twisted. The fire had happened before the explosion and wall breach, then. Whoever was on the other side of that door had taken shelter from the fire.

"Don't get between me and the light; I'm still reading the message," Salima said.

"Sorry," April said, catching hold of a girder and pulling herself closer to the wall. The magnets on the soles of her boots caught, and she walked slowly up to the door, crouching low to be out of Salima's line of sight. It was harder work than floating, but she had more control over her movements this way.

She hated waiting. Especially after already waiting for an hour in the airlock.

"Any word from Hakim?" she asked.

"No," Salima said, only half distracted.

"He was with you at dinner, though?"

There was a long gap of dead air hissing inside her helmet before Salima spoke again. "No. He left before the explosion."

"To the barracks?"

Another long pause. "Not sure."

April squeezed her eyes shut, knowing what Salima was dancing around on the mic. No one else was on the line, but in the command center, every word they spoke was being transcribed by a computer to be perused later. She couldn't say what she was fearing, but April knew. Hakim wasn't going to give up on getting access to more computers.

Something tapped against the hull under her magnet boots, under her very fingertips, as she crouched out of the way. She took a multi-tool off her belt and clanged back. The person inside tapped once, then twice, and she copied. Then they tapped once, twice, three times, five times, eight times.

"Fibonacci sequence," April said, interrupting the tapping to clang back the same sequence.

"What's that?" Salima asked, once more distracted.

"I think Hakim might be in here," April said. "Someone in there is tapping a Fibonacci sequence to me."

"OK, confirmed Morse code," Salima said as if she hadn't heard. "They are saying there are ten of them in there, three already injured. And they only have a few minutes of air left."

Somehow, April didn't find this news discouraging. She knew, just knew, that she was going to get Hakim out of this alive.

"How do we get them out in time?" April asked Salima. "It's way too far to the airlock."

"Ted is working on it."

"The fire must have started near here; the walls and floor are like Swiss cheese." April pushed at one of the walls and it bent briefly before snapping away. The interior walls were nowhere near as thick as the hull had been, and the hull was gone. "How did the room survive?"

"It's a fireroom; it's designed to withstand the heat," Salima said.

"It's like a lifeboat," April said. She could imagine Hakim finding it, knowing it for what it was, guiding others inside. Only she supposed they already knew, working there every day as they did. "If we could get it out of here, you could tow it to the airlock."

"I don't think I can get the hole large enough," Salima said, but despite her words, her robotic arms were once more peeling back fatigued metal.

"It's not a big room," April said, circling around it. "Just a closet, really. I'm surprised they could even fit ten people in there."

"Can you cut it free?" Salima asked. April felt around her belt, past the tether spools to her cutting tool.

"I'm going to try," she said, firing up the cutter and bringing it close to where the remains of the wall met the edge of the boxlike room. It sliced through easily, but there was a lot of wall, floor, and ceiling to get through. April bit down on her lip, ignoring the countdown of minutes in her head, and concentrated on working quickly.

"I have ahold of this end of your tether," Salima said. "Tie the other off on the latch by the door panel."

"What if it's not strong enough?" April said, cutting away the last of the floor and putting the cutter away.

"It has to be. Do it." April could hear the growing fear in Salima's voice, the fear she was trying to keep pushed back in her own mind. They had to move faster. She crawled around the outside of the box, setting it on a slow spin now that it was free-floating. Then she latched on her tether and jumped out of the way.

"Go," she said, ducking into a doorway as the blast from Salima's forward rocket filled the hallway, licking over the sides of the fireroom. The tether straightened, snapped tight. Slowly, the room turned and followed her ship, bouncing against the walls and nearly hanging up on the edges of the hole. Then they were clear and Salima fired again, increasing her speed to get them to the flexible airlock as soon as possible. April crawled out of the station, all too aware of the voice in the back of her head lecturing her about never going EVA without a tether. She made sure to have a firm grip with her outstretched hand before letting go with the other hand, making slow, lurching progress until she reached the tied-off end of her longer tether.

Text scrolled past her HUD, all in caps, to catch her eye. APRIL, COME BACK IN. She was still on channel 12, the designated line for Salima. She switched back to 1, the main line, and heard a confusing flurry of words. She let the spool pull her back to the last rung of the intact hull as she listened. The shuttle pilots were all docking now, taking on passengers as quickly as they could be loaded and making way for the next shuttle to dock. Ted was giving orders but there was a breathless sound to his voice; wherever he was, he was moving while he talked. That text must have come from Lars, then.

April reached the end of her tether, detached it from the last rung, then turned to follow the row of rungs back to full gravity. Her muscles were beginning to tire, not a good thing when she was still outside in the void where a single slip up could send her tumbling off without hope of rescue. She bit her lip again, focusing past the weariness.

At least Hakim was OK. He had to be.

She could see Salima's ship anchored to the hull, the fireroom laying on its side but still attached to the flexible airlock. April crawled inside the airlock proper and sealed the hatch behind her, grateful to once more be within solid walls.

April stepped out of the airlock and wrenched off her helmet. The air in the corridor had a distinct metallic tang, and the main power was still down, leaving nothing but the red glow of the emergency lights. She could already feel future nightmares of running through corridors just like this one, waiting for the second explosion to come. April pushed back the sense of doom that wanted to wash over her and went down the corridor to the sound of people talking, coughing, sobbing.

"You need to get on the shuttles as soon as possible," Ted was saying as he helped people out of the flexible airlock.

"Everyone inside made it out?" April asked. A few had slumped to the floor just outside the airlock, some bleeding from head injuries or clutching sprained limbs, but no one looked too seriously hurt.

Hakim was nowhere to be seen.

"They made it out," Ted said, his mouth a grim line. "Anyone not in the carry-over staff has to get on shuttles and off the station at once."

"I'll help," April said, reaching for the nearest person still on the floor, a woman she didn't know. The woman clung to her gratefully and April helped her limp down the corridor towards the elevator to the docking hub. Perhaps Hakim had already made it to the docks.

"Is there going to be a second explosion?" she asked, her voice as low as she could make it.

"No, nothing left to blow," Ted said. "But we can't have this many people breathing what little atmo we have left."

April left the woman waiting for the elevator and ran back down the corridor to help another person get moving. Some of the others were pairing up, using each other as well as the wall for support to make their way to the elevators. Ted held the elevator until everyone was on board, then pulled April inside before shutting the doors.

"I wanted to find Salima," April said.

"She's at the dock with the others by now," he said.

"And Hakim?"

"Everyone is either at the dock or heading that way now," he said. Or dead, April also heard, although he didn't say it out loud.

The elevator carried them up the long spoke of the station wheel, the pull of the station's spin lessening as they approached the hub. The doors opened at the docks, already full of shaken but less injured people. April stayed at the doorway opposite Ted, helping the injured out of the elevator before following him out.

"We need twelve more for shuttle one," Marie-Therese was calling over the hubbub of the crowd. "This way, quickly please, so the next shuttle can dock."

"Everyone is leaving?" April asked.

"Nearly," Ted said. "Essential personnel only until we get another atmospheric unit back online."

"That won't be soon." At the sound of her voice, April turned to see Salima holding onto a wall rung just behind her. April gave her a quick smile that widened when she saw Hakim just behind her, unhurt.

"I knew we'd rescue you!" she said, throwing her arms around him.

"He wasn't in there," Salima said, and April pulled back to see Hakim looking puzzled, if pleased.

"But, the Fibonacci sequence," she said. "Someone inside was tapping it."

"During the lull, when it seemed like we weren't grasping the Morse code," Salima said.

"It was full of engineers," Hakim added. "Lots of people know the Fibonacci code." But the pleased look didn't quite leave his face. She was getting points for trying to save his life, she guessed.

"You're going to refuse to stay," Ted said to Salima, not a question.

"I won't stay without my brother."

"We just can't afford even a single person breathing air who can't do the work of four," Ted said. "You're good, but you're not quite up to the work of eight."

"I understand," Salima said.

"What about you?" Ted asked, and April was startled to see he was addressing her.

"Me?" She was salvage, and definitely not worth four people. Unless he was talking about her ghost skills? But none of the founders had struck her as particularly superstitious.

"We lost all of our other suits," he reminded her. "We could really use you now. There is going to be a lot of EVAs to make repairs. You strike me as a quick study."

April didn't know how to respond. Suddenly she was being offered everything she had ever wanted: a real job she could do and feel good about doing. A position as a valued member of a real working crew.

All she had to do was leave the Littles behind.

"We would need your answer pretty much now," Ted said. Lars floated up behind him, catching his shoulder to pull himself closer and speak directly in his ear. Ted held up a finger for April to wait as he listened and nodded. April turned to look at Salima and Hakim.

"You should stay," Hakim said. "It's what you wanted."

"But this was something we planned to do together, and now you have to go," April said.

"You don't owe me anything," Hakim said.

"I know," April said. "I just don't think I want to do this without you. Both of you," she said, looking to Salima. "You'd think they could average out between the three of us..."

"Will you stay?" Ted asked. He and Lars were both looking at her intently. She could feel how much they both wanted her to say yes.

"I really can't," she said.

"April," Hakim started to say.

"No, I've already made my decision," she said, stressing the "my" ever so slightly.

"In that case, would you be willing to sell the suit?" Ted asked.

"My suit?"

"If you can't stay, at least we can find someone else who can use the suit, if you'll part with it. We could really use it."

"They won't get the station back up without it," Lars said.

April hugged the suit to herself, feeling the warmth of the circuitry hidden in the layers. It was like a part of her. But she was already refusing to stay and help, as much as they needed her.

"How much?" she asked.

He said an amount. April looked to Hakim and Salima. It would be enough to keep them fed for months.

"What do you think?" she asked Salima.

"It's your decision, your suit."

"But I can stay with you if I leave here? We can find work somewhere else together?"

"Of course."

April ran her fingertips over her palms, so sensitive even through the gloves.

But it was already a tight fit. Another month of three square meals a day and it would be too tight. She would have to voluntarily go hungry to keep the suit hers.

"I'll sell the suit. We can live on that until we find other work."

"Are you sure?" Hakim asked.

"You'll take good care of it?" April asked Ted.

"We'll have to. Our lives are going to depend on it. And when we have finished the repairs and have the atmospheric systems back on full, we'll be sending out word to return."

"And our names will be in the first batch to be asked back, all three of us?"

Ted sighed, then looked at Salima, whose face was as calmly inscrutable as ever.

"Yes, all three of you."

April nodded and put her helmet in his hands so she could start peeling the tight suit off her body.

"My name as well," Lars said.

"What's that?" Ted asked, distracted.

"I think it would be better if I left as well," Lars said. "You don't have any need for a large-groups organizer at the moment, no reason for me to be breathing air that could be going to a more useful worker."

"We're not asking you to go," Ted said. "We owe your parents, and you, so much."

"I know," Lars said. "But I think this would be best."

"And now we owe you even more," Ted said.

"I'll be here the instant I hear your call," Lars promised.

April squirmed the suit past her hips and tumbled in free fall as she untangled it from her legs. The air was cold on her sweaty skin, but before she could even regret her lack of substantial clothing, someone was pressing her station jumpsuit into her hands.

"Martha," April said questioningly.

"I'm staying," Martha said. "I wish you were staying, too. I'll have to be extra brave without you."

"I would be more afraid of something else failing than of ghosts," April said.

"I am," she said. "But fixing things, that's something I can do. Ghosts, I'm powerless."

"There is no reason to fear the dead," April said. She wanted to say again that ghosts weren't real, but it didn't feel like the moment just then, when so many more people had just died. "I think what we perceive as coming from ghosts is really a reflection of our own feelings. It's OK to feel sad, even guilty to be alive. It's human. Don't punish yourself too much for it. You don't need to make an angry ghost."

"I won't."

"This will probably be yours," April said, catching the suit floating near her and putting it with the helmet and skullcap into Martha's hands. "There aren't many as tiny as us." And Martha was a few years older, probably done growing. It could be hers forever.

"I'll take care of it for you," Martha said. "I'll see you when you come back. And I'll be working hard to make sure that's soon."

"Thanks," April said, then found herself giving Martha a hug of genuine affection, something she would never have imagined herself doing just hours before.

"We should be on our way," Salima said, leading the way to where her little ship was docked. All but one shuttle had already departed; they were nearly the only ones left on the dock. Ted slapped Lars on the shoulder, then sailed off down the corridor, back to the elevators and all the work that waited for him at the other end. Lars held out a bag full of coins for April, payment for the suit that was already gone from sight.

"Can I tag along with you three?" Lars asked. "I don't really have anywhere to go. I could use some pointers on the itinerant lifestyle."

"Please do," Salima said, then disappeared down the airlock, leaving her brother gaping behind her. He quickly propelled himself after her.

"Salima, it was crowded with three..."

"The decision has been made," Salima said.

"But why?"

Salima turned to look back at him. April, hovering over his shoulder, felt the secondhand heat from that glare and was glad she was not the target.

"Fine, decision made," Hakim gave in.

"We can use some of my money to expand the ship," April said, following Hakim inside.

"I don't mind being a little friendly in the meantime," Lars said, floating in after them with a rucksack over his shoulder, then shutting the hatch and sealing it. "We all came very close to dying today. Many of us did. It would be churlish to complain about being uncomfortable."

It was indeed very tight quarters. Salima had moved to the front pod, speaking to the station crew who were already retracting the airlock so they could depart. April bumped into Hakim, then floated back into Lars.

"How long to the next station?" Hakim asked as Lars gently moved April to neutral space between the two of them.

"Eight days," Salima said over her shoulder. "Don't worry, we have food enough."

"Eight days," April repeated. Then she started to shake, the events of the day starting to catch up with her. But she was plain cold as well, the station jumpsuit nowhere near warm enough for the interior of Salima's little ship. She pulled herself close to her bungeed bag and dug out a sweater and a pair of jeans she could pull over what she was already wearing. Then socks; things never looked so bleak when her feet were warm enough.

"That money will last us a long while," Lars said. "But not long enough for us to just wait for the station to be open to us again. We'll need jobs." He took out his notepad, tapping away at the screen. "Knowing the founders, those are mixed coins. We should plan to stick close to the stations they were minted from. They are supposed to be freely transferable, but in my experience, there are always excuses to favor the home money." He was a planner; he was going to deal with his sudden change of fortune by excessive list-making. April would happily let him take the lead, but then she saw Hakim bristling at Lars' words.

"Salima and I have been on our own for years," Hakim said. "We know how to get by."

"Of course," Lars said. "This being-on-one's-own thing is new to me, though. What do you typically do?"

"April, we can dip into your funds?" Salima asked from the fore pod.

"Of course," April said. "I was thinking we'd want another pod or two to add onto this ship. I think I have enough for that, right?"

"You have enough for me to do it," Salima said. "I can expand enough to let us take transport jobs. Goods, even people moving from station to station."

"Is it wise, spending so much time out in deep space?" Lars asked.

April wasn't sure what he was worried about, but Salima knew. "The ship has magnetic shielding I've tinkered with. It's safe from background radiation. You're safer with us than you would have been on one of the shuttles," Salima told him.

April shivered at the thought. She had never even thought to ask about such things, just climbed aboard and flew away. The universe had so many ways to kill you, it was hard to keep track of all the dangers.

"We're going to be OK," Hakim said, and April realized he had been watching her, watching emotions wash over her face as she remembered all the things she couldn't unsee from the long day behind her.

She smiled and nodded. She hoped it was true.

16

JOB-HUNTING BLUES

APRIL FOUGHT FOR BREATH, HER THROAT CLOSING IN FEAR, TOO TIGHT FOR her to pull air through. The weight on her chest had forced it all out of her and her lungs were empty, empty and aching. She tried again, tried to push the weight off her, tried to draw in air, but all she managed was to twitch her fingers and gasp mutely.

"April!"

Her eyes snapped open at the sound of her name and, just like that, the weight was gone. She sat up, slumping forward over her knees as she hauled in lungful after lungful of air in great sobs.

"The nightmare?" Lars asked.

April looked up at him standing in the doorway of their narrow rented room. She nodded, then dropped her head down again, pressing her forehead to her bent knees and focusing on slowing her breath. Someone was sitting on the edge of her cot, the hand that had shaken her awake still on her shoulder. Hakim.

"We tried to wake you before we went out, but you wouldn't open your eyes," Lars said. She could hear the regret in his words. "You told us to let you sleep, so we did."

"I don't remember that," April said.

"I don't think you were really awake," Hakim said. "How do you feel?"

April wrapped her arms around her knees and pulled them up to set her chin on them. She knew he was worried because her headaches were coming almost daily now, and because she slept all the time but never ceased to feel exhausted. But when she heard the word "feel," all she could say in response was, "I hate this place."

"I know," Hakim said. "We all do."

"I really, really hate this place," she said, shivering, and he picked up her shawl that had fallen to the floor and wrapped it around her shoulders. "It's horrible here, always dark and melancholy, full of unhappy people. Why is it so horrible here?"

"Only a few more days," Hakim promised her. "Salima says the part is on the way. Once it's here, she just needs to snap it into place and we're gone."

"I know," April said, wiping tears she didn't remember shedding from her cheeks. "I'm sorry. I'm being a problem."

"Not even," Hakim said at the same moment Lars said, "Don't worry about it." They exchanged a long glance. With Salima always off on her own working on whatever she could find to work on and April often unwilling to get out of bed for more than an hour or two at a time, they had been thrown together whether Hakim liked it or not. Still, it gave her a chill. The situation really was bleak if it compelled Hakim to unbend enough to befriend Lars.

"I promised myself I would get up today and go with you to look for work," April said.

"It scarcely matters; there wasn't any," Hakim said.

"We did try to wake you," Lars said.

"What's wrong with me?" April asked, rubbing at her face until her cheeks warmed. "Why am I letting this place get to me like this?"

"I, for one, don't think you're just having a mood," Hakim said, getting up from her bunk. "You must have caught a bug or something. This isn't like you."

"It's a shame there's no doctor on this station," Lars said. "I'd feel better having someone take a look at you."

"Bug or whatever else, I'm sure I'll feel better once we've left this place behind us," April said. "It's so depressing here. Don't you feel it? It's like there's a pallor over the whole place. I try to cheer up, to focus on something productive, but it's like there's something in the air that just makes me go back to my bunk and lie here staring at the walls. Like it's not worth trying to do anything. I know you know what I mean, Hakim. When's the last time you worked on a proof? You can't concentrate either, can you?"

"How's your head?" Hakim asked, dodging her own question. April touched her forehead.

"Nothing yet." She didn't add that, in a way, the few hours of the morning when her headache had not yet settled in were almost worse: the endless anticipation of pain to come. Then the first twinges would hit her like needles behind her eyes and she'd remember that no, the pain was definitely worse.

"Salima earned enough yesterday for us to have a treat today," Hakim said. "Special breakfast. Lars and I were thinking the teahouse."

April smiled at them both. She knew full well neither of them would have picked the teahouse with its delicate pickled vegetables and mellow cheeses. Hakim seldom bothered to eat anything unless it came in a bowl with noodles, and Lars preferred meat of any kind, but the redder the better. Not that they were getting much of their preferred food these days. Hakim had started all lean muscle and bony joints and little had changed, but Lars's rounded face was growing gaunter by the day. It hurt her to look at him. He would have been so much better off staying on the *Chandrasekhar*.

"Let me clean up a little first, OK?" she said, then untangled herself from the bedding to head out the door, bag in hand. It was midmorning, so she had the little bathroom at the end of the hall to herself. She washed her face and brushed out, then rebraided her hair. For whatever reason, they kept the station at a temperature much cooler than April would have preferred, forcing her to wear the same warmer clothes over and over. When the money had run out, she had sold off all her other clothes item by item until she was down to just her carpetbag again. Having to wear the same schlubby clothes day after day was just one more way this place was depressing her.

The door behind her slowly opened, then slammed shut with a

bang. She turned to see who had come in, but she was still alone in the bathroom. The sound of one of the showers leaking, a slow drip, was all she could hear over her own fast breathing. She shut her eyes and took a slow, shaky breath, then a more confident one. Then she opened her eyes again.

Totally alone.

April turned back to the mirror, brushing tendrils of hair out of her eyes and wrapping a scarf warmly around her neck. Of course, no one was there. No one was ever there. She desperately, desperately hoped that no one ever would be there. If she started seeing things, she would be lost for sure.

April clutched the edge of the sink, taking more calming breaths, trying not to think of her mother's friend, the one with the haunted shuttle full of sounds. The crazed look in her eyes that had only gone away when April had repeated the little performance that had worked such wonders with her own mother's torments.

April squeezed her eyes tightly shut. She wouldn't. She wouldn't do it. Not even if no one else would ever know, not even if it made her feel better. Especially if it made her feel better.

What was wrong with her, really?

April let go of the sink, thrusting the rest of her things back into her bag a bit too aggressively, then marching back to the rented room where Hakim and Lars were sitting close together, whispering. April shoved her bag back into the space under her bunk and tossed her braid back over her shoulder.

"Let's go. I'm starved."

If Hakim and Lars traded another one of their significant glances, she didn't notice, just marched off down the narrow hallway between the rented rooms. The floor was a grated walkway, letting her see the levels of similar walkways above and below her. The station had origi-nally been built for military uses, with barracks enough to house battalions, although what battalions of soldiers would be doing on the far side of the moon April couldn't guess. As depressing as this place was, one thing it wasn't was crowded. But they were at the very end of the line, as far out from Earth as it was possible to get until you reached the first of the asteroid mining stations. Salima had gotten a very lucrative trading run that had brought them all the way out here. Then something had broken on her ship, some small but rare thing, and while they waited for a replacement to be located and shipped to them, they had burned through all of Salima's trade profits, then through April's remaining suit money. They had nothing left but what Salima could earn day to day.

April had longed to leave this place even before she had become convinced it was haunted.

Down long flights of steep, narrow stairs and past what must have once been a duty station, and they were out of the cramped barracks and out on the docks. Some ships had been hauled in through the massive airlock to be worked on in atmosphere, just as once ships of the sea had been hauled into dry docks for repairs. Salima's was among them, once more reduced to two tiny pods and a rocket. The extra cargo space had been dismantled and sold bit by bit, and now there was nothing left to sell. Salima was nowhere in sight, but this didn't surprise April. With nothing left to be done with her own ship, she was tinkering with other ships, April suspected often for free just to have something to do. April couldn't see her at the moment, but it was a large dock, large enough to see the curvature of the station at both ends.

The marketplace was on the lower level, a perceptible change in the feeling of gravity given the relatively small size of the station wheel. The station had been designed chiefly to be a military support structure, to monitor communications, repair ships, and house troops on a short-term basis. There had been no shopping area, so a series of warehouses had been repurposed. The warehouses-cum-marketplaces, the docks, and the barracks were, in fact, the only inhabited parts of the station. The remaining spaces where the military had once worked were sealed off. Everyone they asked had insisted those parts of the ship were severely haunted; no one ever went beyond any of the sealed doors for any reason. When they had first arrived, they had all scoffed at that idea. April was no longer so sure it was all a superstitious joke.

The teahouse was in the far corner of the largest warehouse space, set on a platform that let its customers watch people moving around the rest of the marketplace as they sipped their tea. April's steps slowed as she drew near, enough for Hakim and Lars to finally catch up with her. The man who worked in the machine shop across from the teahouse always made her heart clench, like he represented the end of the long road she was starting to walk down against her will. He yammered constantly, sometimes murmuring, sometimes shouting, but always quite alone in his little shop.

She heard footsteps when no one was there. She heard soldiers marching up and down the metal catwalk outside the door of their rented room, although all the soldiers here had died long ago. She heard knocking on the walls, scratching like someone trying to paw their way in, and now doors slamming. Honestly, how much longer would it be before she too heard voices?

"April?" Hakim said, and she realized she had stopped walking outside the machine shop, watching the little man babble to himself as his hands deftly moved over the coffeemaker sprawled out before him. He might be crazy, but he could still fix anything you put in front of him.

"I'm OK," April said.

"Tired?" Lars asked.

April sighed. "Aren't I always?"

Hakim frowned. "I'll get the food. You two grab that table over there." He pointed to one on the far side of the platform, away from the machine shop. Most of the restaurant was empty, there was no reason to grab a table in a hurry, but April was grateful to sit back down. The adrenaline burst that had sent her marching down here had burned out. She fumbled with the chair, the legs tangled up with the legs of the table and other chairs in a way she didn't have the energy to sort out. Lars took over, helping her into her chair before sitting opposite her. He grabbed her hand, and her brain came back out of the fog with a start at his tight squeeze.

"What is it really?" he asked.

April felt hot tears building behind her eyes and stared down at their two hands, willing them not to come. "Don't tell Hakim."

"Don't tell Hakim what?"

"I think," she said, then stopped, swallowed hard, and tried again. "I think I'm becoming like my mother was."

"The nightmares?"

"It's just like hers were," April said, her voice falling to a whisper. "But there's other stuff, stuff when I'm awake. I'm hearing things. All sorts of things, but there's never anything there. Worse is when I'm not sure if I'm awake or if I'm asleep. When I'm somewhere in between, usually when I'm alone when the rest of you are out and I'm trying to nap, but sometimes even when you're all there with me, sleeping. I can feel someone in the room, looming over me. There's definitely someone there, and he presses down on my chest and I can't breathe."

"It's all right," Lars said, squeezing her hand again.

"I really don't think it is," April said with a too-shrill laugh.

"Well, no. But it's not just you," Lars said.

"You hear things too?"

"I think, sometimes. Echoes of footsteps." He sat up straighter. "It could really be footsteps. Those barrack hallways with the grated catwalks—it could really be someone walking in some distant hallway and a trick of acoustics makes it seem closer."

"But you don't think so, do you?"

"It's happening more and more," he said. "Plus, look at these people around us. Have you talked to many of them?" April shook her head. She had been exhausted by the end of their first week on this station, back when she still thought they were leaving right away, before the ship broke. "These people are constantly hearing things, seeing things."

"They say the station is haunted," April said.

"And not just the sealed parts," Lars added. "That's just where it's so bad they won't go anymore."

"I've been in so many haunted places," April said. "I've never seen anything. Before now, I never even heard anything." Hakim turned away from the counter, a tray loaded with food balanced in his hands. "Don't tell Hakim," she said again.

"I won't if you don't want me to," Lars said, "but I think you should. I don't think he's going to be judgy like you're afraid he will. He probably is noticing things, too. You know, I hadn't noticed about the math until you said something, but you're right. He hasn't shut out the world while scrawling away on that tablet since we got here."

"I don't want him to know," April said desperately, and Lars nodded his agreement. He released her hand as Hakim approached so he could put the tray on the table and start distributing teacups, teapot, and plates of little sandwiches and raw and pickled vegetables and even cookies.

"That's too much," April said. She hadn't had sugar in longer than she could remember.

"It's medicinal," Hakim said, setting the now-empty tray on another nearby table before sitting down. "Best cure I know for the over-whelming fog of malaise that hangs over this place. Well, after chocolate, but good luck finding that at any price."

April took a sip of the tea, a strong black blend heavily laced with more sugar. Her brain sang happily.

"April and I were talking about the sealed-off parts of the station," Lars said, although that hadn't really been the topic. "She wasn't with us the other day when the stationmaster gave his little speech."

"What speech is this?" April asked, selecting one of the sandwiches and biting into it. The bread was on the dry side, but the fish paste inside was salty and delicious.

"You know the people here are overwhelmingly superstitious," Hakim said, and April nodded, carefully not looking at Lars. "The stationmaster is an exception to that rule. He wants to go into the sealed parts of the ship. There are rooms there that used to be used for hydroponic farming. Small-scale, but something is better than nothing."

April shivered in real fear. Food was more and more the topic of conversation on every station they passed through. Things were going to get bad all over the solar system. She brushed the thought aside, although it took a few attempts to get it out of her mind enough to focus on Hakim's story. "What happened?" she asked.

"There was nearly a riot," Hakim said. "Unsealing the doors would release the murderous ghosts, blah blah blah."

"It nearly got very ugly," Lars said. "The stationmaster and his assistant managed to calm everyone back done, swearing no one would touch any of the doors, but they had to assign a rotation of door guards before the crowd relented."

"Poor people," April said. "It's so miserable here. I can't wait to leave. Why do they all stay?"

"Passage on a ship is beyond what any of them can afford," Lars said. "Without Salima's ship, I don't think we would have an escape, either."

Hakim saw her shiver. "It's on its way," he told her. "Just another day or two and we can leave this place well behind us."

April nodded, taking another sandwich, but then setting it untouched on her plate. Her appetite disappeared as the first twinge of her headache came like an athlete stretching out before really showing his stuff. She tried to keep eating, especially as Lars and Hakim were both conscientiously making sure she got more than a third of the food they were all sharing, but she couldn't keep it up.

"Take these," she said, pushing her plate away from her. "I just need to lie down."

"Not even the cookie?" Hakim asked.

April shook her head, unable to open her eyes. The light was just too bright. Hakim wrapped the cookies in a paper napkin and put them in his pocket, then he and Lars devoured the rest of the food. April knew they were hurrying so they could get her back to the room, but she also knew they really were just that hungry.

April managed to get back to their room under her own steam, although the headache was continually building and she couldn't manage to move very fast. Hakim and Lars walked behind her, speaking to each other in low voices she tuned out.

She stopped outside the door to the room, blinking confusedly at the crate at her feet. That hadn't been there when they had left. She squatted down to look at the label. It was addressed to her, at this station, but had no return address. Of course, her mother and Ivan knew she was here. Since leaving the *Chandrasekhar* she had kept in contact wherever she could. This station had powerful broadcasting equipment and could send messages even as far as the Belt. She had thought of asking for Ivan's help, but when she had casually asked if he had any holdings in the vicinity, he had only confirmed what she knew already: they were very far off the edge of civilized space. Nothing he sent her way now would get here faster than the part.

She saw her mother's name as the sender, courtesy of one of Ivan's businesses orbiting the moon. She must have sent it soon after they had all arrived here, but had never mentioned it in any of their messages. A surprise?

"What is it?" Hakim asked.

"I don't know," April said. It was a plastic crate with a grill in the middle of the top. She peered into the darkness inside.

A pair of eyes peered back up at her. They seemed to float on their own in the darkness, but behind the eyes was a ghostly white mass.

"Wait!" Lars said, but it was too late. April had unlatched the grill and reached into the box. Her hands found something warm and covered with fine, straight, short hairs. She lifted it out and brought it up close to her face.

"A puppy!" she cried, sitting back on her heels to examine the squirming thing. It was so tiny, with floppy ears and deep, dark eyes. Its body was bright white, but from the neck up, it was inky black. It had seemed to be headless in the dark, but in the light of the hallway it was adorable. April tucked it close against her, feeling its little body trembling under her hands. It pushed its head up against her chin and she laughed, stroking the softer hair around its dark ears. "I love it!"

"Who would send you a puppy?" Lars asked, examining the crate and finding latches on the side. He unlatched them, lifting the top half of the box. The bottom was a mess, and April was vaguely aware that the puppy itself wasn't smelling so good.

"It must have been your mother," Hakim said.

"It must be thirsty," Lars said. "There is a water bottle in here, but it's completely dry now."

"Poor baby," April said, snuggling the puppy close despite the smell. "Let's go to the end of the hall and have a drink and a bath, yes?"

"April..." Hakim started to say.

"We'll be right back," she told him, cradling the puppy in her arms as she walked back to the bathroom. She ran the cold water tap and held the dog close to the flow of water until he had drunk his fill, then turned on the hot water and held a hand under the flow until it felt warm enough not to chill her puppy. She pumped soap into her palm, then ran her hands all over his squirming body, cleaning days' worth of filth out of his fur.

He would have arrived here on a shuttle, after spending days in free fall confined inside the crate. How miserable for the little fellow. Probably not a joy for the shuttle crew either; that open grate was necessary for the little guy to breathe, but as much of a mess as the inside of the crate had been, just as much must have floated out to contaminate the rest of their cargo with puppy mess. What had her mother been thinking?

The white hair now clean and shiny, she ran her hands up his neck to his dark head and found a collar all but invisible against his darker fur. Her fingers found a little bone-shaped tag in the front and she held the puppy up in front of her eyes to get a closer look.

"Boo. Is that your name?"

The puppy licked her nose. He was trembling worse than ever and she finished up his bath as quickly as she could, then unwound one of her scarves to wrap around him like a towel. She rubbed him all over, and this part he actually seemed to like. Then she picked him up again to cradle him in her arms as she headed back down the hall to their room. Lars and Hakim had brought the crate inside, but had left the door open. April came in and sat down on her bunk, still cooing at the puppy as he tried to climb all over her.

"You know we can't keep it," Hakim said.

"Of course we can," April said. "He won't be any trouble at all, will you, Boo?"

"Boo?" Hakim repeated.

"His name. It's on his collar."

"Why would your mother send you a dog?" Lars asked. "I thought you hadn't even heard from her in weeks."

"Not since three stations ago," April said. "But she must have gotten my messages if she sent Boo here to me."

"But why would she send you a dog?" Lars asked again.

April looked down at the dog, turning around and around in her lap. "His name is Boo. I have to imagine she thinks he's a ghost-hunting dog."

"But she knows you don't do that sort of work anymore," Hakim said.

"She knows," April said. "She's not entirely happy with it." The version of the events leading up to them leaving the *Chandrasekhar* that she had related to her mother had been heavily edited to downplay the danger she had been in, and she hadn't mentioned Martha and the pool haunting at all. But her mother must have suspected something was left out. She mentioned again that April had given her word not to turn down people in need, and she mentioned it more and more forcefully as April messaged her from station after station with news of their transport business. The word 'vocation' came up a lot.

"Did you tell her about our current financial difficulties?" Lars asked.

"No, she doesn't need to know that," April said. She tried to remember the last time she had sent a message to her mother. It had been a long time, maybe only once since they'd arrived on this station.

"Then why send something to prompt you back into your ghost work?" Lars asked. "She knows how you feel about it."

"She thinks I have a calling. That I'm meant to be doing it. She's only OK with me traveling and trying new things because she's certain in the end I'll go back to the ghost work."

"You have to send him back," Lars said.

"I will not."

Lars began, "But if she thinks..."

But Hakim cut him off. "It doesn't matter what April's mother thinks," he said, but before April could thank him, he went on. "We can't afford to feed a dog. We don't have the space for him, not here in this room and not on Salima's ship when we leave in a few days. We can't deal with a dog among us in free fall. I'm sorry, April, but it's just not possible."

"He can't eat much," April said. The dog stopped turning around, finally slumping down with his head on her ankle and closing his eyes.

"We can't keep him," Hakim said again.

"I'm not giving him up," April said.

"You just got him. How are you so attached already?"

"I am," April said stubbornly. "My headache's gone. I feel almost human. I need him."

"The headache will be back," Hakim said. She knew he was trying to be as gentle as he could, but with Hakim, that was still all too brusque.

"Surely she can keep him until we have to go," Lars said. "There is some food left in here."

"She's only going to get more attached," Hakim said. "It's only going to be that much harder to leave him behind when we do have to go. April, you know I'm right."

April put her hand on the puppy's head, softly, so as not to wake him. "Maybe he and I can stay here."

"You hate it here," he reminded her. "There is no work for you here, and now you'd have two mouths to feed with no Salima earning enough for all of us."

"There is work for me here," April said, barely more than a whisper.

"No, there isn't," Hakim said. He was standing over her, arms crossed, chin raised ever so slightly. April gathered the puppy up in her arms, the little guy complaining about having his nap so rudely disturbed. Then she pulled her bag out from under the bunk and stood up.

"Yes, there is," she said, raising her own chin. He was still taller than she was by more than a head, but she refused to let that cow her. She pushed past Lars, who reached out a hand to catch her.

"Let her go," Hakim said. Whatever he said next was lost beneath the echoes of April's feet on the hallway grate, but it must have been compelling, for Lars just stood in the doorway, watching her go.

April buried her nose in Boo's soft fur. She was being impulsive, she knew that, but she wasn't being silly. Her mother had sent her a responsibility, and she wasn't going to shirk from it.

And there was work—work only she and Boo could do.

April wasn't exactly sure where the stationmaster was to be found. She went to the marketplace first, but she saw only the same shops she'd been strolling through since arriving on the station, no strange buildings or doors she'd overlooked before. She was loath to ask for help, not from these strange people with their glassy, dead eyes. She went back up to the docks and started walking along the far side, away from the airlocks that led to the shuttles and ships.

She was nearly halfway around the station—fewer people working on fewer ships, nowhere near as much cargo moving in and out—when she saw the open door. She drew closer, hugging Boo as she peered inside. It was a small room, a woman working at a desk, two empty chairs opposite her.

"Excuse me?" April said. "I'm looking for the stationmaster?"

The woman looked up at her, and April saw to her relief that her eyes were bright and present, so unlike most of the residents of this station. She gave April a confused look, not certain why a girl and a dog were at her door.

"You're in the right place," she said. "I'm Mara, the stationmaster's assistant. Can I help you?"

"I'm here about the sealed-off parts of the station," April said. "The haunted ones. My name is April Nguyen. I eliminate ghosts."

17

———————————————

BOO PROVES HIS WORTH

"For what it's worth, her name is coming up a lot," Mara said from where she was sitting on the far end of the stationmaster's desk, scanning through files on a tablet. "High praise from lots of folks rid of ghost problems."

Alexei, the stationmaster, turned his attention back to April, who stood in front of his desk, Boo scampering about her feet, sniffing at everything.

"You are who you say you are," he allowed, crossing his arms as he leaned back in his chair. "But I'm not sure you are *what* you say you are."

"You don't believe in ghosts," April said, remembering what Lars and Hakim had told her before. "But that's not important."

"It's not?"

"No. It doesn't matter. Because those people do. And it doesn't matter what happens when I go inside the sealed-off part of the station. The only thing that matters is that they believe I did something. That belief will make them feel safe, and that feeling of safety will let you get in there and start using those hydroponic bays."

"That *sounds* reasonable—"

"Between you and me, I don't believe in ghosts either," April said.

"So you're admitting you're a con man," Alexei said, raising his eyebrows.

"Con woman," Mara said.

"It's not a con," April said. "There definitely is something going on here. This place, this station, it just isn't right."

"She's not wrong," Mara said.

"A lot of people died here," Alexei said. "The memory of it hovers over everyone here. It's smothering."

"That's not what I mean. I've found in my work that with something like this that affects so many people, all seeing things or hearing things, something else is usually going on. Some real danger that needs to be dealt with. My dog and I will go into the sealed part of the ship and make a show of sending the ghosts on to the next world, but I have something to ask in exchange." April took a breath, then went on. "You have to look for what's really going on."

"I have been," Alexei said, rubbing at his head. "The hydroponics bays are the public reason I want to get into the other part of the ship. What I haven't been telling the others is that I also want access to the environmental controls and medical bays. You're right, something is making us all a little off. I feel it. Mara feels it."

"Headaches," Mara said, ticking off a finger. "Fatigue, hearing things when there's no one there. The damnable depressive feeling that never relents."

"Exactly," April said. "You knew about all this?"

"We haven't found a cause," Alexei said. "Nothing is in the food. There are no organisms in the air infecting us."

"No black mold," Mara said. "No weird hallucinogenic fungal spores."

"It didn't use to be this way. I don't know when it started to change, it was so gradual. But something is definitely wrong and getting wronger. So, you see, we have no problems with the terms of your condition," Alexei said with a soft smile.

"We should get in there right away," April said. "I swear I can put on a show everyone will believe. No one will doubt all the ghosts are gone. Short term. If people are still hearing things or seeing things, the ghost stories will come back."

"I doubt we'll ever get rid of them completely," Alexei said. "Stories are powerful things."

"That's why what I do is effective," April said. 'It becomes part of the story."

"Well, so long as I've made sure my people are healthy, they can believe whatever they like."

"Agreed," April said.

"Do you need to get any supplies or anything?" Alexei asked.

"I have everything here with me. I'm ready when you are."

"Which door..." Alexei mumbled to himself, touching his desktop screen to life, and Mara leaned over his shoulder to press a finger to the screen.

"That one. It's closest to environmental; that's definitely where you should head first," she said.

"Medical second," Alexei agreed. "Once we know what we're dealing with, we can figure out how to treat it."

"We'll need a witness," Mara said. "Maybe two."

"No more than two," April said. "That's enough to spread the story. I don't really like working in crowds."

"As you like it," Alexei said. He looked up at Mara.

"Melanie, from the teahouse. And Hugo."

"Hugo? He's a bit young," Alexei said.

"Melanie is a believer, and she is very persuasive. She's the one who convinced the others to set up their own guards on the doors to make sure you don't try to get in. Hugo, on the other hand, is considered a bit of a brain. Yes, he's young, but people trust his judgment because they know he always thinks things through."

"That could go either way then," Alexei said. "He might figure out what April is really up to and tell the others."

"If he does figure it out, I think he'll keep his mouth shut. Because if he's figured that out, he knows what we're really after."

"True," Alexei said. "Plus, the kid is going to be doing my job some-day. Might as well start showing him the ropes."

"I'll go fetch them and meet you at the door." Mara took her notepad and went out the door, leaving it open behind her. Alexei got down on one knee and held a hand out for Boo to sniff. Boo approached eagerly.

"He's a friendly one," Alexei said, tousling the puppy's ears. "Do you know what breed?"

"No, my mother sent him to me and she didn't say," April said.

"It looks like a sort of terrier, but the coloring is pretty striking," Alexei said, picking Boo up and examining him closely. "When I was a boy, we had rat terriers here on the station. They were smart dogs."

"What happened to them?" April said.

"The number of live births started to dwindle, then the puppies themselves died off. Soon we only had older dogs, too old to breed, and then we had none at all. It's a mystery. Although," he said, the thought seemingly striking him, "if I'm remembering correctly, the problems with the dogs started about the time we started feeling strange ourselves. I'm not sure; like I said, it was all pretty vague for a long time."

"Still, it could be related."

"Indeed." He set Boo back down on the ground and straightened up, taking a moment to stretch his back. "Shall we?"

April followed him back out through Mara's office to the open space of the dock. "I should warn you about Melanie," he said as they walked along the dock, back toward the barracks and marketplace. "She can be a little intense. She's superstitious, but she's not dumb. She has two daughters, about your age, who seem to be the worst afflicted with whatever is going on. They hear things constantly, voices that whisper to them from the other parts of the station. They've been telling Melanie and others the things they hear, dire warnings and threats and the like. I've been there when they are doing their channeling bit and it certainly feels like something otherworldly is going on. I don't know. Sometimes it's hard to think; this fog in my brain only lifts for rare moments. It's like trying to parse what's happening in a dream sometimes. It's hard to care if there's no logic."

"I just feel an overwhelming sadness," April said. "Not quite to the point of despair, but yes, it feels like it's much too much work to care about things."

"I wouldn't worry about Hugo," Alexei said. "He will observe without telling you what he's thinking and he'll reach his own conclusions. Nothing you can say is going to sway him. But her you need to convince."

"I understand," April said. A wave of exhaustion washed over her, reminding her that by this time of day she was invariably back in bed again, trying to sneak moments of sleep around spasms of headache. The headache was still gone, but the tiredness was like a heavy cloak on her shoulders, weighing her down.

Boo trotting beside her looked up at her, seeming to be smiling at her with his eyes, and she smiled back.

"Here we go," Alexei said. April looked back up to see they were approaching a door in the busier part of the dock. When she had passed this point earlier, there had been two men nearby working on an engine of some sort. She realized now that they had also been the door guards, as they were now on their feet in front of the door. The taller of the two was towering over Mara, arms crossed as he repeatedly shook his head. Behind Mara was a boy of about twelve, more roly-poly than most boys on the station, but with serious eyes under shaggy bangs of dark hair. Beside him was a woman April recognized from the teahouse, tall with whitish-blond hair and a faded shawl pulled around well-muscled arms. Melanie. She saw them approaching and stepped up to meet them, tugging her shawl closer around her.

"I'm not sure this is a good idea, Alexei," she said. "The girls, they said never to go past these doors. You heard them yourself."

"I did," he allowed. "May I introduce you to April Nguyen? She is here to help us."

"April Nguyen?" Melanie said, looking her over appraisingly. "I've heard of you. I have a cousin on the *Triomphe* who swears you helped a family there with the ghosts of their daughters."

"I remember," April said. "Twins. They had died from a gas leak."

"And you sent them on?"

"Yes."

"To where?" Melanie asked.

"That I don't know," April admitted. "But I believe wherever they are, they are happier there than where they were, being a constant reminder to their grieving mother. She couldn't let go while she was still seeing them, hearing their laughter, feeling their presence."

Melanie's face was unreadable and April bit down on her lip to keep herself from babbling on. She was skirting around lies she didn't want to have to tell. She didn't want to unleash the hard sell her mother was so adept at; she didn't believe it enough herself to be convincing to others. But she did believe she had made that mother able to move on. That wasn't a lie.

"Then there was a killer ghost?" Melanie prompted.

"Yes, that wasn't on the *Triomphe*, though. It was a smaller station."

"You must be very brave," she said.

"I have nothing to fear from ghosts," April said.

"Let us go past the door and she can show you," Alexei said.

"Have you been told the story of this place?" Melanie asked.

"I don't think I need to know," April said. "Ghosts are ghosts."

"Without knowing what transpired here, how can you show the proper respect?" Melanie asked. Then she looked to Alexei. "You know what they've been saying through my daughters. Respect must be shown. Those ghosts have killed before and will kill again if respect is not shown."

April could see she had made a misstep. She just wanted to get to work, but of course waving her arms and saying nonsense words wasn't really the work. Building the story, that was the work. "Please, tell me. I know bits of it already, but I think there are large parts that are no longer spoken out loud. Those felt like taboo to me; I didn't want to pry."

"I can imagine what you already know: that refugees came here after the plague, just as they came to every station in the solar system."

"And death followed, just as it did everywhere in the solar system," April added.

"Not like this," Melanie said. "And not at first. No, at first the soldiers stationed here broke their orders and let the refugees onto the station. They were supposed to keep the docks sealed against any nonmilitary ship, but they created a quarantine area, this part of the docks, some storage spaces where the marketplace is now, the barracks. They had left out as much food as they could spare, sealed the doors, and let the refugees disembark.

"Unlike most of the refugee ships, this one had had not a single carrier among them. There was no recurrence of plague among them. Still, stories of the other stations hit by wave after wave of mutating virus decimating their populations made the soldiers extra cautious. They kept up the quarantine. There was no plague here, but they did feel the effects of it. The supply runs stopped coming through—too many sick or dead along the chain for shuttles to make it here, at the end of the line. Rationing was implemented, then more severe rationing, but still supplies did not come. The refugees begged for more food, but the soldiers would not break the quarantine. Old ones and young ones started to sicken and die and the refugees got desperate."

April picked Boo up and hugged him close. It wasn't hard to guess where the story was going.

"One of the refugees found a way to sneak into the other part of the station, a way to break past a sealed door. No one knows how many were with him when they infiltrated the soldiers' part of the station. They found a weapons locker first, then found the soldiers. There weren't many left. Not realizing the supply runs would stop, they had left nearly all of their food inside the quarantine zone for the refugees. They had some fresh food from the hydroponics bays, but that didn't last long." Melanie looked April right in the eyes, making sure she had her full attention.

"Do you see what I'm saying? The soldiers were starving first. They knew the refugees had enough food left to last their fewer numbers a long time. They knew there was no danger of plague here. They could have broken quarantine at any time and taken the food back; they had all the weapons. But they didn't. They gave everything they had and were still desperately sending communications back to Earth to send more food. Daily, asking for more help. And the refugees, our ancestors, broke out of quarantine, found the guns, and murdered every last one of them. For nothing; there was no more food."

"Starvation can drive anyone mad," Alexei said. "And it wasn't all of them, only a few."

"We're all tainted by what they did," Melanie said. "It was unjust."

"And the ghosts of the soldiers remain, looking to even the score?" April guessed.

"Indeed. At first, our refugee grandparents spread throughout the station, but the ghosts were not quiet. They tricked the living, lured them into dangerous places, distracted them at key moments when doing dangerous tasks. After one too many accidental deaths, our grandparents retreated to these places, and for a time, for a long time, the ghosts were satisfied."

"We have to go inside," April said. "They are no longer satisfied, are they? They want the whole station now. Whatever they are promising through your daughters, you know I'm right. People are seeing things on this side of the doors. How long before the first fatal accident?"

"It's already happened, actually," said Hugo. "A man on the dock got crushed under a load of crates when the chain snapped."

"No one was there," Alexei said. "We don't know what he saw, if anything."

"He was seeing things," Melanie said. "He told others about it before he died. I've heard the stories circulating."

"We need to deal with this," April said.

"I agree," Hugo said. After a long moment, Melanie nodded.

The two men by the door stepped aside, letting Mara press her palm to the lock. The door sprang open, the hallway beyond lit only by red emergency lights, much darker than the brightly lit dock.

"Mara, wait here," Alexei said. "If we run into difficulties, I'll give a shout."

Mara nodded. Her face was as stern as ever, but April sensed a bit of relief in her body language.

April set Boo on the ground in front of the door. He looked up at her, tongue panting.

"Go on, boy," April said. "Show me where the ghosts lurk."

He kept looking at her for what felt like far too long, but then trotted forward into the dark hallway. April clutched her bag close and followed. She still had a few things from the old days, the bells and a few wispy scarves that would function as a veil for the ceremony. Hugo and Melanie came next, Alexei bringing up the rear.

If anything, the feeling of oppressive quiet, that depressing detachment from everything, was stronger here. April felt a stabbing behind her eyes, brief but intense. Her headache was threatening to return just when she needed to focus.

The hallway crossed another, but Boo kept going forward without hesitating and April followed. The puppy's head was low to the ground, and it was sniffing madly, just like it really was tracking something down. As if ghosts had smells. But was that idea any crazier than being able to see and hear them? To feel cold when they were near? April took a deeper sniff herself. She smelled nothing, but for a moment her head swam, her vision tunneling like she was about to faint. She put a hand out to lean on the wall.

"Are you all right?" Alexei asked.

"Yes, just need a minute," April said. Hugo was watching her closely, his face expressionless. Melanie was looking all around them, her hands half raised as if ready to make fists. At last April's brain cleared, or at least settled back to its recent customary fogginess, and she raised her head. "Where's Boo?"

"He kept going," Hugo said, pointing further down the hall. April walked briskly but on her toes, careful not to make too much noise. The stifling silence of this place seemed to demand not to be disturbed. Then she heard Boo barking urgently somewhere up ahead and she broke into a run.

Boo had turned off the hallway to explore a large room with walls covered with control panels, all dark, and a maze of workstations. The room was divided into three long sections, each a step down from the last. April didn't see Boo at first, but then he barked again and she saw the ghostly white of his body on the far end of the room. His black fur blended with the semidarkness, making him appear headless even as he barked again and again at the empty corner of the room. April knelt beside him, quieting him with a hand on his back. He promptly sat down with a low woof, but kept staring at the empty corner.

"What's there?" Melanie asked from the doorway. "Do you see something?"

"No, but something is upsetting Boo," April said.

"This is the communications room," Alexei said and Melanie gasped.

"What does that mean?" April asked.

"Most of the soldiers were herded up here and executed," Melanie said. "They were cooperating. Right up until the shooting started."

"Probably right here then," April said, looking around as if she expected to still see blood staining the floor. She did see bullet holes in some of the equipment along the back wall. "Definitely here." She straightened back up, then quickly grasped the edge of the nearest workstation as the world tried to tip away from her again.

"April?"

"I'm OK," she said, but her voice seemed to be coming from far away, muffled in her own ears. She focused on her breathing and willed herself not to faint. The pain behind her eyes stabbed her again, and she whimpered, fingers clutching the edge of the workstation, trying to dig into the metal. Slowly, slowly, it receded, but not completely. It threatened to stab her again if she moved too quickly. The low, red emergency lights were suddenly a blessing.

"What's wrong with Boo?" Hugo asked.

April opened her eyes despite the crushing ache and saw Boo lying motionless on the floor.

"Boo!" She dropped back to her knees and picked him up. He didn't rouse even when she gently shook him. She pressed her face to his round belly. He was breathing, barely. She struggled to her feet, stumbling across the room to press him into Hugo's hands.

"Take him outside," she said. "Go now, run! All the way across the docks, get him away from here!"

Hugo nodded and ran, the puppy cradled close to his chest.

"What is it?" Alexei asked.

"Something is very wrong there," April said, pointing to the far end of the room. Melanie was looking at the ceiling, but Alexei saw what April was pointing at.

"Engineering," he said. "It's a level down from here. There's a stairwell at the end of this hall."

"Take a mask," April said, and he nodded and ran back to the docks to fetch one.

Melanie had taken two steps into the room. April reached out to catch her arm and pull her back, but Melanie fell to her knees, moaning and hugging herself.

"Melanie, you should get out of here. It isn't safe," April said. "Come on, we're both going."

"We can't leave!" Melanie said. "Don't you hear them? The screams of rage. They are going to kill us all. You have to stop them."

"I will, but you have to go," April said, trying to pull her back to her feet. Melanie twisted out of her hands, pointing at the far end of the room.

"The lights! Don't you see the lights? They're coming for us." Then she wailed, her head pressed between her hands. "They're in my head. Oh, I can't breathe..."

April's headache tried to blind her again, but a sudden surge of adrenaline beat it back. Tiny as she was, she managed to haul Melanie to her feet and propel her back out into the hall. Melanie slumped to the floor, weeping as she clutched her head. April's heart lurched as she heard footsteps echoing down the hallway. Someone was running right at them—but it was only Alexei, an oxygen mask over his nose and mouth. He pressed another into April's hands as he ran past. April put it on and turned on the little tank.

The sudden rush of awareness nearly made her weep. She had been in a fog for so long she had forgotten what clarity felt like.

Melanie was still sobbing on the floor, nearly hysterical at the things she was hearing and feeling in her head. If her headache was anything like April's had been, if she truly believed something outside of her was causing it just to hurt her... April could see how that would be terrifying. Especially since Melanie believed her daughters would be next.

"Melanie," April said, her voice muffled by the mask. She took a few more deep breaths, then slipped the mask off her own face and onto Melanie's. "Here, just breathe. It will pass."

Melanie clung to April's hands holding the mask to her face, but she grew calmer with each breath. April drew her to her feet and the two of them, leaning on each other, stumbled back out to the dock.

Melanie let the mask drop once they were past the door, and April took a few more breaths of oxygen to keep the headache at bay.

"You did it!" Melanie said, laughing and crying at once. April didn't know what to say to this. Then Melanie turned to the two men standing with Mara and said, "She did it! She really did."

"What happened?" Mara asked. She was looking at April, who gave a small shrug, but Melanie rushed to answer.

"They were there, all the ghosts. They were still right where they had died, lurking. The dog flushed them out."

The word "dog" hit April like an arrow and she dropped her mask, looking around for Boo. She saw Hugo sitting on the floor with his back to her further down the dock and ran to his side. Boo was on Hugo's lap, Hugo holding an oxygen mask over the dog's tiny snout. There was no way to make it fit, but just having the oxygen blow over him was doing the trick. His eyes were locked on Hugo's, but when she leaned closer, he saw her and his little tail thumped against the floor.

"Thank you," April said, and Hugo just nodded and handed her Boo. April settled both him and the little tank in her arms and walked back to the others, still holding the mask over his little nose. She had come very close to losing him, she knew.

Melanie was still trying to describe the ghosts she had seen, formless figures of light that twisted around each other but separated before rushing at her, into her. Mara had an arm around her, patting her back as she nearly broke down again just describing the pain.

"You felt it too," Melanie said, looking at April. "You were so brave. I saw them attack you and you held your ground. You fought them back."

"I've had some experience with it," April said, glancing at Mara. Mara gave her a little nod.

Alexei emerged from the hallway behind them and pulled the door shut, spinning the lock.

"We're sealing it back up?" Mara asked.

"Just for a few hours," Alexei said. "I've boosted the air recyclers up to full."

"Something was leaking," April said.

He nodded. "We never should have left this for so long, not getting into that part of the station. Maintenance checks were neglected."

"It won't happen again," Mara said.

"They're all gone," Melanie said, only half listening to them. "The ghosts are gone. She sent them back into the light and they just zoomed away. The pain in my head went away like flipping a switch, just gone, and everything was clear again. In an instant."

April nodded. That was a pretty accurate description of the effects of oxygen.

"We can't thank you enough," Alexei said. "Honestly, we owe you our lives."

"If we're talking payment, I could use some food."

"You've earned more than a few meals!" Melanie said, putting an arm around her to lead her back to the teahouse. "But we can certainly start there."

April ended up with more than she could carry and Hugo had to go with her back to the rented room, both of their arms loaded with boxes and bags, Boo trotting happily at their heels. It was past dinnertime and Salima was back in the room as April kicked the door open. Clearly, she had interrupted some intense conversation, but she just beamed at them all.

"Udon noodles with chicken," she said, pressing a covered bowl into Hakim's hands. "Kebab." She handed a box to Lars. "And chicken and olive tajine," she said to Salima, who raised her eyebrows with something almost like a smile. Hugo stepped forward and set his stack of boxes on the end of April's bunk, then left with a nod of farewell to April. Boo hopped up onto her bed and circled around her pillow three times before flopping down and falling promptly asleep.

"What happened?" Hakim asked.

"Boo and I did a job," she said. She sat in the middle of her bunk and opened the last of the boxes she had been carrying. It was full of sandwiches, cookies, pickled vegetables, and a little pot of tea and a cup. She took a bite of a sandwich, not quite able to stop smiling. Breathing pure oxygen had really sharpened her appetite.

"What kind of job?" Hakim asked.

"Eat your udon while it's hot," April said.

He dug his spork into the bowl and stuffed noodles into his mouth, then looked at her questioningly as he chewed.

"This station has been declared ghost free," she said. "Boo found the source of the haunting and I did something spectacular, apparently. That bit's all a bit muddled, since the carbon monoxide level was so high there that Melanie from the tea shop and I were nearly killed."

"Carbon monoxide," Lars repeated, in the tone of someone just realizing what should have been obvious from the start.

"One of the heaters in engineering was not operating within parameters. The sealed-up part of the station contained most of the gas, but it had been slowly working its way into the inhabited sections for some time now. The stationmaster shut down the faulty heater and is running the air recyclers on full."

"That explains the breeze," Hakim said, putting a hand over the vent in their room. "And your headache, and the fatigue."

"It explains everything," she said with a glance at Lars. He winked at her around the kebab he was biting into.

"Good work," Salima said. "Did you get paid?"

"Not coin, but gifts," April said. "No one out here is exactly rich, but they're very grateful. The whole marketplace is one big party. We'll be eating for free until that part for your ship comes. I got some new clothes and things too. More importantly, I have a referral, another similar job on another station. And that one will pay in coin."

"Another ghost job?" Hakim asked.

"That's how Boo and I earn our keep," April said. "Boo and I are a team. Inseparable."

"No reason why this can't dovetail with the cargo work," Salima said.

Hakim scowled but said nothing.

"I know some people," Lars said. "If you are looking for more jobs like this, I can put the word out."

"That would be perfect," April said. He could take care of all the parts of the job her mother used to do and she could focus on crafting the story people needed. "Hakim, we're going to need you too."

"For what?" he asked.

"For finding the real problem."

"There might not always be one," he pointed out. "Sometimes ghost stories are just stories."

"That's all right," April said. "I'm OK with just making people feel better. What I don't want to do is miss something like this, a real problem that needs to be fixed. Or like back on the *Triomphe*—something killed those girls, and no one was looking for it. I don't want things like that to happen, but we can work to stop them, can't we?"

He shrugged noncommittally, but Lars was grinning broadly.

"We can do this. It fits in nicely with the transport work."

Salima nodded in agreement, her attention mostly on her tajine.

"Let's go back down to the marketplace," Lars said. "I want to see how people are doing. You've lifted a great darkness off their lives. You're like a hero in a fairy tale."

"Not really," April said, but she knew she was glowing all the same. Lars put Boo in her arms and they went out to join the celebration.

18

THE SHUTTLE VILLAGE

April gathered her hair at the nape of her neck and secured it with a loose elastic band, then separated it into plaits for braiding. Without the band, she never got all the hair into the braid, not in free fall. She braided it all the way to the end, tied it off, and carefully slipped off the band before wrapping the braid around her head and securing it with a few pins. The more time she spent in free fall, the more she appreciated Salima's close-cropped hair, but she knew she could never bear to cut her own. She kept it braided, so it was out of everyone's way, but now that she and Boo had a pod of their own, she could let it down when she wanted, spinning in a cloud of her own glistening black tresses. Not that she did it a lot, especially after Boo got too excited and tangled himself up in her hair, but still. Her own pod. Not a bad thing.

April opened the hatch and floated out into the open pod that only served as a connecting space for all their personal pods. From the outside, it looked like the narrow waist of Salima's ship had four bubbles erupting from it up, down, left, and right. Aft of their personal pods was the cargo space, lots and lots of cargo space. Fore was the enlarged common room, then the cockpit, the engine room tucked beneath both of them, a long, narrow space that was Salima's personal domain even more than her sleeping pod.

It was nice to have money. And not just money, but a steady, reliable supply of it. Salima was hauling enough cargo to make a nice little sum and was establishing regular clients, but it was April's work that was really bringing in the coin. And for once, she could feel proud of that. She wasn't just deluding people; she was taking the opportunity to dig into the "hauntings," she and Lars working together doing the "ritual" while Hakim ruled out any other possible cause for people seeing things. Not every job had an underlying cause that he could find, but enough of them did that she felt justified in continuing to play her charade. Gas leaks could be deadly and were certainly harmful, and they had found five of those so far.

Stranger to April was the low-frequency sound, something Hakim had discovered in a community that was living in the machinery of a station, much like that job she had done on the *Triomphe* the day she had met Hakim. Sound waves too low to be audible to human ears, and yet humans still perceived them as a smothering feeling of dread. Hakim said that at certain frequencies it could even vibrate the fluid in your eyeballs, making you see dark smears at the corners of your vision. This wasn't particularly dangerous, but while April was doing her dispelling of spirits routine Hakim had adjusted an exhaust fan, and when they had left, that feeling of being choked by despair went with them thanks to the fan no longer putting out those sounds. She had totally done what she'd been paid to do.

"Anything interesting?" April asked as she floated into the kitchen area and opened a cabinet to take out a bowl of dried oatmeal. Peaches and cream, her favorite.

"That demon exorcist messaged you again," Lars said. "I sent him another polite refusal."

"Thanks," April said, sliding the opening in her bowl over the hot-water nozzle and turning on the tap. "It sounds interesting, but it's just too far away."

"Agreed," Lars said. "You still wanted something that would take us back towards the *Triomphe*?"

"Yes," she said, pulling herself into the chair next to him. Whether they got a job there or not, she wanted to go back to the place where the two girls had died and make sure nothing had been missed. Maybe it was the noise thing again and they could find what machine was vibrating at that low frequency and adjust it, or maybe it was something much more dangerous. The girls had died from gas, after all. A gas leak that had been fixed before she'd ever gotten there, to be sure, but still. It ate at her.

"This one would be on the way, but it's not even a station, just one of those floating villages of tethered ships. I only mention it because, aside from being on the way, the tone of the message makes me think you know these people," Lars said.

"Mama Rosa," April said. Memories washed over her: the smell of spicy sauces simmering for hours, the warmth of Mama Rosa's arms when she would gather April up in one of her frequent hugs, the happy ring of her laughter.

"So you do know them?"

"I lived there once," she said. "That's where I was when I stopped my mother's night terrors."

"I'll go talk to Salima and work it into her transport schedule," Lars said.

"Thanks," April said. She had never thought she'd go back to that village, had often actively wished not to ever go back, but now that the opportunity had arisen, she knew she absolutely had to. She had never properly thanked Mama Rosa for everything she had done for April and her mother. Especially April; the months they had spent there had been some of Melena's darkest, and without Mama Rosa's abundant mothering, little April would have been truly lost.

April ate her oatmeal, still thinking of her time at that village. She didn't remember much before that time, truth be told. A few snatches of images of a time when they had nicer things, her mother with a man who always smiled at April, caught her up in his arms and tickled her with his beard. She couldn't remember his name now, she realized with a stab of regret. He had been a good man, but he had died and without him, Melena and April had nothing.

April put her dishes in the recycler, as well as the empty coffee bulb Lars had left behind when he'd gone to find Salima. She could hear their voices in the cockpit, or rather Lars's voice, pausing occasionally for Salima to nod or shake her head. April smiled, imagining the conversation, then went aft instead. The hatches to the personal pods latched against the walls of the core pod, and by habit, they all left them open except when they were sleeping or changing. She found Boo still sleeping in her pod, wrapped in the end of her hammock, ears floating straight up from his face, making him look bat-like, especially as he was upside down in relation to her.

Hakim was in his pod, curled over his tablet, stylus moving at a steady pace over the space, occasionally scrolling the screen to make more open space with a quick flick of his other hand. The stylus was a gift from her, one of a large array she'd acquired for him. She still occasionally found him using the end of a spork or one of Salima's finer tools, but the stylus he was using today was her favorite. She was certain it wasn't actually gold, but it looked real enough to her eye. She hovered outside his pod, not wanting to interrupt his work but equally certain that if she didn't, he would entirely forget to eat.

"What is it, April?" he asked, not looking up.

"Did you eat?"

"At some point," he said vaguely. "I'll stop when I hit a wall. I feel one coming."

Still, he didn't look up at her. She had expected him to be more enthusiastic with their work, especially considering how many problems they had fixed, how many lives they had improved. She had tried soliciting his input when she and Lars started altering the rituals her mother had crafted, making them less supernatural and more psychological, addressing the living people gathered around them rather than the "spirits," but he hadn't been interested. She missed the companionship of the old days when he would check her progress on her reader and explain things that were tripping her up.

Most frustratingly, no matter how closely she observed his every gesture and word choice, she couldn't tell if he was withdrawing from her because he was mad at her or because he was just that caught up in the math. She was too afraid it was the former to ask. And he didn't seem to notice all the things she did to try to make it up to him for something she wasn't even sure she had done to make him angry.

Hence the gifts. The stylus had been an easy find, but the math texts she had dug out of sharing libraries on the stations where she did jobs had required hours of careful searching. The few real dead tree books had been a real coup. He had taken what she had given him without quite looking at her, and she had to be satisfied with knowing he appreciated them because she saw him using them constantly. He was never going to thank her, not without some cutting remark about where the money came from or how it sullied him to take such gifts, she was sure.

He was still lost in his math, likely not even hearing her, but she found words tumbling out of her mouth, anyway. "We're going to a shuttle village next, one of the places I lived when I was little. You'll get to meet Mama Rosa. You'll love her. She's going to make way too much food for us and stuff us silly before she'll even let me get to work, just you see. You with your love of noodles, you're going to be out of your mind when you taste her pasta. Do you have any idea how hard that is to make from scratch in free fall? You have to see how she does it. It's so clever."

Hakim made a sound that could mean anything, but mostly meant he wasn't really listening. April hovered awkwardly for a minute, then pushed off the wall to sail into her own pod and tease the lazy puppy awake. He needed to get his walkies in or his muscles would atrophy. Salima had rigged up a treadmill just his size. It had taken him a while to get the idea, but now, so long as April was there to encourage him to keep running, he would let her strap him into it and move his little legs, always looking to her for the next treat. She wondered if he imagined he was chasing things as he ran, and if so, what he was chasing. Ghosts or rabbits? Or maybe ghost rabbits?

But even as she laughed and encouraged Boo, giving him another treat every so often, her mind was still on Hakim in his pod, back to the rest of them. Mama Rosa had a way with people. Perhaps she could draw him out with her food and hugs.

"We're there," Salima said. "They're having a little trouble with the airlock on their side, but they'll have it sorted in a minute."

"I'm not surprised," Lars said, looking out the window next to the kitchen area. "It really is just a bunch of old ships tied together."

"What did you expect?" Hakim asked.

"I don't know. It always sounded like maybe that was metaphorical or something," Lars said. "I assumed they had to be attached somehow; how does anyone move from ship to ship?"

"One of Mama Rosa's boys has a suit, and he transports people in sort of a plastic bubble..." April began.

"Ugh, no. Nightmare fuel," Lars said, holding up a hand.

"It's perfectly safe," April said, "although it does get cold. But you're never out there long, just ship to ship."

"I should message them again," Lars said, mostly to himself. Getting back to the *Chandrasekhar* was feeling more and more like something that was never going to happen. April realized with a little smile that the thought no longer sent a wave of panic washing over her. They were doing OK out on their own.

There was a knock at the aft hatch and Salima knocked back, then spun the wheel, swinging open the heavy door and locking it out at a ninety-degree angle. The airlock beyond was barely large enough for her to manage even that much. April, Boo in her arms, went through first. The door on the far side was just swinging open.

"Tony?" April guessed hesitantly. It had been more than ten years, but she thought she saw something of the awkward teenager she remembered in the slightly pudgy man before her.

"April!" he said, pulling her into a hug just like his mother would do. Boo yelped and he let her go with a laugh. "You've got a dog there."

"Yes, this is Boo," April said, holding up the dog for him to pet. "He works with me."

"I bet that's a sight. Housebroken?"

"Yes, and he just went. You don't need to worry about him. He's a good boy."

"Come on in, then, and say hello to Mama. She's in the kitchen, of course."

"Are your brothers here?"

"A few, about the village. It's Marco's shuttle you're going to be cleansing, so you'll see him for sure." April remembered Marco, the youngest of the brothers. He used to tease her mercilessly until Tony found out and twisted his ear until it was dark red and twice its usual size. He never spoke to her again. That was going to be an awkward meeting.

"Tony, these are my friends Salima and Hakim Little and Lars Gundelach. Everybody, this is Tony."

Tony hugged a rigid Salima, then pulled Hakim and then Lars into a tight handshake and slap on the back that was just on the edge of being another hug. April pulled herself further inside the shuttle. Her memories of the place superimposed themselves over what her eyes were actually seeing. Very little had changed. The racks of bunks were gone from the storage area, no longer needed now that her sons had grown and gone, a little hydroponic garden under grow lights in its place. April followed her nose fore to the kitchen, where Mama Rosa was frowning and adjusting the dial on a cooker.

"Mama Rosa," April said shyly. Mama Rosa held up a finger, watching through a window built into the lid of the cooker, then nodded her head in satisfaction and turned to pull April into a tight hug. Boo once more barked in protest.

"What's this?" Mama Rosa said, the dog all but lost in her bosom. "You brought a critter into my kitchen?"

"He's very well behaved," April said. "And he's part of my work now."

"Equal partner, I'm guessing," Mama Rosa said, still frowning at Boo. Boo looked up at her, his tail under April's arm giving a few uncertain wags. "Well, I've put up with worse. And these are your friends?"

April quickly made introductions. Mama Rosa hugged both of the boys but did a better job than Tony in sensing Salima's reticence and satisfied herself with a brief touch on her shoulder.

"The sauce is nearly there," Mama Rosa said. "Just us and Tony for now, but Marco will be here shortly to take you out to the shuttle. You know the story?"

"Just what you said in the message," April said. "He found it adrift with no one aboard but a hull breach large enough to account for the lack of bodies." April shivered. "I don't really need to know more."

"Any idea what hit it?" Lars asked.

"Not really my area, but you can ask Marco," Mama Rosa said. She hooked one of her sealed cookers up to a hose to drain out the water, and April noticed Salima watching with acute interest. Mama Rosa had designed all of her cookware herself, letting her cook all of her favorite dishes even in free fall when most made do with freeze-dried food and hot water, microwaveable meals if you were really fancy. But Mama Rosa always said there was a difference between heating up food and cooking it. Salima would surely be getting a closer look at all of her gear while April was off working. Lars would be eager to learn every aspect of shuttle village life, and Mama Rosa would happily share every family story she knew. And Hakim?

April imagined he'd find a quiet corner somewhere to get back to the math, but as they gathered around the table to eat she saw he too was looking all around them, taking in all the details, occasionally looking her way, his expression inscrutable. She felt her cheeks heat. Was he judging her for coming from such a place? Like all the gaps in her knowledge made sense now, or that it was a marvel she was literate at all? She knew he took a dim view of her love of nice things; was seeing where she had once lived making him kinder or more judgy? April sporked noodles thick with red sauce into her mouth and carefully ignored his looks. It's not like he was going to tell her what he was thinking, anyway.

Marco joined them just as they were all too stuffed to eat another bite. Mama Rosa tried to get him to take her place, but he refused with a shake of his head.

"To be honest, I'm anxious to get this done. Are you ready, April?"

April nodded, looking around for Boo. Salima had him on her lap, floating scraps of bread for him to snatch out of the air. Boo looked like he would have loved to keep playing that game all day, but came eagerly when April called to him, pushing off Salima's stomach to sail into April's arms.

"Be back in a bit," she said to her friends. Lars smiled and Salima nodded, but Hakim was engrossed in something on his reader and didn't look up. April turned and followed Marco to the airlock opposite of where Salima's ship was docked.

"You remember how to do this?" Marco asked.

"Yes, we'll be fine," April said, climbing into the plastic bubble with

Boo in her arms. She hesitated to look Marco right in the eyes. She was remembering the time he had tied her braids to the back of the kitchen chair, and every time she had tried to extricate herself, she had only gotten more tangled up. She had been so afraid Mama Rosa would have to cut her hair.

"I'm sorry," Marco said, as if reading her mind. "I did a lot of unforgivable stuff."

"We were kids," April said.

"And my dad had just died, and my mother was fussing over two refugees instead of her own family, and that excuses nothing," he said. "I was a jerk."

"You're not a jerk now?" April asked.

"I try not to be."

"Then I forgive you. You're going to tow me out to your shuttle?"

"Yes. Thanks for doing this."

"Your wife is on the *Triomphe* until she has the twins, right?" April said, remembering the message.

"Yes, should be any day now," Marco said.

"Then let's get your new home to a livable state," April said.

Marco gave her a smile of genuine warmth, so different from the cruel twisting of the lips she remembered, then shut the hatch. April let Boo paddle through the air while she sealed up the inside of the bubble. It was not exactly like being inside of a bubble—the surface was quite a bit thicker than that—but it did feel like surrendering everything to the mercy of the guy towing you and to the universe at large. April, knowing she would be traveling this way, had worn her thickest sweater, but she was soon shivering. There was a little heater against the wall of the bubble, but it barely made a dent in the cold. Still, better than traveling in full sunlight. The cold could be combated with sweaters and blankets; the heat was intolerable.

The bubble jerked, then began to move. Boo gave a bark of alarm and bumped up against her thigh, and she caught him and stroked the back of his neck to calm him. Outside, Marco in his much-patched space suit was towing her on a long tether as he climbed from ship to ship. The walls of the bubble were opaque; April had no sense of where she was going or how far away it was. But it was a small village, and soon the bubble brushed up against something solid, then settled into it as Marco outside locked her onto the airlock. He patted the wall twice, her signal to unseal the inside.

This moment always sent a chill up her spine. Any little thing he missed noticing and she would be like a balloon released to vent out every bit of air, propelling so far away from everyone no one would ever even see her bones again.

She bit her lip, reminded herself that Marco had been doing this for years before she'd even met him as a kid, and unsealed the bubble.

19

A FAMILIAR GHOST

THE SHUTTLE BEYOND THE AIRLOCK WAS DELICIOUSLY WARM. THE LIGHTS were on, set to low, but it was still better than the red glow of emergency lights she had expected. Marco had already done all the rehabilitating work, then.

April stepped into the large cargo area, not yet divided into usable spaces like Mama Rosa's. The far wall had a large sheet of dull metal carefully welded onto it. So that had been the site of the hull breach. She floated over to touch it, admiring Marco's careful work. No one knew what had happened; had a small meteor or some bit of space junk struck? It was such a large hole it would have vented all the atmosphere almost instantly, not giving any passengers on board any chance to save themselves. There was no corresponding hole in the far wall, though. It must have been a glancing blow.

Boo pushed out of her arms, eager to explore. April looked over the cargo area, but there was nothing of particular interest to grab her eye. However many passengers there had been, none of them had actually died inside the shuttle, had they? They would have been sucked out into space too quickly. But perhaps someone farther aft had been able to cling to something, to hold on until their strength or their air gave out, only then tumbling out to the void? April shivered despite the warmth and followed Boo up the hallway.

This was an unusual job for her in that no one had actually seen a ghost. Marco and a few friends helping with the repairs were the only ones who had even been on board, and none of them had even gotten the willies. But Marco's wife Yolanda was nervous about bringing her babies back to a home where an unknown number of prior occupants had died in a single horrific moment. April couldn't really blame her; it was hard to live with nothing but a thin hull between your family and death. You were never not aware of it. April had brought some plastic flowers, the closest she could find to forget-me-nots. She would hang them on the walls throughout the shuttle as a remembrance of the dead and declare the ship free of angry spirits.

She was just reaching up to tape the first bunch high on the wall at the end of the hallway when Boo suddenly started howling, insanely loud in the enclosed space. This was very out of character for her happy-go-lucky dog, and she pushed hard off the cargo hatchway, propelling herself past sleeping chambers, kitchenette, and common area to the shuttle cockpit. Boo was behind the pilot's chair, fear and duty wrestling for control of his mind as he barked, then cowered behind the seat, then barked again. The cowering was particularly ineffective in free fall, more of a full-body flinch than a means of getting out of sight behind the seat back.

"What is it, buddy?" April asked. She saw nothing, but a feeling like cold water running down her spine made her shiver. Boo never behaved this way, and he was clearly deeply freaked out by whatever he was perceiving. Some sound out of her hearing range? Some smell she couldn't detect? April pulled herself further into the cockpit and Boo whined, as if his fear were morphing into actual pain. Her heart clenched at the sound of it, but she could see nothing harming him. She climbed over and around the seats, but found nothing.

Boos howling whine went on and on and tears clouded April's vision, unable to spill down her cheeks in free fall. She pressed her hands to the sides of her head in frustration, curling up into a tight ball.

She felt something behind her, standing just over her shoulder. It wasn't exactly like her nightmares back on the other station—no stifling feeling like someone sitting on her chest—but there was definitely something standing behind her, looking at her, reaching out for her. April untucked herself, spinning around to once more see nothing there. She backed out of the cockpit, catching Boo by the collar and holding him in her arms. The puppy still howled like his soul was in agony despite her hand caressing his neck.

Then the feeling was there again: something just behind her, trying to reach out for her. She spun again but still nothing there, like it had just been a vapor blown away by her movements.

She thought of the words she usually said, the gentle encouragement to move on, to go into the light and leave the living to their grief, but Boo's cries made it impossible to find those words now. Instead, she fell back on her first ghost dispelling, the one that had saved her mother from her personal nightmares, and screamed, "Go away! Just go away!"

The feeling was gone, and Boo quieted, although he still trembled in her arms. April wiped the tears from her eyes and looked around again. She pulled herself back into the front of the cockpit, examining every panel, but nothing was on. An air vent was putting out a soft blast of warm air, but that was all. April hugged Boo close. She no longer felt like someone was standing behind her, reaching for her, but she was afraid to move lest it happen again.

She had to move; she still had work to do. Boo slowly stopped shaking, but April kept him tucked under one arm as she taped a sprig of forget-me-nots to the middle of the control panel. She put two more in the cockpit, one behind each of the pilot seats, then drifted back down the hallway, putting one in the kitchenette and another in the common room, then going through each of the sleep pods, a sprig over each doorway. It was a lot of purple; April hoped Yolanda wouldn't mind.

Then something caught the corner of her eye, a brighter, shinier slash of purple. April pulled herself back into the last sleep pod and reached into the cargo netting meant to hold personal effects in free fall.

She pulled out a doll she knew all too well. A superhero whose name she had never learned. A superhero with a purple cape just beginning to fray at the hem.

"Mom?" April said softly.

Of course, there was no answer.

Numbly, April clutched the doll and her dog both and made her way back to the bubble. She sealed them in, then tapped twice on the surface of the bubble. Marco tapped back and soon she felt the jerk of them getting back underway.

That feeling of presence, of someone standing behind her, reaching for her. That hadn't been...?

April clutched her dog closely, aware that she was the one trembling now. Boo licked her chin, but it was like something happening far away, to someone else. Her ears were full of a rushing sound that never built up to anything or receded, just rushed on and on, too loud for thoughts to form.

The bubble bumped back against the airlock of Mama Rosa's ship and after a short interval, Marco tapped that she was good to go. April reached out for the bubble liner, but stopped. Once she got out there, among people, this was all going to be real. This numbness lost in a rush of sound might be better.

But she couldn't stay in the bubble forever. Swallowing hard, April unsealed the liner and crawled back out into the cargo area. She could hear laughter, Mama Rosa's boisterous cackle booming over Lars's smaller chuckles. Boo squirmed out of April's nerveless arms and propelled himself forward to scramble down the hall back to the kitchen full of tasty bits. April came behind more slowly, doll still in her hand.

"April?" Mama Rosa said, the first to see her lingering in the hallway just outside the kitchen. The others looked up, puzzled concern on their faces. "What is it, dear?"

April lifted her hand, opening her fingers enough for Mama Rosa to see the doll. April didn't have to explain. Mama Rosa knew as well as she did what that toy meant.

"Oh, April," she said, pushing away from the table to gather a once-again-trembling April into her arms. That was all that was needed for the dam to burst, giving way to wracking sobs that quickly flooded her eyes with hot tears. Vaguely, she heard Mama Rosa explaining the doll, then asking Lars for a tea towel. Then Mama Rosa was gently wiping the tears from April's eyes, again and again, as they refused to stop coming.

"I felt her there," April said. "I really did. I didn't know it was her. I sent her on and I didn't know it was her."

"She's at peace now, child," Mama Rosa said. "That's the important thing."

"I'm so sorry, April," Lars said, touching her shoulder, and April moved from Mama Rosa's embrace to his, still clutching the doll. Lars held her close, taking over tear-dabbing duties and murmuring words without real meaning, but with a comforting sound to them. Salima drew near, placing a worried Boo back in April's arms, and April managed a tearful smile of thanks. She was upsetting her puppy; she had to pull herself together. She took a shaky breath and brought her puppy up close to her face so he could lick her as much as he'd like.

April took another deep breath, then looked around for Hakim.

He wasn't there.

20

———————

NUMB NOT NAPPING

April was only vaguely aware of the others moving around her, their voices a low murmur she couldn't properly focus on. Her eyes were hot and dry and crying again would be a relief, but the tears didn't come. She couldn't feel the soft warmth of the puppy in her arms, and the comfort and joy he always gave her wasn't there. Salima touched her shoulder and April knew she was talking to her, but she couldn't summon up the energy even to listen. Then Lars's arm was around her, guiding her gently back through the airlock to their own ship. She couldn't look up at him either.

Somehow she ended up snuggled into her hammock with Boo curled up against her belly. She wasn't sure if she'd gotten in herself or been helped in by one of the others. She still couldn't cry. She definitely couldn't sleep. She just stared at the wall in front of her eyes, not really seeing that either.

A deeper murmur among the other voices: Hakim was back. April shut her eyes and ducked her chin under the hammock zipper, feigning sleep until the feeling of someone lingering at the hatch to her pod dissipated.

There was a jolt, then the harder jerk of Salima firing the engine. Then the engine cut off again, and they were moving at a steady velocity that felt the same as hanging motionless. Boo whimpered and April summoned enough energy to put a hand on his head and stroke his ears until he quieted.

She alternated sleeping with staring at the wall for countless hours. Occasionally someone would hover at her hatchway, watching her, trying to guess if she was awake, but never disturbing her. At some point Boo fought his way out of the sleeping bag and she unzipped enough to release him, but she just zipped herself back in again and went back to that place that was not quite awake, not quite asleep. Someone else would take care of Boo if he went looking for it.

The station they docked at was under spin and April jerked out of her doze when Salima set them down, the sudden pull of simulated gravity rocking her hammock. It might have been nauseating if her stomach wasn't a hard, empty knot. Her mouth was sticky, but getting up for a drink of water was too much effort. She snuggled deeper into the hammock.

She heard the others talking in the common area, the deep murmur of Hakim's voice brushing off the others just before the sound of the airlock opening and closing. He was gone.

"April."

Lars. She ignored him. Then there was the skitter of nails on metal floors and Boo hopped up onto her bunk, putting his front paws on her hammock and setting her swinging once more.

"Let's unhook her," Salima said, and she and Lars unhooked her hammock and set her gently on her bunk. Boo, tail wagging madly, burrowed into the sleeping bag until he found her face and licked and licked, ignoring her moans of protest.

"I'll take the dog out," Salima said, picking up a squirming Boo. "Make sure she eats something."

"Yes," Lars said. The airlock door clanged open and shut again, and then it was just her and Lars.

"April, we're at the station. We need to talk about what happens next."

April didn't answer. Then she felt his fingers in her hair, all that poked out of the top of the sleeping bag.

"April, come on. Don't do this—this isn't like you. Come on, we're sitting up." He unzipped her sleeping bag and gathered her up in his arms, hugging her tight against him. "You're scaring me here."

April rested her cheek against his chest and listened to his heartbeat. Her head felt deeply itchy, and she was becoming aware of a sour smell that she suspected was coming from her own body. How long had she stayed in her bag without stirring for more than the most basic of necessities? Days?

Just like her mother used to do.

"I have to clean up," April said, wrinkling her nose at her own personal aroma.

"Yes, you do," Lars said, tightening his arms around her. "Then you have to eat something."

"OK," she agreed, but making the decision to get up seemed big enough for the moment. Actually doing it could wait a bit.

"Then we have to talk about this job," Lars said. "They are waiting for us. Messages were waiting for us before we even docked."

"I won't do it," April said.

"I know you're not up to it, not now. I'll go extend our apologies. You don't need to worry about it. But before I go, I need to know how long you think you'll need. A day or two? A week? Whatever it is, it'll be fine. I just need to tell him something."

"Lars," April said, pushing away from him to sit up on her own. "The answer is never. I'm never doing this again. I'm sorry, but I just can't. No, that's not what I mean. I *won't*."

"April—"

"I won't be changing my mind."

Lars looked her over, tucking a stray strand of her unwashed hair behind her ear. "I'm sorry. This isn't the time to talk about it. Get cleaned up, get something to eat, go take a walk. Whatever you need."

"It won't change my answer," April said. "I won't do this anymore. Not now that I know firsthand just what it is. It's not a comfort, not remotely."

"Did you see something?" Lars asked. "Is that what happened? Did you finally see something?"

"No," April said, just short of scoffing. "There's nothing to see, Lars. I've known that pretty much forever. Now I also know that all the lies

I've been telling myself about what I do and why I do it—they aren't real either. I won't do it again."

Lars chewed his lip for a moment, then stood up, brushing his hands down the legs of his jumpsuit. "I'll make our excuses."

"It's not a postponement, Lars," April said. "It's a cancellation."

He looked back at her for a moment, his eyes full of things she couldn't put a name to. But in the end, if he wanted to say more he didn't, just nodded curtly and left the ship.

April longed to leave the ship herself, to find a bathhouse and make a day of cleaning up, but if she wasn't working anymore, then what money they had left was going to have to last. She took a quick shower instead, but just being in clean clothes and putting a fresh braid in her clean hair made her feel immeasurably better. Salima and Boo returned just as she was putting on her shoes.

"Did he feed you?" Salima asked. April shook her head, and Salima jerked her head for April to follow her into the galley.

"I'm not working anymore," April said as Salima selected a container of miso soup with udon noodles and added hot water from the spigot. "At least not in the ghost business."

Salima nodded and set the soup in front of her with a spork. "We'll get by. We have before."

April ate her soup slowly under Salima's silently watchful gaze, then went back to her bunk, Boo once more curling up against her belly. It was strange that she was still so tired. Or maybe not. She wouldn't describe anything she had done in the hammock as proper, restful sleep.

April woke again when Boo suddenly jumped up and leapt off the bunk, using her belly as a springboard. Someone was coming through the airlock. April got out of the bunk to stand in her hatchway and watch the airlock open. It was Hakim and Lars both. Hakim bent to give the excited Boo pets but Lars headed straight for April, coming to stand so close to her she had to tip her head back to look up at him. She missed free fall, where the fact that she was a head shorter than everyone but Boo didn't really matter.

"Feeling better?" he asked.

"A little more human," she said.

"I have canceled our job here," he said.

"Thank you."

He glanced back at Hakim, still tussling with the puppy, then leaned even closer to her, squeezing her arm as he spoke into her ear. "Are you sure? We have other clients waiting for us on other stations. I will cancel every one of them if you say the word, but are you sure you won't change your mind? We don't have to be hasty or burn any bridges."

"I'm sure," April said.

"Then I'm sorry," Lars said. "I've enjoyed this."

"It's not honest work."

"I'm not talking about that," Lars said. "I've enjoyed working with you. Spending time with you building a business. Turning a vision into a reality. We did well with it. You can't deny that."

"We did well," April allowed. "And I liked working with you, too. That doesn't have to change. We just won't be doing this. I can't lie to people anymore. I wish you understood."

"I do," Lars said, straightening with a sigh and rubbing the back of his neck. "I do."

April watched him disappear into his own bunk. She didn't think he did understand. But he wanted to. That was something.

"April."

April blinked and realized she was alone with Hakim. Hakim, who had been avoiding her since her world fell apart. Hakim who hadn't even stirred himself to give her a hug when she was consumed with grief.

"Hakim," she said, as coldly as she could, then turned and went back into her bunk. She had left clothes strewn about when she had dressed earlier, and she stooped to pick things up and pile them on her bunk. A trip to the bathhouse might be a luxury, but a trip to the laundry was definitely not.

"April," he said again, this time from her hatchway. Boo was engrossed in something red that squeaked when he bit down on it; Hakim had given him a new toy. She fought the urge to smile at the dog's obvious joy. Looking up at Hakim was enough to quench that urge, but the pang of hurt she felt every time she remembered him just not being there wasn't something she wanted to show him either. She summoned her anger once more.

"What is it?" she demanded, gesturing with a kurta in one hand, an inside-out pair of jeans in the other, so he would see how busy she was.

"I have something to show you," he said. "I wanted to wait until I was sure, and now I'm close enough to be sure."

"What are you talking about?" she asked, with no need to feign exasperation.

"Here," he said, pushing her laundry to the back of the bunk to sit on the edge with his tablet on his lap.

April tried to summon more annoyance, but curiosity was winning out and she sat beside him, tossing the kurta to the back of the bunk but keeping the jeans in her hands, turning them right side out as she watched his fingers dance over the tablet.

"Look," he said, turning the tablet screen towards her. "I downloaded the shuttle logs. They are pretty Spartan and clearly not updated as often as they should be, but it gave me a place to start."

"A place to start what?" April asked.

"They weren't thorough enough on their own to share with you, not as you were," he said, turning the tablet back to her and tapping away at the screen as if he hadn't heard her at all. "But this station's name was in the last log entry, so when we arrived, I went to the dockmaster and downloaded his logs."

He found another screen of information and showed it to her.

"I don't understand," April said. "What are you showing me?"

"Look at the first one again," he said, summoning it back up. "Your mother was on that shuttle. Her name was added to the passenger list here, about a week ago."

April didn't know what to say. Was this meant to be comforting, to know she was right? Perhaps to someone like Hakim, coldly logical, this was a comfort: the comfort of certainty and facts. To April, it just felt like he had waited for her to feel human again before stabbing her all over again. She blinked tears from her eyes, focusing on the letters of her mother's name there on the screen.

"Wait, April," he said, bringing back the other screen. "See this? The shuttle docked here five days ago, just for an afternoon, but during that time, your mother disembarked. The shuttle didn't update its passenger list, but the dockworkers here recorded her as leaving the shuttle for the station proper."

"She's here?" April asked in barely more than a whisper, her tears flowing faster, as if the first few bitter tears had been necessary to prime her tear ducts.

"Not anymore, I don't think so," Hakim said. "I'm still working on it, but I wanted you to see this much first. April, I don't know what happened on that shuttle when you were over there alone, but I can tell you that it looks to me like your mother wasn't on board when it suffered its explosive decompression. She got off here and disappeared into the crowds, but with time, we can track her down."

"So what I saw wasn't my mother's ghost?"

"Did you see a ghost?"

April wiped at her tears, wishing they would stop, although she supposed she had several days' worth backed up and there was no shutting it down now that it was started. She glanced up at Hakim. He didn't sound accusatory or sarcastic or anything she would expect. He just sounded curious.

"I didn't see anything, no," she admitted, sniffling. He turned on the bunk to dig through her laundry, finding a relatively clean handkerchief to hand her. She put it to use, then took a deep breath. "I didn't see anything. I definitely felt something. It felt so real. Like she was there with me."

"She had been there not too long before," Hakim said. "She left the doll."

"I felt her there before I saw the doll," April said.

"Before you saw it consciously," he allowed. 'You might have glimpsed it out of the corner of your eye. Or maybe you didn't; maybe you smelled her perfume, maybe you were just thinking of her being back in that place where the two of you had spent so much time."

"I wasn't imagining things," April said.

"I didn't say you were," he said with so much kindness it almost started her tears going again. "I don't want to deny your experience. It was clearly something very meaningful for you. I'm just telling you, I don't think your mother was there when the accident happened. And now that you've quit your ghost work, we can take some time and follow up my leads. We can find your mother."

April took the tablet from him, looking more closely at the entries now that tears weren't blinding her. It was clear that the shuttle logs were barely maintained, but the station dock logs were meticulous. She scrolled through them, just appreciating the thorough bureaucracy of it all, then switched back to the shuttle logs.

"This is where you were," April said, touching her mother's name on the screen. "You went to get this."

"It seemed like the most useful thing to do," he said. "I didn't think you even noticed I was gone."

April felt her face crumpling again. He took the tablet out of her hands before she dropped it and put his arms around her, letting her cry into his shoulder.

"I noticed."

He held her until she was calm once more, exhausted and nearly slipping away to sleep, when a thought nagged her back to alertness.

"Where are we now?"

"The *Triomphe*," Hakim said. "That was where we were going next, remember?"

"But we're docked."

"I've been messaging Ivan EchoHawk in the Belt," Hakim said.

"For how long?" April asked, sitting up to look at him.

"Just since we left Mama Rosa's," Hakim said. "He arranged a space for us on one of his personal dry docks; we can stay here as long as we like. He also offered us the hospitality of his home if we wanted it."

"My mother was here," April said. "She might have gone there."

"I agree. That's where we should start."

"Let's go, now. I need to get started on this. I need to be doing something."

"That I understand," Hakim said.

21

THE HUNT BEGINS

APRIL WALKED THROUGH ALL THE ROOMS OF IVAN'S APARTMENT, BUT THERE were no clues. She wasn't sure what she had expected—a note under a fridge magnet, a travel itinerary left on the nightstand? The only sign the two of them had ever been there was the H. G. Wells book in the room she had slept in for one night. She had tucked it under the pillow after leafing through the pages that night and it had been missed when Hakim and Ivan had packed up her things the next morning. Now it sat waiting for her on the little reading table between two cozy chairs she had never so much as sat in. She ran a hand over the leather cover but left it where it was. If she had taken it with her, she would have just sold it when the money ran out, not getting a fraction of its actual value. It was safer where it was. She didn't deserve such a thing; she wasn't capable of taking care of it.

She walked back out to the common room, Boo close at her heels. Hakim waited there with the assistant who had let them in.

"Mr. EchoHawk is already underway on his return trip," she told April.

"Did he finish his work?" April asked.

"Near enough. He brought a replacement for the manager with him, one of his higher-ups here, and she can take over for him at any point," she said. "He's anxious to be back here to help you find your mother, I know that. Will you stay until he gets here?"

"I don't think so," April said. "That's weeks away, isn't it?"

"I'm afraid so. But all of us are at your disposal. We have been doing all we can since she disappeared."

"Weeks ago," April said bitterly. Hakim and the others kept telling her that Ivan had kept that secret because he was hoping he could find her before April noticed she was missing. With all the traveling they had been doing lately, never spending more than a day or two on one station, April had chalked up the lack of messages from her mother to them not being able to catch up with her. But she should have noticed how long it had been. She should have been worried. Instead, she had been caught up with her new business, with earning money she felt good about.

The assistant's watch chimed, and she glanced at its face. "Message arrived. Would you like to view it here?"

April looked around, then followed the direction the assistant's arms were sweeping. The wall on the far side of the conversation nook had the faintest of rectangular outlines traced on it. When April nodded, the rectangle came to life, filled with the paused image of Ivan's face. A distressed murmur escaped from April's lips; he looked so distraught, thin and disheveled and with despairing eyes. Hakim sat on the arm of one of the chairs, but April stayed on her feet, arms wrapped tightly around herself as the message began to play.

"April, I'm so sorry," he said, and April dropped her gaze, not able to look into those eyes for a minute longer. "I promised you I would take care of your mother. I failed you. I just never thought she would do this. I still don't understand why." His voice cracked and April hugged herself tighter. She was nearly in tears again herself, but he took a deeper breath and spoke again, more calmly. "I've been talking with Hakim about what you found. I have investigators searching for her all over the solar system, but this really refines their search. That's a good thing. I still hope that she's trying to find you. If she just left the *Triomphe* and now you've arrived... you barely missed each other. I'm hoping you will stay there and wait for me. Wait for your mother. I'm sure she will be back. She'll learn that you are there and return. The others can follow up every lead and anything else you can think of that they might try, just say the word. Just please, sit tight and wait for me to come to you. I await your response."

The message flickered and faded back into the even taupe of the wall. April stayed where she was, hugging herself and looking at a random spot on the floor. She heard Hakim behind her, the rustle of his cargo pants as he turned on the arm of the chair.

"Can we have a minute?" he asked the assistant.

"Certainly," the assistant said. "I'll be just outside that door when you need me. Or you can send the message yourself. The controls are just here."

"Thank you," Hakim said. The assistant's footfalls were muffled by the thickly carpeted floor. Then the door clicked discreetly shut, and they were alone with Boo.

"April?"

April took a breath and turned around but didn't drop her arms. "What do you think? Do you think I should just wait here?" Then more softly, as if just to herself. "Perhaps I should. Perhaps that's best. No more ghost hunting, no more waiting for word from the *Chandrasekhar*. Just waiting here for my mother and Ivan to come back."

Hakim moved closer to her but still stayed perched on the arm of the easy chair. "Is that really what you want?"

"When has doing what I want ever worked out?" April sighed.

"Do you think waiting here is the best way to find your mother?"

April bit her lip, the tears pricking at her eyes again, but she blinked hard, driving them back. "No," she said at last. "I don't know. It depends."

"On what really happened in the Belt," Hakim guessed.

"I don't think Ivan is lying," April said. "But my mother has her own version of those events, and I'm sure they're very different. But I don't know. I'm trying to remember how she seemed, the last few messages I got from her. But they were all so short. How can I gauge what the meds were doing to her from that?"

"We can play them again. Salima keeps all communications on a dedicated hard drive."

"I have copies saved to my reader too," April said, brushing a hand over the hard rectangle pressed as always against her stomach. "I'll watch them in a bit; I'm not ready yet."

"OK," Hakim said.

"You think we can find her? On our own?"

"Yes," Hakim said. "But that doesn't even matter. Even if we leave here, Ivan is going to keep looking. And the investigators he's hired, they're going to keep looking. She's going to be found."

"Sooner or later," April agreed.

"And you know, April," he said, copying her own arms-crossed, looking-at-the-floor posture. "If you decide to stay here, I'll still look for her. Everywhere Salima and I go. And I'll message you anything I find out. If you want to stay here and wait for your mother, I understand."

"Oh," April said, caught off guard. She had been assuming that if she decided to stay, they'd all stay with her. But of course that would be ridiculous. She knew Ivan wouldn't mind, and he certainly had room enough for all of them, but they had lives to get on with.

Hakim was looking at her again, waiting for her decision. She felt a tugging at her shoe and looked down at Boo, who had succeeded in untying one of her once-white canvas sneakers and was busy tangling himself up in the lace.

"There's something else?" Hakim guessed.

"I don't know," April said. "I wish I could talk to my mom."

"That would make a lot of this easier," Hakim said with a soft smile.

"I don't think Ivan did a thing wrong," April said again. "But for whatever reason, my mother left, not to get back to me, but to get away from him. Or maybe just away from the Belt. She always hated it there, but I'm afraid it might be him. And if it is, waiting here for her just isn't going to work."

Hakim caught one of her hands and pulled her closer to where he sat on the arm of the chair. "No one knows your mother better than you. Even if it's just a hunch, I think that should be the plan. But we'll be vocal about our comings and goings. We'll make sure every dockworker knows. If she's trying to find you, we'll make it very easy to do so. And we'll stay in contact with Ivan and his investigators. We're going to find her. And then she can explain it all to us."

April looked down at her hand in his, his thumb running over her knuckles. She stepped closer, reaching out a hand to touch his hair, when Boo came barreling out of nowhere to tackle her still-loose shoelace, colliding with her leg hard enough to buckle her knee.

"Ow, Boo!" she protested, untangling herself from where she'd collapsed on Hakim, and stepped back. "Too much time in free fall. I don't have the reflexes for your shenanigans."

Boo looked contrite for about half a second, then found the shoelace lurking under his own paw and pounced. April shooed him away and sat down on the couch to firmly tie her shoe.

"So," Hakim said.

"So," April repeated. They had almost had a moment, a moment where all worries about her mother had fled her mind, but it was gone now. The worries were back in full force, but she knew how to combat those. "What's the plan?"

"First, we have to talk to the others," Hakim said. "I have a list of places to search, but they likely won't coincide with Salima's transport opportunities. Some might, but it won't be like how you and Lars worked around her schedule. It's going to have to be the other way around."

"And we can't just commandeer Salima's ship," April said, nodding. "But what if she says no? How are we going to get around? I don't think Ivan will loan us one since I'm leaving when he asked me to stay."

"She'll say yes," Hakim said.

"What about Lars?" April said, mostly to herself. She imagined what was running through Hakim's head—they didn't need Lars to execute their search plans, and had they ever really needed him at all?—but he didn't say a word, just looked over the list displayed on his tablet. "Well, I guess I tell him what's going on and he can decide."

The two with Boo made their way back up to the dry docks. Boo loved the half-gravity, bounding ahead of them with his leash trailing loose behind him, April not having the heart to confine him when he wanted to run. Salima was working on something on the outside of her ship, making the most of the rare dry-docking opportunity to tweak something.

"Is Lars here?" April asked.

"Yes," Lars said, appearing in the airlock doorway. "What's up?"

"My mother isn't dead," April said.

"That's good news," he said.

"Kind of. She's missing. Ivan is looking for her now, but I think maybe she doesn't want to be found by him."

"Why?"

"It's just a hunch," April said. "I don't think he did anything, but sometimes my mother... well. She might think she needs to be away from him. I want to be clear. All of this is based on a gut feeling I have. Nothing concrete. And it's clearly my personal business, looking for my own mother who's probably perfectly fine, just not with Ivan."

"I don't follow," Lars said with a frown.

"We're going to go find her," Hakim said. "Ivan has people looking for her, but April and I think we'd likely find her first, especially if she's hiding from Ivan. I have some leads. Salima..."

"I fly wherever you need me to go," Salima said before he could even ask.

"It might make you miss some transport jobs," April said.

"We have some money saved up. It'll be enough," she said, turning her attention back to her tweaking.

April shot Hakim a questioning glance, but he just shrugged. His sister did what she did for her own reasons, and a yes was a yes, even if it seemed like she was only half listening to the request.

"Lars," April said, turning her attention back to him. He was staring at the two of them, or rather at their hands. They were standing nearly half a meter apart, their hands nowhere close to touching, but it looked like he had to tear his gaze away from them to look at her when she spoke. As if they had gotten their DNA all over each other earlier and Lars could see it. April folded her arms. That felt like too aggressive a pose, but to change position again would just highlight her nervousness, so she held it. "You don't have to go with us," she said at last.

"You don't want me to come with you?"

"That's not what I said. I just mean, who knows where this quest is going to take us, or for how long, and I don't want to tie you up if you have other things you want to do. I know Ivan will let you stay; he has plenty of room," she finished lamely.

"Why would I want to stay?"

April clenched her hands on her arms to keep from squirming, looked over at Hakim for help, and realized that was probably a mistake. "I don't know."

"We've been wandering about since we left the *Chandrasekhar*. This is no different. I understand you don't want to do the ghost thing anymore. If this is the new thing we're doing, I totally want to be a part of it."

"OK then," April said.

"I'll be about an hour," Salima said, looking over the disassembled parts spread around her.

"I'll stock up on supplies," Lars said, grabbing their pooled savings in its imitation leather pouch and stepping between Hakim and April to head for the elevators.

"That went well?" April said, and the corner of Hakim's mouth twitched in a near smile.

April found Boo and brought him back inside the ship. Their sleep pod was set to the left of the hub, and she set Boo inside. Hakim's pod hatch was in the middle of what was currently the hub's floor, currently open. She sat cross-legged at the edge and looked down into his space, expecting to find him with his tablet and stylus lost to the world. Instead, he was organizing the dead tree books she had given him, lining them up in the niche in the wall, the bungee that kept them secure in free fall hanging loosely in the half-gravity.

"How is the math going?" she asked and immediately wanted to rephrase. He was going to answer with a slew of words that were technically English but that were completely meaningless to her. But if she had asked how he felt about how his math was going, which was what she really wanted to know, he would have just rolled his eyes.

"I'm currently taking a break," he said.

"A break?" Hadn't he said math was life? How did one take a break from life?

"Yeah." He glanced up at her hovering over him and seemed to find it disconcerting. April dangled her legs inside his pod, then dropped down to land neatly on his bunk.

"Why?"

Hakim didn't answer, apparently engrossed in the spine of one of the books. April thought back over the past few days.

"I've been kind of out of it," she said. "You were working on something up until Mama Rosa's. What happened?"

Now he did look at her, with such blatant exasperation she nearly flinched back.

"Me and my mom?" she said incredulously.

"Well, obviously not directly," he said, still sounding annoyed, although he was back to arranging his books.

"Even indirectly, I don't get it. Did I ruin your concentration or something?"

"No," he said. "It just all at once felt really meaningless." He looked down at the book in his hand. "Do you think math is a solitary activity?"

"Isn't it?"

"No," he said. "That's why all these mathematicians wrote these books. To share what they learned with other mathematicians. The ones too far away to talk to and work with directly." He put the book on the shelf next to the others and locked the bungee into place, then sat next to her on his bunk. "I have no idea if my work is as new and exciting as it feels to me, or if I'm just rehashing someone else's work, or if I'm on a wrong track entirely. And I have no way of knowing. April, I don't think there are any other mathematicians out there. Or if there are, I don't know where to start looking for them. And I'm not sure if I can keep doing this alone. It feels meaningless."

"But I thought you enjoyed doing it," April said. "Like running marathons with your brain or something. The effort was the point."

"I did. But once I started thinking about how it could all be wrong, or even if it's right, no one else would ever see it and build from it..." He turned his hands palms up.

"I'm sorry you feel that way," April said, still not sure how all this had been triggered by her. "It's a huge part of yourself to give up. I hope you change your mind."

"I don't see our circumstances changing. We're better off now than we were just a few weeks ago, but we're still not on Earth or on a corporate station. And I don't know where else to find someone in a position to be able to devote their lives to mathematics. The rest of us are just out here, scrambling to stay alive. I'm blessed to have the sister I have, who can take care of the two of us so well that I have nothing but time for math. But we're still nearly always one minor accident away from a fast death. Or worse. Salima protects us from cosmic radiation, but I know we've been in places without adequate shielding, even if just briefly. We've been exposed; that's a roll of the dice."

"I was in the shuttle village for months when I was a kid," April said. "I'm OK."

"You seem OK now," Hakim said. "I don't want to be morbid, but you might have the first stages of the cancer that is going to kill you one day already growing inside you. So might I. So might any of us. So why do math?"

"Because," April said, "math is life."

"Not only math," Hakim said. "I think there's maybe something more."

April wound an arm around his and rested her head on his shoulder. "Yes, but I'm sure math belongs in your life. And when your break is done, you'll think so too." He stiffened for a moment, but then relaxed, his cheek on the top of her head. "This just came up after Mama Rosa's?" she asked.

"That was the flash of insight after a long mental struggle," Hakim said.

"Oh," April said, remembering how difficult it had been trying to talk to him the weeks before. "I thought you were mad at me."

"How could I be mad at you?" he asked.

"The ghost business," she said.

"Well. It's not what I would have liked best for you, but I wasn't mad at you."

"If you don't do math, what will you do?" she asked.

"I don't know," he admitted. "For now, let's just focus on finding your mother. No ghosts, no math, just find your mother."

April couldn't argue with that.

22

THE HUNT ENDS

April held the last corner of her sandwich on the palm of her hand and offered it to Boo, who took it with more relish than she had managed to muster for the first bite. Hakim raised an eyebrow but said nothing. It wasn't a waste; Boo was hungry, too. She only hoped that everyone considered him too much a part of their family now to discuss leaving him behind again, now that the money had run out.

"Not a single lead, then?" Lars asked when the last crumb was found and licked off the wrapper, all of them still just a little bit hungry.

"I don't think she was ever here," Hakim said. "I'm sorry I dragged us all out here, halfway to nowhere, chasing a bad trail."

"It seemed plausible," April said. "She might have been trying to get back to the Belt if she thought Ivan was still there."

"If she was looking for Ivan, she would only have to message him, talk to any of his endless employees," Lars said.

"We don't know her state of mind," Hakim said. April felt like putting her hands over her ears to shut out the latest iteration of the same old arguments. Boo nuzzled her palm in search of more treats, then curled up in her lap, resting his head on her leg with a pronounced sigh.

"We have to get back to civilization," Lars said. "April, I'm not saying we're giving up on the search, but we need to get some transport jobs, save up some money—"

"I know," April said. "I'm sorry we came out all this way for nothing."

"Knowing she isn't here is still information," Salima said. "I've been offered a small cargo to take back to the *Triomphe*. Not much, but it pays in advance, and it will be enough for the fuel to get back there, plus a bit extra for food if we're frugal."

"Very, very frugal," Lars said, looking at the tablet she'd handed him. "But doable."

"Let's do it," April said. "We've wasted enough time out here already."

Lars and Salima headed out to meet the client and secure the cargo. April gathered up the food wrappers and put them in the recycler, then went back to the aft pod to go through her bag one last time.

"There's nothing left to sell," Hakim said, watching her sort through her small pile of clothing.

"There's always my reader," she said.

"Never," he said.

"You're only saying that because your reader would be next," she said with a smile she wasn't quite feeling. "We could share just one, I suppose."

"Take turns?"

"I was thinking I'd just read over your shoulder." April looked at her remaining belongings. All her jewelry was gone, even the cheap plastic stuff. She was down to two changes of clothes, a single pair of shoes that had seen better days, and her mother's doll. She looked at the purple figure in her hand. Even if she could part with it, it wouldn't buy enough to fill even Boo's little belly. Realizing Hakim was right, she repacked her carpetbag. "We've lost everything on this pointless quest. All of your beautiful books, gone. I'm—"

"Don't you say you're sorry again," Hakim said sternly. "You think this is all on you because it's your mother we're looking for, but we all agreed every step of the way. Every bit of the ship we've sold, every personal item exchanged for food. You don't owe anyone an apology."

"We have to get back to the *Triomphe*," April said. "There will be work there. Ivan can find something for all of us."

"You want to give up the search?"

April zipped her bag shut and bungeed it to the wall of the pod. "We don't have a clue where to go next, do we? We'd just be randomly searching. We might as well randomly search wherever Salima is transporting goods. If something comes up..." She bit her lip. It just didn't feel like anything would be coming up. Her mother might as well be a ghost for as much trace of her as April and Hakim had been able to find. Always stories of a glimpse, a brief passing through with no discernible purpose. None of it added up to even a clue what her mother was up to, let alone a path to finding her.

Lars and Salima returned with the cargo, a dozen small crates that, once stowed, just highlighted the emptiness of the rest of the cargo pod.

"At least there will be room in here for some of us to sleep," Lars said.

"Especially the freakishly large amongst us," Hakim added.

"That would be the two of you," April said, looking at the small crate of food Salima had brought into the kitchenette in the fore pod. She opened the lid and looked at the contents: freeze-dried packs of algae soup. The labels announced a variety of flavors, but April knew from experience that there was no detectable difference between "rich roasted chicken flavor" and "hearty beef flavor." Boo peered over the rim of the crate and sniffed, then looked up at her with big sad eyes. "Maybe I should do a ghost job. There must be one somewhere on a station this size."

"I could look," Lars started to say, but Hakim cut him off.

"No. We're not so desperate as all that." He ignored Lars's annoyed look. "Are we?"

"No," April said, not quite adding, "not yet." Even knowing her mother had never been dead when she had experienced that feeling of presence on the shuttle, she still felt that a game of pretend was no true comfort. She stowed the soup packets and double-checked their water supply.

Salima might not have had Hakim's flair with theoretical math, but she could calculate their fuel-versus-food needs instinctively and fire the rocket for whatever rate would make their food stores match their velocity. Food was still cheaper than fuel, especially in the form of algae-based anything, and so the journey back to the *Triomphe* was slower than the trip out; they were conserving fuel, but it made for long, boring days of being piled up on top of each other in the once-again-reduced size of Salima's ship. Salima was usually left to herself in the fore pod, tinkering with whatever she was working on. April and Boo spent hours in the nearly empty cargo pod, literally bouncing off the walls in her attempt to keep Boo strong despite the lack of treadmill. Lars would often join them, but Hakim stayed in the aft pod where they all slept, poring over his tablet. She had seen him looking over his saved files, endless scrolls of numbers and symbols in his own precise script. She didn't ask him about it, afraid that, like popping a soap bubble, she would destroy whatever he was up to by trying to touch it. All of his styluses were gone now, but she watched for the moment he would reach for something and start writing again. So far he was only reading and, she presumed, thinking, but she took to wearing a hair stick or two when she wrapped up her braid, just in case he needed something pointy close to hand.

It was late in the evening on the second day out from the *Haru*, April just thinking about mooring her sleeping bag and crawling inside with Boo, when something banged so suddenly her yelp of alarm almost seemed to come first. She caught a handhold, expecting the ship to lurch or spin, but it remained still. Hakim looked up from his tablet, eyes wide. Then Lars boiled up from the cargo pod and slammed the hatch shut behind him, spinning the wheel to seal it shut.

"Boo!" April cried, afraid he was on the other side of that door.

"He's here," Hakim said, giving the dog's rump a little nudge to send him into April's waiting arms. "What was that?"

"There's a sizeable hole in the side of the cargo pod," Lars said. "It just... appeared."

A crash in the fore pod made them all jump.

"Salima?" Hakim called, leaving his reader spinning in the air as he pulled himself into the other pod.

"Hull breach," Salima said grimly, digging a hand through the spinning collection of tools she had upended from their box until she found the torch. She already had a small square of metal pressed to the hull between the recycler and the water tank, the vacuum beyond holding the patch tightly in place, but she still welded it neatly down.

"What happened?" April asked. "Did something in the engine blow?"

"No," Salima said. "The engine is fine." She pulled herself back to the front of the pod and examined her screens.

"Something hit us," Lars said. "It was weird. I was floating in there, half asleep, and it was like the panel in front of my eyes just popped. I didn't even see what hit us. It must have been tiny."

"The cargo," April said.

"It might be OK," Lars said. "The atmo in the cargo pod is gone, but I think the pod will hold together."

"Unless something else hits us," April said, hugging Boo tightly. "Are we in a debris field?"

"Two hits at once," Hakim said, looking around.

"We're still losing atmo," Salima said.

"Another breach?" Hakim asked.

Salima shook her head. "I'll make another pass on my patch," she said. "But it might be the seal around the cargo pod."

Lars examined the hatch closely, holding his palm around the edges to feel for any movement of air, but in the end, he just shook his head.

Salima finished her second weld and went back to her screens. "Still losing air," she said with a frown.

"How long do we have?" April asked.

"It's a slow leak," Salima said. "But we're not making it back to the *Triomphe* in this state."

April buried her nose in Boo's fur. Her mind kept imagining other, larger pieces of whatever had hit them coming their way. Bits of asteroid, probably. What had hit them already had been too small to see. What if the next was the size of a pebble, or more?

"We're unlikely to be hit again," Salima said, as if reading her mind. "I think what pierced the kitchen broke off of whatever hit the cargo. Didn't you hear? It wasn't at the same time. It was one-two."

April hadn't heard, but she trusted Salima. "What do we do now?"

"Find a closer station," Salima said, already scrolling through screens.

"But we're so far out. What could possibly be out this way?"

"Chapelier," Lars said suddenly.

"*Chapelier* station?" Salima repeated doubtfully.

"Not a station, a man," Lars said. "On the *Asteroidi*, remember? We're much closer to it now than to the *Triomphe* or even the *Haru*. He was the exorcist that wanted to hire you as his apprentice, but you turned it down—"

"—because it was so remote," April said, remembering.

"And also you were your own boss," Lars added. "Let me find his messages. We can head that way now."

"How big is the station he's on?" Salima asked.

"I don't fancy getting stranded on another end-of-the-line station waiting for parts that might never reach us," Hakim said.

"At least we know I'll have work there," April said. "We won't go hungry. We'll need money for repairs and fuel, and to replace the cargo if we lost it."

"Here," Lars said, finding the messages on his tablet and pulling himself to hover over Salima's shoulder as she found the station and plotted a course.

"I'm worried too," April said to Hakim. "I don't want this to be another extended stay. I don't want to get trapped with this Chapelier fellow."

"You didn't want to do this work anymore," Hakim reminded her.

"I'll do whatever needs to be done to get the ship up and running back to the *Triomphe* again. If there's other work there, we can do it. I don't know anything about this place we're going to except this Mr. Chapelier says there are demons there."

"Demons," Hakim repeated. "Not ghosts?"

"They're inside the children," April said, hugging Boo again. "There were lots of reasons I avoided this job even when I was doing this sort of work. On the other hand, what is really wrong with these children? Maybe we can still do some good."

Hakim smiled and scratched Boo between his ears. "That's so you."

"What's me?"

"Taking a near-death experience and finding a way to use it to help others."

April smiled back, trying not to think about how they could still lose the "near" from that experience before reaching Mr. Chapelier. There were so many ways to die in space, and no one would ever know what had become of them.

23

———————

THE NICHE

April slept little during the journey to the *Asteroidi*, her ears always straining as if she could hear something approaching before it punched through their hull like a cannonball. She tried to do some research into demons and demonology on her reader, and while her encyclopedia had extensive articles and a labyrinth of links to related articles, she couldn't focus on any of it. Lars went through what material he had gathered when the messages had first come in, about Mr. Chapelier and the station *Asteroidi*, but he seemed as distracted as she. Even Salima took to staring at the open back of the machine she was working on, twirling tools in her fingers without quite doing anything with them.

Hakim, by contrast, was consumed once more in math. April had given him one of her hair sticks, and when the anxiety built up to scream-out-loud levels she would watch the tip of that hair stick dance across the tablet screen, the finger of Hakim's other hand occasionally scrolling up to get to more empty space with a little flick, and the familiarity of it comforted her.

Finally, after one last sleepless night shift, they approached their goal. "We're five minutes out," Salima said. "No one is responding to my pings; I hope they've left the door open."

"I wonder how many people are living there," April said. She tried to catch a glimpse of the asteroid through the window, but her breath fogged the glass. Boo, asleep in her arms, made a little complaining sound at her movement disturbing his nap.

"Potentially thousands," Lars said. "I downloaded the specs to my tablet when we got the first message from Mr. Chapelier, but they're incomplete. I don't think its construction was complete before the plague and exodus happened. The *Asteroidi* was designed to turn an asteroid into a spaceship that would go further out to the asteroid belt to exploit more asteroids. It would be a rotating cylinder large enough to support some agriculture. It could be a nice self-contained community, or it could be a half-built shell full of squatters."

"No one on the comm suggests the latter. But the cylinder looks complete," Salima said as she fired a short burst of directional rocket. "It's spinning. I'll fly us down the center. There must be some sort of dock."

April looked out the window, this time holding her breath. At first, she saw nothing but stars; then the station was all around them, slowly rotating. She could see green fields, trees, clusters of houses, even a glistening body of water.

"It's gorgeous," she said. Boo lifted his head to look. "Like a little piece of Earth."

"Look, lights are on," Lars said from over her shoulder. "They have the power on. Why not the comms?"

"I found the dock," Salima said, firing the directional rockets again. "The door is closed."

"Do we just wait until someone responds?" April asked.

"We can't," Salima said. "We need to get out of this ship."

April shuddered and decided she didn't want to know why. Something that Salima had been keeping an eye on but not warning them about; she didn't need to have retroactive nightmares about it. "If only I had my suit," she said.

"I still have waldos," Salima said, grabbing the controls and bringing the robotic arms to life.

"They should know we're coming," April said. "I sent my response days ago. This was a really bad idea, wasn't it?"

"It's going to be fine," Hakim said, shutting his tablet off with a click and tucking April's hair stick into his own hair. "We can see it's livable from here. We just need to get inside."

"It's so big," April said. She could see dark space at the very center of her view through the door, but everything else was green and blue.

"The *Triomphe* is more than twenty times bigger," Lars pointed out.

"Yes, but I never saw it from this angle. It's like the Earth is orbiting around us instead of the other way around."

"Door's open," Salima said. "Hold on, I'm firing."

April clutched Boo in one hand, holding on to part of the ship with the other. She twisted around to look over Salima's shoulder as she piloted them into what looked like an open skylight in the roof of an immense skyscraper. The space within was clearly a dock, but there were no other ships. Salima guided them to the top of a transport elevator.

"We're not exactly compatible with this elevator," Hakim said. "It's designed to secure around landing gear, which we don't have."

"The magnetic harpoon will do," Salima said. She let go of the waldo controls and pulled a trigger set into the hull beneath her floating folded legs. For a moment, they stayed where they were; then, with a jerk, the harpoon tether snapped tight, and they were pulled along with the elevator. Gravity slowly increased as they were pulled out to the edge of the rotating cylinder. The ship settled onto the elevator floor, then, having nothing to rest on, tipped to one side. Then the elevator stopped. April set Boo, suddenly heavy in her arms, down and made her way to the door as Salima shut down all her equipment.

"Is there air?" April asked Lars, who was looking out the window in the hatch that no longer led to an airlock.

"I think so," he said, pointing up. Instead of a long shaft going up into space, there was a closed hatch above them. "The elevator functions as an airlock."

"Yes, there's air," Salima called back to them.

"Air, comfortable temperature, lights," Hakim said. "Somebody must be home. Let's go find them."

"I'm going to stay with the ship," Salima said. "Get started on the repairs."

"Stay near the comm in case we need you," Hakim said, and she nodded, then walked around to the front of the ship to inspect something. April carried Boo out the door and set him on the ground. He smelled the air nervously, pressing close to her calf.

"I can see people," Lars said suddenly.

Hakim and April went to where he was standing at a window on the far side of the room. The elevator had not taken them all the way down; they were still about fifty meters above the ground and could see clear to the end of the cylinder. Sunlight directed into the space by reflectors lit up everything like daylight on Earth. A paved trail ran from nearly directly below them around the edge of the lake to the village on the far side. People were indeed moving about, between the houses, along the edge of the lake. Not many, but more than a few.

"That big house on the far side of the village," Hakim pointed. "The one on the little bit of a hill. That must be Mr. Chapelier's place. Ready to meet your future instructor in all things nonsensical?"

"I want to change first," April said. "I don't want to meet him dressed like this."

She expected Hakim to scoff, but instead, he just nodded. "Lars and I will wait out here," he said. "I'll keep Boo out of trouble."

April smiled her thanks, then went inside the ship. It suddenly felt more cramped than ever on the inside, even though she was alone and not floating about with three other people and a dog. Funny what just a bare minute in an open space would do. April dug through her bag, finding the last of her scented wipes to take some of the edge off her stink. Five days in the same clothes built up a funk even when it was too cold to sweat. The outfit she put together could not be as flashy as her usual working clothes; all of that was gone now. But presumably this Mr. Chapelier was already certain of her skills; if so, he would likely not be impressed by such shallow gestures as appearing otherworldly. Instead, she wanted to give a sense of competence and reliability. She pulled out the plain white kameez she had worn the first time she'd played Reversi with Hakim, then a shalwar of a deep navy blue. She didn't have any nice shoes anymore, only functional canvas Mary Janes that weren't as white as they used to be, but hopefully, he wouldn't be looking at her feet. She brushed out and rebraided her hair, leaving the braid loose down her back; it was so nice to be in gravity again. She regretted the loss of her bell earrings, the pair that tinkled so softly only she could hear them. Bells dispelled demons and bad spirits in lots of cultures, and Mr. Chapelier would no doubt appreciate the little authentic touch, but alas, they had been exchanged for mystery meat jerky weeks ago.

April carefully climbed down from the tilted ship and found Lars and Hakim watching Boo sniff around a pile of discarded ship components.

"Ready?" Hakim asked.

"Yes," April said, twisting her hands together nervously. Lars was trying not to stare at her. That was a good sign. "Boo, come on."

Lars and Hakim had already found the elevator, and they rode down to the ground floor, then exited into an empty reception area. It was built to hold crowds of milling people, making them feel like ants as they crossed it.

"So many people could live here," April said. "Why doesn't anybody know about it?"

"We will definitely be finding out the answer to that question," Lars said. "With every other station, ship, and port in the solar system so overcrowded, this just feels wrong."

"I don't think they're actively keeping people out. It was easy for us to get in," April said.

They went out one of many pairs of glass doors and down five wide, shallow steps to the path. April stopped to kneel down and touch the grass, and Hakim and Lars immediately did the same. Boo ran across the green carpet, turned and sprinted back to them, then ran out again, this time stopping to pee.

"Everything around us is alive—isn't it amazing?" she said with a wide grin.

"It's growing everywhere, and it's not even for eating," Lars said.

Boo gave a sharp bark, and they stood back up. A young boy was standing in the middle of the path, watching them. He had the rosiest cheeks April had ever seen.

"Hello," she said. The boy just blinked. "English? Français?"

The boy rubbed at his eye with a mottled pink hand but said nothing.

"He doesn't look well," Lars whispered.

"Hello," the boy said at last, as if it had taken a great deal of thought to come up with that response.

"Hello," April said again, walking up to him with her brightest smile. "My name is April Nguyen. I'm here to see Eldon Bell Chapelier. I'm going to be working with him."

"Mr. Chapelier," the boy said with a little nod.

"Do you know where I can find him?" she asked.

He nodded again, then waved for them to follow him.

"What's your name?" April asked as she fell into step beside him.

"Charley," the boy said. "You came from outside the station?"

"Yes," she said. "Do you not get a lot of visitors?"

"No one since Mr. Chapelier came when I was a baby," Charley said. "But he told my dad he was going to find someone who could help us. That must be you."

"I hope so," she said. "Do you know what I'm here to help with?"

Charley stopped walking to give her a hard look, like he was trying to decide how trustworthy she was. She waited patiently, still smiling, but not too much. She didn't want him to feel like she was conning him.

"You know there are demons, right?" he said, his voice low.

"That's what Mr. Chapelier told me," she said. "But are there really?"

"Yes," Charley said, his young face suddenly so weary. "They attack all of us, but some of us more than others." He looked down at his own feet in tattered canvas shoes, and April suspected he was in the "more" category.

"What's it like?" she asked, but he shook his head, eyes still on his feet. "It's OK, Charley, you don't have to tell me. I'm sure Mr. Chapelier will explain it all to me."

"You've beat demons before?" he asked, risking a little glance up at her.

"Not demons. Ghosts, though," she said. She expected Hakim to interrupt with some comment or even just to scoff, but he was as silent as Lars. She shot him a look of thanks and he lifted his chin in acknowledgment.

"I've never seen a ghost," Charley said.

"I've never seen a demon," April said.

"Me neither," the boy admitted. "It's not something you see. It's something inside you, inside your mind." He dropped his gaze again. "I don't like it."

"I don't blame you, it sounds deeply unpleasant," April said. "Shall we continue our walk to Mr. Chapelier?"

Charley nodded and led the way, this time threading his hand into hers. It felt so tiny, the bones delicate like a bird's, like she daren't squeeze it too tightly.

"How many people live here, Charley?" Lars asked as the path brought them to the far shore of the lake, where it lost itself among an orchard of trees.

"I don't know. Lots," Charley said.

"Do you have a school here?" Hakim asked.

"Yes," Charley said defensively. "I can count. I've just never counted the people."

"I bet you could if you thought about it," Hakim countered. April worried that it would come off like an attack, but Charley decided to rise to the challenge.

"You mean, like, put them in groups? Most houses have six or eight people living in them. The houses are in four quadrants around the central square. There are... twenty-four houses per quadrant. So..." He clucked his tongue against his teeth. "Somewhere between 576 to 768 people, plus Mr. Chapelier."

"Nice mathing," Hakim said.

"Like I said, lots," Charley said.

Clearly, Charley had never been on any other space station or had any idea what constituted "lots of people" everywhere else in the solar system.

The path emerged from the orchard to rows of houses, each with a walled garden around it, tree-lined alleys running between the walls to interconnect everything. April tried to imagine what it would be like to grow up here, to think so few people in so much space could be considered "lots." Most places she'd been as a kid had six or eight people fighting over a square meter or so of space in a hallway or crawlspace because everything else was already overflowing with occupants.

"We're being watched," Hakim said. "But no one is coming out."

"Everybody!" Charley yelled. "We have guests! People from outside the station!"

"I think I should meet Mr. Chapelier first..." April said as people began to emerge around them, gathering in the tree-studded central square of the village. At the very center was a massive fountain, no longer running. Everyone summoned by Charley's words was gathering there, clustered in family groups, holding their children close as they watched the three strangers approach. No one spoke, just stared at them with wary eyes. All the children had flushed cheeks, and many had blotchy red skin on their hands. Even some of the adults had it. The eerie quiet of the crowd was making even Boo nervous; he pressed close to April's calf.

"They're here to see Mr. Chapelier," Charley announced. "I'm taking them there now. She's going to help Mr. Chapelier fight the demons."

April felt eyes on her, weighing her, judging her ability to fight the invisible. She stood straighter and tried to look up to the task.

Charley took her hand again and led her on down the path, past the silent crowd. Somewhere behind one of the garden walls she could hear someone, perhaps a child, babbling incoherently, a string of words that rolled from whisper to roar back down to whisper. The fact that no one in the village found this worth reacting to made a chill run down her spine.

"Charley, what's wrong with everyone here?" April asked.

"Wrong? The demons," Charley said as if that were obvious. She looked back over her shoulder at Hakim and Lars.

"They seem well fed," Lars said. "But they are reacting to something. All the rashes."

"Maybe the plants," Hakim said.

"That's my thinking too. It's the one unusual thing here. But people lived with plants all the time back on Earth. Was this sort of reaction common?"

"Research," Hakim said. "Always start with research."

"There might be sanitation issues we want to look into," Lars said, taking his tablet out of his pants pocket and tapping away. "The plant thing, too. Maybe look around that main building more. There might be a working computer with complete specs for the station there. Someone here might be original crew, but I doubt it. They looked old, but..."

"But prematurely old," April said, and he nodded. "Is their behavior strange because they've been shut off from the rest of the solar system here since, I'm guessing, the plague and exodus, or is something else going on?" April wondered.

"You think we're strange?" Charley asked.

"You seem very friendly, Charley," April said, squeezing his hand ever so lightly. "But no one else said a word. Isn't that strange?"

"We talk to each other all the time," Charley said.

"But no one spoke just now, to us."

"They just want Mr. Chapelier to talk to you first," Charley said. "We knew you were coming, he told us."

"It didn't feel like we were expected," April said. "We had to let ourselves in the dock."

"We don't go into that building anymore," Charley said. "Only Mr. Chapelier sometimes."

"Is it haunted?" April asked.

"Like with ghosts? I don't think so. There's just nothing to do in there. We farm the fields on the other side of those hills, and we fish from the lake, and when we make things, we're in the village. There's nothing worth bothering with in the tall building."

"I'm amazed you're all still alive," Hakim said. "Stations require maintenance, and none of you have been doing any of it? You're very lucky indeed."

"Maybe Mr. Chapelier does it," Charley said, but he didn't sound like he believed it. "You can ask him; this is his house."

24

MR. CHAPELIER

THE HOUSE HAD A FENCE AROUND IT, PURELY A SYMBCLIC GESTURE; IT WAS far too delicate to keep anything out. The path continued past an open gate in the fence to end at the steps up to the porch that wrapped around the front of the house.

"Big place for just one man," Hakim said.

"Nothing here is crowded," April said. "It's going to be a nice change, for as long as we stay here."

"The neighbors are a little strange," Hakim said.

"I'm sure you meant 'strange' in a heartbreaking way," April said as Lars skipped up the steps and knocked on the front door.

Nothing stirred within.

Somewhere, something made a sound like a whistle.

"Was that a bird?" April asked, looking all around. There were trees dotted everywhere, but she could spot no movement.

"We have those," Charley said. "Some you can eat, and some aren't worth the bother." He knelt down and held a hand out for Boo to sniff. Boo slowly came out from behind April's leg to investigate.

Lars knocked again, more loudly.

"Do they have the reflectors set to simulate day and night, or is it always day here?" April wondered.

"It gets dark," Charley said. "Ten to six, no sunlight. That's when we're supposed to sleep. Is it always light where you come from?"

"Some places," April said.

"Someone's coming," Lars said, straightening from where he had been pressing his ear to the door and taking half a step back. April came up the steps to stand beside him as the door slowly swung open. The man within was rail thin, pale except for a decided pinkness to his cheeks, with a wild thatch of black hair that grew all around his head in a maze of curls and spirals. He looked them over one by one, raising a handkerchief to his mouth as he gave a small cough.

"Mr. Chapelier?" April said, trying to summon up a smile. "I'm April Nguyen. These are my friends Hakim Little and Lars Gundelach."

"Ah, yes," he said. "I am very pleased you've arrived at last. Won't you come in?" He smiled, but the smile melted into a worried frown as he saw Boo peeking around April's legs.

"This is Boo," April said. "He's sort of my assistant."

"I see," Mr. Chapelier said. "I rather think he should be happier in the yard, yes? If you just shut that little gate behind you, he shall be quite contained. Charley can keep an eye on him, can't you, Charley?"

"Yes, sir, Mr. Chapelier," Charley said, already spinning the dog in circles as Boo tugged at the end of his sleeve.

"Have you received any of my messages?" April asked.

"I received a polite refusal several weeks ago, and then an acceptance a few days ago," he said with a bored air.

"Ah, yes. We were in a very different situation a few weeks ago. It seemed unlikely we would be out this far, but circumstances changed," April said. "Also, we had some troubles with our ship."

"I don't travel myself these days, but I do recall the tiresome unreliability of transport," he said, closing the door behind them, then leading the way down the hall past several closed doors to one that had been left open. "Please, come into my library and have a seat. I shall fetch some tea."

"Thank you, that would be lovely," April said. Mr. Chapelier stopped at the doorway to usher them all in, then smiled again before disappearing further down the hall.

April scarcely noticed he had left, not surrounded as she was on all sides by books. Every wall was a shelf stuffed with books, and every table between the stuffed chairs was covered with stacks of more books. There were more books packed in half the space as in the library on the *Moreau*.

"Where did they all come from?" she wondered, picking up a book from the low table around which all the chairs were arranged. It was an encyclopedia of psychology. Underneath it was a book on demonology.

"There doesn't seem to be a system," Hakim said, running a finger along the spines of the books as he read the titles.

"Lots of psychology," Lars said. "Medical textbooks, anatomy and physiology—"

"Biology, chemistry, even physics," Hakim said.

"You can all read—how wonderfully rare," Mr. Chapelier said. He was carrying a tea tray so large he had to turn sideways to get it through the door. April gathered the books off of the low table so he could set the tray down. She looked around, found no uncluttered surface, and instead stacked them neatly on the floor under the table.

"You have lots of science books here," Hakim observed.

"Yes, food for the mind," Mr. Chapelier said as he poured out the tea. "I'm particularly interested in psychology. The human mind is endlessly fascinating. All my work is thoroughly grounded in science."

"But I don't see any math. It seems a strange omission. Math is the backbone of science. Without math, science just doesn't hold up." His tone was lightly conversational as his gaze continued to sweep down the shelves, perhaps in search of a Euclid or a Newton.

Mr. Chapelier stopped pouring, setting the pot down with a sharp click. Then he straightened, his eyes full of dark fire and the pink of his cheeks deepening to a frightening shade of scarlet. "You, sir, are not welcome in this house."

Hakim blinked in surprise. "I meant no offense. It's just that my personal interest is in mathematics."

"I have spoken. I will not speak again. Go!"

"Hakim," April said.

"It's all right," he said to her. "I'll be with my sister."

They shared a long look and April realized he was not angry, just puzzled by this man's strange behavior. He knew this was important to her and he wasn't going to mess it up, at least not more than he had already without meaning to. He lifted his chin in farewell and left the room. Only after they heard the front door shut behind him did Mr. Chapelier relax his rigid stance. He took a deep breath, then melted into one of the chairs.

"I do apologize, but I cannot abide impertinence," he said, picking up one of the cups and its saucer and blowing over the surface of the tea. April watched him closely, but no sign of the sudden anger remained. His eyes were once more a warm dark brown, not unlike the tea before him, and his cheeks had faded back to what she supposed was his normal coloring.

"I should be the one apologizing," April said. "Although I promise Hakim did not mean to upset you."

"There is very little value in a secondhand apology, isn't there?" Mr. Chapelier said and took a sip of his tea. April didn't know how to answer that. It sounded far more unspeakably rude than anything Hakim had said.

"May I ask how you heard of me?" April asked instead.

"My mentor, retired now, lives on the *Triomphe*. He heard some stories of your skills and even witnessed you working once. When I wrote to him for assistance, he regretted not being able to come in person but passed on your name," Mr. Chapelier said and blew again on his tea.

"I've only worked with ghosts before," April said, fighting the urge to squirm in the chair. Clearly, there was no other work on this station. She wanted to be more honest, but what if that meant she didn't get the job? Would they be trapped here like before, only this time with no part on the way to rescue them?

"I will teach you what you need to know," Mr. Chapelier said with a little wave of his hand. "The important thing is the ability to focus, to bring all of yourself into the fight until it is done and not lose yourself in the process. My mentor was very impressed with you."

April gave a wavering smile, trying to work out which of her performances on the *Triomphe* he might have been witness to, but coming up empty.

"This is a very strange place," Lars said, helping himself to one of the other teacups. "We have a great deal of questions."

"Hmm," Mr. Chapelier said.

"Lars is a community organizer," April said. Perhaps there was a chance for other work after all, if not for her. "He gets people to work together to improve their living conditions. Although this place seems like heaven itself. I've never seen so much green!"

"So few people live here," Lars said.

"Yes, we don't advertise ourselves," Mr. Chapelier said calmly.

"But so many more people *could* be living here," Lars persisted. "You do realize how much overcrowding is a problem everywhere."

"Yes, of course," Mr. Chapelier said. "We are not unfeeling. We would love to open our doors wide and take all we can fit, but we can't just yet. It would be unethical."

"Because you don't know what everyone is reacting to?" April guessed.

"What do you mean, reacting?" He frowned, puzzled.

"The reddening of everyone's skin. Some of the children look almost chapped, like frostbite, only it isn't cold here."

"Oh, that's just a rash, not to worry," he said with a dismissive wave. "I was speaking, of course, of the demon problem. I've been trying to rid this place of demons since I first arrived, and lately it seems like the demons are winning. And they particularly target the children. I have a few who I've had to exorcise nearly a dozen times, but the demons keep getting back in. It's..." He broke off, anguish washing over his face, making him look suddenly older, every fine line on his pale skin more prominent, as if this emotion came to him so often it was responsible for every premature wrinkle. He sighed deeply and took another sip of tea. "You'll see tomorrow. Pointless to try to explain the inexplicable when, by this time tomorrow, you will know."

"Tomorrow, so soon?" April said.

"I have waited too long already. Some of the worst cases... the demons grow stronger the longer they dwell inside a host. Again, you'll see tomorrow."

"Is there anything I should do to prepare?" April asked. "A book perhaps?"

"You are both welcome to peruse any of my texts. I ask only that they remain within the confines of this house," he said. "And you are both welcome to stay here. I have plenty of room."

"Hakim..." Lars started to say, but April quickly cut him off.

"Hakim will likely want to stay with his sister, and she will likely want to stay with her ship. That's all right?"

"Hmm?" Mr. Chapelier raised his eyebrows as if he didn't under-stand the question. "It certainly makes no difference to me where he goes. I don't own the station, only this house."

"So, no one is in charge?" Lars asked.

"In charge of what?"

"The station. I mean maintenance, just to start," Lars said.

Mr. Chapelier shrugged. "I wouldn't know where to start with such things."

"But if something were to break—"

"My dear boy, I didn't say I considered such things unimportant, only that I wouldn't know where to begin. It seems to me a lovely way for you to occupy your time whilst April and I are working."

"I'll start looking into it tomorrow then," Lars said.

"And I can help you when I'm free," April promised.

"Well, we shall see," Mr. Chapelier said. "Our work is very weary-ing. Very draining. After tomorrow, you'll know what I mean."

25

———————————

BATTLING DEMONS

April had nearly refused to participate when she first saw the chair with its metal clamps that tightened down to hold pinned even the tiniest, thinnest of the children. It looked like a device for torture. Just being held in that chair, clamped at knees and ankles, elbows and wrists, chest and even neck, would be deeply disturbing no matter what else followed. But Mr. Chapelier had wearily repeated that she would understand soon enough.

Sadly, she did.

The girl currently in the chair was a little slip of a thing, like a puff of air could knock her down. Or she had been. She had climbed into the chair of her own accord and put her arms and legs where they belonged, holding still as April tightened the clamps and Mr. Chapelier discussed her recent behavior with the girl's parents. They reported waking screaming from nightmares, sullen tempers that ended in long strings of profanity, not in her own voice, and most recently, the gory slaughter of all the family's chickens. April brushed the loose blonde hair back from the girl's face, trying to imagine this girl killing chickens with her own bare hands, smearing the garden walls with blood and feathers. The girl gave her a shy little smile. No, it didn't fit at all.

She changed her mind minutes later when Mr. Chapelier had

commanded the demon to show itself. The girl had gone rigid, her entire body straightening at the clamps, her tendons popping out like cords against her pale flesh. Her eyes rolled, she drooled, she pounded her little feet with so much force the floor beneath them shook.

And that voice. That voice could not possibly be hers.

Hours passed as Mr. Chapelier fought with that demon, trying to convince it to go of its own free will, then chanting prayers in one language after another. Some the demon laughed at, others drew it into a rage so violent April worried the girl would do herself fatal harm, even bound as she was.

Mr. Chapelier's energy was flagging, and he turned aside to pour himself a glass of water, and April wet a cloth and approached the girl. Her demon had worn itself out again, and the girl was panting like a dog, looking at her with sullen, distrustful eyes. April brushed the hair back from her face, then wiped the cool cloth over her sweaty skin, finishing under her chin where the drool had left slick, sticky paths down her neck.

"Maybe she needs a drink too," April said to Mr. Chapelier. He shook his head.

"She'll just bite the glass," he said. He didn't have to add that he spoke from experience; April believed it. She could even picture it: glass in the girl's mouth, cutting up her lips and gums and tongue. The girl looked at her out of the side of her eyes as if she, too, were picturing it, but relishing the image.

"Emma," April said, brushing back the girl's hair again and trying for all the world to look at her like there was nothing more than a sweet little girl before her. "Emma, can you hear me?"

"Emma gone," the girl growled. Her eyes were watching April gleefully.

"That won't work," Mr. Chapelier said, his voice weary. "The demon is stronger than the girl."

"I don't believe that," April said. "Emma, do you believe that?"

"I am no ghost," the girl said in her low, rumbling voice, "to obey the commands of one such as you."

"Emma," April said again.

"You think you have power, commanding wisps of memory? Now

you see real power. I am no figment of light, no trick of perception, no desperate hope for wish fulfillment. There is no hereafter for me to happily fade into. I am ancient power you cannot fathom, and now I am this girl."

"Enough," Mr. Chapelier said, pulling himself up straighter and approaching the chair.

April fell back, shaken. Everyone in the village knew she was famous for her work with ghosts, but how had this girl gotten to the heart of her fears about what she was really doing? Could a ten-year-old be that perceptive?

Mr. Chapelier was rubbing his hands together as he towered over the girl clamped to the chair. Then, all of a sudden, he put his hands on either side of her face, forcing her to look into his eyes. April turned away as Mr. Chapelier shouted for the demon to leave and the girl screamed back, first at her low roar as her heels once more beat the floor, but then finally in a high-pitched shriek that ended in sobs.

"You may release her now," Mr. Chapelier said, slumping back against his worktable.

April rushed to do so, unlatching clamp after clamp and taking the still-sobbing girl into her arms. Emma clung tightly to her as April lifted her to carry her back out to where her parents waited on the other side of the closed French doors. The curtains had been drawn before they started working; what must it have been like for them to hear all of that screaming and shouting, powerless to intervene?

"Emma!" her father cried, leaping to his feet to take his daughter from April.

"I'm sorry, Papa," she said, burying her face against his neck. "I didn't mean to. I didn't want to. I loved my chickens and now they're all dead!"

"Hush now, child, it's all right," he said, stroking her hair. "We can start again from chicks. As long as you're well, we can always start again."

April watched the family go, Emma still in her father's arms but now pulling back to look up into his face, babbling all her plans for her new chicks, her mother beside them smiling over them both. She had that same warm glow in her chest she used to get, seeing grieving parents come to terms with the loss of their child. Only this family got their daughter back.

But her warm glow faded as she saw the others waiting. While they had been with Emma, the waiting room had filled with sullen children and their distracted, exhausted parents. April tried to summon a smile, waving the next child to step forward for his turn in the chair.

This was going to be a very long day.

The exorcisms continued until the station cycled from day to night, a transition that happened within the space of a minute. Some of the children had been easier to deal with than Emma, but a few had taken even longer. April was bone weary, and she could see that Mr. Chapelier was only staying on his feet from sheer force of will.

"It's like that every time?" April asked, closing the French doors on the empty waiting room.

"Every time," Mr. Chapelier whispered. The incessant shouting had destroyed his voice and even his whisper gave out on him.

"I've made some food," Lars said from the doorway. "You've neither of you eaten since breakfast."

"Thank you," April said. Mr. Chapelier nodded his own thanks, coughing discreetly into his handkerchief. They followed Lars to the back of the house, where there was a little kitchen. Another pair of French doors opened onto a formal dining room, but Lars had set out the food on the cozier kitchen table. Mr. Chapelier collapsed into a chair, at first seeming too deflated to move, but then stirring himself to pull the mug of tea closer to him and fill it with cube after cube of sugar.

"That sounded intense," Lars said as he put buttered slices of toast on both of their plates and topped them with warm, poached eggs. April poked at hers with a fork, but Mr. Chapelier only sipped at his sweet tea, eyes closed. He looked even older than he had the day before.

"It was," April said.

"May I let the dog in? He's been missing you terribly," Lars said. "And I know you miss him."

"May I?" April asked anxiously.

Mr. Chapelier, eyes still closed, waved his hand vaguely in the air.

Lars opened the back door and Boo came bouncing in, and April slipped out of her chair to crouch down on the floor. Boo was beside himself with delight, trying to lick her and jump on her and press his spinning body up against her all at once. April laughed, catching him in a tight hug and burying her nose against his warmth. She couldn't hold his squirming form for long and he danced away, but then danced back to her.

"So much noise," Mr. Chapelier said, and April felt her heart sink. But then he added, "I suppose it's a happy sort of noise. Perhaps I see the appeal."

"He helped me find ghosts in my old career," April said, climbing back into her chair to eat some of her egg and toast. "I'm not sure how he can help with this, though."

"If he has a restorative effect on you, that might be use enough," Mr. Chapelier said. His eyes were open once more, but he still looked like lifting the mug of tea to his lips was almost more effort than he could summon.

"What is really going on here?" Lars asked.

"Lars, if you could see. Those kids—there really does seem to be something else inside of them," April said earnestly.

"Maybe," Mr. Chapelier said to her surprise. "I've never quite worked it out myself. Is it an ancient evil, something supernatural? It feels like it sometimes, doesn't it? But I'm not convinced."

"What do you think it is, then?" Lars asked.

"Psychology," Mr. Chapelier said, setting his empty mug down on the table. Lars refilled it for him, but he didn't pick it up again. "Take Emma, for instance. She has been in here many times."

"Charley said some kids are attacked more than others," April said.

Mr. Chapelier tipped his head noncommittally. "The kids who are in here the most often, it's not hard to figure out why. They enjoy the attention. They are miserable at home. They can't deal with all that they're feeling, so they act out. You noticed not all the exorcisms were particularly difficult?"

"You're saying they're faking?" April asked.

"Eh," Mr. Chapelier said, closing his eyes once more. "Some, definitely. Some, I don't think *they* think they're making it up, but it gets easy to let yourself feel possessed if it lets you do things you normally wouldn't let yourself do. The early teen years, that's where most of my patients are at. It can't be a coincidence."

"So there are no demons? Then what are we doing?"

"That's what I'm saying: psychology." He sat up, the conversation pulling up the last reserves of his energy. "They have real troubles, which they deal with by externalizing them into a demon. It's a psychological construct. My exorcism finishes that process for them, taking what they were externalizing and getting rid of it entirely. For some, that's enough, and they only come here once. Others have relapses. Others have lots of relapses." He started adding more sugar to his tea, cube after cube.

"And Emma is one you think is faking?" April remembered the way the girl had looked right at her, all the things she said that she shouldn't know. "It seemed real to me."

"It's early days for you yet," Mr. Chapelier said, stirring his tea. "You'll get better at judging."

"It felt real," April said, looking down at her own eggs.

"So you don't think anything supernatural is going on here?" Lars asked. "Yet you sent for April."

"I said I wasn't convinced," Mr. Chapelier corrected him sharply. "For a long time, I was sure there wasn't. But lately, I'm becoming less so."

"Why? What changed?" April asked.

"I've changed. I am changing." He reached up, touched his own cheek. "The demons are starting to bleed over into me. And that can't be true if they aren't real, can it? The children show certain symptoms in the early days of their possessions, very strong similarities in their behaviors and what they complain of. I'm starting to have some of those symptoms. I've reached the point where I can no longer tell myself it's just the exhaustion of the work. That's why I sent for you. I may soon be in need of a trained exorcist myself," he said with a dry laugh, then took another long drink of tea. "If you don't mind, I think I'll turn in now. I am quite tired."

"Of course," April said. She and Lars got to their feet as he rose shakily to his, only sitting back down when he disappeared down the hall. Lars looked at the plate full of food Mr. Chapelier had never touched, then set it down on the floor for Boo to tear into.

April propped her head up on one hand, watching Boo licking away at the runny yolks.

"April," Lars said, she realized not for the first time, and she sat up to look at him. "You look exhausted. Shaken." She shrugged, pulling her tea closer but not drinking any. "You really think there was something there, in those kids? I admit, the sounds coming from that room... I can't imagine what it was like to be in there."

"I don't know," she admitted with a weary sigh. "I've never once seen a ghost. But I've seen people reacting to what they've seen, and there really did seem to be something there. This, maybe it's like that. Especially with Emma—it felt like there was something there that I couldn't exactly see but was having such an influence on her."

"Was it like before, with your mother in the shuttle? You said you felt... what did you call it?"

"Sense of presence," April said. "No, it wasn't like that. That was all around me; this was definitely just in the girl. The things she said. We've never even met; how could she know exactly how I feel about all that ghost business? What's more improbable, that something inside her was telling her or that she just guessed? I'm not sure which is scarier."

"You're tired," Lars said, catching her hand and giving it a squeeze. "You'll see things differently in the morning."

"I want to talk to Hakim," she said. "I was going to see how he and Salima were doing today, but the workday was so long. Did you go?" Lars shook his head. "I should have gone. He must think I've abandoned him."

Lars let go of her hand and got up to clear the dishes away from the table.

"I suppose it's too late to go now. In the morning, then," she said mostly to herself.

"I'm sure he understands. Mr. Chapelier was very anxious to get started; he could scarcely blame you for digging right in to the work we came here for you to do."

"He can be funny about that stuff," April said, and Lars snorted.

"Anyway, I really want to talk to him about all this. I wish he had been able to stay here."

"What would he say?" Lars asked.

"Well, I'm sure he could blow all sorts of holes into Mr. Chapelier's theories," April said. "First of all, no math. Second, I'm guessing the same set of phenomenon has all sorts of potential causes we're not taking into consideration because his theories fit everything so neatly, but there could be lots of things going on here, maybe more than one thing at a time. It would be very hard to separate and test them all."

"See, you don't need him here to think things through; you've got it on your own," Lars said.

"Maybe," April said.

"Do you want to see what I've been working on?"

"Yes," April said, straightening and trying to perk up.

Lars took out his tablet and set it in front of her with a flourish. "Station schematics. All of them."

"You found a working computer here?"

"There is a little hill next to the village; it disguises the doorway to a staircase down into the belly of the station. All the systems are running, which is good news, but a few things have problems. For instance, what I plan to focus on first is the water and sanitation. All the houses are equipped for running water and toilets, but none of it is working. Hence the outhouse here and the buckets of water someone from the village delivered to our front door this morning. I'm guessing it comes from the lake. I'm not guessing just how clean it is; I'm not sure where the outhouse contents go just yet."

"That wouldn't be making everyone pink and the children strange, though," April said.

"It's just an obvious start," Lars said. "If I fix it, it will be apparent to everybody that we can make good things happen by digging into their problems. Then when I dig into things with less obvious benefits, like clean water running through the taps, I'll already have their trust."

"Parasites might be part of the collection of causes I was talking about earlier," April said. "I can't think of any connected with sanitation that could change a child's behavior as radically as I've seen, but they certainly can't help."

"I don't think Mr. Chapelier is wrong with his psychology," Lars said. "People can be feeding off of each other."

"Yes, but it's not the root cause, right?" April looked up at him. "And he knows it, whatever he says. It's why he won't let other people come here."

"He's not entirely consistent," Lars said. "He tells us he's not sure he believes in demons, but that's not how he talks with the villagers. I think he's very invested in them believing, which if he really thought it was a psychological condition, would be abominable, to lure them into that sort of belief."

April nodded, yawning hugely.

"Right," Lars said, getting up to clear away the last of the dishes. "Bedtime for you and Boo before you fall asleep at this table."

April was all too happy to comply.

26

THE CURATIVE POWERS OF A GOOD BATH

"How about now?" Lars's voice barely reached her from deep within the bowels of the station.

April glanced up at the monitor. "Still red!" she shouted back.

"This has to be it!"

"Do you want me to help?"

"No, no point. Plus, it's really unpleasant in here."

April didn't doubt that. He had crawled for minutes down an access corridor too low to stand up in. The floor was covered with something black and gritty, and the distant echo of something dripping made her certain at some point gritty had become muddy.

"I think I got it!" He gave a growl of frustration, then a cry of victory. "Definitely got it! I can hear it running."

"It's green!" she confirmed, watching the pipe on the schematic go from red to green section by section. "Yes—the village has running water again!"

She squatted at the opening of the corridor, the hem of her white kameez just dusting the ground. Boo laid down next to her, nose on his paws as he watched the darkness, tail occasionally giving a quick wag of anticipation as they waited. The sound of Lars's breathing and the scrape of the toolbox across the floor grew louder. Then she saw his sweaty face shining in the light from behind her.

"Good thing, you look like you could use a shower," she said.

"Not as much as I smell like I could use a shower, I'm sure," he said, shoving the toolbox into the room, then standing. He had unzipped his jumpsuit to the waist, the tank top underneath sticking to his sweaty skin. Boo was jumping all over him and Lars bent to give him a hard rub along the ribs and a tousle of his ears.

"Let's go try out a faucet," April said. He grinned at her and they walked together out of the maintenance hub. From outside, it looked like part of the station landscape, an ordinary hill that just happened to have a door in it.

"One of the houses?" she said as they walked along the path to the village.

"No, the fountain in the center of town. Once everyone sees that running, they will surely try out their own faucets," Lars said.

"I thought by now more people would be friendly with us," April said.

"They're friendly enough," Lars said. "We're outsiders; I don't think they are ever going to consider us one of them. We'll always be kept at arm's length, like Chapelier."

They reached the fountain in the village square and Lars walked all the way around it before finding the access panel. He popped it off, then turned the spigot on. The fountain made a dry coughing sound, letting forth a little dribble of water, then coughed again and suddenly water was shooting up into the sky, falling back down to collect in the wide basin. Boo barked repeatedly, not sure if he trusted this new thing.

"We did it," Lars said, snapping the panel closed before coming to stand beside her, hands on hips as he admired the sparkling fall of water.

"More you than me, really," April said. "You found all the maintenance programs and figured out how to use them. And crawled down the tunnel to fix the problem."

"That's only true because I had more time for it," he said. "You were right there with me every minute you were free."

"Yes," April said, a sudden weariness washing over her. Tomorrow was another exorcism day. Her fifth. It wasn't getting any easier. And on the rare chance she got an hour away from Mr. Chapelier to go find Hakim, he was always bent over his tablet, methodically writing line after line of numbers and symbols she had no hope of understanding. He would occasionally glance up at her when she spoke to him, but she never had his full attention. She wanted to be happy that he had found his own happiness again, but mostly she felt like maybe he was punishing her for dabbling in the supernatural world again. She couldn't get him to talk to her enough to know for sure.

"You OK?" Lars asked, leaning forward to look into her face.

"Yes, just the usual," she said, trying to muster up a smile. "Shall we bring Salima her tools back?"

"Just a sec," Lars said, pulling off his boots and stepping into the fountain. He put his head into the spray, then turned to let it run down his back. He rubbed the streaks of black grit from his arms and shoulders. The white tank top clung wetly to him, nearly transparent now. April blinked and forced herself to look away. A child was watching them from the doorway of his house, a finger in his mouth, his eyes wide with astonishment. "OK, I'm ready now," Lars said, once more at her side. April smiled at the kid, who ducked out of sight and then peeked out again.

"He's going to be in this water the minute we go," April said. "Watch him."

Lars picked up his boots and the toolbox, and they started down the path to the dock building. Sure enough, they heard a splash and a shriek of delight before they had passed the second house. He was soon joined by others, all laughing and splashing.

"I really hope it was the lake water making them ill," Lars said. "I'm certain if these people were healthier, you and Mr. Chapelier would be doing a lot less business."

"I think so too," April said. "But I doubt the first thing we change is going to work. The lake water and the station water probably come from the same place. If one is contaminated, the other will be too."

"Maybe not," Lars said. "Certainly having functioning toilets is going to make life better for everyone."

"No argument there," April said. "I know *I'm* looking forward to getting home and taking a long hot bath."

"You called it 'home,'" Lars said. He stopped walking and turned to face her. "It feels like home, doesn't it?"

"I didn't really think about it. I just said it," she admitted. "I don't think I really know what that word means. Or what 'home' feels like." She watched Boo cruising along the shore of the lake, nose so close to the ground he was in danger of trodding on his own ears.

"I do," he said. "It's being with family, working together, supporting each other. We have that, don't we? Look what we just did."

"What we just did is very cool," she admitted. He smiled down at her, then set the toolbox down to use as a seat as he put the socks and boots back on his now-dry feet.

"I like it here," he said. "I like living with you in Mr. Chapelier's house, eating together and talking together and romping with Boo together. Working together. It feels like home to me, like when I was a kid. My parents always worked together, helping people make their communities stronger. They were always figuring out ways to improve things, bouncing ideas off each other, inspiring each other."

"Do you miss them?" April asked as he stood up and picked up the toolbox. They continued on to the station building, Boo running to catch up.

"I missed them more when I was on the *Chandrasekhar*. Maybe because I'd just left them, or maybe because I never felt as much a part of things there as I do here," he said. They pushed through the glass doors into the cavernous atrium.

"Not a part of things? You were practically one of the founders," April said. "You were a level above the rest of us, literally."

"Yes, but that was the problem, really," he said. "I was outside the group of the founders. They were very tight, so good at finishing each other's thoughts that half the time they didn't bother speaking more than a shorthand that I never could follow. And as you said, I was above everyone else. Not a part of any of the work crews."

"You seemed like you had lots of friends," April said. They stepped inside the first of the elevators and Lars set the toolbox on the floor.

"I was friendly with a lot of people," he said after a moment's thought. "But I didn't really have friends."

"I never had friends until I met Hakim and Salima. And you," she added.

"Ooh, just made the list," he said.

"I wasn't ranking."

"Weren't you?" His voice said he was still joking, but his eyes were watching for her response far too closely.

"What are you asking me?" she asked.

"I'm not asking you anything," he said, taking a step closer. "I was just telling you, I like being with you. All day, every day. I like it a lot."

"Likewise," April said. She had to tip her head back to look up at him, he was so close. He took hold of her hands, thumbs brushing over her palms in a way that made her shiver.

"Good," he said, then bent his head to kiss her. April froze, but the warmth of him so close to her was too inviting and she rose up on tiptoes, pressing up against his still-damp chest. His hands were just coming up to frame her face when the elevator dinged and the doors opened.

April stepped back, drawing a long breath as if she had been underwater. Then she turned and saw Hakim digging through the rubbish pile by the elevator. Had he seen?

Lars picked up the toolbox and crossed the dock to Salima's ship. April hesitated, but Hakim seemed engrossed in whatever he was doing and completely oblivious to her presence. She ran to catch up with Lars, Boo close on her heels.

Lars set the toolbox down near the ramp up to the ship, but there was no sign of Salima. He walked around to the front of the ship, calling her name, but April hovered near the toolbox. She felt flushed, like her lips were branded for all to see. In just a few minutes she was going to be back in that elevator with Lars again, then walking with him back to Mr. Chapelier's house, then probably alone with him there, since Mr. Chapelier always cloistered himself on the nights before exorcisms. She wasn't sure she was ready to be alone with him again. That kiss had seemed to come out of nowhere, but now that she was really thinking about it, a lot of looks he had been sending her way were making a different sort of sense. And not just since they had been left alone together with Mr. Chapelier.

April felt a sudden shiver of insight tickling up her spine. Was *she* the reason he had left the *Chandrasekhar*? Should she have figured that out sooner? She had grown up observing her mother closely, looking for signs that warned of impending mood shifts. She had gotten very good at reading her mother. How could she be so bad with other people?

"Salima is scavenging," Hakim said, so suddenly it made her jump. She hadn't heard him approach. She wiped at her face as if that could make her stop flushing. At least he wasn't looking at her.

"You're not lost in your math," she said after spending far too long casting about for something to say.

"Hit a wall," he said. "I'm helping Salima today. Sometimes working on something else helps."

"The ship is looking impressive," Lars said, but Hakim gave a noncommittal shrug. "Well, we brought back her tools. And the village has running water and sanitation again, so that's good."

"You OK?" Hakim asked, peering at April closely.

"Yes, fine," she said, trying not to turn pinker than she already was.

"Tomorrow is an exorcism day," Lars said to Hakim in lieu of explanation. "In fact, we should probably be getting back..."

"Go ahead," April said. "I'll catch up."

Lars's eyebrows furrowed quizzically. Hakim had wandered off again, and she had no reason she could give for wanting to stay alone in the dock. He reached out to catch her hand, and she twined her fingers in his briefly, then pulled away. Everything felt like it was making too profound of a statement. She should have realized a long time ago how he was feeling. But she hadn't. She was going to have to figure out what she was feeling, fast.

"I just need a minute," she said. "I want to talk to Hakim about some of Mr. Chapelier's theories. I haven't had a real chance to talk with him lately, what with my work and his math. I won't be long; we can have dinner when I get back."

"Yes, well," he said, clearing his throat nervously. "I'll be... home then."

"Thank you, Lars," April said, managing a little smile. He nodded, then headed back to the elevator. Boo followed along, but when he saw April wasn't going he sat down outside the elevator and watched Lars leave, tail thumping the ground until the doors closed and he was out of sight.

April climbed up the ramp to the ship but the interior was empty, no sign of Hakim. Salima had been busier than April had realized, adding more pods to her ship, along with a lot more equipment than April could identify. When they left the station, they would be in better shape than they'd been in her best ghost-dispelling days. And it wasn't costing them a thing. When April had asked if Salima could scavenge the wrecked ships on the dock for parts, Mr. Chapelier had just given that same vague hand gesture she always took for "Yes, just don't bother me." Since neither she nor Lars were being paid in anything other than room and board, she decided taking what they needed was fair trade. The work might feel like it was killing her, but at least something grand was coming out of it.

"Boo, where did he go?" she asked the dog as she came back out of the ship. "Where's Hakim?"

Boo wagged his tail at the name, but didn't seem to have any idea where to start a search. April crossed the dock to the door to the dock manager's office. It was empty, but the computers were on and running, so he had spent some time here. She leaned over the screen, looking at the data scrolling by. It didn't seem like anything a dock-worker would be running; he must have accessed the main computers.

Hakim started to come into the room from the back door, but stopped when he saw her. She suddenly felt like an intruder in his space and backed away from the monitor. "I was looking for you," she said lamely.

"You found me," he said, then continued into the room, sliding into the chair at the desk and setting down whatever he had brought with him. A computer component. The desk was littered with them. He peered into an open casing, then turned the component around in his hands, examining the ports.

"I wanted to talk to you," she said.

"That would be what you're doing," he said, reaching into the casing to fetch a cable and snapping it into the component. Was he being more obtuse than usual? Hard to say; she'd never been good at figuring out what he was thinking. And she had worked hard at it, so hard she'd never paid much attention to Lars's very clear signals.

April gave a frustrated sigh but pressed on. "Mr. Chapelier has these theories about his exorcisms." Hakim scoffed at that but didn't look up from his work. "Yes, I know. But he's read a lot of psychology. Some of it sounds like things you've told me, about how our brains can fool us. Even healthy brains can make us think we perceive things that aren't there. Especially if we believe those things are there already."

Hakim still wasn't looking at her. She slumped down into the other chair in the room, on the other side of the doorway at a separate workstation. These screens were still dead, and she fiddled with the buttons absently. "I've been reading some of his psychology books, the ones about unhealthy minds. I think the kids we see are probably suffering from some pretty hard-core mental issues."

"Yeah," Hakim said.

"I wish you hadn't been banished that first day. I wish you could see what it's like. I look into their eyes, and it really is like something alien is inside of them. It's very... unsettling. I look into the eyes of a ten-year-old kid and it's like what's inside is ancient and not really human. My rational mind can explain all it wants, but that feeling is too visceral to ignore."

Hakim hesitated midway through screwing the component into the casing, still not quite looking at her. "You're saying you're a believer now?"

"No," she rushed to say. "I don't know what's going on. That's why I wish you were there to see. I would really love to know what you think about what's going on, in that minute. I kind of need to know."

"Chapelier would never allow it," Hakim said and resumed turning the screwdriver.

"I know," she said, flipping a switch up and down, up and down.

"I don't think I really need to be there," he said at length. "You're there, and I know you're thinking about what you see."

"I don't know what to think," she said.

"You don't know how to synthesize what you're thinking," he said.

"You surely have thoughts based on your observations. There's no 'knowing' there. Tell me those thoughts."

"The kids display remarkably similar behaviors," she said, "but that doesn't necessarily mean much. We have no way of isolating them from each other, and even if we could now, it would mean little. They've already been soaking up the same narrative for years."

"The narrative Chapelier has been feeding them," Hakim said.

"I don't think it all comes from him," April said. "Some of this predates his even arriving here. But he's shaped what he's found, no argument there. I suppose at this point everyone behaves exactly the way he expects them to because they believe that's how they should behave."

She paused, but he said nothing, so she went on.

"Something deeper is going on, that's a given, but whatever it is that is making these kids act kind of crazy, they have been given a set of instructions from Mr. Chapelier on how crazy behaves, and they follow it. And it's a kind of crazy he's provided a solution to. He says they're possessed, they know how possessed people behave, they act accordingly, and he does his exorcism ritual, all according to the narrative.

"The thing is, they really do feel better. When he's done, they can be normal again, for a little while. It doesn't fix the real problem, but maybe that's not fixable. It does give them a few weeks of respite before they cycle through again."

"Stories are powerful things," Hakim allowed.

"The structure of the story is somehow letting them confront what's going on in their own minds? They can deal with things in metaphor that can't be faced any other way?" April speculated, but her frustration was starting to tell.

"You don't look good," Hakim said, finally setting aside his tools and swiveling in his chair to face her.

"Lars and I were in the sanitation station all day, fixing the plumbing," April said, brushing a patch of black dirt from her jeans.

"You know that's not what I meant."

"It's exhausting, this work," she said. "I think it helps, but I worry I'm lying to myself. I don't believe in demons, don't worry on that score, but the more Mr. Chapelier talks about demons as a powerful metaphor... I don't know. I'm starting to think there might be something there. I've been reading the books. Our minds, the power of language and story..." She trailed off, aware she was starting to talk in circles.

"Your cheeks are pink."

"Still?" she asked, touching her face, but then she was blushing again for what that single word implied. Hakim gave an impatient sigh and got up from his chair, pulling her to her feet so he could peer at her skin.

"It's not just you blushing. It's always there."

"I hadn't noticed," she said.

"Lars should be noticing," Hakim said. "No point in him always being with you if he's not." She looked at him closely but still had no hint of whether those words were meant to be as pointed as she was taking them.

"He's not always with me," April clarified. "He has work he does."

"Open your mouth," Hakim said.

"What? Why?"

"Humor me."

April opened wide, and he took the little flashlight he had been using to see inside the computer casing and shined it into her mouth.

"What is it?" she asked when he straightened back up, turning off the light with a click.

"I'm not sure."

"I'm starting to look like the villagers?"

"Not that bad. Chapelier, his cheeks are pink."

"He scratches a lot, too. His forearms are often bloody from it," April said. "He says it's 'bleeding over' from the exorcisms. Like the demons he expels, since they pass through him, leave something behind. He's not possessed, but he's infected."

Hakim gave a dry laugh. "These are his metaphors leaving residue behind?"

"I admit his thinking is not consistent. He talks at length about psychology but always ends with saying he's not sure he believes in any of it anymore. I think he's having a hard time thinking, like something is fogging his brain. That's why I'm trying to formulate my own theories."

"Do you itch?"

She shook her head.

"Anything else that might be a symptom? Do your gums hurt? Headaches? Weird visual changes? Anything?"

"I didn't even know I was pink until you mentioned it," she said.

"The sanitation system, that's separate from the lake water?"

"Yes, that's why we wanted to get it up and running."

"Good," Hakim said absently, picking up his tablet and quickly tapping out a note to himself with one hand.

"What are you thinking?" she asked.

"I'm working on lots of theories," he said. "I'll let you know when I find anything concrete."

"But what should I be doing now?"

"Use the clean water, but I scarcely need to tell you that," he said. "Watch yourself for symptoms; anything at all, no matter how minor, could be a clue. Watch Lars too," he added.

"I will."

"And maybe don't eat the fish from the lake. If you can help it. The chickens are probably OK."

"You think there's something in the lake?"

"I'm working on it," he said, and she looked again at the data slowly scrolling down the screen. "I've ruled out a bunch of stuff, but since I didn't really know where to start, I feel like I'm still throwing darts in every direction, trying to find the target. It's nice to rule things out, but it's not giving me hints as to where the target really is. I'm hoping I'll know when I get close, but I might not know until I accidentally hit a bull's-eye."

"I've missed you and Salima," April said. "How is she doing?"

"Same as always," Hakim said. "Perfectly content alone with her ship, building and rebuilding."

"It's looking really good," April said, glancing out the window at the increasingly hulking form.

"We can leave at any time," he said. His voice was low, and he spoke with his mouth close to her ear as if afraid of being overheard. "You say the word and we're gone. On to the next thing."

"Have you heard from Ivan?"

"We've exchanged some messages," Hakim said. "You know, if I heard anything about your mother, anything at all, I'd march right up those steps into Chapelier's house and tell you. Even if the two of you were in the middle of one of his exorcisms. I wouldn't hesitate."

"I know," April said. "But he's still looking?"

"He and his team are still searching every station and every domed city in the solar system," Hakim said.

"Then I can't go just yet," she said. "I'll leave in a heartbeat if Ivan finds my mother, but until then I have to understand what's going on here."

"You're not just getting sick in a way that, frankly, I find a bit frightening. You're also completely exhausted," Hakim said.

"I'll be OK," she said. "It's weird how draining it is, and it doesn't even feel like I'm doing anything. When I'm not doing anything with ghosts, I don't wind up feeling like I was wrestling with a bear all day, exhausted, yes, and frankly a bit sore. Well, some of the kids lash out; I guess that's some of it. Look, we can figure this out, right? We can help these people?"

"Of course we can," he said and stepped back from her. He looked down at Boo lying in the doorway, watching them both. "And you, you mutt you. Tell that great useless Dane to take better care of your girl. You got that, Boo?"

The dog wagged his tail like mad at the sound of his name, and Hakim bent down to give him pets. April watched the two of them tussling together and realized just how much she had been missing having him near. And he kept talking about Lars being with her now like it was a thing, like he already thought of the two of them as a couple. Of course, how he felt about that was information hidden behind a brick wall.

"Tomorrow is an exorcism day, but I'll stop by after," April said. "To see how your research is progressing."

"Won't you need to be resting?"

"I can handle a walk. Unless you'll be back at the math?" She knew the short walk from Mr. Chapelier's house to Salima's ship was going to be almost more than she could do at the end of a day of exorcisms; it was definitely not going to be worth it just to find him lost in thought and not even aware of her presence.

"No," Hakim said, and she almost got a glimpse of something before he looked away. Chagrin, maybe? "No, I'm sticking with this problem until it's solved now. There will be time enough for math after we've figured out what's happening to these kids."

"Thank you," April said.

He gave her a short nod, then turned his attention back to his tinkering.

27

─────────────

PERSPECTIVES

April stumbled into her bedroom and collapsed onto her bed, drawing her knees close to her chest and burying her face against them. She needed Boo, but he was playing in the yard and she couldn't bring herself to go back downstairs for anything. Her body shook with silent sobs, but tears wouldn't come. Screams might.

She tried to take deeper breaths, to get control. She wasn't succeeding.

"April?"

April's body went still at the sound of Lars's voice, then his footsteps as he came to sit beside her on the bed. She was curled up with her back to the door, her hair pulled loose from its braid spilling over her face. Lars brushed it back gently, but she kept her forehead tight against her knees.

"It was bad?" he guessed.

"It was *Charley*," April said, and the tears came at last, stinging around her left eye.

"I heard him break loose," Lars said. "He caught your hair?"

"Yes," April said. It felt like he should be able to see that for himself, like great patches were missing, leaving behind throbbingly sore bits of scalp. She had seen her hair in Charley's hand when she had at last gotten herself free, Chapelier still chanting his exorcising spells, but making no other move to help her. So much hair.

"That must have hurt," Lars said. "I mean, because it was Charley. We all love Charley."

April nodded against her knees, then took a deeper breath, managing to pull herself together this time. She sat up, flinching as she wiped tears away. Lars was looking at her in horror.

"He hit you?" he said, taking her face in his hands and delicately touching around her left eye.

"I don't remember," she said. "Feels like he must have."

"Yes, it's going to be quite a black eye," Lars said. "I tried to get into the room but Chapelier would not unlock the door to let me in. I jimmied the lock with a knife from the kitchen, but you were already gone."

"I ran," April said. Charley's voice echoed in her ears, screaming and cackling as she fled the room.

It hadn't been Charley; it couldn't have been. Some of the kids might be playing games of pretend, but never Charley. And Charley would never hurt her, never mock her like he'd done. She had looked right into his eyes and it had not been Charley looking back. April pressed a trembling hand to her forehead, flinching again as she touched too close to her eye.

"He's OK," Lars said, rubbing a hand up and down her back.

"Mr. Chapelier?"

"No, Charley," Lars said. "Mr. Chapelier finished the exorcism on his own, and Charley is resting on the couch downstairs. You can see him if you like."

April kept her hand over her closed eyes. "I don't think I can do that. Not yet."

"Charley is upset too," Lars said. "I guess he remembers some of what happened. I think he'd like to see you, to know you're OK."

April dropped her hand at that and looked Lars straight in the eye. "Do I look OK?"

"Well..."

"I can't see him like this," April said.

"I can shut the blinds. If the room is dark, maybe..."

"I can't see him now," April said, wishing he would just understand. How could it not be clear how close she was to not holding it together?

"All right," Lars said, too placatingly for April's taste, and she bit back the urge to say so. "You should rest."

"I'm not going to rest," April said. "I have to see Hakim."

"Hakim?" Lars repeated as if he'd never heard the name.

"He's working on what's really going on here," April said, her voice catching on the word "really," but she soldiered through. "I told him I'd check in today."

"I'll go," Lars said. "I'll talk to him while you rest and then, when you're feeling better, I'll tell you all about it."

"No," April said, swinging her feet to the floor and gripping the edge of the bed, unable to stand just yet. "I have to go myself. I'll have questions, and his answers are going to spawn more questions, and I really just need to be there."

"Mr. Chapelier wanted to talk with you about what happened as well."

"He can talk to me later," April said through gritted teeth and pushed herself to her feet. She still felt a bit trembly, but anger was making her far from weak. "I'll be back in a bit, and then I can talk to Charley and Chapelier and anyone else you want to summon up with a dire need for my time and attention. But right now I'm doing this."

"OK," Lars said, recoiling a bit from the forcefulness of her words.

She felt a stab of regret and one of her hands twitched with the desire to reach out to him, to say something to soften her words, but the watery feeling in her knees reminded her that she still needed to hold on to that anger for a bit. She raised her chin, then made her way out of the room, down the stairs and out of the house.

Her anger wavered when Boo fell into step beside her, turning his black face up to hers with happiness in the way his ears were perked up at her. But at that point, she had enough momentum to keep moving.

April felt her energy begin to flag as she pushed her way inside the administrative building and stumbled across the atrium. When the elevator doors opened, she pushed the button for the dry dock and slumped to the floor, Boo rushing to lie down beside her, his head on her thigh. She stroked his ears absently. Her eye was throbbing, swelling enough to partly block her vision, and her throat felt raw, as if she had been screaming for hours. When the elevator dinged and the doors opened, she swallowed gingerly and got to her feet. Sitting down made her feel more exhausted than before and she put a hand on the elevator door for support as she stepped out into the dock.

"Hakim?" she called, her voice low and hoarse. Had she been screaming? She had thought that had been all Charley, but perhaps it had been both of them. The memories now were like those of a nightmare and she very much wanted them to fade and fall away, but images kept erupting back into her mind's eye, not letting her forget.

She made her slow way across the dock to the workstation where Hakim had been the day before, only to find it empty. The computers were all running, but the text and graphs on the screens meant nothing to her.

"Hakim?" she called again, heading for Salima's ship. Not just her legs, but her whole body was shaky, and she could feel the tears like a tidal wave hovering over her, ready to pound her to the ground. She stopped for a moment, biting her lip hard until the feeling subsided to a level she felt she could be master of.

A metallic crash startled her: a tool tossed casually back into a bin of other tools. Boo yipped in surprise, then raced around the corner of the ship to find Salima. April followed more slowly. Salima was leaning into an open panel in the side of her engine, only her legs visible. Boo was sitting nearby, having learned long ago not to disturb Salima when she was busy but still giving his tallest, most formal sit posture, the one that usually earned him treats for being such a good, patient boy. April watched Salima bend without quite emerging from her engine, one hand groping until it found the tool she had dropped a moment before. Clearly, she was deeply in the zone, probably not even aware of Boo and April there with her. April could ask where Hakim was, but she likely wouldn't get an answer.

The idea of walking further to continue her search was too much; April slumped down onto a crate, brushing back hair that fell over her face as she slumped over her knees. It was still loose from Charley yanking on it, but she lacked even the energy to rebraid it.

"I can't do this anymore," April said, mostly to her own knees. "It's all too much."

Salima's hand appeared, groping for another tool. Boo's ears perked, hoping for a bit of attention, but the hand and tool disappeared once more inside the engine and he settled back into his waiting posture.

"I don't think I've ever had any of this stuff sorted out in my head," April said. "My mother's nightmares—those were real, and scary. But why did I do what I did? Why did I tell things I couldn't see to leave her alone? Why did I think to do that? Sometimes I think maybe I did see something, but I've forgotten it now. Like it's a forbidden thing, I'm not allowed to see those things anymore, so even the memory has been taken from me. Why else would I think to tell things that weren't there to leave? No one had suggested anything like that, not at that point."

Something inside the engine started to hiss loudly, and the muscles in Salima's legs flexed as if she were putting her whole body into some effort. The hissing sound tightened and then died out.

"Then there was that, whatever, in the shuttle. I didn't see anything, but I would swear there was someone in there with me. Maybe a ghost, I don't know. I have to keep reminding myself that I didn't think it was my mother until I found the doll. But I think I've touched that memory too much now too. Like I remember smelling her perfume, but I don't think I did at the time. But when I remember it now, that smell is there. I know, weird. My mind is clearly far too malleable."

A long coil of wires dropped into view and was slowly reeled back in.

"Too malleable," April said again. "Those kids, when they are in that room with Mr. Chapelier, what is going on? I wish someone else were there with me to tell me what's happening. I guess Mr. Chapelier didn't believe in demons, but now he's starting to, and I don't know, but I'm starting to, too. That couldn't have been Charley, Charley would never..."

The last bit of wire disappeared back up into the engine. Boo sighed and dropped from his stiff sitting position to lie on the dock floor, nose on his paws as he watched Salima's feet.

"Maybe it's just easier to believe it's demons. Then I know what to do, and apparently I'm good at it. I should take pride in that, right? And maybe if I try really hard, I'll see what everyone else has been seeing the whole time. Maybe I'll be sure that my memories are true. That would be nice, frankly—to be sure of anything at all."

Two tools dropped into the toolbox, then Salima squatted low to step out of the engine compartment, shutting the panel behind her with a snap, then wiping her hands on a dirty rag as she approached her computer tablet and looked at the screen. Boo's ears perked up again, but she seemed sufficiently engrossed in whatever was still running through her head that he didn't bother to sit up again. April stayed slumped over her knees, regretting not just staying in bed. Where was Hakim, anyway?

"I died, once."

April sat up. Salima's eyes were still on her computer screen, and for a moment, April was afraid she had imagined those words. Then Salima tapped the button to put her tablet in sleep mode and looked directly at April.

"You know that, right? Hakim told you?"

April nodded mutely.

"He doesn't really like to talk about it, but I figured he told you."

"He said he felt himself floating over his body, seeing the both of you lying there with everyone crowded around you, trying to revive you, then there was a light at the end of a tunnel, then he was awake again."

"I was dead longer than he was," Salima said.

"Yes, he said."

"I saw the same things he did. When we compared stories later, they were identical, except for one thing."

April waited for her to continue, afraid that she wouldn't, afraid that prompting her to go on would make her drop the matter entirely. Salima looked down at the rag in her hands, tucked it into the pocket of her jumpsuit, and came to sit on a crate near April, bending to pet Boo as he scrambled to follow her and flop down on her feet.

"I saw all the same things, but I had a different feeling. I can't really explain it. The words are too small for what I felt. But it was like I could look within myself and see the whole universe within me. Like I could look all around at the universe around me and know that all of that was me. Both at once, bigger and smaller. But also, I felt the most profound sense of peace. It sounds trite; I don't have the words for how it felt to be in that moment, that one moment for an eternity. Then I was awake, back in the world. Sometimes at night when I'm in that place between being awake and being asleep, sometimes I feel that big/small, that peace again. But it's always just a little version of that other experience, gone the moment I become aware of being in it. Still, I live for those moments."

April brushed the hair back from her eyes, still not wanting to intrude on what were easily the most words Salima had ever said to her all at once.

"I did some research," Salima said. "I wanted to know why my experience was so different from Hakim's. Why didn't he feel the same peace? Was it because I was dead longer, my brain without oxygen longer? Was it because our brains were different to start with? I don't know. Still. It's not a problem I can solve."

There was just the tiniest edge to that statement, like it wounded her, that lack of solution. Then she sat back, leaning against her hands curled over the edge of the crate behind her, and looked up at the dock ceiling.

"'The tao that can be put into words is not the real tao.' Have you ever heard that? After I read those words, I just let go of trying to explain my experience to myself or others. It just was. It happened. How it made me feel, that's important. It's part of who I am now, for always. But I don't have to explain it to others. No explanation is going to approach reliving the experience for me or make the experience real for anyone else. But it happened, and it changed me.

"You had something happen to you that you can't explain. Well, I imagine Hakim has tried. And he's not wrong that our brains are strange, fascinating things. But in the end, no explanation is going to really change how you feel about what you experienced. And at the end of the day, what you felt, what you took away from it, that's the only real thing."

"But what did I take away from it?" April asked, her voice quavering on the edge of despair. "I thought it was my mother's ghost, but that's not even possible. So what was it?"

"You're still focusing on the wrong end," Salima said. "When you came off that shuttle, you swore never to do this work again. And yet here we are, and you're miserable."

April slumped down once more, unable to argue with that statement.

"Since the day I died, I've felt changed. I had this experience that was the most important thing that had ever happened to me, but I couldn't explain it to others. I was never a talker before, but I think that day made me even more withdrawn from others. I don't understand what goes on in other people's minds; it bothers me. But you already know that day was the day my parents died, and Hakim had no one else but me. It was hard for him, very lonely I think. He doesn't make friends easily. Your joining us has really been good for him. But I could see that maybe we weren't so good for you. You seemed lonely with us. Lars helped with that. We've been like a family all these weeks, but maybe that's coming to an end now. My ship is nearly space worthy and I'll be moving on. The rest of you will have to sort out what you want to do, where you want to go. But our time together has been good for me. It's made me aware of how much I'm missing out on, being remote from others. I know none of you share the experience I had, and that will always be a gap between me and everyone else, but there are other things we have in common. And I should focus more on those." She scratched Boo's ears and his tail thumped happily. "And maybe get a dog of my own."

April didn't know what to say. She had never imagined what Salima thought and felt about them all together. In a lot of ways she had just thought of Salima as part of the ship, if she were very generous as an extension of Hakim, but never really as a person entire unto herself. And yet she was.

"I hope we all leave together and stay a family," April said.

"I would like that as well," Salima said. "But we'll see." She brushed her hands down her pants, then got to her feet. "Hakim is deep within the station; we'd have no hope of finding him without hours of searching that you don't look up to. Come on, I'll walk with you back to Mr. Chapelier's house. I'm curious to catch a glimpse of that man."

"Thanks, Salima," April said, taking the proffered arm and leaning heavily on it.

28

———————

THE CULPRIT

April stayed in her bedroom for five days, either sleeping or sitting in the chair by the window, looking up at the blue sky. She could never get enough of that sky. Boo came and went, and she let him do as he pleased. Fields of grass with butterflies to romp after, or more exciting still, the rows of corn where the field mice lived: there was a lot she would miss when she left this place.

On the morning of the sixth day, she decided it was time to emerge. She hadn't come to any conclusions except that she was certain that Salima's experience of being one with everything and her own experience with feeling a presence she still wasn't sure had been her mother weren't similar at all. She understood what Salima was saying about finding the meaning without need for scientific explanation, but April didn't know what that meaning was. She thought she had at the time: her mother was dead, but still with her. But her mother *wasn't* dead, so what did it mean? She just didn't know.

Mr. Chapelier and Lars were sitting close together at the table in the kitchen, poring over Lars's tablet, empty plates and cooling mugs of tea pushed aside. They looked up when she appeared in the doorway and Lars half got to his feet, but April tiredly waved him back down and went to fetch her own mug of tea.

"Feeling better?" Lars asked anxiously. He had been bringing her food, most of which she hadn't eaten, and she had avoided being drawn into conversations.

She still felt like she would rather not talk, but there was a limit to rudeness. "Yes, thanks," she said. There were two slices of toast in the drying rack, and she pointed at them with raised brows.

"Please, go ahead," Lars said. "Do you want me to poach you an egg?"

"No, not there yet," April said.

"Do you want to see what we're working on?"

"Yes, very much, but maybe in a bit," April said.

"You should call on Charley at your earliest convenience," Mr. Chapelier said. "He's very upset. It's not good for his recovery."

"I will," she promised, still dreading that meeting.

"We will need to work again tomorrow," he went on. "I hope you will be ready."

"Oh," April said, caught off guard. She should have days left to decide what she was going to do; he had just moved up the date.

"We can see how you're feeling tonight," Lars said reassuringly. "But some of the kids, they are getting bad."

"I've been researching some more extreme measures," Mr. Chapelier said. "Not for tomorrow, that's too soon, but we need to do something bigger. We're losing control of the situation here. I'd like your input."

"That's what you're working on here? Bigger exorcisms?"

"We need to cleanse the entire station," Mr. Chapelier said, but Lars nearly cut him off.

"But that's not what we're working on. I'm trying to get us back on a steady supply line. We need contact with other stations, access to more foods and medicine—"

"—under strictly controlled conditions," Mr. Chapelier added.

April nodded, exhausted at just the thought of all the arguing back and forth the two of them had already been doing. Lars looked exhilarated; he was born to organize a committee.

"Boo?"

"Outside," Lars said. April nodded her thanks, stacked the toast on top of her tea mug, and went down the hall and out onto the front porch.

Boo gave a happy yip at the sight of her and ran up the steps to jump all over her. She set her mug and toast down on the porch rail and knelt down to tussle with the dog until he was satisfied and leapt back off the porch in pursuit of something he thought he'd seen skittering in the tall grass at the edge of the lawn.

April sat down on the rocking chair, all too aware of the windows behind her that looked in on the exorcism room, and took a small bite of dry toast. She regretted turning down the offer of a poached egg; soaking the golden toast in a thick, runny yolk sounded really good at the moment. The tea was cold but still good. Mr. Chapelier mixed his own in small batches, each a unique delight of subtle flavors.

There was a lot she was going to miss when she left here.

She had just finished the last of the toast, licking the crumbs from the tips of her fingers, when she felt eyes upon her and looked up to see Hakim standing outside the garden gate. She jumped to her feet, heart beating fast.

"My mother?"

"No," he said, reaching for the gate latch. She jumped down the steps and ran down the path to catch his hand.

"He's near," April said.

"I don't care. I have news. I've figured out, perhaps not all the puzzle, but certainly the major pieces."

"You have? You're sure?"

"Very sure."

"And we can fix it?"

"We can fix everything," he said with a rare grin.

April unlatched the gate and stepped out of the garden to throw her arms around him. "You've saved me," she said. "Just in time. There is no way I could do that again."

He patted her back awkwardly. Boo came racing up to them to jump all over Hakim's legs until she stepped back and let him bend down to pet the dog.

"So what is it? What's wrong with the kids?"

"Better I show you," Hakim said. "Can you take a walk?"

"Of course," April said, latching the gate behind her.

"You know this place was a mining station," Hakim said as they started walking back toward the village, Boo close behind them. She nodded. "These people living here, none of them descend from the original miners. The station was abandoned in a great hurry just before the plague back on Earth and sat empty for decades. These people have only been here for about twenty years."

"And that's relevant? Is this something genetic, then?"

"No. I just think if the miners had stayed on, they would have raised subsequent generations with more knowledge of station upkeep."

"Lars wants to change that," April said. "He wants to set up a sort of school to teach the children station maintenance."

"That's a good idea," Hakim said. "But some things need to be rectified before they can start maintaining."

"OK," April said slowly.

Hakim took her elbow to steer her off the path to the village, back to the doorway in the hill that led to the lower levels. Someone was waiting for them, sitting on an upside-down bucket outside the open door.

"That's Charley," April said, coming to a standstill.

"Yeah," Hakim said. "Look, he feels terrible about what happened."

"If he was really possessed, would he even remember it?"

"We both know he wasn't possessed," Hakim said.

"He hit me. My eye still hurts."

"I can see that," Hakim said, touching her face carefully just outside the edges of her still-black eye. "He wants to make it up to you. He came to find me the day after. I would not have found the answer without him. I was close to solving half the puzzle, but the other half eluded me. I had no idea what the kids were up to."

"I don't understand," April said.

"Charley and I will show you."

April nodded with a sigh and resumed walking up to the doorway where Charley was waiting, on his feet now, hands twisting anxiously together.

"Hello, April," he said, not quite looking at her.

"Hello, Charley."

And he burst into tears. She rushed to hug him as he babbled apologies over and over again.

"It's going to be OK," April told him. "Nothing has happened that can't be made better. I'll heal and so will you."

"Hakim said," Charley said between sniffles. "We can get better."

"Now," she said, watching him wipe his tears with the hem of his T-shirt, "you have something to show me?"

"Yeah. It's a secret place where some of us kids go to play," Charley said. "We didn't know it was bad, honest."

"Some of the kids," Hakim said. "All their names would be very familiar to you. Repeat customers to Mr. Chapelier's little business."

"A secret club of fakers?" April asked, and Charley flinched.

"A club of kids giving themselves a double dose," Hakim said. "Lead the way, Charley."

Charley nodded and went through the doorway, ducking into the narrow hallway Lars had followed when he repaired the plumbing. There was a narrow tunnel running vertically, and Charley grabbed the rungs of the ladder built into the wall and started climbing down. April followed. Hakim tucked Boo into his shirt and climbed down one-handed, keeping the other on the dog.

The ladder ended in another hallway, so narrow April's shoulders brushed the walls on either side but taller than the one above. Charley was already nearly out of eyesight, three circles of red emergency lighting away. April rushed to catch up. He stopped where the hallway opened up into a large, square room and squatted over an opening in the floor.

"Ready?" Charley asked.

"For what?" April asked, but he was already gone, jumping down into the hole. He disappeared from sight with a delighted shriek. April looked up at Hakim, vaguely panicked.

"Mining station," Hakim explained. "This part is under spin, but the asteroid in the center of it isn't. There are mining tunnels. Free fall, but normal air pressure. You just have to jump out into it."

"And we can get back in?"

"Of course. The kids do it all the time," Hakim said. He took her hand and at her nod, the two of them jumped off the concrete edge of the hatch into the barely lit stone mining shaft.

"Charley?" Hakim called.

"Coming back to you," his voice carried distantly.

"Remember to avoid the blobs," Hakim said.

"Yes, boss," Charley said, not quite sarcastically.

"Blobs?" April asked. Hakim was still holding Boo tight, although the dog was starting to squirm a bit.

"Look," Hakim said, pointing. Then he took a light out of his pocket and clicked it on. The cavern around them seemed to swallow up the light, leaving only a small aura around them, but it was enough for April to see what he was pointing at.

"Liquid silver?" April said. "It's beautiful."

"Sadly, yes," Hakim said. "You almost can't resist touching it. But do. Resist touching it."

"What is it?" April asked.

"Mercury," Hakim said. "The kids have been playing with it, poking it with their fingers, batting it around the caves with their hands. Apparently, they've been coming down here since the original squatters moved in, but it was only a month or so ago when one of them found an old canister in one of the deeper caverns and unleashed this."

"And it's been making everyone sick ever since?"

"Alas, no," Hakim said. "Or not just. Only the kids who come down here are exposed directly, a few other people indirectly when they bring it back into the station in tiny amounts on their skin and on their clothes."

"Chapelier," April said.

"Exactly. He comes in contact with these kids in particular a lot, and they are indeed driving him mad. The pink rashes are from this."

Charley finally reached them, a small light of his own in his hand. He was looking all around, carefully avoiding contact with the sparkling blobs.

"And you can fix this?"

"This was a mining station. The mercury is probably here to aid in the extraction of gold or silver. They probably have bots somewhere designed for just this sort of cleanup. Spills happen, right?"

"So we just have to find where the mining station maintenance crew kept the bots," April said.

"In the meantime, Charley is in charge of keeping all the kids out of the mines, right?"

Charley gave a sharp nod.

"But the kids already exposed—"

"I'll get to that, but there's something else to show you first."

"I figured," April said. "You said these kids were getting a double dose, so there's more mercury somewhere else?"

"It's a different sort of thing, which is why the puzzle was so impossible to solve until I talked to Charley. Come on, let's get back in the station proper. Just watch for the hatch to pass and grab a handhold."

Hakim kept a hand on her arm as they floated near the spinning station. Charley leapt first, knowing the station hull well enough to time the arrival of the hatch. Hakim pushed April towards it first, then launched himself off the shaft wall to catch one of the handholds that ran in a continuous sequence all around the station. Charley was already in the hatch when April reached the edge and he helped her pull herself back inside. She turned to take Boo from Hakim and watched him pull himself up and out of the hole.

"The water reservoir is also on this level," Hakim said. Charley was already leading the way back down the hallway and April followed, Boo in her arms.

"Did the kids do this too?" April asked. She remembered the water tanks in the *Triomphe* and couldn't imagine anyone wanting to play in such a place, not when there was sunlight and green grass so close at hand.

"No, this was probably done when the original miners left," Hakim said. "I've located the canisters. This isn't the same as what's in the mines. The canisters aren't labeled, but I think someone was using them to store the byproducts of some process, which happens to contain methylmercury, among other things. Three of them somehow ended up in the reservoir, and two have rusted through. This problem would have come up so slowly it's not surprising no one noticed."

"Methylmercury in the water," April said. "But Lars fixed the plumbing. The water running to the houses should be clean now."

"It is, and that's a big help, since the worst point of contamination was the lake itself."

The hallway became a grilled catwalk, traversing a room too large for her to see the walls on either side. She could see Charley's hand-held light bouncing ahead, glinting off the dark waters below. Something splashed in the darkness.

"This connects with the lake?"

"Ironically enough, this is supposed to be what filters the lake. The fish pass through here and back up to the lake bottom and then back down here. There are labs on that side of things, with frozen eggs and embryos. The people here are going to be able to start again with even more fish than they have now. They'll just have to wait a bit for them to get big enough to eat."

"The fish," April said. "You suspected. You told me not to eat the fish."

"The fish have been exposed to larger and larger doses of methylmercury. The symptoms were confusing since this kind of mercury poisoning is different from what the kids were exposing themselves to. Eating these fish will turn your brain to Swiss cheese."

"Can we fix it?" April asked.

"We have to get the canisters out of the water, which won't be hard since I already have the submersible drones I used to find these cans. Salima could put some simple waldos on them so they can pick up the canisters and bring them to the surface. Then we need to doctor the filtration systems, make them a lot more thorough on methylmercury. They currently are mostly concerned with bacterial growth. But I think I have what I need to do that in the science station. Then we kill all the fish, every last one. When the water tests clean, we restock the water with the material from the biology labs and just wait."

"But the people already exposed?"

"There are some things we can try," Hakim said. "Such as chelation, but the station didn't keep a lot of those drugs on hand. They never expected widespread exposure like this, plus the drugs have been sitting around for decades. I'm not even sure they are still good."

"Lars is working with Mr. Chapelier to set up a supply route," April said. "For food and for medicine. Do you think someone could find those drugs all the way out here?"

"If not, they can make a humanitarian plea to Earth," Hakim said. "They'd have to respond. But even if we do get the drugs, some of the damage might be irreversible."

"Still," April said. "Stopping exposure now, helping those who can be helped, and making sure the people here will be safe from now on. That's something, right?"

"It's not nothing," Hakim said.

"We have to tell Mr. Chapelier. At once. We need to get started on the fixes right away. And Lars is going to be crucial in getting that stuff done. I can guarantee Mr. Chapelier isn't going to be any real help, but he can be a huge hindrance if he chooses."

"You have to convince him," Hakim said. "Which means I better stay away."

"I'll meet you at the ship dock after," April said.

29

____

COLD HARD DATA

April stood with her hands clasped tightly behind her back, watching as Mr. Chapelier's eyes moved over the data Hakim had downloaded to her reader. He glanced up at her now and again, but mostly just swiped through the pages without a word.

Lars was theoretically reading over Mr. Chapelier's shoulder, but his eyes were more on April than on the data. She fought to keep the heat out of her cheeks. Save the people first, explain her feelings to Lars later.

Mr. Chapelier set the reader down and reached for his tea.

"So you see?" April asked, unable to wait another minute for him to start talking. She was practically bouncing on her toes.

He shrugged absently, and now April's cheeks were flaming with an entirely different kind of emotion.

"You can't not see what this means," April said. "I can show you the canisters, if that's what you need. But we need to start dealing with this now."

"You can show me canisters," Mr. Chapelier said, then paused to take an entirely theatrical drink of tea, "but that proves nothing."

"Nothing?"

"For all I know your friend put them there to back up this... mathematical story," he said, waving a hand in the direction of her reader, which was still showing the results of all the tests Hakim had done on the water, soil, fish, and Charley's blood.

April sputtered, unable to summon words. She looked desperately to Lars.

"What are you proposing we do?" Lars asked mildly.

"Hakim is going through the medical stores now. There are some chelation drugs here we can give to the worst cases, but they are old and there are nowhere near enough of them. That supply route you were going to establish—you need to get that going now. In fact, Salima's ship is ready to launch. You should just talk to her. You know she'd say yes."

Lars nodded, but she could tell he was acknowledging, not agreeing. He picked up her reader and looked at the data.

"And the water?"

"The drinking water is fine since you got it running again; it comes from a different source and is being filtered. Hakim is going to start adding some extra filtration methods to the lake water and get them running as soon as he gets the canisters out. He and Salima are working on adapting the submersible drones for that now. Then..."

Mr. Chapelier had propped his chin up on his hand, watching her with sleepy eyes. Lars prompted her, "Then?"

"We have to remove all the fish. Space them, probably."

"All the fish," Lars repeated. "That's not possible. The people will starve."

"Once the water is clean and safe again, there are fish embryos frozen in the biology lab, ready and waiting to be reintroduced to the lake. But it has to be clean first or this all repeats."

"It will be weeks, months before we can eat fish again," Lars said. "That's impossible."

"No, it isn't," April insisted. "You have enough grain and fruit and vegetables growing here to get by. Plus, the new supply route."

"Food and medicine cost money," Lars pointed out.

"You have things to sell," April said. "This place is a mining station full of equipment you're not using, things of real value in the Belt."

Lars tipped his head, and April could imagine the mental arithmetic whirring through his mind.

"This is all well and good," Mr. Chapelier said at last. "But it doesn't solve the demon problem. Only my mass exorcism will do that."

April opened her mouth, closed it, then opened it again. "This is your demon problem," she said at last, her voice sounding tiny in her own ears.

"Don't be ridiculous," Mr. Chapelier said.

"I'm not the one being ridiculous," April said. "Go to your own library. You have medical texts in there. Look up mercury poisoning and methylmercury poisoning, look at the symptoms and ask yourself if it doesn't explain what's happening to the children, and to you, and to the whole village."

"I'm already familiar with those texts," Mr. Chapelier said. "I concede it explains some superficial aspects, like this damnable pink rash." He gave his forearm a particularly harsh scratch. "But not all, not the chief aspects. You've been there. You've looked into their eyes and heard them speak with a voice that was not their own. Don't be seduced by someone who shows you some numbers of his own devising."

"All this can be replicated," April said. "Lars can do it. He can test everything."

Lars took a deep breath. "All right. Say you're right. We can't kill off the fish. We can't tell these people they have to live in hunger for months, subject their children to needles and whatever side effects the drugs are going to give them..."

"Look what they are subjecting their kids to now," April said, waving her arm behind her in the direction of the exorcism room. "You can convince them of anything if you can make them believe that helps."

"I can't convince them of *anything*," Mr. Chapelier said. "Things have to fit into their own worldview."

"You can make them believe," April said. "You know how to make this fit their worldview. You can do it."

"Perhaps," Mr. Chapelier said with another shrug. "But I choose not to lie to them. Now, if you'll excuse me, I have more research to do on the actual solution to this problem."

April blinked back hot tears as he put the back of his hand on her shoulder and guided her gently out of his way as he passed behind her, out the door and down the hall to his library. The library door shut with a soft click, somehow sounding more final than the loudest slam would have.

"How can you not help?" April said, angrily brushing tears from her eyes.

"You want too much," Lars said.

"This isn't about wanting," April spat out. "This has to be done. Half measures won't solve it. All the mercury has to be removed from everything. Even with that and with the drugs, there are going to be villagers who will never be entirely well again, but without this, they're all doomed."

"This isn't going to end the exorcisms," Lars said. "That's what you're wanting, and it's too much. You can't turn their world upside down and demand that everyone be rational in the face of fear and tumult."

"Psychological prop," April said. "But that's not what he's talking about anymore. This big exorcism thing he's cooking up is going to change nothing, and then what comes next? Burning the witches?"

"Don't be absurd," Lars said.

April wiped the tears from her face with her sleeve. "I don't have the words to convince you."

"I believe you about the mercury," Lars said at last. "But still, we could do everything you're recommending, and these people could go hungry until the clean fish are big enough to eat, and they could submit their children and themselves to these drugs and I'm sure endless tests to see how the drugs are working—they can do all those things and in the end still have the same problems they have now. Because maybe it isn't just mercury poisoning."

"There might be other things going on," April agreed. "But you have no hope of finding the source of those things until you deal with this thing first."

"It's going to be a hard sell without Mr. Chapelier's support," Lars said. "And calling a halt to the exorcisms is not going to get him on your side."

"I never said he had to stop."

"It was very strongly implied," Lars said. "Are you going to carry on as his assistant?"

"I thought I would leave with Salima," April said. "The medicine might not be easy to procure. I want to do what I can on that end of things."

Lars nodded, as if that was exactly what he'd expected her to say.

"I like it here," April said. "It's like a garden in paradise in a lot of ways. But I can't stay. Not if I have to pay my rate by pretending these poor kids are harboring demons. I won't do it anymore."

Lars gave a humorless laugh. "How many times have you said that before?"

"I mean it."

"I assume you meant it all those times before, too."

"I did," April agreed. "I'm not a hypocrite. We always only dealt with the ghosts as a means to find the real problem. Now that we've found it—"

Lars raised a hand, and she let her words grind to a halt. She expected he had something to say, but instead he repeated Mr. Chapelier's gesture, brushing her to one side so he could storm out the door.

April picked up her reader, slipping it into its accustomed place against her belly. Then she went upstairs to pack her few belongings back in her carpetbag. Her time in this hellish paradise was at an end.

April and Boo emerged from the elevator to find Hakim and Charley assisting Salima in mounting arms on two submersible drones. Hakim got to his feet at the sound of the elevator doors and took a few steps towards her, then waited, hands in his pockets. April walked up to stand in front of him, not sure how to start explaining how badly everything had gone at Mr. Chapelier's house. Hakim reached out to take her bag and put it over his own shoulder, and she realized she didn't have to say a word. He already knew just by looking at her what had happened, or close enough.

"We're still going to fix this before we go," he said.

April looked up at him, searching his eyes. He raised an eyebrow at her sudden scrutiny and flinched when she threw her arms around him, then allowed himself to be hugged.

She had had no clue what Lars was feeling until he had acted on it. Maybe the same thing was true with Hakim? She decided to test it and tentatively rose up on tiptoes to press her lips to his. He stiffened for an instant in surprise, then melted into her, awkward arms around her, suddenly knowing just what they wanted to do.

April could have stayed in that moment forever, but Boo wouldn't allow it. They broke apart, both kneeling to reassure the little dog that he was still the center of everyone's world. Hakim tousled Boo's ears, but his eyes were on April's.

"I just wanted to be clear," April said. "It's not remotely the most important thing going on here, but I think Lars is confusing the two, and I wanted not to do that."

"OK," Hakim said. "I'm not sure I understood that."

"That's all right," April said. "I wanted to be clear to myself, about what I'm doing and why, and now I am."

"Happy to be of service," Hakim said. "You're going to have to explain it all to me later, in exquisite detail, with I hope more demonstrations to illustrate your points..." April felt her cheeks flushing again, deeper than the normal pink of her reaction to mercury exposure. "... but right now we have work to do."

"Of course," April said, and followed him to where Charley and Salima were making no attempt to pretend they hadn't stopped all tinkering on the drones to watch the two of them. April twisted her braid in her hands, searching for words to break the moment.

"Are they going to be big enough?" she asked at last.

"They're stronger than they look," Salima said, her thumbs on the remote making the waldos on one of the drones pivot and clamp together.

"Cool," Charley said.

"Charley had his first treatment already," Hakim said and Charley pulled up his sleeve to show her the brightly colored bandage on his upper arm.

"Did it hurt?" April asked.

"It burned a little, but Hakim said that was perfectly normal,"

Charley said, dropping his sleeve and turning his attention back to the drone.

"You'll need it too," Hakim said, touching her cheek.

April shook her head. "Not from the limited supply here," she said. "Later, when we have more to bring back here. But it's good that Charley has already had an injection." April took a deep breath, and all three looked at her expectantly. Even Boo sat down and gave her his full attention, head tipped and one ear cocked up as he listened.

"We are on our own in this," April said. "Mr. Chapelier wants nothing to do with this, and Lars isn't going to be any help." Her voice cracked on his name. "But we have Charley. Charley who helped find the source of all this, Charley who is helping to solve it with these drones, and Charley who's already had an injection he's going to have to help us convince the others will help. It's a big ask, Charley—"

"I can do it," Charley said. "I knew this was probably the next step. Hakim has explained everything to me so clearly. I knew it was because I'd have to explain it again to the others."

"Actually, that was just because I like to explain things," Hakim said, but there was a certain beamish pride in how he was looking at Charley, like the kid really was his protégé.

"Let's get the canisters out of the water first," Salima said, loading the two drones onto a handcart that Charley ran to be the one to push. "Once we have them out and the filtration running on high, we can go talk to them about the fish."

"The open can in the mines?" April asked.

"We need a different sort of drone for that," Salima said. "It will need a cleaning apparatus, some sort of suction—"

"There are cleaning drones listed on the original mining specs, but they weren't in the lockers where they should have been," Hakim explained. "I'm sure they're around here someplace. Once everyone is on board with the plan, they can help search. In the meantime, it's merely a matter of no one going into the mines."

"Let's get started, then," April said. "I'm just going to put my bag and Boo into the ship. Which is my berth?"

"You'll be able to tell," Salima said, gathering up the drone remotes and looking around to make sure she had everything. April whistled for Boo to follow her, then climbed up the ramp to the airlock.

Landing gear to hold the ship upright, a ramp up to the airlock, everything up and down inside the ship itself. Salima really had sweetened up her ride. A walkway ran through the cargo space before stepping up into a hub between the four sleep berths. April felt a stab of sadness. She didn't see any end to all this that would include all four of them traveling together again. She had been too oblivious for too long and ruined what could have been a really nice friendship. If only she could have sorted out her own feelings before Lars had kissed her, but she couldn't quite regret it.

Boo yipped and jumped through the hatch to the berth on the left. April followed, stepping through the round hatchway into a sleep pod hung with sheer fabrics, violets and blues with silver threads, decorated here and there with tiny silver bells. They hung in drapey waves, but on closer inspection, April found that they were attached to the walls with innumerable small patches of Velcro, so in free fall they would stay where they were. Boo yipped again and April saw that in addition to the usual bunk in the far wall where she would moor her hammock in free fall, there was a smaller bunk in the shorter wall to her right, a little cubby just Boo's size.

A purple curlicue design ran in circles and spirals around the perimeter of the room, which, when April blinked, resolved itself into an elaborate calligraphy. Salima's handwriting? It was gorgeous. She leaned closer to read the words and found them to be poetry. "My external sensations are no less private to myself than are my thoughts or my feelings. In either case, my experience falls within my own circle, a circle closed on the outside; and, with all its elements alike, every sphere is opaque to the others which surround it... In brief, regarded as an existence which appears in a soul, the whole world for each is peculiar and private to that soul. T.S. Eliot."

April smiled in wonder, that Salima would put so much effort into something that had nothing to do with a machine or an engine. To sleep surrounded by soft beauty. And that fragment of poem, a reminder of their conversation, words she could meditate on. She was certain Salima already had. It felt like a deeply personal passage, like Salima was sharing a shining piece of her own soul.

But it wasn't time for her to enjoy her berth, not yet. April tossed her bag onto the bunk and persuaded Boo to wait for her there. The little twist of very hard jerky that had been left in the cubby helped. She shut the hatch behind her, then ran back out to join the others at the elevator.

Things were going to be OK. She just knew it.

30

FINALLY SOME GOOD NEWS

"ARE YOU SURE THIS IS ALL OF IT?" APRIL ASKED, PAUSING IN HER WORK TO stretch her back. She had no idea what time it was, but she guessed the night shift was half over, at least.

"No," Hakim said. "This station is in such disarray there could be more anywhere, but considering its storage requirements, I checked all the obvious places."

"I'm not finding much," April said glumly, then got back to work lifting each vial one at a time out of the rack that fit one hundred and reading the label before setting it back. A much smaller rack sat at her elbow, containing the few vials of chelate she had found.

"We'll come back with more from the *Triomphe*," Hakim reminded her. The computer on the lab table in front of him beeped, and he leaned forward to read the screen. "Luckily, all the embryos are still viable."

"Fish is rare," April said. "Once they get their lake restocked, they'll have another valuable trade good." She looked at a few more vials. "Why have they been living this way? Didn't they realize what they'd found when they came here?"

"The stations were all isolated from each other for a long time," Hakim said. "It was only a year or two before we were born that people started moving around again. No one wanted to risk spreading plague mutations around. These people came here before then and I guess never realized. Or they never needed to know; frankly, mercury aside, they are quite self-sufficient."

"Mr. Chapelier knew," April said. "I guess he really believed something was going on here that needed to be dealt with before bringing other people in, to live or even just to trade. Still, it feels like he kept them isolated on purpose."

Hakim shrugged. "I don't know if it really matters if his motives were noble or nefarious. The result is the same."

April looked up at an excited whoop from Charley. She glanced at Hakim, then the two of them rushed out of the lab onto the catwalk overlooking the water reservoir. Salima and Charley were both bent over their controllers, watching the movements of their submersed drones on the screens in front of them.

"Success?" April asked.

"The canisters are all inside the container," Salima said, still staring at her screen with a studious frown. "Now to bring it up—"

"I'll get under it," Charley said, fingers flying over his controller. By the smile that quirked the corner of Salima's mouth, April guessed that Charley was a quick study in drone piloting. The two of them worked together, leaning to one side or another as if it would assist their distant drones.

"Hello?"

The voice echoed through the chamber and April looked toward the doorway they had come through, but it was empty. Hakim nudged her shoulder and pointed in a different direction.

"That tunnel comes from the basements of the administration building," he explained.

"Lars?" April called back.

"There you are!" Lars appeared behind Salima and Charley, glanced at what they were doing with a puzzled frown, then found the stairs up to the laboratory catwalk. "I've been looking everywhere for you."

Hakim exchanged a quick glance with April before heading back into the lab to continue his work.

"Did Mr. Chapelier send you?" April asked, still hoping her mentor might change his mind.

"No," Lars admitted. "He's not bending. They are removing the contamination?" He jerked his chin back over his shoulder towards Salima and Charley.

"Yes, they've nearly got it. Then we have to turn the filtration systems up to maximum. Salima has also doctored the filters to bind and remove the methylmercury. It will take time; there's a lot of water." Lars nodded gravely. "Then there's the fish."

"April," Lars said. "There's a message for you on Salima's ship. I went there first to find you. That's how I saw the light flashing."

"Did you play it?" April asked, realizing belatedly that he must have, to know it was for her.

"It's Ivan. He's found your mother."

"Alive?" April asked.

"Of course alive," Lars said.

It took several long moments for this news to penetrate April's exhausted mind, but finally she gave a little happy cry and threw her arms around Lars, hugging him tight. Hakim emerged once more from the laboratory and Lars stepped back from her, his cheeks flushing as he avoided looking at either of them. "I was going to talk to you about all this, but, of course, that can wait."

"I have to answer him," April said.

"Who?" Hakim asked.

"Ivan. Hakim, my mother is alive!"

Hakim opened his arms, and she fell into him, happy tears wetting his shirt.

"Go ahead, go message her back," Hakim said.

"I'll take over for you here," Lars said, "if you'll show me what she was doing?" Hakim nodded.

"Thank you. Thank you both!" She spun and ran down the stairs.

"Good news?" Salima asked as April jogged past.

"The best!" April said. "I'll tell you all everything when I get back."

April could hear Boo pawing at her pod hatch and let him out. He had been cooped up for hours while they worked. As anxious as she was to play the message, she gathered Boo up in her arms instead, taking him back down the elevator and out of the building so he could run to the nearest tree and relieve himself. He wanted to romp about, despite the darkness, but reluctantly returned to her side when she whistled. He sulked when she put him back in her pod but then rediscovered the chew and got back to work on it, propping it between his paws almost as if they were proper hands and working the slimy edge with his back teeth.

April settled herself in Salima's usual spot in the cockpit, cross-legged on the floor, looking up at monitors that would be at her level if she were in free fall. Then she keyed the message to play.

"April and Hakim, if you are there," Ivan said, his eyes bright with his upcoming news. "I believe you are still on board the *Asteroidi,* so I am sending this transmission that way. If you've moved on, I ask whoever receives this message to forward it on or return a message to me."

He took a breath, then leaned forward ever-so-slightly closer to the camera. "I've found Melena. She has quite a tale to tell, but suffice it to say she is alive and now quite well and back with me on the *Triomphe.* She is resting now—it was a long journey to bring her back to me—but I didn't want to wait until she was ready to message you herself to let you know she was OK. I'm hoping you're in a position to return here soon; I know she is very anxious to see you again. Message me back; I don't think I'm getting any sleep myself until I hear from you. Ivan out."

April's heart was beating in light fluttery beats. Her mother found! And waiting for her on the station that was already her next destination.

April recorded her own message. "Ivan, Mother," she said, and she could see from the little image of herself in the corner of the screen that she was glowing despite her exhaustion. "Oh, I'm so relieved you're OK. We are already preparing to get underway for the *Triomphe* in a dozen or so hours. We have some work to finish here first. I'll explain it all when I see you. Ivan, we have some supplies we need to acquire for our return run. I'm hoping you can help me track down as many chelation drugs as you can find. The people here have been exposed to high levels of organic and inorganic mercury for quite some time and we're trying to help them get healthy again. They have things to trade. Salima has the specs on everything. I'll have her message you those once we're underway. Mother, Boo is with me. Thank you so much for him. I can't wait for you to meet him. But please, I can't wait until we meet again to know what happened. Where have you been all this time?" She felt the prick of tears at the corners of her eyes and took a deeper breath, bringing her smile back. "I have a lot to finish up here before I can head back, so I'm going to get to it. I'm very anxious to see you again, both of you. Ivan, thank you so much for everything you've done. Mother, I'll see you soon. April out."

She pushed the button to stop the recording, then the other to send the message *Triomphe*-bound, encoded to go directly to Ivan once the station received it.

She got to her feet and walked the length of the ship, but stopped at the airlock door. She could still see the communications screen from here and would see the light if an incoming message was received. Was her mother still sleeping? She had no idea at what point of the day cycle the *Triomphe* was at; every station kept its own clock. She longed to wait around, to play the message the minute she received it, but what if that was still hours away? She should get back to work.

The elevator dinged opened and a large silhouette emerged from the lighted interior, joining her in the semidarkness when the doors hissed shut again.

"Hello, Lars," she said. She'd know those shoulders anywhere.

"April," he said as he approached, hands in pockets.

"You abandoned my task?"

"Charley and Salima got the container out of the water and tossed it out into the mines. They took over the vial search so I could come see how you were doing."

"I'm waiting for my mother to message me back," April said, sitting down on the edge of the airlock. Lars gestured to the space beside her and she nodded an invitation for him to join her.

"I'm sorry about before," Lars said. "Sorry doesn't quite... I'm frankly ashamed. We're a team. I should have backed you up. I mean, I wish you had talked to me about it and then we could have gone to Mr. Chapelier together, but I handled it badly."

"It's not about you and me," April said.

"I know." He ran a hand through his curls. "There is no you and me. Is there." Not a question.

"No," April admitted. "I mean, I like you. We'll always be friends."

"I get it," Lars said before she could go on. "Well, I'm sorry about that. I thought we had a real connection. I guess that was just me."

In a rush, April's mind whirled over every moment they had spent together. It hadn't been just him, but defining every nuance of her own feelings would take hours, and in the end, they would just end up in the same place, so she said nothing.

"We're going to be leaving soon," April said when the silence between them grew intolerable. "We're going to the *Triomphe*. I've asked Ivan to help us find medicine for the people here. I'll get a variety of foods, too, as varied a diet as I can pull together. We can make it a regular route. Lars, these people need a constant, reliable connection with the rest of humanity."

"I know," he said. "I've been working to bring Mr. Chapelier around on that idea for quite some time now. I nearly had him until all this."

"It's more important than ever, because of all this."

"I know," Lars said. "I just wish, really wish, you had come to me first. I could have presented it differently, maybe won him over."

"How?"

"I don't know. I didn't get any time to think on it."

"Too much time has gone by already," April said.

"Maybe," Lars said, but he sounded unconvinced.

"You know," April said after another long silence, "you're always welcome to continue traveling with us. Salima specifically said so to me, and it's her ship."

"Thank you, that's good to know," Lars said, "but I'm really needed here." He stood up, brushing the backs of his pants legs as he straightened. "I'm going back to Mr. Chapelier's house. Sometimes at night he needs me; I'd hate for him to find I've abandoned him."

"You two are closer than I thought," April said.

Lars shrugged. "You've been focusing on other things," he said. He started to walk towards the elevator, but he stopped and turned back. "You won't leave without saying goodbye?"

"Of course not," April said.

He nodded and continued on to disappear into the elevator.

April rested her head against the edge of the airlock. Her eyelids were heavy, each blink harder and harder to recover from.

Then the communications station beeped, and she was fully awake once more. She scrambled back into the cockpit and played the waiting message. Her mother's image filled the screen. The rush of happiness that filled April's chest turned to ice water. She looked thin, pale, her gorgeous hair shaved close to her head. What had happened to her?

"April," she said as the message began to play. "My dear, you look as lovely as ever, although a bit tired. I hope you're not working too hard? I'm so glad you were already planning to head this way. I don't want to interrupt anything you have going on, but I'm so eager to see you again. Just seeing your face... you look well.

"I'm sorry I worried you both. All. Ivan tells me you've been looking for me. I don't know what clues you've been following—the whole thing is so odd. I was shopping at that station with Ivan's men and stopped in that little shop to find something I could send to wherever you were. The man in the shop recognized me, can you imagine? But I suppose you get that a lot. He knew who I was, and he was the one who recommended that dog for you. I arranged for it to be sent to you, but then the man started telling me about this boy with gifts like yours, but he had no control and the ghosts were a torment to him. He asked me if I would visit the boy and I said yes.

"I should have asked where the boy was first. I see that now. There were so many little asteroids in the area, I thought that was where he was taking me. And he said the boy who fetched my bags would explain to the shuttle crew where I was going and when I would be back, so they could wait. Honestly, I don't know what the man was up to. Ivan intends to ask him...

"At any rate, I was taken from shuttle to station to shuttle and ended up at last in a dome on the moon. No mistaking when you're in one of those; no one else deals with that level of gravity, such a nuisance. At this point, I was running low on my medications, even though I had been rationing them since my impromptu journey had started. Apparently, I'm not supposed to do that, to space them out to make them last. They don't work the same. I felt kind of foggy, just letting this man lead me around. But at the end of it there was a boy, and he was clearly in real despair because of the ghosts constantly whispering in his ears. Poor boy. I tried to help him, to teach him the rituals you and I worked out together. But I didn't get much of a chance to help him before I fell ill. Damn lunar dome settlements. The boy's family was beyond poor, and the shuttle that had dropped me off wasn't coming back anytime soon, and no one had a way of communicating with the wider world short of donning a suit and walking to the closest city.

"They took care of me as well as they could," she went on, touching her nearly bare scalp self-consciously. "And I recovered, eventually. It was a near thing. There was a point where I felt like I was balancing, tipping in and out of this world and the next. It was so peaceful, like I was ready to go. Sometimes I felt like you were there with me, sitting near my cot..."

April felt a shiver run up her spine. She and her mother were going to have to compare story chronologies, but April was certain that when they did, they would find that her moment of feeling her mother near would overlap with her mother's. It had to. She knew in her bones it would.

"Well, that's all in the past now. Oh, I can't wait to see you so we can talk properly. Take care of yourself."

Her mother gave one last smile, and the message winked out.

April sent one last message, a short one, just to confirm she was on her way and promise to give an estimated time of arrival just as soon as Salima had them underway.

Then April emerged from the airlock to find the others. It was time to finish her work here. It was time to go.

31

THE FINAL CHOICE

APRIL CURLED UP IN A NEST OF TARPS AT THE EDGE OF THE CATWALK. SHE hadn't really been sleeping, just drifting in and out of a doze. She was vaguely aware that the soft tink and occasional ratcheting sound of Salima working on the drones had stopped a few minutes before, and she had an even more ephemeral memory of Hakim resting his hand on her knee in a not-waking-her farewell some time before that. And she snapped awake just before Salima's hand closed over her shoulder to shake her, as if sensing Salima's urgency itself.

"What is it?" April asked, sitting up and rubbing at her face to get her blood moving. Salima's eyes were filled with shock and the beginnings of panic, something April never thought to see. "What's happened?"

"I'll explain on the way," Salima said, pulling April to her feet. April's body complained of the position she had napped in and the cold dampness of the air over the water reservoir made her stiff, but she kept her legs moving, stumbling along beside Salima's long strides. "Charley and Hakim went up to the village to start the treatment on the children while it was still the middle of the night shift."

"Is that what we agreed?" April asked. Her memories of everything after she had finished sorting through vials were fuzzy. Exhaustion had caught up with her the minute she had put the last of the chelation vials in the designated carrier and returned the rest of the drugs to the storage unit.

"We never agreed," Salima said. "Our discussion was going in circles and then you fell asleep on us."

"Sorry," April said, cheeks flaming. She knew full well everyone else's tasks had been much more involved than hers. Even Charley had outlasted her.

"Charley went up to the village at the end of the day shift and talked in secret to a few of his friends. Apparently, things are getting chaotic up there. They know we're up to something down here, and Lars keeps going into the village to talk to them about it, but there's a lot of suspicion. No one has seen Mr. Chapelier, but there are rumors he is sequestered working on this master exorcism spell. Charley says some of the rumors are completely insane, like some epic battle of humans versus demons is about to unfold.

"At any rate, Charley felt like it would be a better idea to just treat the children and show them to their parents once they start visibly improving, then explain the rest. If they can see what we are doing in a concrete way, it will go a long way towards getting them to listen to us."

"That sounds like a good idea," April said. They had reached the door that led to the station environment and Salima stopped, turning to face April.

"They left hours ago. I got worried and went to check on things. What I saw—I came right back to get you. I don't know if this madness is part of what you do. I've never watched you work, but it's beyond me. Everyone up there is mad. Mass hysteria maybe? I've never seen the like."

"Did you find Hakim and Charley?" April asked.

"I saw them," Salima said, her voice choking on her. "I couldn't get to them. I hoped you would know what to do."

It was like a stab to the heart, seeing Salima so past the point of coping. April nodded with all the confidence she could muster and opened the door to the sunlit station interior.

Beyond the door, everything was so quiet that April felt a warm wash of relief. Whatever Salima had seen, it was past now. Perhaps Mr. Chapelier had finally emerged from his house and taken things in hand.

As if in answer to that hope, April heard someone cackling at her. She looked around, but the houses at the edge of the village all stood empty despite the midmorning hour. Then she saw him, an old man sitting in a doorway, rocking back and forth as if to comfort himself. His laugh went on and on and sounded like a wail of despair, or perhaps that despair was just in the look in his eyes, as if he couldn't stop laughing and feared it was killing him, consuming all his breath until he fell blue to the dust blowing in his doorway.

But what terrified April was the sound his laughter was not quite drowning out: the roar of voices without distinguishable words. Salima looked over at her out of the corner of her eye, as if gaging her readiness for what she was about to see. April pulled herself taller as they walked, running her hands over her hair, adjusting her braid to lie straight down her back, smoothing out her clothing. She had nothing with her like she used to use in the ghost-dispelling rituals, and she missed the layers of veils and jewelry that announced who she was and what she was about. Now she had nothing but body language to command the attention of these people.

The rumble of noise ahead of them built to a roar like a wave breaking on a beach just as Salima and April reached the last row of houses before the square. The entire village was there, fishing and farming implements strewn about as if the villagers had been called here from other tasks. Some stood close to the houses in anxious little huddles, watching and murmuring to each other but making no move to stop whatever was happening around the fountain.

The crowd there was too dense to see what was happening at its center, but April could hear water splashing. Salima, tall enough to see over the crowd, cried out and surged forward, pushing her way past villagers too slow to catch her. She left enough of a wake behind her for April to see as she reached the fountain's edge and was at last caught by two of the larger villagers and pulled to her knees. Salima fought and shrieked, so unlike her usual self, it was as if she truly were possessed. Then the men pushed her down to her elbows and knees and April at last saw what was going on in the fountain.

"Stop! Stop this at once!" April said, summoning every bit of authority she had as she marched through the gap still left in the crowd. She was recognized at once, and many dropped their gaze as if ashamed, but others stared back defiantly at her. April ignored them all, never looking away from the two men in the fountain holding Hakim's head under the water. She wanted to run as Salima had run, to fight them off him, but she knew she would fail at that even faster than Salima had. Instead, she kept to a purposeful marching walk, concentrating on not letting her hands curl into fists as they longed to.

"Let him up," April said. "Now."

One of the two men faltered, not enough to let Hakim go but enough for Hakim to get his face back out of the water. He drew in an immense breath that caught in his throat and ended in coughing and retching. Salima wailed and sobbed, still unable to overpower her captors, although a third stepped up behind her to assist the first two.

"What is happening here?" April demanded. "Do you even know what you are about?"

"We know," said an old woman, even shorter than April. She leaned on two walking sticks, her hands twisted to uselessness and shaking constantly, but her eyes were bright and clear. Methylmercury might have taken her hands and was attacking her ability to walk, but her mind was still unaffected.

"Explain to me," April said, crossing her arms to listen.

"Mr. Chapelier warned us another demon was coming, one more powerful than the others, one the other demons would all bow to. And he told us true."

April glanced up at Hakim, hanging between the two men holding his arms as if he lacked the strength to stand, head bowed as he continued to draw in breath after precious breath. April stepped up into the fountain, shoes and all, and stretched out her arms, shaking her hands out before gently placing her palms against Hakim's cheeks and drawing his face up to look into his eyes. He looked up at her, his eyes all anger. She blinked slowly, all the sign she could give him of the importance of remaining calm. His breath seethed for a moment, his body tense all over, but after a few more blinks he relented, letting himself hang once more from his captors' grip.

"I see no sign of it," April said. "And I know this one well. He has been without food and sleep for far longer than was good for him, and I've borne the brunt of his ire before, but I promise you, it's just him. All human." She risked a little smile.

"He has you fooled," the woman said. "But he is the one we've been awaiting. The demon inside of him was guided here by another of the demon-possessed, and the first thing he did was gather the other demons to him. And they shared a foul liquid between them, something that burned at what remained of our children, hurt them further to keep them weak and the demon strong. But we caught them at their little ritual before it was complete."

April's heart sank. It wasn't hard to guess what had really happened. Then the woman extended one trembling hand and April saw an upturned medical carrier containing a mess of broken glass, the last of the liquid evaporating into the air or soaking into the dirt of the village square. Every vial she had spent so many hours gathering together, all destroyed.

Then she saw the children, every one of Charley's friends, sitting on the ground with adults in a ring around them, effectively prisoners. Charley himself was being held down by his own mother and grandmother, a gag tied around his mouth. His eyes pleaded for help, and April again fought the urge to run to him, to beat his captors away and run with him in her arms to the safety of Salima's ship. Such a plan would never succeed.

"There has been some confusion," April said. "What you saw was Hakim giving medicine to your children. They've been poisoned, those children in particular, and he was trying to make them well again."

"Demon lies," the woman spat.

"No, no. I promise you, and I can prove it to you. The only lies you've been told are about the demons." The last was clearly too much, April realized as the crowd around her began to murmur angrily. She put up a hand to ask for silence, but she didn't get it. In the end, she had to raise her voice to be heard over their arguing amongst themselves. "Please, listen. We've found out what's really going on here, or at least the largest part of it. You've all been exposed to methylmercury in the lake water and especially in the fish you've been eating out of the lake. It's been slowly increasing over time, but it's over now. Charley has assisted us in removing the contamination from the lake, and we're filtering the water even now. The water inside your houses is completely safe, and soon the lake will be too.

"I'm sorry that the medicine was... lost," April said at last, trying not to let her face show how she felt at her work of hours destroyed in one swift, impulsive motion. "But there will be more. We are leaving today to get more medicine as well as food and anything else you might need. You won't be kept apart from the rest of humanity any longer."

The crowd grew really ugly at those words, and April was confused. She had not mentioned the need to kill all the fish, expecting that they would take that hard, but she'd still managed to upset them with something she had said. Was this still distrust of the medicine?

"I'm not asking you to take anything on faith," April said. "I can prove everything I've said, although it may take some work for you to understand what I have to show you. The numbers and the like." The crowd rumbled and the old woman arched one eyebrow. "But I know you're all suffering from methylmercury poisoning. It attacks your nervous system. You've all been exposed, too. It's just a question of how much. Have any of you had trouble with your coordination? Stumbling when you walk? Can't move as fast as you used to? How about when you eat? Are you having trouble chewing and swallowing?" The crowd started murmuring amongst themselves again, but less angrily. "How is your vision? Cloudy or blurred? Maybe the edges are closing in, like looking through a tunnel? How are your hands and feet feeling? Numb? Painful? Do they move on their own? Twitch or shake?"

April watched the people in the crowd confer with each other. She was winning them over at last.

"The demon did all this," the old woman said, pointing a shaking, twisted hand at Hakim. "The one you brought here with you."

"No, that's not true," April said. "And you know it isn't true. You were all showing symptoms before we even arrived. All of those things

I just described to you—you've been dealing with them for years now, haven't you?"

"How do we know you're really fixing things?"

April found the source of the question: Emma's mother, standing near the children. Charley, still gagged, got a hand free and held it up in the air. April thought he was asking permission to speak, but then she realized what he was really doing. She climbed back out of the fountain and slapped wetly across the square to catch his hand, then Emma's, and held them together. All the parents gasped. Charley's skin was nearly normal once more, after several chelation treatments. Emma's was as mottled and angry-looking as ever.

"It's a trick," said the old woman as she struggled to make her own way across the square. Her knees wobbled, and although the walking sticks helped, her twisted hands couldn't grip them properly and her progress was slow. At last she reached April's side and made her own examination of the children's hands, but dismissed them both with a huff. "It's the demons in the children playing tricks on us. These two have been among the worst, we all know that. Their demons are the oldest, and the trickiest."

"They exposed themselves to the largest amount of mercury in the mines," April said. "It's been changing their behavior."

The woman huffed again. "That's the most ridiculous thing I've ever heard. Don't you know demons tell you exactly what you want to hear? That's their ruse. And you're so easily duped."

"No," April said. "We've been working on this for a long time. Anyone that wants to come to the labs with me, I can show you every test that Hakim ran, every potential cause he had to investigate and then rule out before finding the real source of the problem. I can show you how he found it and how he knows it's true and all the steps he's already taken to fix this. And you can see in the logs how he's done without sleep or proper meals or anything just to make you all well again, and this is how you thank him."

A lot of people wouldn't meet her eyes as she swept her gaze over the crowd, and the men holding Salima had released her, but the men holding Hakim still dug their fingers into his flesh as if he might break away from them at any moment.

"Demons are tricky. They can convince you of anything. Most cunningly of all, they convince the weak-minded that they don't exist," the old woman said.

"How can I make you see? You have a ready answer for everything, but you won't even consider what I'm telling you," April said. Then Hakim's voice carried, the hoarseness making April's heart quell at the thought of the anger and pain that must have vented itself while she slept to leave his voice so shredded.

"It's airtight logic, April. You can't refute it," he said. April's shoulders slumped, feeling the defeat about to come. "Yes, the steps of the logic are flawless. It's just the premises that are wrong."

April looked up to see a smile in his eyes, but the old woman must have seen it too, or taken it for something else.

"Dunk him," she said with a wave of her trembling hand, and the men gripped Hakim tighter.

"No!" April said, then took a breath to get the panic out of her voice. "No. That's not the way. Take him to Mr. Chapelier."

"He's not to be disturbed," the old woman said authoritatively. "He's working on a more powerful exorcism."

"You think you've found your master demon, and you don't think Mr. Chapelier would want to see it?" April asked.

The woman hesitated. "Perhaps," she allowed at last. "Bring him."

Salima tried to reach Hakim's side as the two men lifted him over the lip of the fountain, but she was pushed away from him, knocked sprawling back to the ground. April put out a hand to help her up.

"How is this not just going to make things worse?" Salima demanded.

"It was all I could think of," April admitted. "But Lars will be there. He can help."

"Will he?" Salima said, but April had no answer. She pushed through to the front of the crowd just before they reached Mr. Chapelier's gate.

Mr. Chapelier must have heard them approaching; even now that most of their anger had subsided, the entire village made a good deal of noise just walking, and Hakim was still struggling against his captors. He must have heard them and come outside to wait for them, but rather than standing on the stairs or walking up to the gate, he was slumped back in his porch chair, hands folded over his midriff, eyes lost under the chaos of his hair. April wasn't even sure if he was awake or asleep. She looked to Lars, lingering in the doorway behind Mr. Chapelier's shoulder. His lips were pressed tightly together and his eyes were grim.

"Mr. Chapelier," the old woman said, struggling through the gate that one of the others held open for her. She made her slow way up the path to stop at the bottom of the stairs. "We have found the master demon you've long been expecting. He came into the village in the dark of night and gathered all of his lesser demons in secret to share some elixir that burned the children the demons are still inhabiting. We've brought him to you."

The two men dragged Hakim into Mr. Chapelier's yard. April slipped through the gate behind them, rushing to stand beside the old woman at the bottom of the steps.

"He was giving them medicine for their mercury exposure," April said to Lars and Mr. Chapelier. "Chelation treatment. Some people feel a short burning sensation when it's injected. Apparently, Emma did and cried out. But no one was hurt. It was *medicine*.'

Mr. Chapelier acted as if he hadn't heard her speak at all. Lars stepped up to the porch railing and leaned forward to whisper to April, "You should have come to me first. I thought you were going to, before taking any more steps. Secrecy was not the way to handle this."

"We have to stop this," April said. "They were trying to drown him in the fountain before they came here. I don't know what they think will happen next."

"You must fight this demon," the old woman said to Mr. Chapelier. "If you defeat this one, the ones in the children will flee. Didn't you tell us so?"

Mr. Chapelier still didn't stir, and his eyes were still lost in shadow. April marched up the steps to lean close to his face. "You know this is all nonsense. Somewhere inside of you, you still know that. Help me."

Mr. Chapelier tipped his head to regard her. His eyes were blood-shot, his skin pasty where it wasn't pink. As hard as she and the others had been working to deal with the mercury problem, Mr.

Chapelier looked like he had worked twice as hard on his exorcism research. He was consuming himself, destroying himself, body and mind, all for nothing. Her sudden feeling of pity must have shown in her eyes, because Mr. Chapelier made an irritated grunt and pushed her aside.

"Bring him within," he said to the villagers. "Put him in the chair."

"No!" April said, lunging toward Mr. Chapelier in his chair. Lars caught her arm, pulling her to the other side of the doorway just as the men with Hakim came up the stairs, forcing him down the hallway to the exorcism room. Half of the village poured in after them. April struggled to get away from Lars, but he wrapped his arms around her and pulled her further from the crowd.

"Let me go!" April said.

"They won't hurt him," Lars said in a placating voice.

"Yes, they will. They already have!" April said. She tried snapping her head back, hoping to catch him on the chin, but he was too tall.

"Calm down," he said. "We can deal with this, but we need to be calm."

April smashed her foot down on his, but he just grunted. Then she looked up to see Charley and his friends being herded into the yard, ringed still by their parents. The stress on them must be horrific, caught in this fairy tale turning into a nightmare, perhaps feeling like they were to blame for what had happened to Hakim. Some of them were starting to exhibit their possession behaviors again, chattering and laughing like the old man in the doorway had done, throwing themselves on the ground and shaking, unleashing superhuman strength in an attempt to fight their way free.

"Let me go," April said again, no longer struggling. Lars opened his arms, and she went down the stairs to the children and their parents. Charley was trying to put his arms around Emma, to soothe her as she raged in a variety of cackling voices.

"You made him well," Emma's mother said to April.

"We made him better," April conceded. "But you destroyed the rest of the medicine. We need to leave to get more. Can't you help convince the others?"

Emma's mother looked miserably at her daughter, calmer now but still breathing like an animal as Charley stroked her hair. "I don't know how I can."

"April," Salima called. She had been inside the house but was coming down the stairs now. "Can't you tell Chapelier you want to do the exorcism yourself? You're his apprentice, right? He doesn't look good."

"He's been ill," Lars said.

"I don't think he considers me his apprentice anymore," April said. "But I can try convincing him he's too ill for this." She shot a glare at Lars, but he didn't try to stop her as she went up the stairs and pushed past the villagers to emerge in the exorcism room. Hakim was already bound in the chair much too small for him, crunched down low so the neck restraint would fit, elbows and knees jutting out at all angles. His joints must have been screaming. He would have been screaming too if they hadn't gagged him. His eyes were pure rage and several of the men behind him were sporting new injuries, bleeding noses and split lips.

Mr. Chapelier was pouring himself a glass of water with a hand that trembled so much the task was nearly impossible for him. April took the decanter and filled the glass herself.

"You can't do this," she said. "You've not recovered enough from last time."

"Stop pretending," Mr. Chapelier said. "I know your real reason for being here now."

"You want us gone, we want to be gone," April said. "Let him out of the chair and we will head to Salima's ship. We'll be gone in minutes, I swear."

Mr. Chapelier brought the glass up to his lips. April longed to steady that glass for him, worried he was going to chip his teeth, it shook so strongly, but his cold stare stopped her hand.

"You know we're right," April said. "You have medical books. I'm sure you've consulted them. You and the children have been exposed to mercury; it's why you're all pink and itchy. And everyone in the village has been exposed to methylmercury. It's why you shake. It's why you are having trouble even forming thoughts. An exorcism isn't going to fix any of that." She stepped closer, catching his hand after he set the glass down and giving it a squeeze to ease its trembling for the briefest of moments. "You know I'm right."

He looked up at her, bloodshot eyes glassy. He needed a nap, several proper meals, and then more proper sleep. He needed the medicine the others had destroyed.

"We need to go," April said. "We'll be back with everything you all need. And we won't come back into the village if you don't want us here. Lars can come up and get all the supplies. After that, we leave again, if that's how you want it. But you have to let us go."

Mr. Chapelier squeezed her hand back and a happy, relieved smile started to pull at the corners of her mouth. But then he spoke.

"There's no fixing this," he said, low and close to her ear so the others wouldn't hear. "Yes, I read all my books. You can remove all the mercury, all the methylmercury, but the damage is already done. When I'm dead and you cut into my head, you'll find my brain is now Swiss cheese, and there's no coming back from that. But there is one last thing I can do."

"No," April said, but he was stepping away from her, towards the others.

"I am weak," he told the villagers. "I am sorry. I know how you depend on me to free your children, and I will do it. But I cannot today; I'm not strong enough, not ready enough."

"She can help you," the old woman said, pointing at April.

"No, she's lost the path," Mr. Chapelier said.

The woman nodded. "The demons convinced her to believe their biggest lie."

"That they don't exist," Mr. Chapelier finished for her. "But perhaps she might come back to the side of the light. Come here, April." April stepped closer, ignoring Hakim's eyes pleading with her to do the opposite. Mr. Chapelier put a trembling hand on her shoulder to draw her closer still. "Look into his eyes, deep into his eyes. Tell me you see the demon looking back out at you."

April bent over to put her face close to Hakim's. Her braid swung forward over one shoulder and she fought the urge to twist it in her hands. She could pretend one last time. She could "assist" Mr. Chapelier with one last exorcism, even the big spell he was working on if he wanted. And when they were done, would he let them leave? She believed he would. They would be free to go, to fetch what the village really needed and return in all haste, to save all they could, to give all the care they could for those that couldn't be saved.

She could pretend one last time.

Hakim's eyes were boring into hers. She remembered when they first met, all the hate that had been in those eyes then when he hadn't even known her. She understood better now why he had felt what he had been feeling in that moment. And the dark eyes looking into hers now said that he too knew better what she struggled with every time she had to choose whether to pretend one more time. She didn't know what he was thinking, but she knew he wasn't hating her, whatever choice she was about to make. But a single tear slipped from the corner of one eye, sliding down to be absorbed in the tea towel he was gagged with.

April smiled at him, a sad, tremulous smile. Then she straightened.

"There is no demon," she said. "Only a man being tortured by you all for the crime of trying to save your children from this madness."

She expected roars of outrage, for the old woman to start ranting again, but the room remained in complete silence. Mr. Chapelier pulled his handkerchief from his pocket and touched it to his lips for a moment before carefully folding and putting it away once more.

"Very well," he said. "He will have to await the return of my strength for the exorcism.

"Take him to the mines."

32

———

ESCAPE

The next few minutes were a confusion of pain and noise. The noise receded, but the pain did not. April tried to push up onto her elbows, but her arms were lashed tight to her sides by someone's belt. She rolled to her side and saw Salima looking back at her, tied and gagged, with blood dripping from her nose to the floor.

Someone had hit her on the head, April remembered, and she felt the back of her head gave a sudden twinge of pain. Hit her from behind when she'd tried to throw herself on top of Hakim still strapped to the chair. Then too many hands had been on her, pulling her away, some by the hair, but after that blow to the head her ability to fight them had dwindled to mere twitches and sobs.

From the look on Salima's face, she had fought harder and longer, but in the end, no more successfully.

Footsteps approached from behind her and she tried to wriggle away, but a hand landed on her shoulder.

"Hush, it's just me," Lars said, bending to undo the belt. April groaned when he first cinched it tighter, then nearly started sobbing again when the blood ran back down her arms in a cascade of tumbling, stabbing needles. Lars turned to free Salima, but turned back to push April back down to the floor when she attempted to awkwardly stagger to her feet to follow the mob.

"We have to stop them!" April said. "There's mercury floating free in those mines. They are all about to be exposed."

"I know," Lars said, picking away at knots pulled tight by Salima's struggles. "But you need another approach."

"There isn't time. They might already be there."

"Not yet," Lars said. "Mr. Chapelier is going to want a show." He frowned at the stubborn knot, then looked around the room, spying a ceremonial dagger hanging on the wall as part of a display of historical exorcism equipment. To April's shock, the blade was so sharp the knot fell away under its edge without Lars having to hack or saw at it. She looked up at the other items on the walls, things she had seen a thousand times and dismissed as Mr. Chapelier's historical interests. Did he actually use these things? They looked like devices of torture.

Were they going to be part of this master spell he was planning to use on Hakim?

"If you had just come to me first," Lars said, not accusatorily but with deep regret. "I had nearly won him over. He was getting to a place where he could reconcile his work here with you leaving and bringing back food and medicine, even admitting that there was a mercury problem that needed to be dealt with by medical means. I was so close. And once I had him on our side, the others would have followed."

"I wish we had known better what you were up to, how much progress you were making. Hakim and Charley acted on the best knowledge they had."

"This is why we have to *talk*." Lars set the knife on a table but remained in a low squat between the two of them still sitting on the floor. His shoulders were slumped, his head hung low. April had never seen him so exhausted. But then he took a deep breath and straightened up. "Nothing to do but start again. It's crucial that you all leave as soon as possible. It will take you weeks to get to the *Triomphe* and back, and it will likely take all that time and more for me to convince him to let you and the supplies back in."

"We don't have to come in, just the supplies," Salima said.

"At some point, he's going to have to trust others. This isolation is not good for this community," Lars said.

"First Hakim," April said.

"We'll go get him," Lars said, standing up and pulling April to her feet. "Salima, go ready your ship for departure. I don't think they are going to let Hakim go without a fight. They will try to stop us. Understand that for years now, Mr. Chapelier has told them all that this demon invasion was something they had to deal with before they could open up their station to others. And they believe it. They believe letting Hakim go is letting his demon loose on all of humanity. They take that responsibility very seriously."

"You get him to me; I'll get us all out of here," Salima said, using her gag to staunch the flow from her nose. She gave April a desperate look. "Get him to me."

"I will," April promised, giving Salima a tight hug.

The three of them went out into the yard. The children were still huddled in the corner of the garden, but their parents were no longer ringing them in. Emma's mother was talking to a few of the others in a low voice, then she lifted Emma's and Charley's hands. They looked up when the door banged closed behind Lars. Emma's father, eyes red with unshed tears, rushed up to her, and April flinched back against Lars.

"I've destroyed everything, haven't I?" he said, tearing at his hair. "I thought... but it wasn't, was it? I destroyed their only hope."

"No," April said firmly, catching hold of his arms. "We never had enough. We only hoped to start some of the more extreme cases on treatment. We were always going to have to return with more medicine. And we will. The important thing is that no one goes into the mines. They are contaminated. Also, the fish. You have to catch and destroy every fish in that lake. But once that's done, you can start again with new fish, and we'll be back with enough medicine for everyone."

"I know how to do things," Charley said. "I'm working on making a cleaning drone, and Salima is going to help me as much as she can by messaging from her ship. And Hakim showed me how to wake up the fish embryos and reintroduce them to the lake. I can do it."

"Cleaning drone?" Emma's father repeated.

"For the mines," April said. "The lake is already being cleaned, but in the mines the mercury is free-floating in silver bubbles. I'm afraid..." Her voice caught, but she pressed on. "I'm afraid that Mr. Chapelier is going to put Hakim down there and leave him there until he's been exposed to enough mercury to make a very convincing possession victim. And then..." But memories of that other equipment in the exorcism room closed her throat up entirely.

"We aren't going to let that happen," Lars said.

"We'll go with you," Emma's father said, and the other parents were nodding.

Charley led the way back under the hill and through the access tunnels to the lowest level of the spinning station. The children ran through the tunnels and slid down the ladder rails with practiced ease, but from the wide-eyed look on the parents' faces, they had never come down here, not even when they were children themselves.

April had formed a picture in her mind of Hakim in the chair teetering on the edge of that opening in the floor as the rocky walls of the asteroid passed beneath, Mr. Chapelier working the crowd up into a frenzy before kicking him out of the spinning station to float in the mine shafts, stilled lashed to the chair, unable to move away from the blobs of mercury. Her fear that she would arrive too late, that Hakim would already be in the mines, had calcified to a certainty. What she hadn't expected to find was that Chapelier and the villagers had gone into the mines as well.

"Is he insane?" April seethed when they found the empty room.

"He knows the danger," Lars said, sounding puzzled himself. "He knows that's where all the mercury is."

"We have to go in there," April said, although her stomach tightened into a cold, hard knot at the thought. "The children have to stay. They've already been exposed to so much."

"We have to go," Charley said. "You'll get lost. It's a maze, but we know the way. All the ways."

"Do you know where he would take Hakim?" April asked.

"Mr. Chapelier has never been down here before," Lars said, "has he?"

"We can find him," Charley said. "They'll all be together; that will be loud. Sound really carries down there."

April looked up at the parents.

"We're all going," Emma's father said. Emma was holding his hand and her mother's, and the three jumped together, through the opening in the floor and out of the station. The others rushed to follow. Lars took April's hand, and they jumped together.

"This way!" Charley was calling, bouncing off walls and sailing through the air with practiced ease, the other children right behind him. Lars and April followed a bit more slowly, as they made sure to line up destinations before launching off of walls. The parents, unaccustomed to free fall, were further behind, clinging closely to the walls and reaching out hands to help each other along.

"The deepest shaft," Charley said before disappearing around a rocky corner.

"Coincidence?" April said to Lars.

"I'm starting to doubt it," Lars said. "But did he come down here before or after you told him about the mercury?"

The deepest shaft was also the widest, and even the children stayed close to the walls. There were lights in the mines, but they were dim and spaced too far apart to ever see anything clearly. April looked up to spot her next handhold and noticed something blotting out one, then another of the lights, something floating near the center of the shaft. Then it drifted into the radius of the next light and April saw it was the exorcism chair.

"Hakim," she said, crawling faster to catch up with the children, to reach the voices growing louder.

The shaft ended in a larger cavern, the drill that had dug so deep still buried nose-first in the rock. The villagers were trying to tie Hakim to it with sashes and belts and restraints pulled free from the chair, but he was fighting them with one last desperate rush of adrenaline. He had an advantage; these villagers were no more adept in free fall than the children's parents still struggling to catch up. April searched and at last spotted Mr. Chapelier floating at the edge of the crowd, one hand on the protective cage around one of the lights, the other holding his handkerchief to his mouth. He looked distinctly green, and April suspected not all the bubbles in the cavern would be silvery.

"Please," Emma's father said as soon as he was close enough to be heard. "Stop this madness. We need to get out of here, back to the village square. Assemble the elders at the tree and have a proper discussion. I'm sorry I reacted without thinking, but I'm calm now and you all need to be too."

"What we need," the old woman said, floating gracefully with one toe on the cage around the driver's cabin in the drill, her crutches abandoned in the freedom of weightlessness, "is to bind this demon. He is too strong for us now, but binding him here will weaken him until Mr. Chapelier is ready for the fight."

April didn't think that woman was ever going to deviate from her hard line. Instead, she launched herself over to Mr. Chapelier.

"Why are you doing this?" April demanded.

"I'm doing nothing," he said, tucking his handkerchief away but not quite looking at her.

"You're allowing all this to happen," April said, leaning close to force him to look at her. "You put everything in motion to make this happen. To what possible gain?"

"Gain?" he scoffed. "One doesn't do this sort of work for *gain*. It's a calling."

"You've worked so hard to keep these people apart from the rest of humanity, believing in what you tell them to believe in, turning their backs on real help. *Why*?"

Mr. Chapelier angled himself so he could more effectively look down his nose at her, but said nothing.

"Why did you come here in the first place? I believe it was to help these people. You came with all those books and all that knowledge and all that desire to help others. Then what? What happened to that man? Mercury poisoning, to be sure, but that wasn't your fault. Even not knowing it was mercury poisoning wasn't your fault. Hakim spent days and days uncovering that truth, and even he nearly missed it. Two different kinds of mercury, both poisoning your people. Who could suspect that? But denying the truth of it? What's the point of that, Mr. Chapelier? What are you thinking?"

He took the handkerchief back out, but April doubted he was feeling nauseous again. No, he was looking for anything to put between himself and her words. She caught his arm, pulling herself closer.

"You look tired," she said, gentling her voice. "You look diseased. I know the mercury is eating at your mind, making it hard to think. Won't you just admit you need help?"

"Demon," he said, trying to pull his arm from her grasp but too weak to succeed. "Demon," he said again, half a sob, and she realized he wasn't referring to her, or even to Hakim. "It must be a demon. I try, but I can't make my thoughts connect. My hands move, but it's not my doing. I burn, I itch; something is *inside* me. Why else would I do these things? These terrible things?" She thought he was going to break down into tears and was preparing to hug him until it passed, but instead he found a burst of strength, pulling free from her grip only to dig his fingers into her upper arms as he pulled her closer still to his face, to his wild eyes. She could swear they were ringed in silver now. No, not silver—mercury. But that wasn't possible. Just a trick of the light.

"You have to do it," he said.

"I will. I'll bring back food, medicine—"

"No," he said, more wail than word. "You have to get this demon out of me. I've taught you all I know. You're ready. My apprentice. Please, free me."

"No," April said, and his fingers dug even deeper into her flesh.

"Yes, you must. I'm not me. I'm losing me. Help me..." His final *me* became a shriek that filled the cavern, putting an end to the various arguments occurring in pockets all around the drill. Mr. Chapelier's voice deepened into a growl and began to utter words she did not know, built up to a babbling vocalization that didn't resemble words at all, then descended into a desperate laughter.

"Stop that," April said, low but firm. "You are you. Stop this at once."

He continued to laugh and babble and growl. At times, it seemed like two voices coming out of him at once, a low hum and a high whistling shriek, and April could feel all eyes on them, wide-eyed terror in the parents as much as the true believers like the old woman. She kept her own face perfectly calm, like a mother patiently waiting for her toddler's tantrum to blow itself out.

But Mr. Chapelier was no toddler, and when he released her, it was not to let her go but to start raining blows on her, catching her braid in one fist so that she could not escape him. April cried out, covering her face with her arms. She would never imagine there would be so much strength in that wire-thin body.

Another cry of pure rage filled the cavern and something collided with Mr. Chapelier and April, sending the three of them toppling out into the open space. Another body collided with them and the spin of all that differently directed momentum had them tumbling crazily enough for April's stomach to threaten to spill.

Then someone caught hold of something, and they all jerked to a halt. April lowered her arms from her face. Lars had an arm around her waist, holding her still as Hakim bent back Mr. Chapelier's fingers one by one until he released her braid.

"I should take you up to the airlock and toss you out," he hissed close to Mr. Chapelier's ear.

Mr. Chapelier burst into tears, pulling his knees close to his chest and burying his face against them. Hakim released him with a look of disgust and he tumbled slowly away, pulling himself into a tighter weeping huddle. April pulled away from Lars to float back to Mr. Chapelier, hands landing gently on his shoulders.

"Please," she said, stroking the tangles of hair back from his blotchy face, "won't you accept my help now?"

All of his words were gone, but he nodded.

Mr. Chapelier's breakdown seemed to suck the life energy out of everyone. It was a much more subdued group that helped each other back up the shaft and into the station proper. Some were rubbing at patches of skin, and April knew that whatever they had believed when they had gone into those mines, they were now open to the suggestion that those glittering silvery blobs might look pretty but were deep trouble. And if they believed that, they would believe about the fish.

There no longer seemed to be any reason to hurry back to the ship, so April followed Lars as he carried Mr. Chapelier back to his house and Hakim, his hand in April's, came along without a word. Now that he had exhausted all the nervous energy that had been driving him for the past weeks, Mr. Chapelier looked tiny, more clothes than man, bone thin inside a suit twice his size. Lars carried him up the stairs and placed him gently in his bed. April went into the kitchen to make a pot of his favorite tea and brought it up to set it on the nightstand. Lars was sitting on a chair pulled close to the bedside, Mr. Chapelier's hand in his. Hakim leaned against the far walls, arms crossed and eyes half closed with exhaustion.

"Rest now, teacher," Lars said. "April has made you tea. Just rest, eat a little when you can. I'll be back soon."

Mr. Chapelier roused enough to clutch tightly at Lars's hand. "You'll be back?"

"Yes," Lars said. "I'm just seeing them off. Then I'll be back."

Mr. Chapelier tried to muster a smile, but it slipped away from him. He burrowed deeper into the pillow and closed his eyes.

Lars walked silently beside April and Hakim back through the village to the administrative building. Charley saw them and raced to join them.

"How is it?" Hakim asked him.

"Better," Charley said with a shaky, grateful laugh. "I think the worst is over."

"Yes," April agreed.

"Although," Charley went on, "some are still saying Mr. Chapelier is right. That we really are cursed. The demons just took the form of poisoning all of us."

"It's not a curse," April said. "You did nothing to bring this on yourselves. It's just random chance. It's not fair, but life isn't fair. We just do the best we can with the circumstances we find ourselves in."

"You keep telling the others that," Hakim said. "They might not want to listen, but if you say it enough, they have to hear it. Maybe it will sink in, eventually."

Charley nodded gravely. "I'm going to show some of the others the things you showed me, the tutorials and how to operate the workstations, things like that. And we'll see each other again soon, right? And maybe someday, not when you come back this time, but someday, maybe I can go with you and see other places and other people?"

"Definitely," April said. "And you can tell the others. We can transport passengers as well as cargo. Anyone can leave anytime they wish. They just have to ask."

Charley left them at the doors to the building to run back to the village, but Lars stayed with them up the long elevator ride to the docks. "That kid is going to be in charge someday," April said to fill the silence.

"Yes," Lars agreed.

"We have to give him everything he needs to succeed," Hakim said. "I've shown him how to access all the computer systems, but the library here is woefully inadequate. He'll learn everything he needs to know to run this station, but nothing more. Nothing to aspire to beyond day-to-day maintenance."

The elevator doors opened with a ding and they emerged on the dock, Boo rushing to greet them, tail wagging so hard it was nearly throwing off his stride. Salima wasn't far behind him, rushing up to stand awkwardly before her brother. He pulled her into a tight hug. Lars bent to ruffle Boo's ears, and when he straightened back up, Salima gave him a quick hug he was clearly not expecting. Salima scooped Boo up into her arms as Hakim extended a hand to Lars, and Lars shook it warmly.

"We launch when you're ready," Salima said, then she and her brother and Boo climbed up the ramp to the airlock and disappeared inside the ship.

April realized she was alone with Lars for the first time since he had kissed her and felt awkwardness creeping over her like bugs in her skin. He shifted his weight from foot to foot, rubbing at the back of his neck as he cast about for something to say.

"So much to do," he said at last. "The plumbing was only the most critical system; there are others that have fallen offline. Lucky there are few people here now, or the atmospheric systems running at half capacity would be a serious problem."

April smiled and nodded. "It's a big task, getting this crowd organized, trained, and working. I can't think of a better man for the job, though."

"I hoped..." But Lars shook his head, not going there. "What Hakim was saying in the elevator, that's got me thinking. If you can, try to find some readers like yours, with education programs on them. I'd like to start a school."

"That's a good idea," April said. "But I don't think these are easy to find. My mother technically stole it when she brought it out of the corporate station."

"You and Hakim dig into it. With Salima's help, I'm sure you could not only replicate it, you could make it better."

"Better," April repeated, her mind suddenly flooding with every pet peeve she'd ever had interacting with her reader: her frustration with the math program that Hakim had already fixed, a million other little things that could be tweaked.

"I have a favor to ask," Lars said, interrupting her avalanche of ideas before it could properly get underway.

"The readers aren't a favor?"

"No, that's just like the food and medicine," Lars said. "This is personal."

"OK," April said cautiously.

"When you're back on the *Triomphe*, I'd like you to find Mr. Chapelier's mentor, the one who recommended you, the one who sent him here. I think he should know how Mr. Chapelier is faring, but I'd also like to know more about what Mr. Chapelier was like before he came here."

"I'm curious about that myself," April admitted. "How can I find him?"

"I've seen some of his correspondence with Mr. Chapelier; I'll message you the details."

"OK," April agreed, and suddenly realized there was nothing left to say.

Lars smiled down at her, then bent to kiss her cheek ever-so-slightly self-consciously. Then April turned to climb the ramp to the airlock. Lars had put his hand at her neck when he'd kissed her and she could feel a slight tugging as her braid moved through his fingers, the end slipping away as her hand closed around the rail that ran around the hatch. She turned back to give him one last wave goodbye, then stepped inside and pulled the hatch shut behind her.

Boo's nails skittered over the catwalk as he raced to jump all over her. She had been neglecting him horribly while working around the lake reservoir and she bent to pick him up and bury her nose in his fur, keeping her face there as she walked past the sleeping pods and through the common room to the cockpit. Hakim got up when she stepped inside, letting her take his place as he went aft to secure the ramp. Salima gave her a quick smile before busying herself with the controls. Lars must have gone into the dock control room because April felt the lurch of the dock floor rising to take them back up to the airlock.

Hakim came back into the cockpit and dropped to sit cross-legged beside April. April set Boo down on her lap and wrapped an arm around Hakim's, laying her head on his shoulder.

"You've had an epically terrible day," she said, touching his abraded knuckles gently.

"It ended all right," he said, kissing the top of her head.

"Lars wants readers like mine to start a school."

"I was thinking, there is so much empty space in the station hard drives. Do you remember the media file sharing drive on the *Chandrasekhar*? I think we should start collecting media files. Every station we go to when Salima transports goods, we should collect copies of everything we can find and bring it all here. One location everyone can come to and find anything at all."

"A library," April said, closing her eyes as she imagined it. "What a fantastic idea. And so perfect to put it here."

The motion from the elevator stopped and April realized that sleepy, floaty feeling she had was because she really was floating, back in free fall once more. Salima gently coaxed her ship out of the dock, through the center of the station's cylinder, and back out into the black of space.

"Next stop: the *Triomphe*," she said.

"The *Triomphe* and my mother," April said. "And Mr. Chapelier's mentor. I owe him a visit and a long conversation."

"And the water treatment area," Hakim added. April opened her eyes to look up at him quizzically. "You have unfinished business there, don't you? You never found the source of that haunting."

"That's right," April said. "There must be something."

"Low-frequency sound from a machine needing adjustment, perhaps," Hakim said.

"We'll find out," April said.

Hakim put an arm around her to pull her closer and Boo climbed until he was half in her lap, half in his. Hakim put out a hand and Salima took it, not just letting herself get pulled into their group hug but hugging back, burying her face in Boo's neck just like April loved to do.

April still felt all the cold vastness of space around them, but she didn't mind. She was part of a warm node of human comfort. It was all she needed.

NEW SERIES: THE FORGOTTEN PLANET

Coming soon from Ratatoskr Press Books, the new YA sci-fi series THE FORGOTTEN PLANET starts with book 1: Raiding the Forgotten Derelict.

History sleeps beneath them all, but only she sees it.

Lafayette Eloi always knew her parents thought differently from others. They kept their books buried beneath her mother's house. They spoke an old language in the dead of night, whispering behind closed doors and bolted shutters. She grew up in a village where no one was related to her, and she never knew why.

Then, after her mother died, her father came to fetch her. Now she and her mother's dog assist her father in his work. The work discussed in whispers in the dark. The work that had cost Lafayette so much all her young life.

But now she learns just how much her father's work means to their entire world. Only no one knows anything about it. Only her father. And only Lafayette.

Because the work that consumed her father's entire life and her mother's too now nibbles at the fringe's of Lafayette's own life. And she cannot refuse its call.

Raiding the Forgotten Derelict, first book in the new YA sci-fu series THE FORGOTTEN PLANET, available in September 2024 from Ratatoskr Press Books.

COMPLETE SERIES: THE RITCHIE AND FITZ SCI-FI MURDER MYSTERIES

The Ritchie and Fitz Sci-Fi Murder Mysteries starts with Murder on the Intergalactic Railway.

For Murdina Ritchie, acceptance at the Oymyakon Foreign Service Academy means one last chance at her dream of becoming a diplomat for the Union of Free Worlds. For Shackleton Fitz IV, it represents his last chance not to fail out of military service entirely.

Strange that fate should throw them together now, among the last group of students admitted after the start of the semester. They had once shared the strongest of friendships. But that all ended a long time ago.

But when an insufferable but politically important woman turns up murdered, the two agree to put their differences aside and work together to solve the case.

Because the murderer might strike again. But more importantly, solving a murder would just have to impress the dour colonel who clearly thinks neither of them belong at his academy.

Murder on the Intergalactic Railway, the first book in the Ritchie and Fitz Sci-Fi Murder Mysteries.

COMPLETE SERIES: THE TRAVELS OF SCOUT SHANNON

The complete six-book series THE TRAVELS OF SCOUT SHANNON begin with book one, Under Falling Skies.

Scout Shannon's whole family died the day the Space Farers dropped an asteroid on their domed city. Now she lives alone, out in the wild with only her dogs for company. She prefers it that way.

But Scout finds herself at a crossroads. One road leads back to a quiet life snug under the protective dome of a city. The other road leads to a life in the rebellion, a life of adventure and excitement but also danger. Dare she try to find the rebels hiding in the hills?

Then a chance encounter with a stranger from the other side of the galaxy threatens to derail what remains of Scout's life. The entire galaxy awaits her, if she survives the next four days.

"Under Falling Skies", a young adult science fiction novel, set on a remote planet with a distinctly Old West feel. For fans of gunslinging women and young girl assassins. And dogs.

Under Falling Skies, the first book in THE TRAVELS OF SCOUT SHANNON, available everywhere now.

SCI-FI SERIAL PODCAST!

Check out my new monthly podcast of serialized science fiction: THE TALES OF THE CHAI MAKHANI TRIO!

Elyot loathes the massive Commonwealth ships that hover menacingly over his home world of Adghal. He hates the Commonwealth enforcers who harass the populace even more. But with his mother missing and presumed dead, Elyot keeps his head down and strives to avoid notice. And he succeeds until the day two strangers enter his life...

New episodes of this sci-fi serial drop every 1st of the month.

Now streaming on Apple Podcasts, Google Podcasts, Spotify, Stitcher and more. Also available in eBook and print everywhere books or sold. For a complete episode listing, check out the page on my website.

THE THIRD POLE JOB, the first novella in the Vic Harper Caper series. For those who love capers, heists and other impossible missions.

ALSO FROM RATATOSKR PRESS

Also from Ratatoskr Press, The Witches Three Cozy Mystery Series by Cate Martin, a mix of mystery and magic that begins with Book 1: Charm School.

Amanda Clarke thinks of herself as perfectly ordinary in every way. Just a small-town girl who serves breakfast all day in a little diner nestled next to the highway, nothing but dairy farms for miles around. She fits in there.

But then an old woman she never met dies, and Amanda was named in her will. Now Amanda packs a bag and heads to the big city, to Miss Zenobia Weekes' Charm School for Exceptional Young Ladies. And it's not in just any neighborhood. No, she finds herself on Summit Avenue in St. Paul, a street lined with gorgeous old houses, the former homes of lumber barons, railroad millionaires, even the writer F. Scott Fitzgerald. Why, Amanda can practically hear the jazz music still playing across the decades.

Scratch that. The music really, literally, still plays in the backyard of the charm school. Because the house stretches across time itself. Without a witch to protect this tear in the fabric of the world, anything can spill over. Like music.

Or like murder.

The complete series is out now, and it all starts with Charm School.

FREE EBOOK!

Like exclusive, free content?

To get two prequel short stories to THE RITCHIE AND FITZ SCI-FI MURDER MYSTERIES as well as a bonus prequel novelette to the completed six-book series THE TRAVELS OF SCOUT SHANNON, signup for my monthly newsletter at KateMacLeodWrites.com.

Thank you!

ABOUT THE AUTHOR

Photograph © 2016 Jonathan Conklin

Kate MacLeod has written stories which have appeared in Analog, Strange Horizons and Mythic Delirium, among other places. She is also the author of two young adult science fictions series: The Travels of Scout Shannon, and The Ritchie and Fitz Sci-Fi Murder Mysteries. She also contributes to a serialized science fiction podcast called The Tales of the Chai Makhani Trio. She currently lives in Minneapolis, Minnesota.

Find out more about the author and sign up for her newsletter at KateMacLeodWrites.com.

ALSO BY KATE MACLEOD

Novels

The Slums of the Solar System:

Mitwa

The Mars of Malcontents

The Whole World for Each

Books 1-3 Box Set

The Travels of Scout Shannon:

Under Falling Skies

In Quaking Hills

Among Treacherous Stars

Against Impassable Barriers

Over Freezing Altitudes

At Galactic Central

The Travels of Scout Shannon Books 1-3

The Travels of Scout Shannon Books 4-6

The Travels of Scout Shannon Books 1-6

The Ritchie and Fitz Sci-Fi Murder Mysteries:

Murder on the Intergalactic Railway

Murder in the Skies

Body in the Catacombs

Death on the Summit

An Undiplomatic Murder

A Lethal Betrayal

The Forgotten Planet

Raiding the Forgotten Derelict (Forthcoming September 2024)

Sci-Fi Novellas

The Intergenerational Tree

I Rise into a Daybreak

Caper Novellas

The Third Pole Job

The Twelve Days of Christmas Job

10-Story Collections

Tales of Blood and Ink

Tales of Old Gods and New

5-Story Collections

Tales from Heian-Kyo and Others

Tales from the Edges and Ends

Tales from Forgotten Days

Tales from Ancient and Future Times

<u>Tales from Across Space</u>